Books by Niki Livingston

Theia's Moons Series

Eyes Wide Shut

Enyo's Warrior

Protectors of the Stars

Guardian

The Chaos Awakened Saga

Marked Chaos

Expanded Chaos

Transformed Chaos

Novels

Be My Leprechaun

Novellas

Wrong Side of the Mirror

Novelettes

A Web Through Time

Wicked Heart

Wicked Soul

Jolly Old Monster

Unable to Wake

THEIA'S
MOONS
Protectors of the Stars

NIKI LIVINGSTON

Protectors of the Stars

This book is a work of fiction, including, but not limited to, characters, events, and features. They are all the imagination of the author and any resemblance of any aspect or persons, living or dead, is entirely circumstantial.

Copyright © 2017 Niki Livingston

Publisher: Unbound Wonders Press

Editor: Erin Sandlin

Cover art © Niki Ellis Designs

nikiellisdesigns.com

ISBN-13: 978-0-9976644-5-4

To connect: www.NikiLivingston.com

To my sisters, Michelle and Rachael.

Thank you for your guidance

and love. You have both been my examples and

I appreciate your loyalty and support.

Love you forever.

Our greatest glory is not in never falling,

but in rising every time we fall.

-Confucius

ONE

Grief's Darkness

STANDING ON THE balcony, just outside her daughter's room, Malkia examined the sky, longing to see her father's ship reappear. It had been two days since he fled, leaving her broken on his stone path. She had wept and screamed for an entire day, shifting between rage and pain, and wondering if she would ever feel whole again.

Her eyes scanned the landscape, clutching tightly to the piece of parchment that held her only known clue to find her daughter, while eyeing the Erebus Forest to one side of her, and the rugged mountains to the other. The Artemisians and deimoses that had escaped, hadn't returned, and after Tantiana and her group scoured the forest, they'd concluded they were in the clear for the time being.

The vegetation near the edge of the forest rustled as Tantiana peeked out, eyeing a large critter scurry across the fields towards the fortress. The dragon tilted her head to the side, snapping forward and snatching the rodent in her mouth.

Malkia's lips twitched slightly, enjoying the playful way Tantiana hunted small pests. As if her dragon read her mind, Tantiana twisted her head back and winked at Malkia, before returning to her hiding spot in the trees.

"I warned you this would be a disaster." Malkia heard her Esaki mother whispering frantically, somewhere on the lower levels. Malkia knew her intrusion on their conversation was wrong, but she had lost all empathy or respect for the three women she loved. "You two insisted this was the best way, but from the beginning I knew Malkia would resent all of us. Now even more so, since our actions caused the loss of her daughter."

Haltia cleared her throat. "There is a flood of information Malkia doesn't know exists and she may despise me, but everything I have done has been to protect her. If she could only travel back in time and witness the amount of disarray and turmoil both Thane and my father brought into this world—" Her voice trailed off.

"I don't think Malkia cares about the past." Alyssa interrupted, her tone snapping harshly, then receded back into a whisper. "And neither do I."

Turning away from the outside world, Malkia blocked their conversation from her mind, drained from their excuses. She strolled into her daughter's room, closing the double doors behind her. She had spent the past day rummaging through Esta's room, searching for a clue to where her father would hide. After hours of examining on the first day, she'd reclined on the floor, defeat sweeping through her mind and resentment devouring her heart.

Now she stood, staring at the room that had been the sanctuary where her daughter slept and played. Her heart ached for the lost time and the possibility of never finding Esta. Broken was an understatement for how Malkia felt, as her eyes wandered over portraits of her baby girl, noticing how happy and content she had been.

Malkia shuffled over to the bed, picking up the pillow before crawling back beneath the covers. Her thoughts returned to that moment she witnessed her father's ship disappear into the clouds. The events of that day had spiraled so quickly and looking back, she wished she had done everything differently.

Haltia had begged for forgiveness, asking for some time to explain her story and reasons behind her actions.

"You're dead to me, Haltia," Malkia had said, her eyes narrowing with disgust. "All three of you." She pointed at Asha and Alyssa. "You all had your own agendas, and from what I have heard and witnessed already, you were all out for yourselves. My daughter is gone, and it all could've been prevented if just one of you hadn't been thinking of yourselves." She had turned away from them, hiding away in Esta's room ever since.

Malkia buried her face deeper into the pillows, wanting the ache in her heart to disappear, but not knowing how to halt its consumption. She'd never felt this hopeless in all her life. Squeezing her eyes shut, pleading to drown out the pain worming its way through her soul, the creak of the door brought her back to reality. Perching up on her elbows, her eyes darted to the doorway, checking to see who was intruding on her solitude.

She sighed, shaking her head. "Damon, I need to be alone," she pleaded, her face sticky with the remnants of her tears. Snuggling back into the covers, she clung to Esta's blankets, inhaling her lingering scent.

The cushion shifted, Damon obviously ignoring her request as he reclined next to her. She bit her lip and closed her eyes, holding back fresh tears as he reached over and swept her hair away from her face, and ran his hands through the locks. He didn't say a word. His hands were soft on her hair and his presence quieted her pain.

They lay in silence for some time, his fingers combing continuously through her hair, before Malkia shifted her body and nestled her face into Damon's chest. He wrapped his arms around her, cradling her protectively against his body. His breath became unsteady and Malkia heard the beat of his heart quicken.

She breathed in deeply, looking up from his chest, and stared into his dark eyes. Her hand touched his cheek, his eyes longing for her touch as she reached up and kissed his lips. Sighing deeply, he pulled her tighter and pressed his lips to hers. His tongue invaded her mouth, exploring every inch.

Malkia eased up on her knees, straddling his body, and again melting into his embrace. His hands ran down her back, firmly gripping her hips as she pressed into his body. Drawing away, she grabbed the bottom of her shirt and eased it over her head. Damon stared in amazement, touching her skin softly and running his hands over every section of her body.

Rising swiftly into a seated position, his lips met hers again, their tongues exploring each other's mouths as he removed his own shirt. She ran her fingers across his chest and down his arms, drawing him towards her and covering his neck with soft kisses. He moaned, grabbing her face with both hands and pressed his lips hard onto hers, their breath coming in quick.

Malkia sighed in longing, as he removed the remainder of his clothes. She gripped his arms, kissing him firmly and easing him onto his back. The motions came with unbridled enthusiasm, as if they were always meant to be one. Their bodies moved in unison, and she moaned with pleasure, their union almost instantly climatic. Her pulse quickened and a rush of pleasure raced through every inch of her body. Crying out as the exhilaration sent shocks throughout her exhausted muscles, straight down to her fingertips, reviving her body and heart all at once.

Several moments later, she collapsed breathless next to him, after feeling his climax end and witnessing the pleasure rush through his eyes. Her body tingled from head to toe, and for the first time in days she felt some peace within her heart. She nestled into Damon's chest, listening to his racing heart.

The silence was filled with their heavy breathing, and Malkia inhaled deeply, allowing the serenity to continue its flow through her body.

"I love you, Malkia," Damon whispered, kissing the top of her head.

She smiled to herself, closing her eyes, and for the first time in two days she allowed sleep to take her mind.

"Malkia, wake up!" She heard her name being called from the blackness, but her mind was reluctant to wake. "We're under attack. Malkia. Wake up!" This time she sat straight up, her eyes darting around the shadowy room, resting on Damon's face, his brows furrowed staring at the doors that led to the deck.

"What is it?" Malkia asked, easing the blankets off her body and swinging her legs over the edge of the bed.

Damon slid past her, grabbing his daggers before slithering towards the window. Crouching near the floor, he shifted the fabric from the window and peered into the night sky. Malkia glided towards him and stared over his shoulder, searching for whatever Damon thought was attacking them.

"What did you hear?" Malkia whispered into his ear, not seeing anything out of the ordinary outside.

Damon turned to face her, his eyes wide as he licked his lips. "I didn't hear anything. I had a dream." He paused, his eyes glazing over. "A nightmare."

Malkia stood up, a smile surfacing on her lips. She reached down to help him up, but he shook his head and pulled her back down to his level. "Damon, it was just a nightmare. We can go back to bed."

"No." He shook his head again, turning back towards the window. "Ever since I arrived on Eris, I've been having dreams and visions about real events. I had them as a child, but they didn't return until I set foot on Eris." His face turned enough to make eye contact. "You never asked how I knew your father had a message."

Malkia inhaled deeply, digesting this new information. She settled onto the ground, closing her eyes for a moment. "Why didn't you tell me?" She opened her eyes, lifting them to meet Damon's distraught expression.

"I wasn't sure what it all meant. The visions were out of order and chaotic, but they began manifesting into reality and to be honest, I was petrified to speak it out loud." He glanced over his shoulder, his forehead creased with worry. "All my abilities are intensified here and the power coursing through my body can be overwhelming." He shook his head. "But the thought of what I can do—" His voice cracked, as he closed his eyes. "What you and I can do as a team, I can't say it doesn't scare the hell out of me."

Malkia curled her hand over his knee. "I understand how you feel, but now we need to make sense of your dream. You said we are under attack. What happened?"

"The Artemisians sent their deimos into the fortress to slaughter us. It's going to happen tonight. Your father is *not* finished with us." His eyes wandered back to the window, fear sweeping across his face, as he recalled his nightmare.

"Let's go wake the others," Malkia said, rising from the floor and gliding towards the door. "If the deimoses are on their way, we'll need everyone to be prepared. I can surround the fortress with my light, but if they know of any underground routes, I won't be able to hold them off."

Damon rose from his position, following after her. She grabbed her staff and daggers before easing the door open. Damon curled his hand around her side, protectively holding onto her, but not intruding on her desire to move through the door first. They both peeked into the corridor, searching for anything out of the ordinary, and exhaled quietly as they were met with silence and the dim light down the hall.

Sprinting down the corridor, Malkia knocked softly on Haltia and Asha's door, her eyes scanning down the wide hallway, watching for any sudden movements. Damon stood a few feet away, his stance guarded as he turned his back towards her.

The door cracked open and Malkia sighed with relief. "We need to wake everyone," she said to Asha. "Damon has had a vision and we believe the deimoses are on their way for another onslaught."

Asha opened the door wide and stepped out, eyeing Damon suspiciously. "When did you start having visions?"

Damon pivoted to face the women, his lips pursed tightly. "When I arrived on Eris, but I didn't fully understand them or realize their significance." He shook his head in frustration. "But they keep occurring and I can't ignore this one."

"What did you see?" Haltia moved out of the shadows, standing behind Asha with her arms folded over her chest, her eyes puffy and red, with streaks of dried tears standing out starkly on her cheeks.

"I just told you what he saw," Malkia snapped at her mother.

Haltia stepped forward and around Asha, ignoring Malkia. "I want to know details. Did you see the Artemisians? Did you see where they were and what they were saying?"

Damon closed his eyes, his face softening in concentration. He exhaled softly and then inhaled deeply. "I saw a structure inside the Erebus Forest." He paused, breathing in and out a few times, while his forehead creased with concentration. "It appears small from the outside, but when you enter, it stretches downward for miles. Artemisians by the hundreds inhabit this establishment and their deimoses live on the lower levels." He stopped talking, but his eyes remained closed.

Malkia glided towards him, but Haltia gripped her arm, drawing her back. "Give him a minute. If he has the sight, he'll remember his full vision. Let him be." She searched Malkia's face, her irises showing the deep pain she was enduring as a tear escaped her eye.

Malkia backed away from her mother, sagging against the wall behind her and closing her eyes in an attempt to connect with anything but Haltia and Asha.

"There are tunnels that lead to our fortress," Damon spoke up. Malkia's eyes snapped open, standing straight again. "The Artemisians ordered the deimoses to break through the barrier in the sublevels and murder every living thing they find." Damon's eyes opened, his hands slowly curling into fists. "I know where the entrance is."

"We're right behind you," Malkia blurted out, stepping towards him. "Lead the way."

"I'll wake the others," Asha announced, turning the other way. "We will catch up with you three."

Malkia nodded, before racing after Damon and Haltia.

Halfway down the staircase, Malkia knew they were too late, her stomach knotting from the presence of the beasts in the home. She halted in her tracks, gripping Damon's arm to make him stop. His eyes flashed over to hers and inhaled sharply when he saw the look of dread melt down her face.

"We are out of time, aren't we?" Damon asked, his eyes darting down the dark staircase.

Malkia nodded, taking a step back up the stairs. "I can feel their closeness. The deimoses are already in the fortress." She clutched Haltia's hand and towed her back up towards her. "We need to move into a closed area and protect it while we devise a plan to stop them."

"Go," Damon ordered. "I'll bring up the rear and make sure nothing follows us."

The two women turned on their heels, bounding lightly back up the stairs, nearly colliding with the rest of the group as they rounded the corner.

Skye jumped back, her eyes wide. "You scared me! What's happening? Why are you returning?"

"The deimoses are already here," Malkia replied, moving through the group towards the far end of the hallway. "Let's converge in the study. I can protect it with my light barrier, while we decide how to destroy them and the entire Artemisian hide out."

Standing in the study, Malkia watched as Damon and Koleton barricaded the doors with furniture. She closed her eyes, concentrating on her light as it flowed from her and grew in strength, encompassing the room's perimeter. The snarling of the deimoses could be heard stirring down the corridor, and Malkia heard someone gasp loudly from the sound.

"We were just in time," Bella whispered, her hand curling around Malkia's forearm. Malkia opened her eyes, observing her friend.

"Any chance we can find an alternate route out of this room?" Malkia asked. "If I can sneak around the deimos herd and find out where they are entering, I can travel to the Artemsians and put an end to their bunker."

"Your father had all kinds of secret tunnels throughout this house, but I was never privy to any of them." Haltia replied, sliding her hand along the wall next to her. "I'm not sure if this room has any, but it wouldn't hurt to search. Asha, Alyssa and Bella can use their magic to detect any interior exits."

Malkia nodded, sliding her arm around Bella's waist and giving her a sideways hug. "Thanks for being here with me." She whispered to her friend. "I'm struggling and I hope you know none of my resentment is directed at you."

"I know," Bella smiled at her friend, squeezing her arm and kissing her cheek. "We all understand."

Kolten snuck up behind the women and enclosed them both in his large arms. "Let's kick some ass, ladies." He stepped back, winking at the duo.

Malkia and Bella laughed, pushing Kolten away, before turning back to the group. "Let's see what we can find," Malkia said, gliding towards the wall of their temporary sanctuary. "With Tantiana outside, I fear it will only be a matter of time before the Artemisians direct their energy towards her, in order to eliminate that threat."

The other individuals nodded, as the three witches gathered into a small huddle, chanting quietly while the others searched every nook and cranny of the room. The group shuffled away from the doors and into the middle of the room as the clawing against the wood intensified. The snarls seeped underneath the door and filled the air around them, causing them all to sidestep towards the outside wall.

"We found it." Asha looked up from the witch's huddle after several long minutes, a ball of light moving from the middle. It flew over the group's heads, illuminating an area on the wall adjoining the outside section.

Malkia moved towards the light, noticing within the witch's magic light, a handle was on display. She reached forward and tugged at the handle. The door remained sealed. Malkia searched for a latch, but couldn't find any. Skye slid up next to her and took the handle from

Malkia's grasp. She pushed in the center, and they watched as the wall slid to the left, revealing a doorway with a stairway leading down.

"That's my girl," Koleton boasted, winking at Malkia and Skye.

Malkia grinned over at Skye. "You have the magic touch."

Skye flashed a smile at Malkia, taking a few steps back, and allowing the rest of the group to see the stairway. A musky smell lingered near the doorway, and darkness enveloped the bottom of the narrow staircase. Alyssa opened her hand, tossing a ray of light down into the blackness.

Another doorway stood at the bottom. Damon edged forward, clasping Malkia's hand as he moved past her. "I'll go first."

"Wait." Malkia whispered. "I think only a few of us should go. The rest can stay here inside my protective light."

As she finished speaking, the fortress shuddered, followed by violent shaking. Screams filled the space around them as each person scrambled to find something to steady themselves. The walls swayed with the motions and the doors quivered and shook from the pressure, but continued to hold the creatures at bay.

"Change of plans," Malkia yelled above the rattling. "We're all going."

TWO

Fighting for Their Lives

BELLA TOOK THE lead, while the rest of the group quickly bounded down the narrow stairs behind her. Justin secured the door behind them, being the last one through. The shaking continued but lessened as they approached the other door.

Stopping at the bottom of the stairs, the group held their collective breath, waiting for Bella to check the other side of the door. She exhaled softly, waving for everyone to follow her, giving them the all clear signal. Each of them slid over the threshold, glancing in every direction before following the one in front. Moments later, they were all gathered in a lower-level room, the eerie stillness engulfing them.

Koleton tiptoed towards the door in the room, placing his hand on the frame and his ear against the door. Putting his finger to his lips, he motioned for them all to stay quiet, listening intently to the movements on the other side. Nodding his head, he pulled on the latch and eased the door open.

Malkia peeked through the doorway first, enclosing the group in her protective light. She signaled Damon to show them the entrance the deimoses were using to infiltrate the fortress. He slid past her, into the corridor, hurrying towards the far end with the rest of the group in tow.

Easing through the doorway at the end of the hallway, Malkia noticed the open entrance to a hidden corridor. The deimoses had all made it through and what stood in the doorway with its back turned towards them, sent shivers down her back. The group skidded to an abrupt halt, scampering to find shelter from the massive Artemisian.

The demon grunted, hearing their hustle and shuffled to face them. Malkia stood her ground, glaring at the creature who was determined to see her dead.

His eyes narrowed, seeing her standing in the open room. "It's you," he grumbled. "The one who destroyed my home. How did you make it past my pets?"

"Does it matter?" Malkia asked, stepping towards him, strengthening her protective light. "Do you realize it was my father's plan all along to have me burn your moon, in order to obtain dominion over your people? Are you all that foolish to not see his hand in this?"

"Who's your father?" the creature replied, moving his weapon in between him and Malkia.

"I thought you knew who I am," she said.

"I do!" He bellowed, his face flushing to a dark red. "You're the witch who devastated my home. Why are you taunting me?"

"Who instructed you to slaughter me?" Malkia wiped the beads of sweat from her forehead, feeling the heat from her light intensifying.

The Artemisian whistled loudly. "No human gives me orders. I only take orders from the High Lord. I don't know who your father is and I don't care, but I do know you will die today."

"Maybe your High Lord will know who my father is," she replied, wringing her hands together, her eyes shifting around the room, searching for her comrades. *They must have hidden themselves before he turned around.*

The Artemisian took a step forward, his eyes slanting into thin slits. "You won't live to meet the High Lord."

Malkia could hear the growls of the deimoses moving down the corridor, towards them. She turned on her heel, slamming the door shut. "It's time to go," she instructed her friends, keeping her eyes on the demon.

Without warning, the Artemisian raced towards her with deceptive speed for a creature so large. She dove out of the way, tumbling into Asha's arms on the other side of the room. Gathering herself, she turned to face the creature, her light bursting from her body and rocketing towards him. Ducking out of the way, her light grazed his shoulder, causing him to curse loudly and stumble to the ground. He struck with a deafening thud, as her light hit the opposite wall, shaking the entire room.

As he attempted to rise, Koleton and Damon hurdled out of the shadows, their weapons drawn. Koleton's large dagger cut deep into the demon's throat, and Damon shot a massive hole into his sternum with one of the Artemisians laser weapons. Choking on his own blood, the demon's eyes widened for a moment, before he fell forward, landing face first on the cold floor.

Malkia inhaled deeply and sagged against Asha, who was still holding onto her. Closing her eyes, she took a few deep breaths before straightening back up and glancing around the room. "Their deimos pets are right outside the door. I think we need to lead them back to their bunker and then destroy their entire hideout."

"Agreed," Haltia responded, stepping up behind her. "We need to end whatever hold your father still has on this area. However, he has to be in communication with the Artemisians. So, although I agree with you on terminating their bunker, I do believe we need to find his whereabouts first."

Malkia nodded, looking over at Damon. "Are we all ready?"

The group nodded in unison. Shifting around to the lead, Damon made his way to the hidden entryway, with Malkia right behind him. Each one moved into the passageway, edging cautiously along the blackened path.

It wasn't long before they heard the door that was the only barrier between the deimoses and them, crash violently to the ground, followed by the snarling of the animals, in the wake of their slaughtered master.

"They will follow soon," Malkia whispered. "We need to run."

She didn't have to twist anyone's arm, as each individual picked up their speed, sprinting into the darkness and using only their limited sight to keep them from colliding with hidden obstructions. Within a few minutes, a dim light cascaded into the tunnel. Slowing their pace, they edged towards the threshold, making sure they wouldn't have any surprises.

Damon reached the end first. Clasping his laser weapon with both hands, he peeked around the corner, holding his breath. Malkia's heart quickened, watching his forehead crease and his lips tighten. He stepped back, putting out his hand to signal them to wait. A few seconds later, they saw a small herd of Artemisians round a corner, moving away from them and down a slanted corridor. Damon glanced again, nodding at Malkia and sliding into the room. Each of them moved quickly, hearing the deimoses growing closer by the second.

"Their pets are going to find us, no matter where we go," Skye whispered, her hand curling around Malkia's forearm. "How do you expect to find your father and evade the deimoses?"

Malkia shook her head. "I don't know. Haltia? Do you have a plan?"

Haltia turned towards the two women. "Let's move to the other side of the bunker. If we can put enough space in between us and the deimoses, maybe we can buy us enough time to find out some information and then double back. Then you and Asha can annihilate all of them."

"It's not much of a plan," Malkia muttered, her eyes twitching with irritation. "We need to keep running," she said to the rest of the group. "Let's stay together and move as quickly as we can around to the other side. If any of you see anything of importance, we'll stop."

Sprinting ahead of the group, Malkia watched closely for any Artemisian or deimos. The corridor was dark, with shadows dancing on the clay walls from the lighted lanterns along the way. The entire hallway was embedded with dirt and rock and reminded Malkia of the caves in her dreams.

As she hurried along the rocky path, a cry of a child echoed around Malkia. She stopped dead center in the pathway and glanced back at the group behind her. "Did you hear that?"

"Hear what?" Damon asked, lightly grasping her elbow.

"I swear I heard a child cry. What if my father is hiding here?" Her eyes fluttered down the hallway and then back to the group. "What if Esta is still here on Eris?"

Alyssa stepped forward, her forehead creased with concern. "I think someone is playing with your mind, Malkia. Did you hear the cry in your head or was it out loud?"

Malkia placed her hands on her head, shaking it rapidly. "I swear it was out loud, but I don't know any more. Maybe I imagined the whole thing." She growled under her breath, turning back to the tunnel. "Let's keep going. We don't have any time to waste." She began running again without waiting for a reply. Her head was swimming with doubt and she wondered if the events of the last few weeks had caused her to lose all touch of reality.

Without thinking, she raced around a corner, colliding into two Artemisians. "Ugh!" Malkia choked, falling backwards away from the demons and landing hard on her backside. She jumped up quickly as the Artemisians began firing their weapons.

Her light quickly surrounded her and the group. The lasers beat up against her shield and she felt the heat of the inferno inside of her. She realized how easy it was to destroy the Artemisians and her heart longed to go back to the days where her greatest achievement was successfully avoiding singeing her eyebrows when starting a fire. She closed her eyes and clasped onto Damon's hand.

"I don't want to do this anymore," she whispered, a silent tear escaping down her cheek. "I don't want to do this anymore." Her voice grew louder, as her eyes snapped open. "Stop it!" She screamed at the demons, pleading desperately. "I'm not your enemy. Please stop it."

The Artemisian's weapons stopped firing on her light, but they held them firm and pointed directly at her. A large crowd of demons had gathered behind their comrades, eyeing Malkia with freezing contempt.

"I'm not fighting you any longer," Malkia cried out, her lower lip trembling, biting it to hold it still. "I don't desire to exterminate anyone else. I've been a pawn in my father's ploy for far too long and I refuse to continue on with his charade. If you want to fight someone, find him and battle your way to sweet revenge, because I quit!"

The stillness in the air wrapped itself around the group, suffocating Malkia as she stared at the wide-eyed demons in front of her. No one moved and the silence was deafening.

"You quit?" a voice from the crowd of demons bellowed, breaking the silence. "How can you quit? You started this battle." The group of Artemesians nodded in unison, grunting loudly in agreement.

Malkia stood up straight, staring at the demons in front of her. "I didn't start this battle. I don't even know who began all of this, but I do know my existence was created afterwards." She balled her hands up into fists, feeling the rage consuming her heart, but wanting to weep in defeat instead. "I never wanted this," she mumbled, shaking her head. "I didn't ask for this life and I'm exhausted fighting a war I had nothing to do with. I want out. I want to be done. What do I need to do to end this?"

The Artemisian closest to her growled with fury, his face turning a bright crimson color. "Someone has to pay for the destruction of our moon. You swooped in without any questions and completely annihilated every living thing on Artemis. You're not allowed to just quit. You did start this battle and now we will end it."

Malkia hid her face in her hands, her uncontrolled tears sliding desperately from her eyes, drenching her hands and face. "You really are the barbarians I was warned about," she said through her hands.

"I'm asking for another way and all you can see is the end of my life."
She paused, her hands falling to her sides. "I *did not* want this!" she
screamed at the demons again. "I never asked to be the Erisians
weapon. I only want my daughter and a peaceful life returned to me.
Nothing else."

Another Artemisian chuckled. "You're no warrior. You're just a
frightened woman, afraid to finish what you started. If you are so eager
to give up, remove your shield and allow us to have our revenge."

Damon stepped forward, followed by Justin, Koleton and Skye.
Their weapons were drawn defensively in front of their bodies. Malkia
strengthened her light and could feel the fire taking hold of her heart
again, as she watched red hues bounce rapidly within the purple aura.
Asha curled her hands around the tender flesh of her arms, bringing her
back to reality, just when her face began to flush with heat.

Malkia turned to Asha. "I can't hold it back. I want to, but if they
insist on fighting, I don't know if I can contain it." Her forehead
creased and a sob escaped her lips. "It's consuming my entire soul."

"Don't allow the power to take hold of your soul," Asha responded,
putting her hand under Malkia's chin and pulling her eyes back up to
hers. "You have control of this. If the demons are intent on fighting,
we will do it together."

Nodding her head, Malkia pivoted back towards the Artemisians
and now she could see the deimoses had surrounded them on every
side. "I'm willing to end this battle tonight," she said to the demons.
"We can agree to live in peace and find a way to repair the damage I've
inflicted on your people. I understand thousands of lives were lost, but
I was unaware of the good of the Artemisians until it was too late. I

never desired this outcome."

Shaking their heads with disgust, one of the Artemisians spoke up, his words an ice pick to her heart. "You're a wicked and evil witch and it will be my pleasure to rip you to shreds, the way you did to so many of my people."

Malkia swallowed hard, her pulse quickening and her face flushing with the fire inside. Her breath came in short, as she attempted to calm the rage building rapidly within her heart. "You've given me no other choice."

The light burst from her body, directing itself at the swarm of Artemisians in front of her. The deimoses scurried away, running for shelter wherever they could find it. The explosion surrounded her group, ricocheting violently in every direction.

"Let us help you," Alyssa murmured, grasping Malkia's shoulder. "We can do this together and hopefully keep the darkness smothered in the abyss of your thoughts."

"Thank you," Malkia replied, turning to her Esaki mother. "It's fighting to be free and I'm not sure I can resist any longer."

"We are in this together." Asha stepped forward, clasping Malkia's hand. "We have done this once before and we can do it again."

Alyssa nodded, grasping hold of Malkia's other hand, followed by Bella reaching out and grabbing Asha's free hand. The four women stepped forward, with the rest of the group behind them, allowing their powers to grip onto the lives of every Artemisian and deimos they met. As they neared the balcony opening, Malkia built her powers inside her, only allowing the purple light to flow from her body. At the edge of the Artemisian bunker, the four women stared down into the deep tunnel, crawling with demons and deimos and allowed their combined powers to spiral downwards, consuming all that it met, until there was only black silence.

THREE
An Unlikely Friend

"SEE WHAT WE can accomplish as a team," Alyssa spoke up as they all trudged silently back to the fortress. "We have the power to plow through your father's blockade of demons and find your daughter."

Malkia glanced over at her Esaki mother, numb exhaustion spreading through her entire body. This wasn't the outcome she had desired. "I heard a child cry out back in the Artemisian bunker. How do I know we didn't just destroy my own child in the process?"

"She wasn't there," Haltia interjected, stepping forward next to the other women. "No one else heard the child, which makes me believe your father has discovered a way to intrude upon your mind. He's determined to find a way around your defense system and if that means he goes directly to the source, your mind, he will. It never occurred to me that he would go in that direction, but it makes sense. He has wanted to either destroy you or control you, since we discovered your intense powers, and he has had twenty-nine years to perfect his techniques."

"Do you mean he has found a way to read my mind from a distance and without my knowing?" Malkia asked, halting in her tracks and looking around at the weary group. "I cannot win with this man." The heat from her inward fire, stung her face as the fury melted through her skin.

Asha clasped Malkia'a hands with hers, holding them between their hearts. "Malkia, I know you are angry and hurt, and I don't blame you for feeling this way. However, we won't survive much further if you don't find a way to control the darkness, permanently. You have many choices, but the one that will ensure your separation from your daughter is giving into that fire." Placing Malkia's hands against her cheek, she continued, "Close your eyes and see your purple light and the brightness it brings into your life."

Malkia inhaled quietly and closed her eyes, sensing Asha's power flowing from her hands and into her own body. The coolness soothed the heat and her heart returned to a steady beat. "Thank you, Asha." She opened her eyes and stared at the purple eyes smiling back her.

Asha kissed her hand before letting it slip away. "I'm always here for you."

The group continued their return to the fortress, sealing the secret entrance once they were safely through. At this point, they could only hope there wouldn't be any more attacks on their group.

Damon followed Malkia into Esta's room, shutting the door behind him. "What do you need from me?"

"Honestly," Malkia replied, turning to face him, her eyes slanted from exhaustion. "I want your touch. Some time to forget my father and his desire to end my life."

Damon reached for her, tugging her tightly into his chest and kissing the top of her head. "You don't have to ask me twice for that. You already own my heart, body and soul."

Releasing her, he led her to the bed, kissing her softly on the lips before he wriggled her shirt up over her head, followed by his own. His hands grazed her sides, moving to caress shoulder muscles taut from emotional and physical stress, gently kneading sensitive flesh, and finally coaxing her trousers from her hips. A moan escaped her lips, as his fingertips pressed between her thighs, drawing a bloom of pleasure and euphoria from the core of her being.

Smiling up at Damon, she clasped the nape of his neck and bruised his lips with the hunger of her kisses, as they slipped onto the bed. The sensations he stirred within her were strange continents of longing never yet mapped. She needed his touch.

The fortress was dark and silent as Malkia slipped from Esta's room, glancing back one last time at Damon. He slept soundly, with his arms curled around an extra pillow. A smile crossed over her lips, remembering their moment together and realizing it was always supposed to be him.

For now, she would have to say good-bye the coward's way. She had left him a note, explaining why she was leaving and that when the time was right, she would return.

...Don't wait for me, if you need to return to Esaki. I will find my way back to you, one way or another. And please, watch over Tantiana and the rest of our friends. All my love,

Malkia.

She floated away from the closed door, moving quietly down to the main level and out the main entryway. The still of the night was calming, and she welcomed the solitude as she swept silently over the forest and away from her family and friends.

As the morning rushed in and the suns peeked over the horizon, Malkia came upon a small village. Reigning in her light, she entered the town, searching for a place to eat. The smell of fresh baked bread filled the air, and Malkia followed the scent, eventually coming upon the bakery.

Opening the door, she was welcomed with the sweet aroma of breakfast, and she slid into the nearest chair, waiting for someone to notice her presence.

"Well, hello there stranger," a young man said, as he walked from the kitchen area with his notebook. "What can we make for you?"

Malkia smiled up at the man. "I would love some of your fresh bread, eggs and some sliced meat, along with fresh juice."

The young man scribbled on his notebook, his smile widening. "Sounds great. I'll have that out for you soon." He turned away from her, just as more customers walked into the bakery.

She inhaled the clean air and smiled to herself, recalling the peace surrounding her as she nestled in Damon's arms. He had told her he had kept his powers at bay with her, desiring for their union to really come from both of their hearts. It was as if they were always supposed to be together, a match made by destiny.

Watching the new patrons settle into their seats, Malkia shifted her gaze to the closest window, watching the suns wake up the creatures of Eris. A small rodent scurried across the dirt in front of her window, racing towards a nearby dwelling. A sapphire bird landed in the flowers, pecking at the ground, as it searched for its morning meal and a horse pranced through the nearby fields, neighing at the people as they idled on by.

Moments later, the young man set a large plate in front of Malkia, filled with all the delicacies she had ordered. She grinned up at him, as she picked up her fork and began eating. He nodded and winked, before turning on his heel and walking away.

Turning her attention to her food, her thoughts bounced around in her mind. *I don't know what I am looking for, but I do know I have to find out more about my father. There is a reason I heard the cry in my mind and I'm beginning to think there is more history to this conflict than anyone is willing to divulge. If they won't tell me, I'll find someone who will.*

Her thoughts absorbed her while she ate. Once her hunger was sated, she glanced around the small room, her jaw clinching as she caught the carnelian eyes staring at her from across the bakery. His long, talon-like fingers tapped the tabletop in front of him, as his skin took on a crimson tint, his anger obviously spiking.

Rising from her seat, Malkia stepped towards the creature, keeping her eyes locked on his every move. "Why are you here?" she whispered, barely standing over him, despite his seated position.

He curled his fingers, a crooked smile sliding across his face, as he leaned back in his chair. "This is my home, witch. Unlike you, I belong here." He paused, watching her closely. "I know who you are and I will dismember you for your invasion of my moon."

Malkia stepped back, glancing over her shoulder at the few humans eating in the bakery. They didn't seem to notice or care that they were in the presence of their enemy. "How is this your home?" she asked the Artemisian, while shaking her head. "Your kind only wants to destroy the human race, not live among them."

"Are all you humans the same?" the creature asked, sitting up straight in his chair.

Malkia's brows furrowed, noticing the stares from the other guests. "No, humans are not all the same. Why?"

His smile widened, enjoying her discomfort. "What makes you think all Artemisians are the same? What gave you the right to judge a whole civilization based on the word of a corrupt leader?"

"You don't know what you are talking about," Malkia replied, taking another step back.

"If you believe you can escape, go ahead and try." He waved his hand, leaning back in his chair again. "I already have your scent and I'm not like the other Artemisians you have met."

Malkia pivoted on her heel, tossing payment for the food on her table and exiting the bakery in a rush. The suns had risen completely and the village was bustling with people. No one seemed to notice her, but when she looked back, the humans and Artemisian were watching her from the bakery.

This is not the place for me, she thought. Observing the structures and mountains towering around the village, she pressed forward, determined to put some space in between her and the Artemisian.

Passing some of the locals, she smiled and nodded, before taking one more glance at the bakery. The Artemisian was now standing just inside the doorway, watching her retreat. Shaking her head, she faced away, sprinting down the first alleyway she came across.

Before long, the small village was behind her and she breathed a sigh of relief. *Maybe it is time to just leave Eris for good.* Pursing her lips, she examined the landscape surrounding her, as she decided on her next step. *Not yet. I need to find out more about my father and hopefully find a way to reach Esta.*

Racing along an over grown pathway, her eyes scanned every inch of her surroundings, wondering how far away these particular structures were. As her thoughts spiraled back over the last few weeks, recalling her abduction, the betrayal of her friends and lover, along with Misty's glass prison, she realized her ensnarement in this life was never her choice. Her father had played her, knowing in advance her every move.

Maybe her mother had a point. He had discovered a way to intrude upon her mind and was using that advantage to set her up for ultimate failure. He had already ripped away her daughter. There was not much more damage he could accomplish that would be more excruciating then that moment.

Malkia slowed her pace, her heart aching both from the memory and wishing she possessed the knowledge to end this charade today and reunite with her daughter, once and for all.

"Oomfff!" Malkia grunted, smashing into a hard barrier that appeared out of nowhere. She stumbled backwards, her hands covering her bruised nose.

The lanky Artemisian stood tall in front of her, his eyes narrowed to slits, and his hand firmly grasping his laser weapon. "Did you really believe I would just allow you to walk away?" He asked, his jaw jutting out menacingly.

Malkia wiped the blood from her nostrils, eyeing the demon with icy contempt. "I just want to be left alone."

The Artemisian laughed out loud, before shaking his head with disgust. "You destroyed my entire moon and left it to burn to a crisp. You are a monster, who deserves to meet her creator, and I'm here to make that happen."

Her light burst from her body, shielding her from the lasers blasting from his weapon. She stepped back, grimacing at the thought of having to battle another Artemis creature, but willed her light to flare from her hands. The force struck the demon in the upper thigh, his body flopping forward, as his legs were swept out from underneath him. Landing face first into the rocky path, he grunted loudly from the impact.

"Stop it," Malkia demanded, stepping back a few more feet and pulling her light back into her body, as she eyed the demon on the ground. "I'm done fighting my father's war and don't desire to end your life. Please walk away and allow me to live in peace."

The Artemisian rose from his fallen position, with a leap that startled Malkia. She skipped back farther, seeing the fury slide across the demons face, as his skin took on a gleam of flawless ruby.

"You are an egotistical parasite," his voice roared over her, like an electric current, causing the hair at the nape of her neck to stand on end. "You massacred an entire civilization, without an ounce of remorse, insisting you deserve to continue to breathe, while my remaining people suffer the aftermath of your actions. How dare you."

Before she had a chance to respond, he dove at her, gripping her hair and tossing her against a nearby tree. She wheezed and gasped desperately for air, her light guttering like as spent candle before it receded entirely. She felt a boulder crush her face, causing her eyesight to falter, just as the sharp rocks on the path dug roughly into the side of her body, driving a groan from her lips. Focusing on her powers, she propelled her light outside of her body, holding it steady and waiting for her vision to return.

"You miserable savage," she heard the demon bellow at her and twisted her face towards it. "You don't deserve these powers. Punishment for your actions should begin with the dismantling of your barricade, followed by an identical torture that you showered down upon my people."

Malkia blinked, seeing his blurred silhouette crouched over her, as her vision began to return. Reaching back, she touched the back of her head, feeling the sticky residue in her hair. Groaning again, she slid away from the Artemisian and rose awkwardly into a seated position.

She shook her head and rubbed her eyes, before focusing on the demon, thankful her light kept him at bay. "I do deserve death," she whispered, as she exhaled in defeat. "What I did is unforgivable and I don't blame you for wishing for my extermination." She paused, scrubbing furtively at her cheek as a single tear escaped. "However, I have to stop my father from creating any more destruction and pandemonium, all because of his resentment towards me. My death won't halt his vengeance and I have to protect my people and my daughter before I'm taken from this life."

The Artemisian took a step back, his eyes softening slightly. "Who is your father?" he asked, tilting his head slightly, his forehead crinkled in speculation.

Malkia inhaled deeply, wiping her hair away from her face. "His name is Thane." She eyed the demon, but he stood quietly, his eyes empty of recognition. "I don't know how influential he is with your people, but he had a large number of them working with him at his fortress on the edge of the Erebus forest. Their bunker was hidden in the thick of the trees, deep inside the ground. However, I was surprised his name is not known among your people."

The Artemisian's skin had returned to the color of wet slate and he stepped a few more feet back, before lowering down into a seated position. He scrutinized Malkia for several moments before speaking up. "I know the man you speak of, however, he's not addressed as Thane. He is the Supreme or High Lord and was only elected because of his invaluable knowledge, along with his endless supply of funds and power." He leaned back, supporting his weight on curled fists. "I have met your father, but did not realize the relation. He has been urging my people to find you and end your life, even before you demolished my moon. Now, I find it odd he sought your death, being that you are his flesh and blood."

The tears came without warning and Malkia felt the ache rise in her chest, knowing she had been used from the beginning to take the lives of so many innocent Artemisians. The sobs gripped her, the molten lead of guilt suffusing her heart and mind, shaking her to the core.

The Artemisian sat in silence, watching her from his perch on the pebbles, his expression remaining calm. The embarrassment of the situation settled her cries, as she wiped away the tears streaming down her face. "I apologize for my outburst. Two months ago, I didn't even know my father existed. Now, I have become his pawn to eliminate your race and ensure his rise to dominance over all the people on Theia's moons." She stared down at her hands, one last sob rising up her throat. "I can see now, he discovered a way to shift the attention from himself and create a war against his own daughter, which enabled his escape."

She rose from the ground, wiping off her backside and legs, and then straightened to face the demon. He slowly stood as well, observing her every move.

"I'm inclined to believe you," he said, after a few moments of silence. "The Supreme Lord has always seemed untrustworthy, but he has kept our civilization safe for many years that I have struggled to refuse his bidding. It has been a mystery to many with his sudden disappearance."

Malkia shook her head, feeling powerless in her explanations, but finally fitting the puzzle pieces together. "His lover was entrusted with making sure I traveled to Artemis and destroyed your moon. Her daughter and grandchildren led me down a path of trust, guaranteeing I felt safe and sure of my decisions. Her grandson was my partner and best friend for many years and now in retrospect, I can see this was all staged for the moment my father could take power over your race and guarantee his supremacy." She closed her eyes, raking her hands through her hair. "He has used all of us and now he holds my daughter hostage in the hopes he can either extinguish me or in the future have her execute me."

The Artemisian stepped forward, holding his hand out for Malkia to take. She stood as if rooted to the ground, staring hard at the demon before finally moving towards him and grasping the long fingers. He held it firmly, staring into her eyes. "I believe you."

She hiccoughed in surprise. "Thank you," she replied, tears bursting from her eyelids, wetting her cheeks once again. "The regret and shame will always be mine to bear, and I take responsibility for following instructions of people who never had anyone's best interest at heart." She inhaled, pausing to catch her breath and wipe away her tears. "All I ask, is to be allowed to live long enough to retrieve my daughter from my father's grasp and place her in safe and loving arms. Then you may have your revenge."

"I don't mean any disrespect, but if what you say is true, you were only a puppet in the destruction of my people. The one who must pay for their deaths, is the same man who is holding your daughter captive." The Artemisian released her hand, straightening his stance.

She sighed in relief. "All I desire is to find my daughter and avenge your people."

"Although, you're a bit impulsive," the Artemisian replied. "I trust we have the ability to work well with each other. My name is Apollo."

"It's a pleasure to meet you, Apollo. I'm Malkia." She grasped his hand once more, his muscles flexing from the spark of their connection. Her smile spread across her face as she picked up the items strewn across the ground, shoving them back into her pack. "Why do you believe that we can work well with each other?"

He cleared his throat, a grin dangling on his lips. "I've never fully trusted the Supreme Lord." Apollo handed her a container of water. "He's not of my race, but he warped many minds into trusting he would keep us safe from the Enyoans and any Erisian that chose to battle against us. He never mentioned a daughter, aside from the one he keeps protected in his fortress. However, he insisted we find a woman of magnificent abilities, who barricades herself in a purple light and can rise with our flying crafts, and end her life or perish in her fire. Those were his words." He moved away from Malkia, signaling her to follow him. "He assured us that our moon would remain unharmed, as long as we annihilated every living soul on Esaki and promised to execute you the moment, we found you."

Malkia trotted alongside Apollo, finding it difficult to keep up with his long strides. After a few moments, she encircled herself with her light, floating quietly alongside him with little effort.

"But you didn't wipe out everyone on Esaki. Many people survived the war. Is that why he turned on your people?" Malkia asked, breaking their silence and craning her neck to see his face.

"I don't believe so. The Artemisians attacked Esaki many years ago, because of his instructions, but after our last battle we were told to leave the moon alone until he had a better idea of your whereabouts." Apollo shot a glance to the sky, shaking his head. "It wasn't until a couple of months ago that he brought you up again, years after the slaughter of the Esakians. Honestly, I believed you were already dead at that point."

Malkia chewed on her bottom lip, her heart pounding from the story Asha had told her about Haltia. *How did my mother convince my father to leave me alone?* She questioned in her mind. Turning back to face Apollo, she could see him peering over at her. "There are many stories floating around and I wish I understood how they all fit together. Too many missing pieces." She paused, noticing his puzzled look. "My memory of Eris and my family was blocked from the age of five, until just a couple of months ago. I had no idea my father desired my death when I first saw him again, nor did I know about the war raging between Eris, Enyo and Artemis."

Apollo nodded, turning his face to watch the pathway. "That makes more sense and explains why he was searching for you on Esaki."

"He knew where I was," Malkia replied. "He took me there himself, back when I was a child. You and your people were just as much puppets in his plan as I was. Do you have any idea how we can end his manipulation or fix this situation?"

"I don't think we will be able to fix anything," he responded, his eyes scanning their surroundings, as they glided through the trees. "We are only capable of safeguarding your daughters escape and assisting my people in rebuilding their lives."

Malkia nodded. "I hope and pray my daughter will have a desire to leave with me, instead of proclaiming loyalty to my father."

"Prayer and hope are unnecessary," Apollo said, halting in his tracks and staring down at her. "I do not understand your people's need to pray. The only way to create the path you desire, is to take action and do the work yourself."

"Do you not believe in a Higher Power?" Malkia asked.

He shook his head, stepping forward again. "A Higher Power has nothing to do with our paths. If any form of God or Creator exists, *It* is not standing around anticipating our prayers. We must take action. Your human beliefs astound me at times." He paused, holding out his arm to stop her. He pressed his talon-like finger to his pursed lips, pointing his other fingers into the thick of the forest. "There are others in the forest," he whispered.

Malkia released the latch on her dagger, holding it firmly in her hands. Following behind the large demon, she peeked around him to attain a better view. Within seconds, she heard the language of the dragons inside her mind and realized they had stumbled upon a nest.

"Stop," Malkia demanded, grasping onto the forearm of the demon. "It's a dragon nest. The mother has departed, but the dragon babies are stirring. We must wait until the mother returns and then I'll be able to speak with her."

"Dragons do not exist on Eris," Apollo stared back at her, his eyes slanted in disbelief. "And how are you able to speak with dragons?"

"It's an ability that was bestowed on me by my adopted mother and warlock. I don't know how she accomplished the feat, but it is a power I have come to enjoy." She pursed her lips, searching the sky for the mother. "They trust me, and I won't betray them. My own dragon, Tantiana, is one of the most exquisite creatures I have ever known, and her loyalty has been refreshing, considering the amount of deceit I've encountered."

Apollo nodded. "I can appreciate and understand that. I will respect your wishes to wait until the mother returns." He paused, searching her eyes. "If you would like, we can proceed with our journey and leave the creatures alone."

"No, I need to see them and make certain they are safe. If they don't belong on Eris, I need to know why they are here." Malkia moved in the opposite direction from the dragon nest. "Let's find a safe distance from those hatchlings and make camp for the night." She halted in her tracks, turning to face Apollo. "If you don't mind keeping me company for the time being."

"I do not believe in prayer, but fate has an amusing way of showing up when we are in most need of it," he responded. "For now, I am delighted to spend my time with you and consolidate our knowledge."

Malkia beamed, following behind Apollo as he stepped towards a new path that led away from the dragons.

FOUR
The Hidden Village

THE MOTHER OF the dragons didn't return until well after Malkia and Apollo had set up camp and finished their meal. The warm fire crackled in the background as Malkia heard the dragon's wings whoosh through the air, followed by the dialect in her mind. The mother was speaking to her hatchlings, ordering them to stay in the nest.

Rising from her perch on a rock, Malkia nodded at Apollo and left the safety of their hideout to confront the dragon in a clearing nearby. The mother had already landed and was awaiting her arrival.

Venturing closer, she gasped when her eyes adjusted to the twilight and clearly saw the massive creature. The red and orange streaks down her sides, glistened next to the intense black skin. The stunning animal appeared as a fire in the night sky. The dragon sensed Malkia's advance upon her, and shifted her body around so they were facing one another.

Language of the Majestics? The dragon asked, tilting her head and staring at Malkia with fire red irises.

Malkia stepped closer, her head bobbing up and down. *The only information explained to me for the means of my ability, was an incantation that was conducted on me when I was in my mother's womb. Whatever the warlock did created what I am today.*

Interesting. The dragon replied. *No human connection before now.*

Why are you on Eris? Malkia asked. *No one has ever beheld a dragon on this moon, aside from the one I brought with me from Esaki. Have you always resided here?*

Hemera is home. The dragon replied. *Artemis warriors forced me here.*

Malkia glanced back towards her camp, thankful Apollo had not joined her. *I'm sorry to hear you were brought here against your will,* she said to the dragon. *What's your name?*

Adelina. The dragon answered. *Escaped captivity, have been nesting my young and searching for a way home.*

I'll help you, Malkia thought. *There must be a way to return you all to Hemera. I'm unfamiliar with that moon, but where I'm going may provide the answers you desire. I would like to return here once I complete my expedition. Will you wait for me?*

Name? Adelina asked.

Malkia touched her chest in reference to herself. *My name is Malkia.*

I fear for my young. Adelina said, her head dropping to Malkia's eye level. *Worry warriors will return.* The dragon paused, searching Malkia's face. *But I trust you. We will wait.*

Malkia smiled, nodding at Adelina. *I'll return as quickly as I can, but it might be a few weeks. Be safe, Adelina.*

The dragon turned, her wings fluttering as she bounded into the air, diving back into the thick of the trees where her babies waited. Malkia wandered back into the forest, edging her way towards Apollo. "What a gorgeous creature," Malkia said out loud, smiling to herself.

Her camp was not far off, but she took this moment to remember why she was here and where she needed to go to end this battle with her father. This moon held her father's darkest secrets and she was going to break them open for all the people to see. Pulling the piece of parchment from her trousers, she used Theia's light to view the etchings. Her first stop was not far from here, but it would be nearly another day before she arrived.

She stuffed it back into her pocket as she neared the flicker of her campfire. Apollo stood, his face dark with concentration, staring into the fire and she smiled to herself, grateful for her new comrade. As she trudged across a collection of dried leaves, the demon's head jolted up, surveying the area from which she was approaching. He beamed when he caught sight of her.

"You survived the beast's breath," he joked, chuckling to himself.

"Were you worried?" Malkia bantered in return, winking at him.

"Not for one moment," he replied. "I'm keenly aware of your ability to handle dangerous situations. Although, encountering one of those fire creatures seems reckless and suicidal, if you ask me."

Malkia laughed, the sides of her eyes crinkling with amusement. "Good thing I wasn't asking you." Yawning with exhaustion, she walked towards the fire and her pack, which held her blanket. "Speaking of, I would suggest you stay far away from the dragon. It appears she was abducted from her home moon and brought here by some Artemisian warriors." She slid down to the ground, leaning up against the tree behind her. "She wasn't impressed by your kind and I would prefer that you survive the breath of the beast as well."

"Good call." Apollo reclined on a rock near the fire. "Thank you for the warning."

Tugging on the soft fabric, Malkia pulled her blanket from her pack, laying it on the dirt and spreading it out. She could feel Apollo's eyes on her and glanced up, making eye contact.

He cleared his throat, his expression softening with admiration. "When I first laid eyes on you, I was overcome with what you humans call, anger. I had just returned from Artemis, only viewing the fires ravaging my home from the safety of high orbit. Honestly, I believed fate had delivered you into my hands and I thanked my lucky stars for allowing my revenge to come so easily." His lips twitched with a crooked smile. "Fate is a fickle creature. As we battled, I already knew I couldn't annihilate you. When your light shot out of your body and protected you from my attacks, I desired to break through and shelter you myself. An internal conflict of sorts squeezed my heart and after watching you gain your eyesight back, I knew you and I would be companions." He paused; his serpent eyes unblinking. "The fate that brought us together is not finished with us."

Malkia stretched out on her blanket, before curling into herself, using her pack as a pillow. "There is something about us, isn't there?" She smiled up at Apollo. "Who knew I would befriend an Artemisian. After everything I have done, I believed I would always be the enemy of your people. Now, I just might have a chance to survive. Thank you, Apollo." Her eyes fluttered, as she attempted to keep them open.

"You're welcome," he replied.

Apollo and Malkia wandered through the trees, the second sun peeking over the hills behind them, as the first sun warmed their backs.

The morning had begun early, and they had been traipsing through the forest for hours in silence. Malkia knew where she needed to go and her companion had never questioned their path.

The parchment was held firmly in her hand and every so often she would glance at it, confirming the landmarks matched what was mapped out on the document. Finding the structures seemed to be the only connection she could make to the other moons, that and her father.

"Do you mind if I ask you a question?" Apollo asked.

Malkia smiled back at him. "Didn't you just ask one?"

Apollo halted in his tracks, tilting his head slightly in thought. "You are correct, I did ask a question." He chuckled quietly, stepping forward once again. "May I ask you more than one question?"

Laughing out loud, Malkia nodded. "Of course you may."

"You've been sneaking looks at that papyrus off and on since we began traveling together. Do you have a destination I can assist you with finding?" He shot her a sideways glance.

Malkia ran her fingers across the parchment, uneasy to reveal what she knew and why she had to find these particular buildings. She glanced over at Apollo, her mouth set in a grim line. "You won't believe me if I told you why I am traveling to this certain point."

"I might surprise you." He attempted to wink at her but ended up blinking. "I wish I had the ability to do your human, one-eyed blink."

Malkia burst out laughing, as she watched his awkward blinking and his contorted facial expression. "Winking is what we call it and it's not as neat as you think it is." She unfolded the parchment and kneeled on the ground in front of her, smoothing the document out on the dirt. "I need to find these structures." She pointed to the three triangles, tucked away in between mountainsides.

Apollo reclined next to Malkia and took a closer look. "I know where these are." He replied. "Your father wanted to find a way inside, but we all failed in our attempts. What is in there that is so important?"

Malkia closed her eyes and shook her head. "Of course he wanted inside the pyramids." She paused, surveying the area around them. "I don't know what is in there and right now I'm not interested in their contents. What I need to find is a symbol of a feather on the outside of the structures."

"Why?" Apollo asked, his forehead creasing with confusion.

Malkia folded the parchment, tucking it inside her trousers, as she rose. "Because it enables my contact with the Light Beings."

Apollo's eyes widened, slowly rising from his perch. "You have seen the Light Beings?"

Nodding, Malkia stepped backwards, unsure of his intentions. "Does this bother you?" she asked, intertwining her fingers and chewing on her thumbnail.

"It isn't possible." Apollo ignored her question, staring at her as if he were boring a hole through her soul. "How are you able to see them?"

"The first time was years ago, back on Esaki," she replied, resting her hands on her hips. "I stumbled across a pyramid and after many failed attempts to find an opening, I touched a symbol of a feather and zap." She spread her fingers out in front of her face. "I appeared in a different place. I met them there."

Apollo's stature had stiffened, and his eyes had glazed over, as he stood silent in front of her. Stepping a few more feet away, Malkia made sure she had the parchment, before turning back to Apollo. His facial expression hadn't changed, and Malkia was beginning to wonder if she was safe anymore.

Clearing his throat, Apollo blinked, returning to reality. "I was told only the Chosen Heir would be able to communicate with the Light Beings or what most others call the Aletheian's." He shook his head, clearly confused. "How are you that person?"

Malkia groaned, tired of explaining herself to everyone who learned of her abilities. "I don't know why I can speak with these Beings and I certainly don't know why you were told only the "Chosen Heir" has the ability to communicate with them. If I was chosen to do anything, it's to stop my father from his desire to control Theia's moons. As for any other chosen missions, I'm opting out, once I have ended his dramatic performance and have my daughter safely out of his reach." She raked her hands through her hair, feeling the pressure she had left back at her father's fortress weigh down on her shoulders. "I told you I don't want to fight any longer and I meant it. I don't want any of this."

Apollo had stepped forward and when he reached Malkia, he grasped her shoulder and turned her to face him. "I'm not here to fight you. Not anymore at least. I am perplexed by this new information, but if you tell me you have the ability to see and speak with the Aletheian's, then I have even more reason to accompany you on your mission and assist you in finding what you desire." He straightened up, smiling down at her. "These Beings are a form of angels to the Artemisians. They have been seen by only a handful of my people that I am aware, and their presence in our star system has always ensured balance and safety."

"Then why did they allow me to destroy your moon?" Malkia questioned.

"There has to be a reason." His smile stretched across his face. "I informed you of my belief in fate and this situation is why. The Aletheian's are always guiding us on our paths. If we have fallen into a dark path and are inflicting pain and strife on others, the beings will interject, but they will use another to complete the work." His eyes swept across the trees. "There is a reason for all of this. I can see that now."

Malkia nodded, inhaling deeply and not wanting to discuss it any further. "If we hurry, we can make the pyramids before the last sundown. I would like to find the feather before it sets, but if not, we can search first thing in the morning." She stepped forward, Apollo moving in line with her. "Thank you for believing in me," she whispered.

Apollo chuckled. "I should be the one thanking you for allowing me to tag along. I honestly believed I would not meet the Chosen Heir in my lifetime, but here I am strolling through the forest with her by my side." His grin expanded, showing off his bright white teeth.

"Please, don't make a big deal out of this," Malkia said, a quiet growl growing in her throat. "If I am this Chosen Heir, I want to find out more of my role before we announce it to anyone else."

"Of course." Apollo shot Malkia a crooked smile.

Malkia rose upwards through the thickness of the trees, searching for the pyramid structures. The mountain sides loomed above them on each side and according to the map they were on the correct trail, but the first sun had set and the second one was casting its final shadows on the valley below them. She cleared the last of the trees, her light shoving the branches out of her way, as she glided past them.

Glancing forward, the tip of one pyramid stuck out from the forest, but the other two remained hidden. At least she knew they were near. Rushing back to the ground, she gave Apollo a half-hearted smile. "They're close."

"I told you not to worry," Apollo chided, jutting his chin out in frustration. "You're an awfully stubborn woman."

"I know." Malkia skipped forward, her light dissipating around her. "Let's hurry. We've lost any chance of having direct sunlight, but I can use my own energy to light up the area."

"Watch out!" Apollo shouted, grasping Malkia's arm and wrenching her backwards, just as a rock swung rapidly over the spot she had been standing. Spikes stuck out in random places, held in by some sort of netting.

Malkia gawked at the trap that nearly ended her life. All this way and some rigged contraption would have been the death of her if it weren't for Apollo. "How did you know it was coming?" She breathed, the air in her lungs coming up short.

"We ran into a number of these traps on our first journey through these trees. The locals desire solitude and will use violence to discourage outsiders, but their methods are old fashion, and my hearing is extraordinary." He grinned down at her. "I heard the pop of the lever as it released. You must have tripped something as you walked by."

Her racing heart beat ferociously in her ears, as she surveyed the trees around them. "Where do the locals reside?"

"They are up in the caves around the pyramids," Apollo answered. "They knew we were here the moment we stepped into the ravine."

"And you didn't think this was information I should know," Malkia's lips drew back in a snarl as she surrounded herself with her light, once again.

"I'm still on your side, Malkia," he replied, stepping back from her threatening glare. "I've been watching for any sign of them and believed they were allowing us safe passage through." He paused, running his finger over his chin. "I apologize for my lapse in judgment. I should've informed you, before it became a problem."

"Yes, you should have." Malkia encircled him inside her light, before signaling for him to stay close. "I have the ability to keep us safe, plus I'm anxious to arrive at the pyramids, so I would really like to move along. We can talk about this problem, after we make camp."

Apollo nodded, following closely behind Malkia. "Why do you trust me?" he asked. "As I realize my mistake in not giving you vital information for your safety, I can see this whole scenario could appear like it is a trap to capture you. How do you know I'm not leading you straight into the arms of your enemy?"

Malkia halted in her tracks and turned to face Apollo. "Please don't mistake this comradeship for trust. At this point, I don't trust anyone, especially not you. However, I have my ways to discover other's true intentions and I believe yours are aligned with mine." She grasped onto her pendant, staring down at the glow of bright blue and smiled. "I don't believe in much these days, but like you said, fate has a funny way of showing up when you least expect it."

"I'm pleased to hear you say that." Apollo's eyes and jaw relaxed, striding next to Malkia as she began walking again.

Without another run in with a trap, the duo arrived at the first pyramid, in one piece. Malkia raced up to the structure, eyeing the etchings in the stone and frowning as she inspected them one by one. The last sun was setting and before she had a chance to finish one side of the base, it set completely, enclosing them in an evergrowing darkness.

The stars above them began to twinkle and Theia's light could be seen, but she was hidden by the height of the mountains. Malkia eased her light into the palm of her hand and slowly began to search for the feather.

Apollo had made his way to the other side of the pyramid and when Malkia reached that side, she could see he had set up camp, with a fire blazing and both their bedding spread out. He had taken the rest of their leftover bread and fruit picked from a nearby tree and had them waiting on a makeshift table near the fire.

Malkia smiled, easing back onto the ground. "Thank you for taking care of the campsite and food. If I didn't know any better, I would think you enjoy my company." She chuckled, stealing a glance at her companion.

"I have grown quite fond of you." He nodded, not noticing her teasing tone. "I'm happy to prepare our needs, while you find a way to speak with the Aletheian's."

She laughed, knowing she was the only one enjoying her jokes and jabs, as she pulled her bread apart and chewed on the crust. They ate in silence and Malkia searched the woods around them, keeping an eye out for any local mischief.

After she finished eating everything Apollo had prepared for her, she gulped down a large amount of water, before bringing her light back to her palm. "I won't be much longer. If I don't find it soon, I'll finish tomorrow. If I do find it, I will let you know before I disappear into thin air." She smiled again at Apollo, this time receiving a chuckle in response.

"Thank you for not just disappearing on me," he replied, a smile surfacing on his thin lips.

Malkia turned towards the pyramid. Deciding to begin at the top, she was grateful this pyramid wasn't as large as the one on Enyo. However, Apollo mentioned the next two were twice as massive, so she was happy to save them for the next day.

By the time her eyes began to droop and her light weakened, she had completed searching three of the four sides. Sighing heavily, she trudged back to the camp, feeling defeated by the long day. Apollo slept soundly on his mat and blanket. She didn't notice the set of strange footprints just outside their camp as she melted into her blanket and succumbed to the blackness behind her eyelids.

The shuffling of feet brought Malkia to her knees. Her eyes heavy with sleep, she rubbed them allowing her eyesight to clear. Focusing on the shadowed trees around her, she searched the tree line for the eyes she felt boring into her.

"Apollo," she whispered, glancing over at her comrade and seeing him standing with his large dagger in his right hand and his staff in the other, scanning the woods as well.

"I heard them," he replied, his voice steady and his grip tight on his weapons. "Show yourself," he bellowed into the night sky.

Malkia rose from her knees, both her daggers held firmly in front of her. The shadows in the trees shifted and a large number of people stepped into the light. She scanned their faces, seeing the eyes of the elderly, along with a few young warrior men and women.

A light haired, older man stepped away from the others, his midnight eyes glued to Malkia. "We must ask you to exit the area surrounding the pyramid and follow us to our dwellings."

"Who are you?" Malkia asked, her daggers shifting as the man stepped closer. "What do you want from us?"

"My name is Duncan and we—" He waved his hand around at his group, "are the keepers of these structures and have been anticipating this day for hundreds of years."

He mumbled a few words under his breath and despite her best efforts, Malkia dropped her daggers. She glanced over at Apollo, hearing his weapons strike the ground as well. Eyeing the man with icy contempt, Malkia moved towards Apollo. "What just happened?" she whispered.

"He's a warlock." Apollo's eyes were wide, but he remained composed, curling a protective arm around Malkia.

"Malkia," Duncan spoke up, his eyes twinkling with delight. "We know who you are and we aren't your enemies. Please follow us to our dwellings and I will explain everything to you there." Leaning over, he grasped her daggers and held them out for her to take. "We mean you no harm."

"And why would we trust you?" Malkia hissed at Duncan, snatching her daggers from him.

His smile didn't fade, as he chuckled out loud. "You don't necessarily need to trust us, but following us back to our homes and learning more about your past might help clear up some of the mystery surrounding your life."

"What do you know about my life?" she asked, shoving her daggers back into their sheaths.

"I know your father," Duncan replied. "I also knew your grandfather, your mother's father. Except the truth is, he wasn't her biological father, and this is why every strange moment that has occurred in your life is significant."

Malkia's eyes widened and she inhaled sharply, as he finished speaking. "How do you know this information?"

"Malkia," Duncan stepped forward, clasping her hands with his own. "I realize you have been thrust into a life that you had no clue about, and I know everything that has occurred since your memory was restored has been overwhelming and absolutely heartbreaking. I'm here to give you valuable information and explain to you why you're different. Please come with us."

Malkia nodded slowly, her pulse quickening in her ears, as she realized she might have found the warlock who knew how to find her father. Gathering up her items, she could see Apollo doing the same, but with his dagger still drawn defensively. She straightened up and swung her pack onto her back. "Apollo, I think we'll be safe." She stepped towards him, placing her hand on his forearm. "Let's do this peacefully and see what information they have to assist our journey."

Glancing around the group, Apollo breathed deeply, before sliding his dagger back in its scabbard and tossing his pack onto his back. "I'm only doing this for you, Malkia," he whispered. "The way they approached us was disrespectful and suspicious in nature and I will continue to have my guard up until I believe their intentions are honorable."

Malkia shot him a wary smile. Grasping his arm, they followed the group of strangers through the trees. Approaching the mountainside, Malkia noticed a trail leading up the side, followed by what seemed like an endless run of stairs. Not wanting to draw any more attention to herself, she groaned knowing she would have to hike, instead of using her light to fly her up.

As they rose above the tree line, Malkia looked over at the tip of the pyramid, longing to search for the etching of the feather and speak to the Light Beings. Moments later, Duncan veered off the stairs and stepped over to a doorway carved out of the mountain. The tunnel was dark, and Malkia hesitated to follow. Apollo stepped forward and gave her a reassuring smile, just as Duncan's wrist lit up and he pushed down on the light.

A door swung open a few feet into the tunnel and yellow light spilled into the darkness of the passage. Malkia gulped, moving her feet in front of each other and following Duncan over the threshold. "What's on your wrist?" she asked him.

Duncan glanced over at her. "It's a device connected to all the doors that lead to our village. As I approach, the signals read each other, and the light lets me know that I can proceed with opening the door. We all have one, but they are engineered to our DNA, so no outsiders could steal one and be allowed in."

"It's amazing that you possess this technology." Malkia smiled, but tightened her grip on Apollo's arm. "Where I grew up, there was technology for a short time, but the battles with the sky people destroyed all evidence of it."

"Esaki is an extraordinary moon," Duncan replied, leading the way through the large tunnel.

Malkia's forehead puckered and her lips pursed. "You know where I grew up?" she questioned.

"I know a great amount about you, Malkia." He paused for a few moments, scratching his crooked nose and squinting at the path ahead. Rubbing his hands together, he continued speaking in a hushed tone. "When we reach the village and have a moment to unwind, I will divulge all that I know. You will both have your own rooms, with a bed as well, and tomorrow I will escort you back to the pyramids, where I will introduce you to the Guarding Statue, as well as assist you with your search for your feather."

Silence suffused the corridor, as tangible as dark water, and Malkia was grateful when they finally caught sight of Theia's light beaming in through a far off opening in the mountain. Moments later they stepped onto a moving platform. One by one, the group slowed their pace and stood watching, as the tunnel widened right before it ended. Malkia gaped at the abundance of trees and vegetation spiraling towards the heavens just under their feet, as the tunnel grew farther away and they descended into a valley, surrounded by the massive cliffs. The stars twinkled above them and Theia's light illuminated the mysterious village below.

"This is amazing," she muttered, smiling up at Apollo. "Did you know this was here?"

Apollo shook his head, his chin jutting out in thought, eyeing the valley as it grew near. "I don't think anyone knows of this sanctuary." He paused, examining the looming escarpments towering above them. "Your father least of all."

"Unless you know what you are searching for, you won't be able to find our establishment. We have remained hidden for hundreds of years and have only relented to reveal ourselves to you, because we know of your significance." He glanced over at Apollo. "Our seer speaks both your names."

They stepped off the moving platform and the rest of the group filtered off to their own homes, while Malkia and Apollo followed Duncan. They approached an oversized home. On the lowest level, light gleamed from expansive windows as if to welcome the travellers. But the darkened stories above offered a somber note of reticence that echoed Malkia's own.

Duncan opened the front door and waved for them to cross the threshold. As they entered, the exquisite beauty of the foyer drove a gasp from Malkia's parted lips. The floor was carved into individual squares of random sizes, with the colors of the suns rays beaming from each one. The walls had etchings of the stars, moons and faraway lands and they reached high, following the massive spiral staircase to the top floor. As the lights flickered on, Malkia stepped forward, her head tilted back to view the highest image.

A painting of a lone, blue planet stood out from the rest. It circled only one sun, with a dead rock circling it in turn. Malkia's breath caught, remembering a similar image in her grandfather's home, back before she was left on Esaki. "Will you tell me about that planet?" she asked, pointing and turning to look at Duncan.

"I will." He smiled. "Is that what you would like to hear about first? It does tie into the story of your grandfather, but if you want to know what it is beforehand, I would be happy to oblige."

Malkia shook her head. "No, please just tell me the story from the beginning."

Duncan nodded and motioned for them to follow him into the room off to their left. Stepping through the doorway, Malkia saw several cushioned seats, with a table in the center. She moved to the one that appeared the most comfortable and reclined into it, a sigh escaping her lips.

Apollo sat in the chair closest to her, setting his staff on the floor next to him and remaining stiff, as he searched the area around them.

Duncan sat across from both of them, his mouth twitching with thought. "This has been a long time coming and I'm honored to be the one to disclose your history and your true origins." He smiled again, leaning back in his chair and crossing his legs. "Let's begin with your history, Malkia. Your grandfather was one of the most influential and powerful leaders of my time. Being that I have been around for nearly a thousand years, I would have to say I have witnessed many leaders pave their way through Eris."

"My grandfather was the leader of Eris?" Malkia asked, biting her lip.

"He wasn't *the* leader of Eris but was a significant influencer of the Eris government. Our moon is small compared to Enyo and Esaki. For the past millennium, we have been governed by a democracy and have ensured that none of our elected officials serve more than five years." He paused, waiting for a question, but when there was none, he continued. "We've discovered that the less time an official serves, the less comfortable they become with corruption and greed. However, your grandfather succeeded in edging his way in with at least three or four of our officials at each election and without fail a battle would arise somewhere in our star system."

"You believe my grandfather created the havoc by having the power over these people?" Malkia asked.

"We know that your grandfather had the ability to twist people around his finger and receive all kinds of favors in the process. He was a malicious man, whose sole purpose in life was to gain as much supremacy over all the civilizations circling Theia." Duncan scratched his chin, a yawn taking over his face. "I apologize. It has been an incredibly long day and I'm nearing the end of my stamina."

"One question before we take our leave of one another." Apollo spoke up, leaning forward in his chair. "If you knew all of this information, why did you not track Malkia down years ago on Esaki?"

"I was one of the warlocks who hid the children on Esaki." Duncan uncrossed his legs and sat up straight. "I knew of Malkia, but I hadn't met her. When she didn't return with the other magical children, I was summoned to her father's home, where he privately requested my assistance in finding and forcing her to do his bidding." He shook his head, a frown creeping over his face. "I declined and told him, he should be ashamed of himself for wanting to control his own daughter. I was banished from Eris and had to find refuge on Artemis for a time. When Thane discovered I had befriended a village of Artemisians, he had the entire group slaughtered, while I witnessed their execution. I escaped with nothing to my name and no allies to assist me."

Malkia had straightened up, her eyes wide as she licked her lips. "That's awful!" Her voice shook with emotion, and she intertwined her fingers, staring at Duncan. "I'm sorry he put you through that awful turmoil and heartache. He's a vicious and horrible human being."

"He is," Duncan nodded. "I was lucky. I stumbled upon a group of star travelers, who allowed me to hitchhike back to Eris and introduced me to the people I now call family." He pointed out the window. "These people sheltered me from Thane and in return I've done everything to find the woman whose advent our seer has prophesied for centuries. It wasn't until the day your powers were unblocked that I realized Thane's daughter and the woman we were seeking were one and the same."

Malkia rose from her chair, smiling as another yawn overtook Duncan's face. Apollo followed suit, gripping onto his staff and circling around his chair to leave. Stepping towards Duncan, Malkia sank onto the chair next to him. "I don't know my father well. I barely remember him from my childhood. However, I do know what a monster he can be, and I intend to halt his dominion over our moons. Tomorrow I would like to hear more, especially the part about the blue planet."

"Yes, tomorrow." Duncan rose, offering his hand to Malkia. She grasped it and stood, following Duncan out of the room, with Apollo in tow.

Duncan led them up the spiral stairs and showed them their rooms. Malkia turned the knob to her room and slid inside, turning to mouth "Goodnight" to Apollo. Switching on the electricity, Malkia smiled at the fourposter bed that stood flush against one wall, while a large wardrobe stood on the other end. "Tomorrow will be a better day," she said to herself, as she stripped off her clothing and crawled under the supple, velvety blankets.

FIVE

A Lost Love

"GOOD MORNING." MALKIA waltzed into the eating hall, a smile plastered across her face and her eyes twinkling with joy. "That was the best night's sleep I've had in ages."

Apollo rose and pulled out the chair next to him. "You look absolutely radiant." He grinned down at her, his slanted eyes blinking at her in another attempt to wink.

Malkia laughed, settling in her chair as Apollo pushed it in. She glanced over at Duncan, who remained quiet but wore a matching smile on his face. "That bed was the most comfortable cushion I have ever slept on. I wish I could wrap it up and bring it with me."

"You always have a home here," Duncan said, dishing up some food onto his plate. "When your mission is complete, we would all be thrilled to see you again."

"Thank you, Duncan," she replied, pouring herself some coffee and sipping on the hot drink. "I just might take you up on that offer. For the bed of course." She winked at Duncan as he laughed out loud.

"Of course," he said, stabbing his food with a fork, his smile dancing in his eyes. "After we finish our meal, I would love to take some time to continue with my story. It wasn't by coincidence that you two met."

Malkia's eyes darted upwards, staring at Duncan and then turning to see Apollo. His eyes met hers and he nodded with a smile. "It's interesting you say that," Apollo said, eyeing Duncan. "We met in the most unlikely circumstances and at first I desired her execution for the damage she inflicted on Artemis. However, once we began to battle, my anger fizzled quickly and I felt a longing to protect her instead."

Duncan nodded, chewing on his food. He swallowed a moment later and leaned forward, placing his elbows on the table. "I can imagine that took you by surprise to have such a change in your emotions. I have a theory to go with your experience." He picked up his fork again, scooping up the last of his food and shoving it in his mouth.

Malkia ate quickly, anxious to hear what Duncan knew. She gulped down her juice and finished her coffee, before sliding her chair back and rising. Duncan followed suit, while Apollo polished off his plate. Moments later they converged in the front room, where they had gathered the night before.

"Where did we leave off last night?" Duncan asked, sinking in his accustomed chair.

"My grandfather and his greed to take control," Malkia replied, sitting in a sturdier, straight chair, just a few down from Duncan.

"That's right," Duncan began, crossing his legs and intertwining his fingers. "Your grandfather was a powerful man and he was not prepared to have a daughter like your mother, Haltia. He adored her and she was his one weakness. There were multiple abduction attempts and her life was always in danger as a child. Everyone knew if they could take her, they would be able to control her father." He inhaled deeply, his eyes glazing over in thought for a moment. "Your mother lived a guarded life, and when your grandfather discovered her secret love affair with another woman, he brought your father into the picture. He needed someone who was already loyal to him to take on the task of keeping your impetuous and headstrong mother under control. Not long afterward, they were married, and your mother became emotionally unavailable to many of her longtime friends, as well as the woman she loved the most."

"You're not speaking of Asha, are you?" Malkia asked, leaning forward in her chair, her brows drawing tightly together.

"No," Duncan replied, scratching his head. "Asha was a dear friend of mine, but your mother only met her while she was pregnant with your sister. The woman I speak about is living here in my village. Her name is Selene, and she and your mother grew up together, becoming lovers in their teenage years."

Malkia closed her eyes, thinking of her mother and all that she must have endured with her own father. "She didn't want to marry Thane, did she?"

Duncan shook his head, as Malkia opened her eyes. "No."

"I have been an awful child to my mother," Malkia said quietly, feeling embarrassment stirring within her and wanting to curl up in a ball from the shame. "I allowed my hurt feelings to decide how I would treat her, and all along she has had her own demons to battle."

"Haltia loves you more than life itself," Duncan replied, sitting up straight. "Don't worry about the past. What's done is done, and the only way to rekindle your relationship is to forgive her and finish this quest together. Knowing her like I did, there would be nothing more satisfying then to have her daughter back in her life and Thane destroyed."

Malkia nodded, leaning back against her chair. "I've already forgiven her."

Duncan smiled in acknowledgment. "Your grandfather discovered a shocking bit of information about your mother, after she married your father. It was nearly the death of him, as he couldn't handle knowing she wasn't his biological daugther."

"That's right, you told us about this back by the pyramid." Malkia slightly nodded her head, pursing her lips. "Who was my mother's father?"

"We don't know his name, but we do know your grandfather sought him out and had him executed before he had the chance to escape. No one knows who he was for certain, except your grandmother. She was put to death alongside her lover." Duncan leaned back against his chair again, his brows furrowed in thought.

"He murdered his own partner?" Malkia asked, her eyes narrowing, as a wave of nausea rushed through her.

"Yes," Duncan replied, his eyes meeting Malkia's. "Your real grandfather was a mystery for everyone. No one even knew he existed and to this day people question whether or not he was actually executed or if Cerce, your grandfather, just made him up to explain your grandmother's disappearance."

"No one witnessed their execution?" Malkia's eyes widened and she gripped the armrests, waiting for Duncan's reply.

"Not that I have been told." A frown melted down Duncan's face. "No one really knows anything, except what Cerce has told them. Your mother was devastated to find out her mother was slaughtered by her own father's hands but was thrilled to find out she was not biologically tied to him. Once we have completed here, I will send you to meet a warlock who knows more about your biological grandfather." He brushed his hands together, uncrossing his legs and leaned forward in his chair. "But that is all I can do. I don't know his exact whereabouts and like myself, he desires seclusion and to remain hidden from the rest of Eris's brash civilization."

Malkia shrugged, bobbing her head up and down. "I can understand. Thank you for assisting me as much as you can." She intertwined her fingers and closed her eyes for a moment. "The blue planet? There was a painting of it, in my grandfather's home when I was young. Will you tell me what he and the blue planet have to do with one another?"

"Oh yes, the blue planet." Duncan grinned, his face lighting up again. "I don't know much, but I do know it does exist and that your grandmother had some connection to it. The painting you remember in your grandparent's home, was drawn by your grandmother, as she painted the one here as well. Your grandmother had similar attributes to you and was able to envelope herself in a white light. Although hers was not as robust, and she rarely could push beyond the confines of her own body." He paused, searching Malkia's expression. "Whatever the blue planet represents to your grandmother, it has something to do with your biological grandfather."

"What is your theory?" Malkia sighed, her mind struggling to put the puzzle pieces together.

Duncan cleared his throat and scratched his chin. "My theory is this." He sat forward in his chair, his eyes wide. "I believe your biological grandfather came from the blue planet. Somehow, your connection to this planet, is why the Aletheian's are so interested in you. Cerce discovered what the planet was and attempted to find his way there, but your grandmother would not divulge the information. This is why I believe she was really executed." He paused, noticing Malkia's glazed expression. "This is just my theory, but many others hold the same conclusion. It seems too coincidental, and no one else can explain why the paintings of the blue planet in these few homes is identical to etchings found in one of our pyramids, along with other pyramids strung across the moons in this region."

Malkia sat up straight. "That is what my father was after when he tried to break into the pyramids."

"Yes," Duncan replied. "He is anxious to find out the blue planet's significance and how you're connected to it all. You are both on the same mission, but for different reasons."

"What about Ginny?" Malkia asked, her brows bumping together into a scowl. "Why were the Light Beings interested in her?"

"She created the illusion of a Chosen Heir and somehow fooled the Beings." His eyes narrowed. "The Aletheian's aren't our Creators, but they are aware of our creation. These Beings can transport and aren't restricted by time and space, but they do have some limitations. Ginny was one of their mistakes, but I'm not positive of why they couldn't tell the difference. Once they realized they had the wrong woman, she was banished from their presence. This is when the darkness gripped her soul and she succumbed to it."

Apollo shook his head, sitting forward in his seat. "If these Aletheian's are not our Creators, then why do they have so much influence over our lives? I have been told stories of their dominion and interest in Theia's Moons, and it seems odd they would remain in our star system, when they have the ability to transport wherever they desire."

"It does seem strange," Duncan said, his lips twisting in thought. "Their focal point has something to do with the blue planet, but you are correct, why do they require souls who are currently trapped in mortal bodies to assist them in their quest?" He shook his head and glanced over at Malkia. "If I were you, I would use caution with any person, creature or being you encounter, including myself. There are too many secrets." He paused, his eyes wandering to the large window at the far end of the room. "Unfortunately, our time is up, and we need to return to the pyramids and find your feather."

Malkia nodded, as she rose from her chair. "I'll grab my belongings and meet you both in the front vestibule."

Moments later, she descended the stairs, eyeing the lonely blue planet and its one star. The moment she had seen it, she knew it was significant and wondered if there was a memory buried in her mind that would assist her in finding out its significance.

When she reached the front hall, Apollo and Duncan were speaking quietly to one another, halting their discussion as she approached. "Am I interrupting something important?" She questioned. "You both look intense."

Apollo glanced away and Duncan shook his head. "We were speaking of the dangers of the pyramids, in case your father has spies watching for you to arrive." Duncan shot Apollo a stern look. "But my people are always guarding the area. We know when someone has invaded our space."

Apollo grunted and stormed off to the door, yanking it open and blowing through the entrance before Malkia could say anything. Her forehead crinkled as she glanced over at Duncan, and then raced to catch up with Apollo.

"Wait, Apollo," she yelled, seeing his large figure maneuver into the streets and disappear down the road. Encircling herself with her light, she flew over the vegetation, settling next to Apollo as he strode furiously along the pathway. "Why are acting like this?" She reached out and grasped his arm.

Halting in his tracks, Malkia nearly collided with him as he turned to face her. "I don't trust anyone. He even suggested that he might be untrustworthy, but he wants me to believe they have every nook and cranny secured over in that wilderness." His face simmered, as his skin's hue darkened to crimson. "I refuse to let you walk into your father's ambush."

Malkia face jerked back in surprise, her mouth setting in a straight line. "You're not in charge of me." Taking a few steps back, she shook her head, her eyes narrowing at Apollo. "I'm capable of protecting myself. Why are you acting like you need to keep me safe?"

"Malkia," Apollo hesitated, his skin cooling. "I know your father, and I've seen what he is willing to do. I'm not suggesting we stop our mission, but I don't want to hear the lies of Duncan guaranteeing your safety, without first checking for myself."

Duncan appeared, sauntering quietly towards them, his eyes fixed on Malkia. She looked back at Apollo, a frown spreading across her face. "We don't answer to these people," she whispered. "If you need permission to search the area before I go in, I give that to you." She searched his eyes, as he nodded.

"We really should move quickly," Duncan said, rubbing his forehead as he approached. "Apollo, your distrust is a valuable tool, especially considering your relationship with Malkia. I want you to know, we have done everything we can do to ensure her safety."

Apollo tightened his fists and puffed out his chest. "I would feel more secure, if you allowed me to survey the area, before Malkia is brought over."

"Fine." Duncan shook his head, his expression hardening. "This argument is a waste of time." He turned to Malkia, gritting his teeth. "I'll take you to the meet Selen, and we will follow after Apollo within the hour." Twisting back to eye Apollo, he said, "That's all the time I can give you."

"That is all the time I require." Apollo glanced at Malkia, before turning on his heel and racing down the street toward the path that led through the mountain.

Malkia watched his fading silhouette, before facing Duncan. "He's an intense creature and is only looking out for my safety."

"I know, but we both know it's unnecessary." He held out his arm for Malkia to take, shifting direction to go down another road, leading her to the woman who once loved her mother.

Selen's cottage was quaint, with two paned windows flanking a bright yellow door. Lush fruit and vegetable plots seemed to embrace the building, along with an array of vibrant flowers and plants. Malkia smiled to herself as she gazed at the striking hues, reminding her of her mother's garden when she was a child.

Knocking on the door, Malkia stepped a few feet back, continuing to admire the view and waiting for an answer. After a few moments, she heard the squeak of the old door hinges and turned to face her mother's past. Standing in the doorway, a striking lady eyed them, her long silky black hair cascading past her shoulders and chest, resting against her hips.

Malkia stepped forward, holding out her hand, "Hello. My name is Malkia. Are you Selen?"

The woman eyed Duncan over Malkia's shoulder, biting her bottom lip. She shifted her gaze to meet Malkia's, recognition dawning on her face as she grasped her wrist, squeezing it the way the Eris people did in greeting. Malkia followed suit, remembering these traditions from long ago. "Yes, I'm Selen. You must be Haltia's daughter." Her breath caught in her throat, and she placed her hand over her chest. "You look just like her."

Malkia smiled, her head bobbing up and down. "I've heard you were my mother's partner, before my grandfather ripped her away from you."

"Yes," Selen replied, waving her hand to invite them in. "Please make yourselves at home. Would you like a cup of tea or coffee?"

"Just water for me," Malkia said, looking over at Duncan.

"I will take a cup of tea," Duncan nodded, reclining on a couch in the sitting room.

Malkia followed him, sitting on the same couch as Duncan and allowing her body to mold into the back of the cushions, enjoying the calm of her surroundings. "I know why I'm so eager to return to the pyramids, but why are you?" she asked, after Selen disappeared into the next room.

Duncan sighed, turning to face her. "I'm worried. Your father is persistent and if he discovered our hidden city, we would be annihilated. The man has no mercy and would stop at nothing to retrieve you, so I worry for the safety of my people." His jaw tightened, a cloudshadow of fear flitting across his face. "I want you to know, once your father is stopped, you'll always have a home here. Until that day, I would prefer if we played it safe and you kept your distance."

Malkia nibbled on her bottom lip, a frown sliding across her face. "I understand. Why did you wait until after our breakfast settled to push us out the door? Why not just insist on our departure when we first woke?"

"Dear, child," Duncan said, his forehead puckering. "There is so much for you to learn, and I possess the knowledge to teach you. Knowing I have to send you on your way is not easy." He avoided her eyes as he fought back tears. "My people are terrified of Thane and his followers, and they would give up nearly everything to see his reign of terror end on Eris, but I cannot sacrifice their lives. We'll assist you in finding your feather and give you aid in discovering all that the pyramids can offer you, but by nightfall, I will insist that you both move on with your journey."

Malkia nodded, sitting up straight as Selen entered into the room, holding their drinks in her hand. She grasped a hold of her cup, sipping mindlessly and thinking about Duncan's words. Selen sank in the chair across from Malkia, a grin sweeping across her face.

"How is your mother doing?" Selen asked, her silver eyes beaming.

Malkia inhaled deeply, her brows knitted with sadness. "My mother has seen better days. I was just reunited with her after twenty-four years and the first thing I do is run the opposite direction, because I allowed my anger to control my head."

Selen's eyes fell, casting Malkia a veiled glance. "Why did you run away?"

"It's a long story," Malkia replied, twisting her fingers together. "I would rather know why you didn't fight for my mother."

Selen laughed out loud, but her eyes remained sad, glistening with tears. "Oh my! I *did* fight for your mother. If you only knew what she and I both endured, just to fall on our faces in the end. Your grandfather and father are evil men and I'm lucky I'm still alive after our showdown."

"I'm sorry," Malkia whispered, sadness clouding her features. "There is so much I still don't know and I'm afraid I sound judgmental, but I'm actually just learning."

"It's your approach," Selen leaned forward in her chair. "I did fight for your mother. I loved her with my whole heart and soul, and the day your grandfather ripped her away from me, was the worst moment of my life. If I could have planned another way or convinced her to not trust her father, we would have had the opportunity to disappear." She sighed, tears shimmering in her eyes. "I gave up so much of my life for her and I still lost. To this day, my heart aches for her."

Malkia nodded. "I'm sure that was painful. Thank you for clarifying." She took a sip of her water, before setting it back down on the side table. "What can you tell me about my father that will help find my own daughter?"

"He stole your daughter?" Selen asked, sitting up straight in her chair, her eyes widening.

"Yes," Malkia muttered, closing her eyes for a moment. "He despises me and will do everything he can to destroy me. I have two missions to accomplish—retrieve my daughter and kill my father. I realize I haven't been patient or understanding or supportive of any of my friends or family, and this decision to stop at nothing until my daughter is out of my father's reach has seriously clouded my judgment." She pursed her lips, staring at Selen's bright eyes and smiled after a moment. "I need to finish what I started here, find this other warlock Duncan has told me about, and then return to my family."

"You should tell them where you are, right now," Selen insisted, rising from her chair and holding out her hand. "You can't expect them to sit around and worry for your life, while you gallivant around Eris."

Malkia shook her head, declining her hand. "No, Selen. Right now, I need to figure out my next step and be more prepared, before I yank my loved ones back into the fight. They'll be angry, but it's not about them right now."

"You're making a mistake," Selen whispered, glancing over at Duncan, who had remained quiet during their exchange. "Why are you allowing this to continue? You know she's better off with her family."

"I'm not Malkia's keeper," he replied, scowling in return to Selen's question. "I wanted her to meet you, because of your history with her mother, but she isn't required to do our bidding because of that. Do you really know if being with her family will be the better option or do we allow Malkia to fix her own issues? I believe once upon a time, you weren't given the option and it nearly destroyed you."

Selen took a step back, her expression sobering. "I see." She gritted her teeth, holding back the fountain of tears threatening to tumble down her face. "You're right."

Duncan rose from the couch, reaching down and helping Malkia up. "Selen, you aren't ready to face this, are you?"

The tears came without warning, streaming down her face. "No, I guess I'm not." She turned to face Malkia, biting her lower lip, attempting to hold back the sobs. "I adored and loved your mother, and I would love to see her happy, but seeing you has stirred up some painful memories and I just don't believe I can handle them right now. It was lovely to meet you and see Haltia's face within yours, but I'm going to have to ask you to leave."

Malkia smiled and gripped Selen's hands. "My mother loved you. Don't forget that."

Moments later, Malkia stood on Selen's sidewalk, staring up at Theia and breathing softly. She heard the click of the door shutting and then felt Duncan's hand on her shoulder. Turning to face him, she could see the terror of their situation overtaking his face.

"Let's go," Malkia said, pivoting on her heel and stepping towards the pathway to the mountain. "Apollo has had plenty of time. We need to hurry."

SIX

Mystery Invaders

DUNCAN TROTTED TO keep up with Malkia. Within a few minutes they were stepping onto the moving sidewalk and watched the small town shrink in size, as they rose towards the opening in the mountain. It didn't take them long to race through the passage. Once they arrived, there were a dozen of Duncan's people waiting to help.

"I want to finish looking for the feather at the first pyramid," Malkia instructed. "With all of us searching, it shouldn't take us long."

She was right. They finished the first pyramid within an hour and on their way to the next one, they ran into Apollo. His eyes were wide, a look of dread spreading across his features. "I don't think we're alone."

Malkia glanced around. "What do you mean?" she asked, focusing on him.

"Something or someone is moving in," he whispered, his breath coming in short. "We need to find cover and draw them away from Duncan's town."

The sound of a horn blasted through the trees and Duncan jumped to attention as the first strike hit the man standing a few feet away from Malkia. His body vaporized with the discharge from the fighter ship.

Another woman who was closer to him skipped back, biting back a scream and racing to find cover as more laser blasts stung the ground around the group. Malkia encircled everyone with her light, searching the skies for the vessel.

"Stay close," she cried, clenching her fists, while her eyes strained to see through the branches above. "How did they see us?" She glanced over at Duncan. "Did you know this would happen?"

Duncan shook his head rapidly. "No!" he shouted. "I knew they were searching for you, but I really didn't believe they would find us so easily."

Malkia raised her eyes to the sky again, but couldn't see anything of value. Just as she turned to face the small group, an explosion reverberated through the trees and vegetation, spraying sticks, rocks and dirt in every direction. Malkia's heart sank, and she choked back her anger as she traced the trajectory of the detonation back to the two pyramids.

Apollo curled his long fingers over her shoulder. "They have destroyed one of the structures."

Malkia's body shook with rage, eyeing the sky, her body's heat building and the fire inside bursting around her. Shooting into the air, she searched for the vessels, seeing one flying directly towards her. *These are not the Artemisian ships,* she thought, shifting out of the way as it zoomed past her. It was slimmer and longer, with a metallic sheen that kept it hidden in the sunlight.

Aiming her light at the flying vessel, she built up the power in her arm, but it fizzled as she noticed the black smoke rising up over the mountain and three other ships rocketing away from the area. Her breath caught in her throat as she glanced down at Duncan and then over at the burning pyramid. Holding her breath another explosion struck the third pyramid, driving the breath from her lungs as it tossed her through the air. For a moment her light faltered and she fell rapidly towards the forest, terrified by the quickly approaching ground.

Her arms flailed around her, just as her light bounded out from her body again, and she was able to right herself. "No!" she cried, seeing the black smolder increase and the screams of Duncan's people filled her ears.

She aimed for the top of the mountain, flying rapidly to protect those who remained. As she descended the other side of the mountain, the smoke curled around her light, pushing to break through her barricade. Reaching the ground, her eyes glistened with tears seeing Duncan's little town in shambles around her. Flames danced from the broken homes and buildings, and bodies outlined the cobble stone roads.

Malkia rushed to the nearest body, pulling the woman over on her back and gasped when she saw the face was nearly ripped off and her body overrun with burn marks. "No, no, no, no, no!" Malkia's screams grew louder, as she backed away from the body.

She raced through the streets, searching for any survivors. Reaching Selen's house, she cried out, clenching her fists as the tears tumbled from her eyes, stinging her cheeks as they ran down her face. The small cottage was completed destroyed. Her garden was on fire, with no sign of Selen. Malkia twisted in every direction, finally curling within herself and digging anguished fingers into her hair as she screamed.

"Why?" she cried, looking up at the blackened sky. "Why would you slaughter these people?"

"Malkia," a desperate voice cried from a few feet away, barely noticeable with the crackle of the fire around her.

Glancing towards the voice, Malkia saw Selen's black hair against the flames nipping at her body. Rushing over, she yanked Selen out of the fire, snuffing out the inferno ravaging her body. The woman's clothes had melted into her body and her crimson skin was blistering with hot welts. One side of her hair was nearly gone, but the flame had barely touched her face and head.

Groaning with fatigue and agony, Selen's eyes watered with what little moisture remained in her body, staring pointedly up at Malkia. "Tell—" she choked on her words, as blood oozed from her mouth, dripping down her face.

Malkia placed her hands over Selen's body, giving her all the healing light she possessed. Selen gripped onto her arm, her hand shaking with fingers black and wooden. Malkia's eyes darted between the fingers and back at Selen's wide eyes. "Tell your mother—," she licked her lips, gagging on the blood that kept filling her mouth. "I will always love her."

Selen's body convulsed, the pain rushing to her eyes and flooding her face. The blood drizzled from her mouth and nose, her chest sinking with one last sigh as her eyes became devoid of life. Malkia sat frozen on her knees, her hands hovering just above the woman's heart, a sob rising from her stomach and catching in her throat.

Her arms began to shake as she folded over Selen's body, weeping into her fisted hands. Her own body rocked incessantly, her screams and cries ripping through her heart and soul, the smell of charred flesh saturating her nostrils and making her retch from the rotten taste in her mouth.

Rising from the ground, she flew through the town, desperately searching for anyone else. As she reached the far end, she saw movement through the smoke. Terrified that it might be the creatures who slaughtered the town, she crouched behind a broken wall, waiting for a better view.

A few moments passed and the wind finally whistled past her, blowing the smoke away from the path. An older child coughed, holding onto a baby, who lay limp in his arms. Malkia rushed from her hiding spot, settling next to the boy. His face was covered in ash and his body shook as he stood frozen to the spot in the middle of the pathway. Malkia reached for the baby, but his grip tightened when she attempted to take the child. His eyes remained wide and his breath came in short rasps, not taking his eyes off the scene in front of him.

Malkia stooped down, looking the boy in the eyes and grasping his chin to make him stare at her. "You're alive, dear child. Let me help you."

His eyes finally focused on her and the tears flooded down his cheeks, as if he had been holding onto a fountain of liquid. He sank into her arms, sobbing uncontrollably and shaking from head to foot. Pulling him close, she searched for the baby's pulse and exhaled slowly when she discovered a faint one.

"Your sister needs help." Malkia twisted the boy's face to look at her. "I want you to hold onto me and close your eyes. We're going for a ride, away from here and somewhere safe."

The boy nodded and closed his eyes as he wrapped his arms around her neck. Malkia pulled the baby close and enclosed them all in her light, lifting them out of the fire and smoke and over the mountain. Moments later, she landed in the spot she had left Apollo and Duncan. Searching the area, she only saw the broken trees and dusty air. She held the boy close to her, looking for a safe place to hide, but nothing stood out to her.

"Hold on again," she whispered in the boy's ear.

She leapt into the air, scanning the mountain for a cave. After a few minutes, she saw Apollo waving his hands at her from a landing near the entrance to the mountain. Touching down softly next to him, she surveyed their surroundings searching for Duncan.

"Where is everyone?" she asked, setting the boy down and easing the baby out of his hands.

"They scattered after you left. Duncan made his way back to his village and I haven't seen him since." He groaned, holding his side with one of his hands. "I waited for as long as I dared for you to return, but after a while I decided to follow Duncan and see what I could do to help."

"Are you well?" Malkia asked, pointing at his side.

Apollo nodded, releasing his side and kneeling down next to her and the baby. "One of the larger tree branches struck me on my side. It is painful, but I'll recover. Who are these two children?"

"I found them," she replied, releasing her healing light into the small child. "I returned to the village, searching for any survivors and these are the only two I found." The tears festered again, as she turned to avoid Apollo's shocked eyes. "I have to save this baby and then return to help. Will you guard these two, while I'm away?"

"Of course I will." Apollo grasped her arm.

Malkia's breath caught in her throat, as she choked back the flood of tears threatening to burst from her eyes. "It was awful," she whispered. "There were bodies everywhere. Who could do such a horrible thing?" She slumped in her despair, feeling the pain wash through her body. "I can't bear knowing I was the cause of this tragedy. Everywhere I go, my father finds a way to destroy anyone I hold dear to my heart. This is why I can't return to my mothers. This is why I need to finish this quest on my own."

Apollo grimaced, sitting back on his heels, his hands balling up into fists. "You can't let your father win." He paused, closing his eyes. "Please don't allow him to control you."

The baby cried out and Malkia picked her up, curling her arms around the tiny child and kissing her forehead. "There, there baby girl. You'll be fine. Your big brother saved you." She made eye contact with the older boy and he smiled back at her, but the sadness in his eyes told another story. "What's your name?" she asked the boy.

"Tristan," he replied, stepping forward to take the baby from her. "Thank you for saving my sister's life, but now what? Where do we go?"

"I don't know yet," Malkia said, raking her hands through her dusty hair and grimacing at all the knots. "I'm going to return to your village and see if I can find any more survivors. Will you stay here with Apollo, until I return?"

Tristan nodded, snuggling his sister close to him as she reached for his chin, beaming up at him. Malkia smiled at the two, glad she was able to find them first. "I'll return soon," she said, directing her gaze towards Apollo. "If I find Duncan, I will bring him back as well."

Moments later, Malkia settled down on the other side of the mountain, her eyes darting around the charred remains of the village she had hoped to have returned to someday. The stench of the burnt corpses flooded the air around her and after a few minutes she had to encircle herself with her light, just to protect herself from the scorched smell permeating the air.

She raced to each building, one by one, but she only faced more death. Within, her rage began to build, as she felt the deep loss of these people's lives rushing through her body. Nearing the middle of the town, Malkia noticed through the nauseating flow of smoke, a few people rummaging amongst the debris.

Gliding slowly towards them, she saw Duncan frantically digging through a mound of rocks, his face marked with the braided remnants of tears as they made paths through his ash-coated skin. Sprinting towards him, Malkia could see he had found someone alive. He glanced up at her for just a moment, a look of terror and pain suffusing his face, before returning his attention to his work. Malkia yelled at the others to help. Together they all dug down into the mound and finally releasing the young woman from her suffocating prison.

Duncan scooped the woman up, as a fit of coughing overtook her frail body. He moved her to the road, where he gave her water and helped clean the soot from her face.

"I can fly her out of here and leave her with Apollo on the other side of the mountain," Malkia offered, kneeling down next to Duncan.

He shook his head, avoiding her eyes, as he continued to clean up the woman. "You've done enough. I asked you to leave and now I really need you to do so." His words cut through Malkia like a knife.

"Duncan, if I had known they could find me, I would've never stayed here. Furthermore, those weren't Artemisian ships, which makes me wonder who actually did this." Malkia placed her hand on Duncan's shoulder, pleading with her eyes for him to listen, pain clawing ferociously at her chest.

"It doesn't matter who it was." He turned to face her, an icy glare distorting his features. "My people have perished, and they've left us in ruins. Two of the pyramids have been destroyed, and no one knows why these people would target the ancient structures. It all leads back to you." His jaw tightened, as another fit of coughing shook the woman. "I know I shouldn't blame you and I realize you will eventually halt the wars that threaten Eris's peace. But until that moment happens, I need you to stay away from my home."

Malkia rose from her perch, her heart pounding fiercely in her chest. "I understand Duncan. Can I help you finish searching for survivors?"

Duncan shook his head again, but this time he looked up at her, his face glistening with sweat and his eyes bloodshot from the smoke. "Please leave. Go to the east and follow the shallow river of Tistaban. When you reach the statue of Dellanti, right before the waterfall, begin heading north. If you remain on that path, you'll eventually run into the other warlock I spoke about earlier. He will have the means to hide you and he can teach you far more than I ever could." He inhaled deeply, giving the woman another gulp of water. "I wish you the best of luck, Malkia and I truly hope our paths cross again under better and safer circumstances. Until then, your departure is all I ask of you."

Malkia nodded. "Apollo has two children on the other side of the mountain. I will let him know to bring them to you." She turned to walk away.

"Wait," Duncan shouted. "Tell him to stay put." Malkia twisted back to face him. "I'll send my people out to retrieve the children and take them to our safe house. They're safer out there, away from this soot and smoke."

Her lips drew in a straight line, as her eyes wandered to the ground. "I'll deliver your message." Taking a deep breath, she turned around again, whispering to herself, "I'm sorry." A silent tear escaped, weaving down her cheek as she shot upwards and disappeared through the stagnant air.

SEVEN
The Aletheian's

APOLLO GNASHED HIS teeth together, clearly frustrated by Malkia's plan. "This is absurd," he bellowed, screwing up his face and throwing her an icy glare. "There's no reason for us to separate, and, after this attack, I would be a fool to allow you to continue on your own."

"Then a fool is what you will be," Malkia grumbled in return. "I'm not asking. I don't want you to accompany me to meet this next warlock." Her breath came out as a whoosh and her eyes closed for a moment, before refocusing on her friend. "I need to know who killed all these people, and you're the one Artemisian I can trust. If you can infiltrate your people and find out what they know, I can spend my time learning the whereabouts of my father." She paused, her eyes shifting to the small cave the children were in. "We owe it to these people."

Pacing the ground away from Malkia, Apollo's eyes met hers and she could see the terror washing over his face. He stepped forward, grasping her wrists and staring down at her. "We do owe them, you are correct. I'm petrified you will be slain if I leave you, but I realize you have a better chance of protecting me, than I you." He glanced over, as the boy peeked out from the cave. "I will await Duncan's retrieval of the children, and then I will return to my commanding ship that is orbiting Eris. How will I find you again?"

"I don't know," Malkia replied, reaching around the large Artemisian and squeezing him as tight as she could. "I'll miss you, dear friend, and I do hope we will cross paths again. Duncan said you were mentioned in the prophecy. I take that as a chance we will be together again, someday." She untangled her arms from his waist and peered up at him. "Be safe, please."

"I will miss you," Apollo replied, pulling her back into a tight embrace. "I'll do my best to be safe and only ask the same of you."

Malkia smiled, stepping away and stooping to grab her pack. "Now, this is just becoming awkward." Apollo half-heartedly laughed and she threw him a wary smile. "I will see you again." She winked at him, before encircling herself within her light and flying off above the trees.

Moving through the air, Malkia searched the area for the two wrecked pyramids. Seeing the destruction of the trees ahead, she flew towards it, intent on finding something to assist her with her questions. As she drew near, she noticed a strange statue sitting off to the side near one of the pyramids. Malkia shifted her aim towards it, noticing how much it resembled a Pegasus, although its face was more like that of a dragon. Its knelt hooves were chiseled to perfection, but the body began as a Pegasus and gradually changed into the neck and face of a dragon.

"What are you?" She asked the statue, walking around the massive beast, scanning over every inch of it.

Touching the symbols on the body, she noticed they were similar to the engravings on the other pyramids. Her breath caught in her throat and her heart rate increased, when she noticed the feather. Bounding up to touch it, she hesitated for a moment, searching the area one more time and hoping this wasn't a trap. Gingerly, she reached over and placed her hand over the feather.

A maelstrom wind buffeted her as she was yanked into the wormhole and plummeted through the open space. She held out her arms, enjoying the fall and knowing she was going exactly where she needed to be.

Moments later, she jolted to a stop, the sound of the surf was close and the stars twinkled in the night sky. She surveyed the trees, noticing only shadows and the sway of the vegetation around her. Stepping lightly onto a nearby path, she followed the sound of the ocean and hoped the Aletheian's would make their presence known soon.

As she emerged onto the beach, she noticed a few homes nestled into the tree line, their windows throwing pools of warm light onto the sand. Malkia halted in her tracks, thrown off by the unusual structures and the sudden realization she wasn't in the same place the Aletheian's took her before.

Easing back behind a tree, she watched the homes and the beach, seeing a person walking along the edge of the water, its waves nipping at his bare feet. The light from the settlement, cascaded across his face, and she could see he was an older gentleman, with snow-white hair and deep lines etched around his eyes and mouth, as well as feathered across his forehead.

"Charlie," a woman stepped onto the deck, her hands grazing the railing, before stepping nimbly down the stairs. "Are you staying out here all night?" A smile crept across the woman's face, as Charlie turned to face her.

Malkia recognized that smile. Her breath came in short as she watched the older couple link arms and kiss, before walking back up the stairs and entering the home. She stood, frozen in place, watching the lights go out, and in her peripheral vision, noticed the Aletheian's step into view.

"Malkia," the taller being called to her. "We have been waiting for you."

"Wh-wh-what is this place?" Malkia's voice barely came out a whisper, as she stumbled over her words, her eyes darting from the Aletheian's and back to the small structure. It held someone she'd never met, but already knew in her heart.

"This is a planet in another star system, millions of light years away from Theia," the petite being chimed in. "We can see you have questions, and in due time you will know the answers, but for now we need to remind you what's at stake."

Malkia shook her head. "I'm quite aware of what's at stake. My daughter has been kidnapped. She's my priority."

"No," the smaller Aletheian spoke, her voice echoing through the trees. "Your daughter will only be saved, if you learn to control your rage and then end your father's dominion over the people and creatures of Theia's moons. This is your only priority. If you don't stop him—."

The taller being stepped forward. "Your moons will be annihilated if you don't halt your father's power. Do you really believe your father is only interested in waging war on you? He was given a mission and he will stop at nothing until it's completed." He pointed at the home Malkia had been watching. "Your mother was a pawn from day one in

Thane's orders. Her father didn't know his plans, but he didn't need to, and now the days are here when two star systems will either survive or collide in a massive explosion. If his plan works, the death toll will be in the billions."

Malkia gasped, her eyes growing wide. "Are we on the blue planet?"

The Aletheian's turned away from her, sliding back into the trees. Malkia raced after them, her heart drumming inside her chest, seeing them begin to fade. "Wait," she yelled. "Please give me some answers. Who are you?"

They turned to face her, their light brightening as she neared. "We are the watchers of this universe, the protectors of our dimension. Some call us energy, while others call us gods, but we are best known as angels. We are here to keep our universe organized and in working order and you were chosen, before conception, to right the wrongs of your star system." The Aletheian's glanced at each other and then back at Malkia. "Unfortunately, another star system was dragged into your mess and now you've been summoned to assist in properly realigning them." Their lights began to fade again, turning their faces towards one another.

"Are you telling me there are no gods or creators?" Malkia questioned, stepping forward in a rush.

"No," the taller being whispered. "That is not our message. Malkia, you will return to Eris soon. Find the warlock Duncan spoke about, unite yourself with your family and friends and finish this battle once and for all."

The Aletheian's faded completely, leaving Malkia staring at the spot they'd been standing, her hands balled into fists and her forehead puckered with frustration. She pivoted on her heel and stormed back to the beach, determined to speak with the older couple before she was yanked back to Eris. Racing towards their home, she pounded on the door, her stomach knotting at the thought she would be forced to leave before speaking to them.

She heard the shuffle of footsteps and saw the windows fill with light. Seconds later, the door creaked open and Malkia stared at the older gentleman from the beach. "It's awfully late, Miss," he said, his eyes blinking to clear away the mist of sleep. "Is there an emergency?"

"I need to speak with you and your partner," she replied, stepping closer. "I don't have much time—."

"Who's at the door, dear?" The woman's voice echoed behind the man, as she moved next to him, looking at Malkia. Her gasp sent shivers down Malkia's spine, as recognition slid over the woman's face. "You?"

"Please," Malkia cried, her voice cracking with urgency. "I need to know your name? Where are you from?"

The woman pushed past Charlie, closing the distance, just as Malkia saw the light surrounding her. She reached out to grab the woman, but only grasped onto the air that was throwing her back to Eris.

Malkia cried out, a rush of emotions racing through her body. "I was so close," she roared, just as she smacked into the ground near the statue. "Ouch!" She glanced up at the sky. "I just needed to know if it was she," she screamed into the open air. "Why do you insist on keeping me in the dark?"

Rising from the ground, she brushed off her backside and stared up at the stars and Theia, realizing she had lost the rest of the day. She shook her head and picked up her pack again, sighing in frustration. Then she flew into the air and headed east, following the Tistaban River.

The river was named after one of the gods who was worshiped by her ancestors, and in her parent's earlier stories she remembered them stating he was the god of mischief and conspiracy. Fitting that a shallow river was named after him. Malkia chuckled to herself, as she thought about meeting this god. *Maybe some mischief would brighten up my life, at this point,* she thought, as she made camp in the early morning.

She had discovered a copse of trees and it was easy to hang her extra blanket above and bundle shrubs around her, to create a small makeshift hut. Listening to the sounds of nature, her thoughts returned to the older couple and the blue planet. Her mind jumped from them, back to Duncan and his people, and then to Mataya and her family and friends left in her father's fortress.

Turning on her side, she curled into a fetal position, her blanket not giving her any warmth or comfort and the sticks and rocks beneath it poking into her body, making her uncomfortable. After tossing and turning for what seemed like hours, she finally surrounded herself with her light, feeling the heat and peace sweep over her. She closed her eyes, but only saw the carnage and wreckage of Duncan's village behind her eyelids. Snapping her eyes back open, she took a deep breath and forced her thoughts to Esaki and Damon.

"I miss that man," she said out loud, watching the brush in front of her sway slightly from the breeze. *And I miss Esaki,* she thought, closing her eyes once again and visualizing her small little town, with all her family and friends—Parowan stomping joyfully, the village people dancing around their town fireplace, and everyone laughing as they enjoyed each other's company.

Tears welled up in Malkia's eyes and she wished to return to her safe life, before the savages ripped her world into shreds. "I can never go back," she whispered to herself. "That life has died with everyone who perished."

The sobs came without restraint. The events that had occurred over the past few months had completely changed her outlook on life, and the empty hole she felt in the pit of her stomach only reminded her of all the deaths that had transpired because of her existence. Her body shook, tears flooding her face, as her heart wept for all the people and Artemisians she had slaughtered, along with all her family and friends who had been caught in the crossfire.

"Will I ever feel whole again?" she cried out, sitting up in her tiny hut. "Will I ever be able to forgive myself?"

The night sky remained calm, and the echo of her voice fluttered off with the wind. Malkia sank back to the ground and closed her eyes, allowing her heartbreak to rock her to sleep.

EIGHT

Ustarum

THE STATUE OF Dellanti rose nearly fifty feet high and seemed to teeter on the edge of the waterfall, as if a slight nudge would send it plummeting over the brink. Malkia stood admiring the winged woman, her hair cascading over her wings and shoulders and her staff gripped across her heart, hitting her hip bone near the base and the shoulder near the top. Her chest and midriff were bare, and she wore a leaf skirt just long enough to touch the top of her knees.

Her warrior pose empowered Malkia and she blew the statue a kiss before turning north and strolling through the tall grass covering acres of land ahead of her. The day rushed by, and Malkia's heart rate increased when she saw the dark forest looming menacingly ahead of her, just as the second sun began its descent behind the distant hills. Glancing around her, she encircled herself with her light and entered the shadows of the trees.

The forest was busy with animal life as they skittered to their homes for the night, while the nocturnal beasts loomed in the background, their eyes burning into her when she eased past them. Moments later, the sun set completely, leaving Malkia to use her light to guide her through the eerie twilight. It wasn't until she was too far in that she felt the presence of another person. Turning to face them, she searched the shadows, petrified by the unknown, realizing this wasn't who she thought she would find or better yet, who would find her.

Malkia could see his eyes staring at her, through the darkness. She knew who he was and had known he would come, but she was not prepared for the robust energy he brought with him. She felt it pulsating through the trees, as he advanced to her position.

"How did you find me?" Malkia asked, stepping backwards as he closed in.

His eyes narrowed and she saw his brow furrow, as he stood still, several feet in front of her. "You can't hide from me." His voice was a knife to her stomach. "You have failed to be the warrior you were designed to be, and for that I am here." His hands clenched fiercely at his sides.

"What are you talking about?" Malkia questioned, shaking her head. She surrounded herself with her purple light, her chest tightening with the same fear that had consumed her the moment she had lost her daughter again.

"That won't stop me." His energy squeezed her light, snuffing it out, right before her eyes. Startled by her nakedness, she quickly stepped back, balling up her energy and directing it at him. Her eyes widened and her pulse quickened, as he grasped her energy and increased it in size, barreling it back towards her.

The blow felt like a hundred bees had stung her all at once, as her body flew backwards, colliding with a large boulder. Gasping for air, she struggled to inhale fully, and faltered to stand.

I have to disappear. He's going to kill me. She glanced around, eyeing his shadow edging towards her through the trees. Her heart was racing, as she staggered back up and floundered blindly through the trees and brush. Sensing her light again, her body began to heal, and her legs sprinted faster, while she surrounded herself with her protective energy.

Lurching high into the sky, she frantically searched for a safe place to hide from the monster chasing her. Malkia felt the impact before she made it more than forty feet into the air. Her light flickered and then disappeared altogether. Her heart dropped into her stomach, as she tumbled rapidly towards the ground, shrieking as the jolt of the collision sent jarring pain throughout her body. Her twisted form lay broken and bent, blood trickling from her nose and mouth.

Malkia willed her body to heal and waited while it mended all the broken pieces, praying the man wouldn't find her before she was able to fight. *Who is this man?*

I'm the one person who can destroy you.

She cringed when she heard the voice, but quickly realized it was in her head. *Please leave me alone. Why are you after me? I've never done anything to you,* Malkia pleaded with the man.

How do you know you haven't done anything to me? The only person you ever think about is yourself.

Malkia glanced around at her surroundings, but with the tall grass, she was unable to discern the shadows. Squeezing her eyes shut in frustration, she willed her body to heal faster. *That's not true. You don't know me at all, if that's what you think of me.*

Then, who are you? His voice echoed in her head.

Her hair was matted against her cheek, as the gummy blood

continued to seep from her forehead. Twisting her head back, she struggled to find her pursuer. *Why can I not live in peace? Why are you tormenting me? I'm not here to hurt anyone. I just want to live my life alone.*

Malkia knew she didn't want to be alone, but she needed this man to know she wasn't his enemy. Asha and her Esaki mother had warned her about him. They had said if she stayed on Eris, he would come for her. She thought back to that moment and wished she had listened more, instead of choosing to be difficult.

Why did you stay here, Malkia? Why have you not gone after your daughter?

"What do you know of my daughter?" Malkia screamed into the chilly air.

"I know more than you would want me to know." His voice was close. She sensed his presence beside her, feeling a hand slide onto her stomach. The silence was deafening as her breath caught in her throat, opening her reluctant eyelids, and staring at the warlock who haunted her dreams.

His hand remained on her torso, his dark face turned towards her with a smile twitching over his lips, "Did you know?" He pressed down firmly, staring at her pointedly. "This one will surpass your abilities, bringing a force into this star system, no one has ever known."

Malkia's eyes widened, her heart accelerating as she edged her fingers towards her stomach. Her hand rested in the spot the warlock's had been, directing her energy into her own body and searching with her mind. Inhaling sharply, she gulped, her eyes darting back to his face, just as the blackness enveloped her sight.

Dimness clouded Malkia's eyes, as she forced herself to focus on her surroundings. Her head was heavy and throbbed with agony. Reaching up, she rubbed her eyes, attempting to wipe the film of sleep from them. As the room came into focus, she eased herself into a sitting position, examining what she could see.

A large, wooden door stood across the cavernous room, with a faint light outlining the edges. The bed she was lying in was enormous, covered with cushions and blankets. A beam at each corner stretched to the ceiling and was draped with flowing fabric. The walls were lined with paintings, and Malkia strained her eyes to see the landscapes on each one, hoping for a clue of her whereabouts.

She finished searching the entirety of the room, not noticing any other living creatures in the semidarkness. She slid her feet out from underneath the warm blankets, hanging them off the side of the bed and easing down onto the ground. Her toes were greeted with the soft touch of animal fur. Looking down, she noticed the shape of some beast lying below her, creating a barrier between the chill of the floor and her feet.

Tiptoeing towards the door, she grasped the handle, twisting and easing it open inch by inch. When there was enough room for her to slip through, she took a deep breath and peeked around the corner. The corridor was quiet and dark, with shadows bouncing from a faraway lantern. Sliding into the hallway, she willed her light to manifest, surrounding herself with her protective barrier and floating soundlessly towards the flickering fire.

Rounding the corner, she noticed a fireplace at the far end of the room with cushioned seats and a large table in the center. A man sat in one of the chairs, reading a paper in his hands. He wore some kind of round spectacles on his face, his nose holding them before his eyes. She floated towards him, ready to strike the moment he tried to hurt her.

He glanced up from his paper as she neared him, a smile creeping slowly across his face. "Fantastic. You're awake. I was beginning to think you would sleep for a week."

As he spoke, Malkia remembered his voice. He was the one who chased her through the trees and eventually caused her blackout. "It's you," she whispered, her brows furrowing, as she blocked him from seeing her thoughts. "Why have you brought me here?"

He placed his papers on the table, rising from his seat and stepping towards her. "We're on the same team, Malkia. I'm only here to clarify your significance and create a more experienced warrior. You were chosen by the Gods to be an instrument in our evolution, and I intend to move that forward. That includes teaching you what your unborn child will become."

Malkia eyes crinkled in frustration, and she pursed her lips in disbelief. "I was *not* chosen by any God, to do anything. I do realize there are certain Beings who desire the end of my Father's dominion and are relying on me to not use the dark magic coursing through my body, but there is no God who wants me to further our evolution."

"You're mistaken, my dear Malkia." The mysterious Warlock stepped closer and for the first time she viewed his entire face. His amber eyes pierced her soul, creating waves of excitement rippling down to her toes. "You have much to learn. It will be sunrise within the hour, so let's make our way down to the eating hall, and I can begin to convey to you the story about your Father and the Gods who want him annihilated. These aren't just Beings, they are the protectors of our Creators." He moved towards her, holding out his arm for her to take. "Let me show you how important you really are."

Hesitating for a few moments, Malkia finally grasped the Warlock's arm, allowing him to lead her down several dark corridors and a flight of stairs. As they neared the eating hall, they passed a large window and she noticed the first sun's rays beginning to touch the sky above. "Are you the warlock Duncan instructed me to find?"

He paused in his steps, glancing over at her. "I haven't heard that name in nearly a century. If you are speaking of one of the two people I trust in this star system, then yes, Duncan would've been inclined to send you to me." He began walking again. "We were the best of friends, once upon a time, but my knowledge of your father far surpasses his, which must be why he sent you, my way."

Once inside the hall, the Warlock eased her chair back and pushed it in for her, as she sank into her seat. He strode around to the head of the massive table where he slid into his own chair. Moments later, a bald, squat man hustled into the hall, carrying a tray of drinks and delicacies. He set them down in front of the Warlock, before rushing away to attain her food.

The Warlock sat in silence, staring inquisitively at Malkia, waiting patiently for his servant to return. A smile rose on his lips, and an uncomfortable, awkward silence pulsated between them.

"Did Asha ever explain to you the significance of the pendant you wear around your neck?" He spoke up, his voice deep and energetic.

Malkia gripped the pendant, glancing down at it for a moment. "No, she didn't." She pursed her lips, staring into his entrancing eyes. "I fled before I had the chance to ask, although my curiosity nearly kept me there." She paused, waiting for him to reply, but when he didn't, she continued, "What do I call you?"

He examined her face a moment in silence. Before he had the chance to speak, the servant returned to the hall with her food, placing it carefully in front of her. Reaching for her glass, he filled it with a rose drink, followed by coffee in another. He turned on his heel and hurried to the Warlock's position, where he did the same for him. Without a word, he bustled out of the room, leaving the two of them in silence once again.

The Warlock placed his napkin on his lap, smoothing it before reaching for his coffee. He sipped at the hot drink, setting it back down and using his fork to begin eating the food in front of him. Malkia watched in awe, wondering if he would divulge his name or if he desired to remain mysterious for the entire time she was his guest—or his prisoner.

Picking up her fork, she stabbed the eggs on her plate, chewing them slowly, as she continued to scrutinize the man in front of her. They ate in silence for some time, before the Warlock cleared his throat, bringing Malkia back to reality.

"My name is Ustarum," he finally offered. "I've been a manipulator of the elements since before your parents existed, and I've observed from afar the deception your Father has proclaimed. What I know about you, your pendant, your reason for living, and your entire family genealogy will astound you." He smiled when her forehead creased in confusion. "Malkia, when your light burst into existence, I remember exactly where I was standing, because your brightness drove straight through my body, like a flaming sword. I can honestly say, I have been waiting for this moment for an agonizing length of time."

Malkia gulped, the heat from the room surrounding her, making her suck up the air in desperation. Sweat beaded on her forehead, and she reached up to wipe it off while sitting forward in her chair. "How do you know so much about me? How could you possibly feel my light kindle?"

"In due time, I will answer all your questions," Ustarum said, picking up a slice of meat and easing it into his mouth. His amber eyes brightened, as a devilish grin spread across his face. He finished chewing and took a swallow of his juice. "When I heard about the destruction you caused to Artemis, I was appalled by your actions. Your parents and mentors have failed you at a paramount level. At that moment, I decided to find you, and teach you what your true purpose is."

"What might that be?" Malkia asked, sipping on her juice and eyeing him, as she attempted to settle her nerves.

"Another question to be answered at a later date. Right now I would like to discuss why you abandoned your family and friends." He paused as the servant returned, sweeping up the dirty dishes in front of him.

The servant surveyed Malkia as he moved towards her, but when their eyes met, he quickly bowed his head, grabbed her dishes, and rushed out of the room. Watching him leave the room, she slowly returned her attention to Ustarum. "Are all your servants so odd?"

Ustarum chuckled, pushing his chair away from him, as he rose. "Don't let Omri frazzle you. He's an intense man, who is untrusting to anyone outside our home, and for good reason. You're not the first to be taken under my wing." He sauntered towards her, holding out his hand for her to take.

Malkia clutched his hand, rising unsteadily from her chair, a rush of vertigo causing her to grip the table as well.

"Are you unwell?" Ustarum asked, grasping her elbow.

Malkia shook her head, as her eyesight returned to normal and she balanced herself. "I must have risen too fast." She smiled at the mysterious man, before following him out of the eating hall. "Where are we going now?"

"I would still like to hear why you ran away from your Father's fortress, without your people," he replied, patting her hand that was gripping his arm. "Your anger and grief appear to have consumed your ability to reason, and I'm curious to why you allowed emotions to dictate your path."

Malkia halted in the middle of the corridor, unwinding her hand from his arm. "I left my people because I'm in desperate need of answers. My daughter was abducted by my father, and I desire to find her before she is turned against me." Fear splintered her heart, grimacing at the thought of not being able to track Esta down. "My mothers abandoned me on Esaki, leaving me with none of my childhood memories, and stripped of most abilities. I'm having an internal struggle with forgiveness." She paused, chewing on her bottom lip to suppress the heartache tearing at her insides. After a few deep breaths, her eyes met Ustarum's. "Knowing they could've prevented the majority of the events that stole my daughter from me, creates an anger and darkness inside me, which consumes me." Malkia stepped away from him, her flame boiling just beneath the surface of her skin. "I need to find my daughter, but before I do, I have to know how to control the raging inferno pulsing through my veins."

Ustarum closed the distance between them, touching Malkia's face with his calloused hands. "It's a good thing we have finally met." He smiled, tightening his hold on her face. "There is much for us to do and I would like to begin today. Please take some time to shower and dress. When you are ready, return to the sitting area where you found me before breakfast. I'll begin the lessons there."

Malkia nodded, as he released her face, turning on her heel and trekking up the stairs, before winding through a few hallways and somehow finding her way back to her room. She shoved the heavy door open, closing it firmly behind her and sagging against it with a deep breath. *If anyone is intense in this house, it's that man,* she thought, standing up straight and examining the room in the light for the first time.

Large tapestries hung from ceiling to floor, surrounded by paintings of Theia, her moons and the ocean. *Does he know how much my soul yearns to be near the water?* Malkia thought. If she ever had the chance to decorate a home, she would fill it with the beauty of the oceans, rivers and lakes, along with the twinkle of Theia. As much as she appreciated the sentiment, she didn't want him reading her mind

Stepping into the shower, she stood under the faucet, allowing the water to cascade down her body, soaking every inch of her skin. She closed her eyes, remembering the sight of Esta the last time she beheld her in Palma's room. The tears came without warning and she squeezed her eyes shut, attempting to block the pain from her heart.

After several deep breaths, she finished her shower, wiped her face of all signs of the tears and dressed in some sleek, black leggings, with a fitted, black shirt. Comfort in all forms was what she was looking for, as she wiggled her feet into a pair of slip on shoes Ustarum had set next to her door.

Making her way back to the sitting room was just as simple as the first time. Malkia saw the flicker of the fire, before noticing Ustarum seated in another chair farther from the heat.

"You made it." Ustarum beamed from his chair. "I would like to speak to you about your unborn child and that pendant. Once we have some rules established, we can begin your lessons." He rose from his chair and sauntered closer to the fire, waving for Malkia to join him in the armchairs by the coffee table.

Malkia sat on the edge of the chair, eyeing Ustarum as he poured himself a glass of water and set it on the table in front of him. He noticed her stare and grinned. "Would you like a drink?"

"Yes, I would. Thank you," she replied, feeling uneasy sitting across from the man who attacked her in the forest. "How did you know I was with child?" she asked, as he sat down in his chair, taking a sip of his water.

"I can sense its strength and powers, just like I did when you were created. They are separate from your own and are beginning to build, even though its form is still that of a seed." Ustarum set his glass down and leaned against the back of his chair. "What you have created inside your womb is by far the most extraordinary human I have ever come across. There is a reason for its existence, and I'm determined to ensure its safe arrival to our star system."

"Do you know what its purpose is?" Malkia asked, wringing her hands together and chewing on her bottom lip.

"Not yet." He smiled. "But that is unimportant right now. Right now, I would like to give you a set of skills that will assist your power's growth and strength. I would also like to teach you how to resist the darkness and use only pieces of it, in times of desperate need." He leaned forward, his eyes dancing with excitement. "Your dark magic is not a curse and shouldn't be treated as such. Most warlocks run from it, but I have trained with the Thalians and they have given me the keys to use the darkness as it was intended."

Malkia's eyebrows lifted as she straightened up in her chair. "The Aletheian's told me I cannot succumb to the darkness, or I'll fail, and destruction will befall ours and the blue planet's star systems."

He didn't flinch from the mention of the blue planet but pursed his lips before speaking. "The Aletheian's only require others to rise above their addictions and fears. The darkness can be both of those, and if you surrender to them and lose yourself, they've failed in their mission." He ran his fingers across his bearded face, his eyes glazing over in thought for a few moments. After some time, he refocused on Malkia and smiled. "Have you ever pondered the beginning of human life?"

Malkia's forehead creased, as she shook her head. "No, I haven't. That seems to be a strange subject to contemplate. Why do you ask?"

"Because someone once prophesied of a woman, who beamed light from her body, who would discover the origins of humans. With her powers and many abilities, she would be able to converse with the Aletheian's or as I call them, Angels, who will eventually bestow this knowledge upon her." Ustarum crossed one leg over another, watching Malkia's eyes. "Most believed it was your father's lover, Ginny, who possessed the ability, but I could never sense her worth. She was filled with a desire for power and greed, which is a definite oneway ticket away from the Angels. They won't tolerate such negativity."

"You believe I can be this woman?" Malkia asked.

"Yes," he replied, stretching out his feet in front of him. "You don't possess an ounce of greed in your soul. I have the sense you enjoy leading and teaching others, but you lack any desire to overpower them. You're impulsive, selfish, and use your emotions far too often to make decisions, but you are teachable and open to new options." He paused, scratching his head. "Your father's family has a long history of control and power over the people of Eris and your mother's father used his dominion to create havoc and chaos for several moons in this vicinity. Being that your mother isn't like either one of them, considering her biological father didn't belong to this star system and you don't carry their greed in your heart, plus you possess the foretold abilities, I believe there is a significant chance you're the Chosen Heir."

Malkia sat up straight, her eyes wide. "What did you just say about the Chosen Heir?"

"They call the woman in the prophecy, the Chosen Heir. She will be the mother of all knowledge and will have the ability to converse with the Angels and possibly travel to our Creator's whereabouts." He rubbed his hands together, a grin spreading across his face. "Have you heard this before?"

She nodded, her shoulders tense as she thought of Apollo. "A friend of mine mentioned the Chosen Heir, along with Duncan. As much as I don't want the job, I'm beginning to believe there are no coincidences."

"There is a purpose for everyone in this life, and you're no exception." His eyes fell into his lap, exhaling a deep sigh. "You haven't asked why I attacked you in the forest. Why is that?"

Malkia shook her head, her hands trembling from the memory. "How do you bring something like that up?" she half joked, a wary smile surfacing on her lips. "Hey, thanks for sheltering me in your home after you threw me against a boulder and then forced me to freefall to a possible demise." Her breath caught in her throat, struggling to forget the pain from the impact. "I would like to know why you didn't just talk to me. Why the theatrics?"

"When I first felt your presence near, I was thrilled." His voice was nearly a whisper and Malkia had to lean forward to hear him. "But then my own darkness surfaced. I thought of all the lives you destroyed, and I allowed a side of me that I haven't felt in ages to surface and take control of the situation. Logically, I believed I was giving you a taste of your own medicine, as well as teaching you a lesson."

"What do you mean, teaching me a lesson?" Malkia asked, her forehead creasing.

He cleared his throat and sat up straight, his eyes meeting hers. "You waved your powers over a whole civilization, with no thought of who you were slaughtering, and destroyed every living thing. When I was able to overpower you and give you a taste of the pain, I felt like I was showing you their pain."

"I did think of them," she whispered, her face and ears burning with shame. "It was too late, and I do deserve to be punished for my crimes, but I want you to know, I did think of them. I wanted the inferno to stop, but by the time I realized my mistake the fires had consumed everything, and now I will pay the price for all their deaths."

"No, you won't," Ustarum said, his eyes widening and his shoulders tensed. "What happened was supposed to happen. I see that now, but until I hurt you myself, I didn't understand why."

Malkia's brows bumped together and heat blossomed in her cheeks. "What happened was supposed to happen? That's ridiculous," her voice shook with emotion, and she let her breath out in a hiss. "Those Artemisians didn't deserve to die, nor was it supposed to happen."

"Malkia, I know you don't see my perspective, but someday you might glimpse it and finally understand. For now, we can agree to disagree." He ran his hands across his beard, searching her eyes. "The point is that my intentions were selfish and fueled by my own pain. It's ironic how all things circle back around, teaching you the lessons you thought you were teaching others."

Malkia leaned back in her chair, still shaking from his words and realizing she had allowed him to control her emotions. "I don't understand right now, but I would like to move forward with our conversation." She breathed in deeply, her eyes searching the room before speaking again. "You weren't surprised by my mention of the blue planet. Why is that?"

He smiled broadly, the twinkle in his eyes returning. "That will be a great story, but today is not the day it will be told." He paused, laughing to himself, his eyes glazing over for a moment, before focusing back on Malkia. "I need one week. You give me eight days to whip you into shape and when all is said and done, I'll divulge all that I know about your family and the mysterious blue planet. Agreed?"

Staring back at him, Malkia thought of grabbing her scanty possessions and leaving, never to return to this man again, but as she peered into his eyes, she realized this was what she left her family to do. All the traveling, the blood loss of Duncan's people, the meeting of Apollo—all of it was so she could encounter this man and discover how to rein in the darkness and learn a better way to use her powers.

She rose from her chair, leaning forward and offering her hand to Ustarum. "Agreed."

He stood and grasped her hand, squeezing in acknowledgement. "This will be quite an adventure, Malkia." He grinned. "You and I will both be much wiser by the end of our week together."

"I hope so." Tucking her hair behind her ears, she turned and looked around the room. "When do we start?"

"Today. We start today." He waved his hands over the top of her head. "I have just blocked all of your powers, but one. It's up to you to figure out which one it is by mid meal."

Confusion swept over Malkia's face as her light refused to surface from her body. "What if I don't discover the one that remains?"

"Then I will have to force your hand," he replied. "Good luck." He turned and left the room without another word.

NINE
Kneeling on Her Knees

BACK IN HER room, Malkia attempted to force her light from her body, but she felt normal again, as she did back before her powers were unblocked on Esaki. Her telepathy couldn't be tested and without her light she was unable to fly or fling her powers. She worked on levitating herself without her light but ended up with a bruised knee and a jammed finger.

"What am I missing?" She asked herself, staring at a painting of Theia hovering over an ocean. "I wonder if my speed or strength has been taken." She didn't usually use her speed, as she had her light to keep her ahead of everyone.

Stepping lightly out into the corridor, she looked both ways, before planting both feet in the middle of the hallway. Focusing on her speed she began running, but by the time she reached the stairway, she knew that ability had been blocked.

"Ugh!" She grumbled, sagging against the banister. "What is this showing me?" she whispered to the painting of a man hung on the wall across from her.

Pushing herself away from the railing, she limped back to her room, feeling the bruise on her knee even more so after running. "I forgot how difficult it is to just be human," she mumbled to herself, as she neared her doorway. "Wait!" She straightened her back and peered around to make sure she was alone.

Closing her eyes, she focused on her hurt knee, willing her powers to heal herself. Within a few seconds she felt the warmth slide over her knee and finger, taking the pain away and fixing the damage done by her foolish attempt to fly.

Striding back down the hallway, she smiled when she ran into Ustarum. "That was an easy one."

"You've discovered the one ability I left you with?" he asked, grinning from ear to ear.

"Yes," she replied, waltzing over to the fireplace and reclining into one of the chairs. "I can still heal my body."

"Show me." He walked towards her and smiled again when he saw the confusion wash over her face.

Malkia sat up straight and glanced around. "How am I supposed to do that?"

Ustarum slid up next to her, a large knife gripped in his hand. He reached over her body and sliced her arm clean open. "Owww!" Malkia screamed, bounding up from her chair and grasping onto the cut. "What is wrong with you?" she yelled at the man, looking down at the blood pouring from her wound. The smell of copper permeated her nostrils and slid down the back of her throat.

Tossing an icy glare at Ustarum, she leaned back on a faraway chair, closing her eyes and focused on the wound. The warmth encircled the affected area and slowly began to twist and twirl around it, until the pain dissipated completely.

Malkia opened her eyes and peered down at her arm, sighing in relief as she wiped the remaining blood away with her hand. The wound had completely healed. Standing up, she stomped past Ustarum, her temples throbbing with rage. "I'm going to clean up. I think we are done for today."

As she passed him, he waved his hand over her again, an amused smile smeared across his face. "I'm sure you would like to possess all your abilities again."

Malkia twisted back around, her body quivering with indignation. "What's the point of all this? Why cut me, just to see me heal myself? It seems like a huge waste of my time, and I don't want to spend the next eight days playing foolish games."

"The point, my dear Malkia, is to teach you to focus on just one ability at a time." He stepped forward, grasping her arm that was caked with blood. Rubbing his fingers together, the blood wiped clean before Malkia's eyes. "You were given all these abilities and absolutely no instructions on how best to use them. What I want for you is to master each and every one of your powers. Don't allow them to control you. Realize that you're in complete control of them. When you can do this, you will be ready to face your father."

Malkia's breath caught in her throat and her head throbbed from her embarrassing tantrum. "Why do I always feel sheepish once you're done explaining yourself?"

"You're a passionate woman," Ustarum said, leading her back to the fireplace. "This can be a strength, if used in the necessary circumstances, but at this point it is only an obstacle in your learning." They reclined in the chairs nearest the fire. "Patience is a powerful ally.

Many times, you'll gain a better outlook on your circumstances if you pause and take a step back. Gain a wider and deeper view of what is truly occurring."

Malkia sat for a moment chewing on his words and staring into the dancing flames of the fire. "What's next?" She focused on Ustarum, crossing her ankles, and leaned back in her chair.

"Like I said, I want to teach you to focus, but not just on your abilities. Controlling your emotions in every situation will make you a far more powerful leader." Ustarum rubbed his hand mindlessly over his beard. "Are you willing to give me your full time and attention for these next eight days?"

Malkia closed her eyes, thinking of her family, friends, Tantiana and the dragon waiting for her in the forest. In eight days, this will all be over and she could finally return to them. Opening her eyes, she lifted her chin and met Ustarum's gaze. "Yes, I'm all yours."

"Fantastic." He sat up straight, his brilliant smile radiating across his face. "I will mold you into the warrior you were born to be."

"Ustarum, I'm doing it!" Malkia exclaimed, her eyes dancing with the beams of light from the bright suns, as she stared down at him. "How did you know I could levitate without my light?"

Ustarum chuckled, shielding his eyes to peer up at her floating body. "Your light is just one of your abilities. You're the one who restricted yourself. Think back to the moment you remembered your ability to fly. Did you have your light surrounding you at that time?"

Malkia eased back down to the ground, shuffling through her memories to that moment when she was perched on Tandi's bed back on Esaki. "You're right. I didn't have my light around me." A puzzled look slid over her face. "Why did I start only flying when I had my light surrounding me?"

"It happens, Malkia. In the midst of chaos, a person will begin a habit and before they realize it, they are using one crutch to solve another solution that never needed the crutch in the first place." He curled his arm around her shoulders. "You'll eventually remember the moment it all began and realize why you did it in the first place, but that's insignificant at this time. Now you know. You're one step closer to mastering all your abilities."

"Four days in," Malkia whispered, looking up at him. "I'm glad I stayed. What I've learned in these few days is invaluable."

"Tomorrow I want to work on your telepathy. You've mentioned you don't like the idea of intruding on others thoughts, who have no idea you are there." He squeezed her arm, as they walked towards the back door of the cottage. "However, when you are searching for your father and daughter, I believe this will be one of your most valuable abilities. Misty could read anyone's mind, with effort, but you can do it with just a twist of the dark magic inside you."

Malkia's heart skipped at the mention of using her dark magic. "Do you think that is wise?"

Ustarum nodded, threading one of his hands through his hair. "Absolutely. As I've said, the dark magic can be a tool, if used properly. Don't allow it to grip your fear, as that will only give it greater dominion over you. Use it as you breathe in deeply and find the calm within the storm."

"I'm nervous about unleashing the darkness." She hung her head, her brows furrowing. "I've kept it buried so well for the past few days, and the thought of just allowing it to escape makes me uneasy." Her jaw tightened in anticipation of what was to come, her eyes shifting from Ustarum and back to the ground.

"Do you trust me?" he asked, throwing her a sideways glance, as he opened the door for her.

Biting her lip, she stepped over the threshold and into the back foyer. Turning to face him, she bobbed her head up and down. "Yes, I trust you."

"Then you have nothing to worry about." He smiled, tossing her the blanket they had brought with them. "Will you give that to Omri on your way to your room? I will see you at dinner." He walked away, stepping lightly up the back stairs and disappearing out of view.

"It's not working." Malkia opened her eyes, frustration crinkling their edges. "We have been at this for hours, Ustarum. Can we pick up where we ended, after our mid meal?"

"No," he barked. "Do it again. Breaking the barrier to a person's mind is as easy as snapping a twig in two. Imagine my blockade being a piece of glass and take a bat to it with your powers. Allow the darkness to drip into the bat before you hit the glass."

Malkia shook her head and closed her eyes again. She could feel his barrier holding strong around his thoughts as she slid into place, a mental bat held in her hands. Her palms began to sweat, as she thought of the dark magic seeping from her mind and she had to take a few deep breaths before continuing. With her last big breath, she sent a wisp of darkness on the wind of her exhalation, twisting it around the bat and swinging it with everything her mind could muster.

The glass shattered and she jumped from the explosion. Her eyes snapped open and noticed Ustarum was smiling back at her. "You're in," he said, rising from his chair. "I told you it would work." He moved across the room and settled onto the couch. "Now do it again."

Malkia groaned, sagging back against her chair in exhaustion. She threw an icy glare at Ustarum before closing her eyes once again. Breathing deeply, she found Ustarum's barrier and noticed how much stronger it was this time. Its full-bodied strength pulsated to her heartbeat, and she sighed, knowing he was pushing her to do better.

Taking a few deep breaths, she imagined the barrier as a thick piece of glass. Dropping the mental bat, she imagined a large hammer appearing in her mind and a moment later allowed a drip of dark magic to slither onto the tool. As it made its way around the hammer, she drew it back and smashed it into the glass, the shatter reverberating inside her mind.

She smiled, keeping her eyes shut and viewing the inside of Ustarum's mind. A flash of a thought went by, and Malkia noticed her Esaki mother's name, Alyssa, mixed in with the words, before Ustarum repaired the glass barrier.

"Good job," he congratulated her, clapping his hands.

Malkia opened her eyes and grinned over at him. "Can I go eat now?"

"Yes," he replied, rising from the couch. "Let's go enjoy a nice meal and then we can return and start again."

Malkia chuckled, but her eyes were tired from the hours of work. "I'm ready to call it a day."

"Not yet," Ustarum said. "I only have three more days after this. You need to have this skill mastered before you sleep tonight."

Shaking her head, Malkia followed the warlock down the stairs and into the eating hall. Omri was already there, setting out the food. He ignored Malkia, as usual, but nodded in greeting as Ustarum strolled by. The two of them settled into their usual chairs, and Omri poured them water and juice before scurrying off to his duties.

"Maybe someday he will like me," Malkia said, raising her juice glass in a toast. "To another lesson learned, but not mastered."

Ustarum laughed. "Cheers to that." They both took a long drink from their glasses, before digging into their plate of delicacies.

"Ustarum, will you tell me about my pendant?" Malkia asked, after a few bites of food. "What do you know about it?"

Setting down his fork, Ustarum wiped his mouth with his napkin and leaned back in his chair. "Asha and Alyssa came to me before you existed. I believe your mother was pregnant with your sister. They were terrified of your father and his power over Theia's Moons. They believed he was the instigator behind the conflict with the Artemisians, but they also feared he was working with the creatures as well." He rubbed his hand over his beard, his eyes glazing over, as his thoughts returned to the past. "Haltia played along with your father, out of fear of retribution. She had met her own father's wrath and knew what both of them were capable of doing. Asha and Alyssa begged me to assist them in the creation of a pendant that would protect its wearer but would also be a catalyst to help transform the wars in the future."

Malkia sat up straight, her eyes growing wide. "What do you mean, a catalyst to help transform the wars in the future?"

"It means, Asha and Alyssa always intended for you to wear that pendant and realized that the combined powers between it and you would pave the way to the end of your father's dominion over our star system." Ustarum leaned forward, picking up his fork and stabbing his food. "This is a discussion you should have with them, but just be mindful of their intentions. It might sound as if they were molding you to be a particular way, but in fact the opposite is true."

"Is that it?" Malkia asked, leaning forward and placing her elbows on the table. "You made a pendant that would shape the future, knowing it would be worn by the daughter of Thane? Why does that sound so unlikely?"

Ustarum chewed on his food, his eyes lost in retrospect. "I didn't agree with Asha and Alyssa, at first," he said, once his food slid down his throat. "In fact, they had to return three times before I agreed. At this point, I knew you were on your way, and just like the child in your womb, I knew you would be a truly extraordinary soul." He speared more food on his plate, glancing back up at Malkia. "You were always meant to wear that pendant. It was made for you alone and because of your union, you have become the strength this star system has prayed for to heal it from your grandfather's wrath."

"Will my child require a pendant, as well?" Malkia gritted her teeth as she picked up her fork.

Ustarum paused, his fork poised before his open mouth. He smiled. "This child will be extraordinary with or without a pendant." He shoved his food into his mouth, a smile spreading across on his lips as he chewed.

The stars twinkled in the night sky, while Theia shone brightly to one side. Malkia stood on the balcony of her quarters, enjoying the quiet calm surrounding Ustarum's home. The past week had been a rush of information, lessons, and an overabundance of constructive criticism. She felt the lassitude of the day's lessons and was looking forward to the next day, when she would be able to leave the dwelling and wander around the forest, practicing all her newfound skills. Ustarum promised it would be a day of enjoyment.

Just as she was turning to go in for the night, she felt the heat of fire race past the dwelling. Turning back around, she gasped to see a dragon soar over the trees, his eyes locked onto her.

You don't belong here, the dragon spoke in her head.

Malkia encircled herself with her purple light, touching her pendant with her hand. *Wait. Do you know me? Why don't I belong here?*

You destroyed the demon's moon. I was brought from Hemera to bring you to their leader. His wings barely cleared the roof of the home as he turned, landing in the clearing, near the front gate.

Malkia's breath came in short gasps, her pulse racing in her ears.

The dragon snarled at her light, his eyes black as night, staring through her soul. She rose into the air, landing softly on the dirt below. *I won't battle you. I've come here to find a way to bring peace to Theia's moons.* She paused, seeing Ustarum slip out from a side door of his home. *We can be comrades.*

The dragon sneered, a loud chuckle rising from his throat. *You mean nothing to me. I have one task and once it's complete, I'll be returned to my home.* The beast stepped forward, his breath hot on her light.

I'm not going with you. Malkia replied, standing her ground, her light remaining a brilliant purple hue, with a new silver tint. The darkness had receded within her to such an extent that it was difficult to remember why it had ever had such a hold on her. *You're free to leave and tell the demons' leader that if he wants me, he can come find me himself.*

The dragon roared, his white scales glistening with a red glare from the fire he had set to the trees behind him. Malkia leapt from her position, flying off into the forest. The massive beast stalked behind her, closing the distance quickly.

You won't escape from me, the dragon told her.

A blinding light arose from the midst of the trees, just beyond Malkia's reach. It raced past her, knocking the dragon off its path. His scream of pain echoed into the sky, as the magic pierced his scales, flowing across his body like an electrical current. She skidded to a halt, breathing deeply to calm her heart as she turned to face the ferocious beast.

I'm tired of fighting, and begging you to leave me alone, Malkia pleaded with the dragon.

His head whipped around, meeting the barrier of her light and hurtling her through the trees. As Ustarum had taught her, she kept control of her protective light, easing herself right side up and facing the dragon again. She glided back through the trees, where the dragon was rising from the ground, his wings slamming into the trees and ripping off hundreds of branches. Several smashed into her light, making her wince.

I will return, the dragon screamed in her mind.

As he cleared the trees, Malkia noticed off in the high shadows another set of wings closing in on them.

"*Malkia move,*" Ustarum yelled from a low hill, over to one side of her.

She shot off into the trees, the collision of the two beasts grinding and gnashing overhead and Tantiana's voice in her head. *I found you.*

The two dragons tumbled back to the ground, grazing Malkia's light, as they collided with the dirt. Malkia's heart raced with fear, seeing a cloud of dust envelope her dear dragon, with the white beast landing on top.

"*No,*" Malkia screamed. "*Tantiana,*" The inferno in her heart swelled rapidly, making the silver in her light bounce erratically around her light. She raced into the dust cloud, searching for her dragon, but came face to face with her foe.

His jaws snapped at her light, yelping when his teeth hit the barrier. *What is that surrounding you?* He screamed again in her mind.

You're going to lose this battle, Malkia warned. *Take this chance to exit. Don't force one of us to end your life, just for the sake of a group of demons who abducted you from your home.*

I will kill you, the dragon whispered.

No you won't, Tantiana's thoughts jumped into the conversation. Malkia glimpsed the flash of her dragon's emerald eyes, as her teeth sank into his white scales.

He screeched loudly, thrashing around violently. Tantiana took a deep breath, rearing back and releasing the inferno from her core. The white dragon leapt away, roaring in pain. Tantiana didn't hesitate as she followed after the white beast, letting more of her fire rush through the trees. His scales protected him from the flames, but it licked ferociously at the chunk of his skin revealed by Tantiana's bite.

His screams filled the crisp night air, while he attempted to jump into the sky. Tantiana reached forward, clutching his tail in her teeth and ripping him back down to the ground. Striking the earth with a thud, he groaned in agony, before stumbling up and running through the trees.

"We must not allow him to escape." Ustarum strode quickly towards Malkia. "The Artemisians cannot know where you're hidden."

Malkia stole a glance at Tantiana, who was tailing after the white dragon, and then back at Ustarum, taking a deep breath. "I'll end it." She bounded into the air, racing over the trees, following the trail of fire, screams and broken branches.

Seeing both dragons up ahead, Malkia balled her purple light into her hand, whispering the paralyzing incantation that Ustarum had taught her. Before she was done, the white dragon reared its head, shooting a heavy flame at her light. When the crimson sheet of light had dissipated, the white dragon was plowing through the trees once again, sprinting towards Ustarum's dwelling, with Tantiana flying just above him.

"Great," Malkia sighed, racing after them. Settling in the white dragon's path, she finished her incantation, just as he came into view. Her light shot out of her hand, striking him with such force he flew back into the forest, nearly knocking over Tantiana.

Ustarum swept up behind her, gripping her forearm. "You need to end his life."

"No," Malkia blurted out, shaking off his grasp. "I'll ensure his safe return to Hemera. There's no reason for him to die."

From afar, Malkia noticed Omri shuffling towards them, a look of dread covering his face. Ustarum turned to see what Malkia was watching and cried out when he saw the flames dancing around his cottage.

"We need to extinguish the fire," Ustarum commanded. He sprinted through the trees, followed by Malkia and Tantiana.

Reaching his home, Ustarum swung open his front door, disappearing out of sight. Malkia encircled her light around the entire house, along with Tantiana, waiting for the Warlock's return.

Without warning, Omri burst up in front of Tantiana, spooking her. Stepping back onto a sharp rock, she yelped, her front knee buckling beneath her and her head swinging violently backwards. The dragon's head returned to the ground with a pop, striking Omri on its way down. Malkia watched in desperation as the events unfolded in front of her, powerless to arrest the progression.

Rushing to Tantiana, she felt the breath of her beast and knew she had been knocked unconscious. Omri's body was sprawled a few feet away, a nasty gash open down the side of his face and chest, with his shirt ripped open. Malkia knelt next to the short man, placing her hands over his chest and whispering the healing spell that would make her own healing light stronger.

Within seconds, her light around them flickered and she yanked her hands away from Omri's chest. Ustarum bounded up next to her, leaning over Omri.

"What happened?" His voice shaking with anger, with his fists clenched at his sides.

"Omri frightened Tantiana," Malkia whispered.

"Speak up, woman," Ustarum yelled. "What did your beast do to my servant?"

Malkia shook her head, running her hands through her hair. "It was an accident." She stared up at her mentor. "He came out of nowhere and Tantiana jumped, creating a chain of bad reactions." Malkia looked back at her dragon. "She only wanted to help."

Ustarum growled, shaking his head. "The fire is growing. You stay here and heal Omri. I'll tend to the mess those dragons created." He stomped off, only glancing back when Malkia didn't release him from her light.

She moved the light over Ustarum, watching as his magic quickly filled the dark sky. Within moments, the thunderous clouds rolled in with a vengeance. The rain came quickly, rolling down her protective barrier and streaming into hundreds of tiny rivers.

Malkia turned to Omri, his raspy breath catching her attention. Placing her hands back on his chest, she began her incantation again, feeling her light shatter around her and then slither from her hands and into his body. Her eyes closed without thought, a rush of ecstasy pulsing over her skin, as the large drops of rain soaked her to the bone.

Moments later, Omri squirmed. Malkia's eyes opened, staring down at the strange, little man. He was watching her, his forehead creased with irritation. "What are *you* doing?"

Malkia shifted her weight, rising from her perch and holding out her hand to assist Omri off the ground. He grasped onto her and stood up, his lips pursed and his eyes narrowed.

"You were knocked out, after you frightened Tantiana." Malkia pointed at the unconscious dragon. "If you wouldn't mind, I would like to tend to her. The fire is being extinguished and your wounds have healed."

Omri nodded and turned on his heel, heading back into the cottage without another word. Ignoring his rude behavior, Malkia hovered next to Tantiana, placing her hands on her scales. Speaking the same healing spell, Malkia's light coursed through her once again, bursting into her dragon's body and rushing to cover the larger body.

"Come on, baby," Malkia coaxed, feeling an uneasy sensation settling in the pit of her stomach. "You aren't allowed to die on me." The uneasiness began to twist into a knot, as her light failed to make much progress. Her energy was draining quickly, and the incantation was no longer assisting. "Tantiana, you're not leaving me!" she cried, squeezing her eyes shut.

There was no response, although the dragon's breathing remained steady. Malkia continued to stream her energy and light into Tantiana, only pausing when she felt the firm grip of Ustarum on her shoulder.

"You're giving her too much," he said, tightening his grasp. "You need to rest and recoup your energy. Then, we'll do it together."

Malkia opened her eyes, glancing over her shoulder at her mentor.

"I can't leave her."

"You have to." He eased her hands off Tantiana's scales, turning her to face him. "I've secured the white dragon in the forest. He will sleep until we are ready to move him off of Eris. I'll place an invisibility spell on your dragon, so while you are recovering, she'll be hidden."

Malkia nodded, stealing one more glance at Tantiana, before stepping towards the cottage. She listened to Ustarum begin his incantation, as she slid inside the front door, trudging up the stairs and winding through the hallways to her room.

Sliding into her bed, she sighed from the coolness of the blankets, before wrapping herself up in the silky blanket and allowing the black of sleep to swallow her whole.

TEN

Sisterly Love

MALKIA GROANED, TWISTING away from the light and burrowing deeper into her blanket and pillows. "Is it really morning?" She asked Ustarum, who had pulled open the fabric from the windows. "My body feels like a boulder was dropped on it."

"You exerted too much energy last night, first with the battle, then with protecting my cottage, followed by healing Omri and attempting to heal Tantiana. Not to mention a full day of finalizing your expert abilities." He stood at the edge of her bed, his arms folded across his chest, staring down at her. "I would say we have discovered your limit."

Malkia sighed, untangling her arms with the blanket and propping herself up on her elbows. "I've battled for far longer and not felt this banged up afterwards. It doesn't seem I did enough last night."

Ustarum's eyebrows furrowed as he leaned forward, using the bed post for support. "Healing others is always an energy drainer and because you attempted to heal a badly injured dragon, twenty times your mass, I believe you experienced far more depletion than you realize." He pivoted on his heel, stealing one more glance as he said, "It's time to rise and eat, and then join me outside to properly heal your dragon."

He shut the door as he left, leaving Malkia to her own thoughts. She closed her eyes, knowing it was time to contact Damon and her mothers. It was time to leave Eris.

Wriggling her body out of the bed, she eased her feet onto the floor, stepping lightly towards her cleaning room. She showered quickly, gathering her hair up on top of her head and yanking on her trousers and boots. She slid a dark blue shirt over her head and smoothed it out over her torso and chest.

Inhaling deeply, she left her bedroom, gliding through the corridors and down the wide stairs, stopping at the bottom. She could smell the aroma of breakfast wafting down the hall, calling for her. Glancing towards the front door and then back towards the smell, her stomach made the decision for her.

Ustarum was reading a book in the eating hall, while he sipped on his coffee. Pulling up a chair, Malkia sat a few seats down from him, smiling faintly when he glanced over at her.

"Are you ready to begin your final lesson?" he asked.

Malkia's forehead creased and her lips slid into a frown. "I thought you had taught me everything."

He nodded. "At the time, I believed I had taught you all that you needed to know, but after witnessing the chaos from last night and seeing you take on so much of the negative energy, while exerting a large amount of your positive energy, I realized you have no idea how to protect yourself."

"I'm not following," Malkia said. "What else do I need to protect myself from?"

"You're not a stranger to energy, am I correct?" Ustarum asked, sitting forward in his chair and placing his book on the table.

"Yes, you are correct," she replied, eyeing Omri as he opened the door, holding a tray covered with sweet bread, sliced meat and eggs. He set it down in front of her and then returned a moment later with a cup of hot coffee. "Thank you, Omri."

He ignored her gratitude, shuffling quickly away and disappearing behind the door. Malkia turned back to Ustarum, who shrugged at her questioning expression.

"Energy swirls in and all around us," Ustarum began. "Every living creature and every object is made out of this energy and we all have the ability to dispense light to those around us. The reason not everyone can do what you do, is because they don't have the magic coursing through their veins." He paused, waiting for her to interject, but when she didn't, he continued. "Every single soul has a light inside them, because they are made out of energy. The issue lies with the negative energy, which forms in people and creatures who are filled with anger, bitterness, or malevolence. There was a time when you had some of this negative energy inside you, and on a small scale, still do."

Malkia sat up, finally understanding what he was attempting to explain. "What you mean is that when the negative energy is directed towards me and I'm open to all energy, I take on that negativity. It literally becomes a part of me and my own energy. Is that what you are saying?"

Ustarum's head bobbed up and down, as he smiled. "Mostly. That is the part in which you'll understand why you have to perform this next spell of protection." He turned back towards his food and coffee, finishing the last few bites and draining his cup. "When you complete your breakfast, please meet me in the front by Tantiana and I will demonstrate how you must protect yourself, every single day for the rest of your life."

"What about the dark magic inside me? Is that negative energy?" Malkia asked, absentmindedly running her fingers over her pendant.

"It can be, but not always. Dark magic and negative energy aren't the same, but one can be converted into the other." He rose from his chair. "I'll see you outside." Without another word, he strode off, leaving Malkia to digest his words and her food.

Gnawing on the sliced meat, Malkia realized she had allowed herself to be vulnerable from day one of this journey. If she'd known how to protect herself, maybe she would have made better choices. She finished her meal, sipping slowly on her coffee, before gulping down the remainder of her juice.

Reaching the front of Ustarum's home, she noticed Tantiana was no longer under the invisibility spell. She rushed to her side, petting her nose and kissing it, but only hearing the soft rasp of her dragon's indrawn breath in reply.

"Let's begin with protecting yourself." Ustarum stepped into view from the other end of Tantiana. "First, you'll need to close your eyes and mentally wrap yourself in an impenetrable light. How you do it and what it looks like is entirely up to you." He paused, waiting for Malkia to close her eyes. Once she did, he continued, "As you become more skilled in this, it will be as easy as your visible light. Now are you seeing the light around your body?"

"Yes," Malkia answered, nodding.

"Now that you have that light surrounding you, here are the words to keep it snug and tight during your encounters with negative energy," Ustarum said. "Shield of protection, safe within my space."

"That's it?" Malkia asked, peeking from beneath her eyelashes.

"Keep your eyes closed," Ustarum demanded. "Yes, that's all you need to say. It's simple, like most incantations, however you need to make sure you circle yourself first with your mental light." He paused for a moment and Malkia was tempted to open her eyes, but resisted against her anxious nerves. "Do it now."

Malkia tightened the light she envisioned. "Shield of protection, safe within my space." The light in her mind brightened and she felt a warmth in her torso and chest. She opened her eyes and stared over at Ustarum.

"Did you feel the light kindle within your body?" he asked, lifting an eyebrow at her.

She nodded, setting her hand over her heart.

"Great." Ustarum placed his hand on Tantiana's backside. "Let's begin to heal your dragon. Stay there and set your hands on her head. I'll take my place by the tip of her tail and ensure your energy doesn't escape. Once you began the healing incantation, I'll follow suit and together we should be able to restore her health."

Malkia nodded, sliding her hands on Tantiana's scales, just above her eyes. Closing her eyes, she willed her light to rush through her body and connect with her dragon. As the light slithered from her hands and into Tantiana, she began chanting the healing spell, focusing on spreading her energy through every inch of the beast's body.

Breathing steadily, Malkia could feel Tantiana's heart rhythm beating in time with her words. The connection grew in strength and Malkia felt a surge of power and ecstasy rush through her arms, as Tantiana and she became one. The words from her mouth flowed like lightning and the electricity surrounding the trio crackled in the air, making Malkia's hair stand on end.

As the incantation came to a close, the energy receded back into Malkia's hands and she opened her eyes to an unconscious dragon. Her eyes shot down to Ustarum who was shaking his head and walking towards her.

"Something isn't right," he contemplated, his brows furrowing, creasing the fine lines around his eyes. "What you just did was astounding and would have shocked a rock to life. Why it's not working on Tantiana is a mystery." He twisted around, checking every inch of the dragons exposed body.

Malkia followed along, her mind swimming with fear. She watched Ustarum investigate Tantiana and wondered what he was thinking he would find.

"Ah-ha!" Ustarum exclaimed, kneeling down next to Tantiana's hind leg and yanking out a long stick, with a pointed end, almost looking like a small arrow. "We have visitors," he said, turning to face Malkia, his eyes wide.

Her light bounded out of her body, encompassing the house and the three of them. "What is that?" Malkia asked, pointing at the stick.

"It's a dart," he replied, rising from his perch. "It was filled with a poison that I was unable to detect. Did you notice anything strange when you were connected?"

Malkia searched her memory, but only remembered knowing

something was wrong with Tantiana last night and now she was kicking herself for not trusting her own instincts. "No, today it felt magical to be connected with her, but yesterday when I touched her, a darkness shot through me."

Ustarum groaned, as he curled his fingers around Malkia's shoulder. "It could be the work of another warlock. Whatever poison was used on Tantiana, it has infected you as well, on an energy level." He waved his hand, enclosing Tantiana in another invisibility spell, before dragging Malkia behind him, back into his cottage. "We need to clear you first and then figure out what poison was used."

"I need to contact my family and friends." Malkia froze just inside the front door. "They can assist."

"Do it quickly and meet me in my study as soon as you are done." Ustarum raced up the stairs, disappearing around the corner before Malkia could say another word.

Rushing into the sitting room, Malkia settled into a chair, squeezing her eyes shut and breathing deeply a few times before focusing on her mother, Haltia. Seconds later, her image bounced into view and Malkia sighed with relief when she noticed most of her friends and family behind her.

"Malkia!" Asha exclaimed, jumping up from her chair. "Where are you? We've been worried sick about you?"

Haltia stepped forward, tears brimming on her eyelids. "Malkia, I've been dying to see your face again." She reached out her hand and Malkia choked on a sob stuck in her throat.

"I shouldn't have been so vague in my note to Damon." Malkia could see most of her friends were relieved she was safe, but there was animosity behind their relief. "It was selfish of me to leave like I did."

"I can't see you Malkia," Skye cried out, tears spilling onto her cheeks. "But you need to know how furious I am with you. How dare you leave without a word! We came all this way, because we love you and this is how you treat us." Skye shook her head, hysteria rising in her inky irises. "Damon left to go search for you and we haven't heard from him in days. Mataya has wept every single day since you disappeared and your mothers have been a frantic mess, not knowing if you were alive. You should be ashamed of yourself."

Malkia nodded, taking in all her words and knowing she didn't have the right to fight this. "Tell her I'm listening," she said to Haltia. "Tell her she's correct."

Haltia repeated Malkia's words to the ones in the group who couldn't hear her. Skye picked up a vase and tossed it at Malkia, before storming out of the room. The crash of the glass, echoed through the room, but the sound of Skye's receding footsteps is what tore Malkia's heart to shreds. *You deserve it,* Malkia scolded herself.

"I know I don't deserve anyone's help right now," Malkia started, looking at Haltia and Asha. "However, Tantiana found me last night and attacked another dragon that was ordered by the Artemsians to capture me."

Haltia gasped. "Were you hurt?"

"No." Malkia shook her head. "But Tantiana was. Not by the other dragon, but by some kind of poison, shot into her by a small arrow called a dart. We just discovered it this morning."

"Wait." Asha cut her off, after Haltia repeated Malkia's words to everyone else. "Who is we?"

Malkia grimaced, her face twisting into a scowl. "I've been staying in a cottage, near a town called Thebes, with a warlock who calls himself Ustarum."

"What?" Haltia shouted, stepping closer to Malkia. "That man has been mortal enemies with your father's family for generations. Why has he taken you in?"

"Why do you think?" Malkia shook her head in mock disbelief. "If he despises my father and he knows I want to exterminate the man, why wouldn't he take me in?"

Haltia cradled her head in her hands, shaking her head in frustration. "You have no idea the history this man has with our family. He's using you."

"You're right. I don't know the history, because I wasn't allowed to be a member of my own family for nearly twenty-five years." Malkia felt the temperature in her body rise and breathed deeply to regain her composure. "I'm letting this go, because right now Tantiana's life is in danger and another warlock has their eye on my whereabouts. I need you to come to Thebes."

"We need to find Damon first," Asha spoke up again.

Koleton stepped forward, his jaw clenched. Not being able to view her, his eyes wandered around the area where Malkia stood. "Malkia, we'll always be there for you and Tantiana, but we have to find Damon. Remember the barbarian you first encountered on Esaki?" He paused for a moment, continuing without assurance she had answered. "He still resides inside Damon. You're his calm and although it isn't your responsibility to keep him from the darkness, how you deserted him has brought his savage instincts to the surface. He held it together for days, but then his visions began to haunt him, spiraling him down a path of desperation. It's our job to protect him from himself and remind him of his importance." Koleton's eyes narrowed as he leaned forward, up against the back of the couch. "And what you did has to be addressed. You abandoned us for nearly two weeks, without a word, aside from that useless note. Your sister is beside herself. This is not something any of us—" he paused moving his arm around the room. "Are willing to let go."

Malkia nodded, looking at Haltia and Asha. "Tell him I understand and I'll do whatever it takes to pay for my transgressions. I do need all of you and I'll update you with everything I have learned, once you arrive. In the meantime, I'll see if I can find Damon as well. I know he is furious with me, but he and I can handle our issues in private. I'll be in contact soon."

As she said the last word, Mataya burst into the room, her face overrun with tears. "Malkia," she cried. *"You're alright,"* She raced forward, throwing her arms around her sister.

Malkia gasped, her eyes widening and her hands circling around her sister's shoulders. "How are you touching me?"

"My abilities have grown since you abandoned me," Mataya replied. "What I'm capable of doing and creating, has only become stronger and this one," she tapped her sister's arms, "is the one where I can bend space." Mataya stepped through the vision, right into the room with Malkia. She turned back to the group. "Bring my things when you come. I will be here with my sister." She waved her hand and the vision dropped.

Malkia's jaw dropped, as Mataya threw her arms around her neck, again. "I'm going to kill you for putting me through this heartache," she scolded her sister. "You're not forgiven, but I love you and I'm here to do whatever we need to do. What's the problem?"

Lifting her jaw off the ground, Malkia blinked a few times, before embracing her sister again, squeezing her tight. "I can't believe you're here. How in the name of Theia, did you make that happen?"

"I told you, my abilities have strengthened since you rescued me from your father. Once his drugs wore off, the natural flow of my powers just ignited." Mataya grinned, her smile beaming from her eyes. "I didn't realize what was happening until a few days after you disappeared, but once I knew what I was doing, I allowed it to pour from me."

Malkia laughed, matching her sister's smile, as she danced around the floor with her. "I told you we were the same. Blood or not, you and I are connected on a much deeper level." She kissed Mataya's forehead. "I'm sorry for leaving you. I was in a dark place and if I hadn't escaped, I think I would have imploded by now."

"I understand why you ran away," Mataya replied. "But you should've taken me with you or at least given me a place to sneak off to when mom and the rest of the group were bickering." She winked at Malkia, giggling at her idea.

Malkia remembered why she had contacted her family and friends and her frown returned. "Tantiana has been poisoned. We need to find out what is in her body and how we can rid her of the darkness."

Closing her eyes, Mataya ran her hands over her face several times, then held her hands in front of her, rubbing her thumbs against her fingers. Before long a spark ignited in her hands, creating a rush of electricity throughout the room. Mataya opened her eyes, scanning the area around them. "The power pulsating through this home is astonishing. Are you protecting it right now?" She glanced over at Malkia.

Malkia nodded, watching the electric current rush back and forth through Mataya's body. "There is a warlock who resides here and I'm protecting the entire area around Tantiana and this cottage. Ustarum believes the poison came from another warlock, but he doesn't know their identity."

Mataya continued to survey the room, before stepping away from Malkia and exited over the threshold, into the front entryway. "Give me a moment to check out the home and grounds. I'll return shortly." Without another word she opened the front door and slid quietly out into the sunlight, closing the door behind her.

Bounding up the stair, Malkia was met by Omri as she reached the top. "What's happening?" He peeked over her shoulder. "Ustarum is waiting for you."

"My sister is here," she replied, glancing down the hall towards the sitting room. "She's searching for the warlock that may have poisoned Tantiana. I need to inform Ustarum, but I want to be back downstairs when she returns." She pivoted on her heel, sprinting down the corridor and nearly colliding with Ustarum.

"Where's the fire?" Ustarum chuckled, gripping her hand.

"My sister," Malkia breathed loudly. "My sister is here."

"I know." Ustarum smiled with a twinkle in his eyes, curling his arm around Malkia's shoulders. "I felt her presence the moment she stepped over the vision's threshold. What an astounding young woman."

Malkia tugged her shoulder away from Ustarum. "I need to meet her back downstairs. Are you coming with me or would you rather I bring her up to meet you?"

"Bring her upstairs. I would love a demonstration of all her enhanced abilities." He smiled, a slight glaze shadowing his eyes. "I can see her becoming an extraordinary warlock someday."

Malkia shook her head, leaving him to his own imagination, as she barreled back down the stairs. Omri was standing near the open door, surveying the outside world. Peeking over his shoulder, she caught a glimpse of Mataya meandering over the muddy puddles, just beyond the pond. Tantiana was enclosed in Ustarum's invisibility spell, but Mataya seemed to know where she was as she eased around the beast, allowing her electric currents to test the air above her.

After several moments observing Mataya, Omri turned back and jumped at the sight of Malkia. "Why did you not inform me of your presence behind me?" he asked, glowering at her.

"What is it about me that you don't like?" Malkia ignored his question, as she took a few steps back. "You speak to me as if I'm the droppings of a deimos beast. I don't know if you're aware, but I'm human, just like you, and I have feelings, just like you." Her blood boiled, as she stared at the small man who refused to give her the time of day.

Huffing dramatically, Omri pushed past Malkia and raced out of sight. She sighed, turning back to see that her sister was on her way back to the cottage. Her olive skin glistened in the sunlight and her dark hair tossed wildly in the wind. She was no longer her baby sister, who had required a gentle hand.

Mataya grinned as she waltzed over the threshold. "What a charming little cottage. Your warlock has picked a divine stretch of land to hide away from the rest of the moon's inhabitants."

"I agree." Malkia smiled in return. "He's excited to meet you. Would you join us in the sitting room?"

"Of course." Mataya waltzed forward, grasping Malkia's hand and allowing her to lead the way. "I'm delighted to be with you again, dear sister. I can't express how full my heart feels in this moment."

Malkia halted in her tracks, tugging Mataya close. "I love you, Mataya. More than words can say."

Mataya squeezed Malkia, planting a kiss on her cheek. "Now, let's go speak to that warlock of yours."

ELEVEN
Negative Energy

"Mataya." Ustarum rose from his chair, grasping hold of Mataya's hand as he strode up to greet them. "Malkia's dazzling and skillful sister. Your abilities are groundbreaking."

A hesitant smile rose on Mataya's lips, eyeing Ustarum while he kissed her hand. "And you are the warlock who has kept my sister from me for far too long."

Ustarum chuckled, turning and leading them both over the sitting area by the fireplace. "Oh, dear child, your sister has come a long way in her powers while she's been under my watch. You'll be astonished by all she has achieved." He offered the women chairs and then sank back into his own. "But first, I would welcome your assistance in finding the dark energy that Malkia has absorbed by attempting to heal her poisoned dragon. Are you willing?"

Mataya's eyes flashed over to Malkia, her brow furrowing with concern. After a slight nod from her sister, she focused back on Ustarum. "I'll do anything for my sister. What do you require from me?"

"Malkia, it will be easier if you are reclined on a couch. We'll need you to be subdued." Ustarum stared at Malkia, waiting for her to reply, his palms resting on the arms of his chair, ready to rise when she agreed.

Breathing in deep and closing her eyes, she noticed she was still wrapped in her protection spell. "Do I need to undo the incantation, protecting me from negative energy?" she asked, opening her eyes.

"No," Ustarum replied, standing and walking over to her. "It will give you strength. We're only using magic to find the negative energy, therefore your barrier won't hinder us in the slightest." He reached down and helped Malkia up, followed by Mataya. "If you would lie on the couch and relax your body as best you can, your sister and I can begin the spell to discover whatever is ravaging yours and Tantiana's bodies. Once we have it out of you, I'll have a better idea on how to heal your dragon."

"I see," Malkia said, reclining on the couch, with her arms lying to her sides. Her eyes wandered over to Mataya, and she winked before closing her eyes.

Inhaling deeply a few times, her pulse settled to a steady rhythm and her body began to relax. Her breathing quieted, and she felt Mataya's hands on her head, as the words for the searching spell began to pour from Ustarum's mouth.

"In search of this blackness, I call upon the Creators of our kind, warding off all outward negative energy and asking for the banishment of inward negative energy. Let the evils twisting through this body flee through space and time." Ustarum paused and a tingling sensation swirled around Malkia's throat. "In search of this blackness, I call upon the Creators of our kind, warding off all outward negative energy and asking for the banishment of inward negative energy. Let the evils twisting through this body flee through space and time."

Malkia's body jolted violently and her eyes sprang open, seeing Mataya'a eyes grow wide and Ustarum's forehead crease with frustration. "Close your eyes, Malkia. Your sister and I are going to need to recite it together." Ustarum placed his hands firmly on her core and Mataya's hands returned to her head.

Closing her eyes again, she began her breathing techniques to calm her racing heart. Ustarum's and Mataya's voices echoed above her. "In search of this blackness, I call upon the Creators of our kind, warding off all outward negative energy and asking for the banishment of inward negative energy. Let the evils twisting through this body flee through space and time."

Malkia's screams of terror filled the room and her eyes flashed open once again, as a shooting pain thrust its way down her spine and into her legs. She gasped for a breath, her eyes widening in fright as she watched a black mist burst from the exposed pores of her skin. Ustarum leapt to his feet, grasping the darkness with another spell and enclosed it in a glass bottle he had set on the table next to them.

Malkia's blood hammered in her ears as she curled her knees against her chest, attempting to calm her harried breathing. Her eyes flashed wildly at Ustarum as he pressed the cork into the top of the jar. "That was inside me?" she shrieked, her eyes dancing from the jar, to Ustarum and then over to Mataya. "That's what's in Tantiana?" Her hand covered her mouth, and she clenched her teeth against a rising bubble of hysteria.

Ustarum nodded, his lips set into a thin line and his eyes closed for a moment. "We'll need more help with Tantiana. What she has writing through her body is far more powerful and deadly then what you caught from her. It's also imperative that we move without delay. Her life is in danger and if we don't remove this hex from her body within the next two days, she will die."

Malkia's breath caught in her throat and she leapt from the couch, sprinting to her room. "The rest of my family and friends can assist," she yelled back at them, leaving her sister and Ustarum staring after her.

Reaching her room, she threw open the door and slammed it behind her. Sitting on her bed, she focused on Damon. The seconds strummed passed, feeling like ages before the vision bounced into view. Damon stood on a mountain ledge, examining the pyramid near Duncan's town.

He turned towards her and stared back at her, not showing any signs that he was surprised to see her. "You finally channeled me," he grumbled, shaking his head in disgust.

"Damon, I know you're furious with me and I'll give you the chance to yell and scream at me later, but now I need your help." Her voice shook and she put her hands up to her mouth and eyes to gain control again.

"What is it?" Damon snapped, stepping closer, his hand resting on the hilt of his dagger.

Malkia took one more deep breath, before her hands fell to her sides. "Tantiana has been injected with a poison that will end her life in the next two days if we don't dispel it. The three of us here are unable to complete the task on our own. I need you to gather everyone from my father's fortress and bring them here." She paused, catching her breath.

"I'll meet you in the small town of Thebes, by dinner time tonight."

"Hold on, Malkia." Damon's arm rose in attempt to stop her from dropping the channel. "I have a ship and it's large enough for everyone, including Tantiana. Once I gather the group, we can come straight to you. Just give me the directions and we'll be there."

Malkia sighed with relief. "Damon, you're a saint. Find the Dellanti statue on the edge of the Tistaban River. Go north. After you pass Thebes on your right hand side, you'll run into a dark forest. We are on the far north end of that forest. You will need to land the vessel in the clearing just to the west." She bit her lip and wrung her hands together. "I'm fairly certain it's large enough for any ship."

"We will be there soon," Damon replied, sprinting out of view without another word.

Malkia dropped the channel, her eyes surveying her room. The quiet was unsettling, but she needed to contact her mothers before returning to Mataya and Ustarum. Taking another deep breath and closing her eyes for a moment, she envisioned Haltia. Opening her eyes, the channel opened and her mother stood in her room with Asha.

"Thanks goodness you channeled again," Haltia said, her eyes wet with tears. "We're gathering up everything we need and then we will begin our search for Damon."

"Damon is on his way to pick you up," Malkia replied, her eyes soft, finally seeing her mother for someone other than the woman who abandoned her. "He has a ship and should be there fairly quick. I gave him directions to our location, so we should see each other again soon." She paused, feeling her heart aching for everything that had transpired over the past few weeks. "Mom?" She whispered.

Haltia paused her packing and focused on Malkia, stepping forward to be closer. "What is it, Malkia?"

A sob rose in Malkia's throat and the tears poured from her eyes. "I'm sorry." Her head shook back in forth, pursing her lips to stop the tears. "I'm sorry for all my ungrateful and selfish acts. I was hurt and scared, and terrified for Esta. I took all my negative emotions out on the three of you, and I realize now that I had no right to act the way I did." Her body shook, as the clenched fist of another sob tightened her throat. "I need you. All of you. Tantiana will perish if we don't banish the poison inside her and we'll need all of you to accomplish the feat. I know you all desire answers and I'm willing to give them to you, but when you arrive, can we please focus on Tantiana's life, first?"

Asha and Haltia glanced at one another, their own tears festering in their eyes. "Of course we will focus on Tantiana," Haltia replied. "We're family, always and forever. We'll be there soon, my sweet child."

Malkia nodded, as the vision dissipated. Her head was pounding and her stomach churned with the thought of Tantiana's demise. Rising from the bed, she dried her eyes and face on the back of her sleeve and walked to the door, tugging it open. The knowledge that she would have to face her family and friends again, along with vanquishing the darkness from Tantiana's body, was draining on her soul. Rounding the corner to the sitting room, she could see Mataya and Ustarum sitting near the fireplace, conversing quietly.

Their whispers were urgent, but they halted once they noticed Malkia approaching. Ustarum rose from his chair, shifting another chair closer to them. "Come and sit with us," he requested, motioning for Malkia to join them.

Malkia sank in the chair, smiling when Mataya reached over curling her hand around Malkia's knee. "We will save Tantiana," she averred, searching Malkia's eyes. "Don't give up hope."

"I'm not." A tired smile surfaced on Malkia's lips. "I spoke to Damon and my mother. They will be here soon, with a massive ship to carry Tantiana away from this place."

"Malkia," Ustarum spoke, as he rubbed his hand over his beard, a motion Malkia noticed he used often. "There is something you will need to retrieve to assist our salvation of Tantiana. It will require you to return to the Guarding Statue by the pyramids. Inside this statue there is a chamber that contains a moss used in a potion against this poison. You will need to find a way in and bring me a large ampule filled with this ingredient."

"Damon just left that area." She rubbed her eyes, sitting forward in her chair. "Is it possible for him to bring this moss to us?"

"Unfortunately, accessing the statue is a chore. You'll need yours and Mataya's powers to find the entrance and ease it open." Ustarum crossed his legs, fidgeting with the hem of his trousers. "As well, there is information in there that might assist you in your quest to find the blue planet, we have yet to speak about."

"What information?" Malkia asked, sitting up straight at the mention of the mysterious planet.

"Today, while we completed your tasks in the forest, I was planning on outlining your history and the significance of the pyramids, along with how they tie into your blue planet, but after all that has occurred I'll have to run through the details as we move forward." He chewed on his bottom lip and then exhaled a gust of air, as his eyes lifted to meet Malkia's gaze. "The pyramids all hold a key to finding our Creators. They also have a connection with the blue planet, as it is a part of the many star systems our Creators have populated. This lone blue planet holds a map to the several other star systems, one of which is the location to our Creators' home world. This is why your father is intent on discovering its whereabouts." He paused, his eyes shifting between the two women, before they fell to his lap. "And that's why it's imperative he's stopped."

Malkia swallowed hard, taking in all of Ustarum's words. "What about my grandparents? How did they leave our star system to live on the blue planet?"

Ustarum's eyebrows shot up, a hint of surprise flashing over his face. "What do you mean? How do you know they reside on the blue planet?"

"I saw them," Malkia replied, threading a hand through the hair at the nape of her neck. "You didn't want to speak about the blue planet before now, but back when I was at the Guarding Statue, I found the engraving of the feather. When I touched it, the Aletheian's transported me to the blue planet, directly to the home of my grandparents."

"I wasn't positive of their whereabouts," Ustarum muttered, rubbing his forearms, his forehead creasing as he spoke. "There have been numerous rumors and lies, but I always knew Cerce never executed your grandmother. I also believed they had somehow made it to this mysterious blue planet, but I could never prove it, and after years of searching, it became old news."

"You say the reason my Father is interested in the blue planet, is because of this map. Was Cerce searching for the map as well?" Malkia asked, folding her arms across her chest and leaning back into her chair.

"I don't believe he was," Ustarum replied, shaking his head. "Cerce was intent on ruling the moons of Theia. Thane was his highest ranked general and was always ruthless to the core. I believe the search for the blue planet began long after your biological grandfather arrived in our star system, which is an entirely different mystery."

"It wasn't Cerce who began the search?" Malkia's eyes narrowed and her jaw clenched, as she began digesting this information.

"He could have, Malkia." Ustarum gritted his teeth. "I honestly don't know, and at this point, I don't believe it's relevant. Your father is determined to take your daughter out of this star system, in search of our Creators. Is that what you want?"

Malkia exhaled in a huff. "Absolutely not." Looking over at Mataya she noticed that her eyes were closed. "What are you doing Mataya?" Her voice harsher then she intended.

Mataya smiled and opened her eyes. "I'm listening and learning. Everything that is being discussed will be important down the road and when I close my eyes, my ability to absorb your words is heightened." She licked her lips, moistening their crimson fullness, as her eyes shut again. "Malkia, my fear petrified me for many years, but after these powers began to course through my body, I allowed myself to give into them fully. I love you with all my heart, so I say this because of my love for you. Stop being so defensive and selfish. Give into the positive energy flowing brightly through your body and you'll finally discover why the stress you're causing yourself is useless."

The sting of her sister's words, rushed to her heart and she struggled to understand why Mataya was calm and collected, while in the same breath, ridiculing her. This wasn't the sister she had known on Esaki. Malkia's gaze fluttered over to Ustarum, who tried to hide a smile with his hand, as they made eye contact.

"Do you agree with her?" Malkia questioned, her eyes narrowing. "Am I defensive and selfish?"

Ustarum cleared his throat, his eyes flashing over to Mataya. "Your sister has a point. You're high strung and worry about every issue. Stress is fear and fear will only make you weak."

She groaned, leaning forward in her chair and raking her hands through her hair. "Seriously you two, let me apologize for not choosing to relax, when my dragons life is hanging in the brink of death and my family, who I abandoned, is about to arrive. Oh yes, and don't forget my father who wants to see me dead. Let me just relax and close my eyes, so all of you can feel more comfortable." Rising from her chair, Malkia tossed Mataya an icy glare, noticing her gaze from underneath her eyelashes, before stomping away. "I'm going to check on my dragon," she announced as she left the room.

Stepping down the stairs, Malkia paused, taking a moment to focus her thoughts back on Ustarum and Mataya.

"She's not ready," Ustarum argued, his voice heavy.

"She is ready," Mataya insisted. "She's tired. I know my sister. Once we heal Tantiana and leave this moon, she will adjust her sails and be prepared to move forward with her next task."

"And what is that?" Ustarum asked.

"We have to return to Artemis, so she can have the opportunity to heal the moon from her destruction." Mataya's voice sounded urgent.

"Her role in healing the moon is an imperative element, and without her the other party will be unable to make the impact necessary to complete the restoration."

"Alright," Ustarum replied. "We need to heal Tantiana first. How do you suggest we speed that along?"

"We don't speed anything along," Mataya expressed. "She's free to live her life the way she deems right. I won't intrude on her choices. Everything I'm feeling right now, I won't force upon her. When she's ready, she will come to me."

Malkia shook her head, dropping their conversation and gliding down the remainder of the stairs. Slipping out of the front door, she moved quickly towards the spot where Tantiana laid. Touching her dragon, she leaned over her head, draping her body over her head and allowing the emotions to settle in her stomach before facing her family and friends.

"I failed you, my sweet and gentle dragon," she whispered in Tantiana's ear. "But I promise to expel this darkness inside you and we'll leave this god forsaken moon, once and for all."

She slid to the ground, exhausted from the emotional tension of the past few days and dreading the moment she had to see her family and friends, knowing they would eventually insist on answers. Leaning against Tantiana, Malkia closed her eyes and allowed herself to unwind, using the energy of Eris to build up her strength.

"Malkia?" Mataya's voice interrupted her meditation. "I know you don't understand me right now, and I don't want to come off as holier than thou, but I do want you to know, I'm always on your side."

Malkia's eyes slowly opened, breathing in the fresh forest air and tilting her head to look up at her sister. "I know you are. How are you accessing all this knowledge?"

Mataya's eyes sparkled and a smile crept across her face. "Remember the day your block on your powers was removed?"

Nodding her head, Malkia pointed at the ground next to her, asking Mataya to join her. "I do." She closed her eyes, as Mataya sank down next to her. "It was one of the most magical moments of my life."

"Keep your eyes closed," Mataya instructed, touching her knee. "Do you remember how the fear dissipated and your emotions distilled, becoming more potent?"

"Yes," Malkia breathed, feeling an echo of that moment, the electricity of the freedom. "I wasn't afraid any longer and my anger became stable and controlled. What happened?" Her eyes flashed open, finding her sister's gaze.

"You allowed the negative energy to consume your heart, weakening your connection. All the lies and heartbreak caused by your father, are negative energy." Mataya leaned forward, her eyes boring into Malkia's soul. "All of that and so much more has broken your spirit. But, dear sister, I believe in you and so do your family and friends. The Aletheian's have put their trust in you, and our beautiful star system is depending on you to let go of the fury, guilt, and sense of betrayal. Forget about the ones who were never on your side and focus on the ones who are here, right now."

Malkia's eyes glistened with her heartbroken tears. "You're right," she muttered, her soul cracking with the realization of her misdeeds. "I've allowed all of this to break me in the most humiliating way. I know I had a choice and I failed all of you, especially Esta and

Tantiana."

"You're missing my point," Mataya replied, scooting forward and gripping her sister's hands. "You're going to make mistakes. Everyone does. It's how you react and rise afterwards that will count. Stop feeling sorry for yourself and the choices you've made. Everyone has a place inside themselves where everything is possible. Seek that place and then rise up to face the problems at hand. Together we will heal the moons of Theia."

"When did you become so wise?" Malkia asked, a weary smile growing on the edges of her lips.

Mataya reached over and embraced Malkia. "You've been my example." Her eyes shot to the sky and Malkia's followed, noticing a substantial ship moving over the cottage towards the meadow. "I'm going to assume that's our crew," Mataya stated, smiling at Malkia.

"Looks like it." Malkia rose from the ground, grasping Mataya's hands and helping her up. "And so it begins."

TWELVE
Healing Elixir

Walking towards the meadow, Malkia's heart raced, anticipating the reunion with her family and friends. It was difficult to pay attention to Ustarum and Mataya's discussion, so she instead focused on placing one foot in front of the other and listening to the noise of the forest. The sticks crunched underneath her weight and the critters in their path, scurried off into the vegetation. An insect flew near Malkia's ear and she swatted at the bug, just as the ship came into view.

Approaching the large vessel, beads of sweat broke on Malkia's brow and her heart jumped into her throat when she saw Damon step down the plank, followed by the rest of their group. Bella raced across the distance, throwing her arms tightly around Malkia's neck.

"You're in deep trouble, lady," she whispered, squeezing Malkia. "But before all of that, I want you to know I love you and we will make it through this." Bella stepped back, looking her in the eyes and wiping away the tears tumbling down Malkia's cheeks.

"Thanks, Bella." Malkia choked on her words, but somehow mumbled them anyway.

Asha strode up next, with Haltia and Alyssa right behind her. Asha put her hand under Malkia's chin, staring into her eyes. "You are most definitely an imprudent and reckless child." She tugged Malkia into an embrace, followed by Haltia's and Alyssa's arms encircling them both.

The flood of tears was annoying Malkia, but she didn't know how to control her emotions. Her sobs shook her body, but for the first time in months, she felt safe in the embrace of her mothers. As they untangled their arms from each other, Malkia glanced over at Damon. He stood stone-faced, ignoring the dramatic reunion of the rest of the group.

Koleton swept in, squeezing Malkia in a giant hug as he swung her around. "What are we going to do with you?" he asked, setting her back on the ground.

"I'm going to strangle her." Skye stepped around Koleton a frown plastered on her face. "But first I want a hug." Malkia sank into her best friends arms, wrapping her own arms tightly around her body.

"I'm sorry," Malkia muttered. "I'm truly sorry for leaving you like I did."

Skye leaned back and wiped Malkia's hair out of her face. "You should be sorry, and I'm not sure I've forgiven you, but I do love you and want to help save Tantiana."

Malkia straightened up, surveying the group and still seeing Damon's cold eyes cutting through her heart. "We ha-a-ave to return to the Guarding St-statue and bring back some moss for Ustarum to create his healing elixir." Her voice shook and her face flushed a dark red as she stumbled over her words. "Just Mataya and I need to go, but anyone is welcome to accompany us."

"We will all go," Damon announced, turning back to the ship.

"Someone has to stay here and guard Tantiana," Malkia spoke up, wringing her hands together, her breath catching in her throat when he shot her an icy glare.

"I will stay," Ustarum announced, handing her a wooden container. "Bring back as much as you can and make sure you find the blue planet's map instructions." He whispered the last few words, patting her hand as she grasped onto his container.

"I will. Please take care of Tantiana." Malkia turned to face the group and nearly ran into Skye and Alyssa.

"We're going to stay and see what can be done to prepare for the incantation," Alyssa informed, glancing sideways at Ustarum and giving him a pointed look. Focusing back on Malkia, she gripped her daughter's forearm. "I love you Malkia. Please be safe."

"I'll do my best," Malkia replied, pursing her lips to press away the shame rising in her chest. "I'll see you both soon." Throwing Ustarum one last look, she noticed his lips were set in a firm line, and his eyes were hard and intense. *What is up with those two?*

Sprinting to catch up with the rest of the group, she grasped Mataya's free hand, watching the back of Damon as he stormed off ahead the group. "This isn't going to be easy," she said, glancing at Mataya and then up at Justin, who was holding her sister's other hand.

"Probably not," Justin replied, shooting her a sideways glance. "Damon has spent the past couple of weeks tearing apart your father's home in order to assist you in finding your daughter. He has kept himself busy, occupying his mind, because he is deathly afraid of his heightened abilities, and your disappearance only made it worse for him." He shook his head, his jaw tightening as his shoulders slouched forward. "That man is completely in love with you, and he will stop at nothing to keep his cool, so he doesn't destroy the best thing that has ever happened to him." He glanced around, his voice lowering. "But after what you pulled, I don't think he knows how to forgive you."

Malkia nodded, her eyelids sagging and her frown lines creasing around her eyes. "I understand." Walking up the plank, into the vessel, Malkia was reminded of boarding the ships on Enyo. She shivered, as the hairs on the back of her neck stood on end.

The flight to the Guarding Statue was quiet and Damon avoided Malkia's eyes, refusing to join in on any conversation. Her stomach churned as she leaned back in her chair, listening to the whispers of the rest of her group, along with the hum of the engine. She couldn't wait for this part of her day to end.

They arrived quickly and exited the ship in silence. Standing in front of the Guarding Statue, Malkia could see the feather pulsating above her, resisting the desire to go back to the blue planet. As the group separated, searching for the entrance to the statue, Malkia noticed Damon outlining a deep groove with his fingers on the far end. Tiptoeing towards him, he jumped when she touched his shoulder.

Glaring down at her, he turned back to his search, ignoring her presence. Shaking her head, she shifted over, so she could see his face. "Damon, I know you're angry with me and you have every right to be, but we can't continue on like this. We're strong enough to work through this." She stepped closer to him, her hand hovering above his tightened bicep. "At least I hope we are," she whispered the last sentence, her heart beating rapidly in her chest.

Turning to face her, the icy contempt rising in his eyes and spreading across his face pushed Malkia back with palpable force. His irises darkened and his cheeks and jaw clenched, not having to utter a word. His silence broke her, an ache rising through her chest, squeezing her racing heart and crushing the trust in love she desperately desired to believe in.

Damon stomped off, leaving her to face her shattered heart as she watched him disappear into the distant trees. Exhaling in a huff, she held back the tears, chewing on her bottom lip, while she searched for the entrance to the statue.

Mumbling some of the seeking spells Ustarum had taught her, she nearly collided with Mataya as she rounded to the back area of the statue. "Have you found anything?" Malkia asked, straightening her back and glancing around to find the rest of the group, avoiding Mataya's knowing eyes.

Mataya shook her head. "Ustarum mentioned something about you and me performing an incantation together. Maybe it's time we combine our abilities and find out what you and I can accomplish when we are united."

Nodding her head, petrified her broken heart would reveal itself if she spoke, she gripped Mataya's hands and closed her eyes. Allowing the energy of Eris to rise to her toes and through her legs, Malkia could already sense a bright light beaming from their bodies. She kept her eyes shut, concentrating on her sister's hands and their united strength.

Mataya's hands began to warm, as Malkia heard her mumble something under her breath. Malkia began chanting herself, keeping her mind trained on the statue and their light searching for its doorway.

A gasp was heard from someone in their group and Malkia's eyes flashed open, turning to face the statue, without letting go of Mataya's hands. The statue was glowing bright blue, and right at the back end, where they were standing, a door outlined the broken edged rocks.

As the women dropped their hands, the outline of the door disappeared. Malkia stepped forward searching for a handle, but couldn't find any trace of the door they had just been gazing upon. "We need to do it again," she insisted, sighing as she turned back to Mataya. "We can't break our bond until the door is opened." She glanced over at Koleton and Justin, nodding for them to prepare.

Mataya grasped Malkia's hands again and together they began chanting under the breath, focusing on their combined energy. The whispers around them grew louder and the wind rustled the surrounding vegetation.

Seconds later, someone gripped Malkia's shoulder and she opened her eyes to see Bella staring at an opened door to the statue. Letting Mataya's hands go, Malkia stepped towards the statue, scooping up Ustarum's container before passing over the threshold and into the chilly, damp air waiting for her on the other side.

The strong scent of stagnate water and mold filled her nose and she reached up to plug it with her free hand, using the outside light to view her surroundings. Turning in a circle, she could see the walls were filled with ancient writings and the beams rising from the ground were glistening with copper flecks, impressing on Malkia how important this structure once was. From her childhood stories, any building that used copper from the ancient eras, was considered sacred. It was made for the Gods.

Edging forward, Malkia felt the presence of someone else behind her and glanced back to see who had followed her in. Damon's eyes danced around her, avoiding making eye contact, but his anger seemed to have dissipated, replaced with a deep sadness. Turning back to the room, she noticed a faint outline of a doorway at the end of the room. Stepping farther in, she used her light to brighten the room, showing her a better view of what they were walking into.

More statues, about two feet in height, lined the walls all the way to the next doorway. Each one wore a unique expression and Malkia mused over the idea they might be sending a message.

She turned to face Damon. "Do you see the odd way each statue is positioned, along with their facial expressions?"

Damon straightened up, regarding each statue, as Malkia shone her light on them. He nodded, his forehead creasing in thought. "Do you think it means something?"

"It could," she replied, sinking down to look at one up close, its eyes staring upwards towards the ceiling and his arms crossed over its chest, while standing on one foot. "But we don't have the time to decipher it. Just something to keep in the back of our minds, in case it is needed later down the road."

Damon pursed his lips, his hand running up down the hilt of his dagger. "Let's find the moss and whatever else Ustarum needs and leave this place. All the eyes on these statues are making me uneasy."

Malkia chuckled, rising from her perch and eyeing the open door. "Did no one else want to join us?"

"I guess not," he replied, his hand mindlessly touching her arm, as his eyes washed across the rest of the chamber.

A sad smile rose on her lips and she looked back at Damon as he yanked his hand away, realizing what he'd done. She shook her head and moved towards the far off doorway, hoping the moss was nearby, along with the clue that would lead her to the blue planet.

Reaching the doorway in a few strides, Malkia could feel a near freezing draft rising from beyond the threshold. Illuminating her light into the next room, she could see the walls were curtains of damp runnels and the bright purple moss filled the room from floor to ceiling. She stepped closer and noticed on a side wall no moss was growing, but possessed an etching of what appeared as a cluster of stars and planets.

Rushing over to it, she ran her hands over the grooves, wondering if this was the map that fit in with the blue planet. Not wanting to waste any more time, she turned to face Damon. "Will you have someone in the group grab a large piece of that thin parchment you have on the ship, along with some black chalk?"

He nodded, ducking his head to go back through the doorway and leaving Malkia to gather up the moss. As she reached for the first handful, it shrank back from her hand. Malkia yanked her hand back and examined the ground. Everywhere she had stepped, the moss had shifted away from her. She sighed, realizing it wasn't going to make this an easy picking.

As she stepped forward and leaned towards the moss, it wiggled away from her again, although she was able to snag a pinch full. She groaned, dropping the small amount in the container, just as Damon returned to the room and held out the parchment and chalk.

"Will you see if you can pick the moss, while I copy this etching onto the parchment?" she asked, gripping onto the items.

Damon took the container without a word and using his lightening speed, grasped onto the moss and yanked out a large amount, tossing it into the container. Exhaling and shaking her head, Malkia turned towards the drawing, placing the parchment up against the wall and rubbing the black chalk across it.

When she was done, she rolled the parchment up and twisted around to see Damon watching her, the container tucked under his arm, filled to the brim with moss. "Thank you," she said, stepping towards him.

He nodded, ducking back under the doorway and leaving her behind. She followed after, feeling the eyes of the little statues watching her leave.

The sun's light blinded her as she stepped outside of the Guarding Statue. Malkia's hand moved above her eyes, shielding herself from the light and glancing around at the group she had left not too long ago. Except now there were more of them. Malkia recognized Duncan's face immediately and his stony expression made her stop dead in her tracks.

"Duncan, what's wrong?" she asked, gripping onto the parchment with both hands.

"I told you to leave, Malkia. Why have you returned?" His jaw clenched, as he rubbed his hands together.

Malkia edged toward him, afraid of his assumptions. "It's a long story, but first off, I found Ustarum. He's the one who sent me back here."

"Ustarum should have known better. My town is in shambles because of your existence and I cannot hold my people back any longer." He waved his hand, a light bursting from his palm and striking Malkia.

Flying backwards, she heard Haltia and Mataya cry out as the wind threw her past the statue. Her light bounded from her body and she straightened herself out, before settling back onto the ground and faced the group around her. Duncan's people quickly surrounded her, their bow and arrows drawn and aimed at her.

Skipping past them, she walked up to Duncan, her light stronger than it had ever been before. "You invited me into your town." She stepped closer, silver sparks blossoming out around her. "Your anger directed at me for someone else's actions is exactly why nothing is being solved. You have every right to be furious, but I suggest you remember who invited whom into their town. I was willing to search for the feather, do what I came to do, and leave." She paused, her eyes scanning over the rest of the group, before coming to rest once more upon Duncan. "You insisted we accompany you to your town and now I have one more battle to avenge."

Duncan lowered his raised hands, waving at his comrades to disarm as well. "It has been horrid, Malkia." His lips trembling from emotion and exhaustion.

"I know. I was there," she replied, allowing her light to dissipate. "What those ships did was inexcusable, and I won't stop until I have brought them to justice. I want to be clear on who did this." She grasped Duncan's arm. "The vessels were *not* the Artemisians. Whoever brought this carnage upon your people, had nothing to do with Artemis."

Haltia moved forward, standing next to Malkia. "Duncan, what happened here?"

Duncan's eyes darted between the mother and daughter a few times, finally resting on Haltia. "We were attacked while Malkia was residing in our town. Whoever it was, they destroyed my entire village and slaughtered the majority of my people." He paused, glancing down at his hands. "Including Selen."

Haltia's hand rose quickly to her heart, when she heard Selen's name spoken. Her eyes widened and her breath caught in her throat. "She's dead?" She whispered, her other hand wiping a flood of tears escaping from her eyelids.

Twisting to face her mother, Malkia gripped onto both of her hands. "I was there with her," she muttered, pulling her mom into an embrace. "She wasn't alone when she moved on."

Her mother's body tensed and she drew away from Malkia, walking towards the ship without another word. Trudging past the group, Haltia's eyes remained on the ground, her hands rolled into fists and her shoulders shaking with grief. Malkia watched her leave, surprised by her reaction and frightened her mother would blame her for Selen's death.

Malkia glanced back at Duncan, who was overcome with grief as well. His eyes met hers, tears pouring down his cheeks. "My entire village has been decimated. I don't know how to fix the wrongs of this world." His shoulders sagged forward, turning his back on her and shuffling away. The rest of his people followed his lead.

Her hand rose to her mouth, as she pivoted to face her friends and the back of her mother. Just as she did, her mother sank to the ground, her screams echoing through the trees separating them. Malkia raced to her side, curling her arms around her frail body and holding her close, as a flood of tears washed down her face and her body shook from head to toe.

"I spent my entire mar-r-riage protecting—" Haltia mumbled, her weeping making it difficult for Malkia to understand.

"It will be okay, Mom." Her words seemed hollow, but in the moment she was struggling to know what to say. Squeezing her mother tight, Malkia stroked her fountain of hair, while thinking back to Selen's last moments. "Selen loved you," she whispered in her mother's ear. "Those were the last words she spoke to me."

Her words only caused her mother's tears to burst from her eyes, her sobs growing louder, wetting Malkia's shoulder. Moments passed and the rest of the group returned to the ship, allowing them the privacy they needed.

"Your father," Haltia stammered, her tears decreasing and her body back under her control. "He despised Selen." She coughed and swallowed hard, twiddling her thumbs and staring down at her hands. "I spent my entire marriage protecting her whereabouts and keeping him from murdering her. His final knife in my back was to ensure her death." Haltia raised her head, meeting Malkia's eyes. "This wasn't about you. He had no idea where you were or it would've been you who perished, not an entire village. This was about Selen and me."

Malkia shook her head, gripping on to her mother's shoulders. "Why? Why would he destroy an entire village, because of your old flame?"

Haltia snorted, laughing bitterly as she rose from the ground, pulling Malkia up with her. "Selen was my first love. He knew he never had my heart, so he was determined to rip apart my soul any way he could. The only time he halted his revenge, was while you and Palma were young. After we left you on Esaki, the quest to find her was mixed in with his desire to overtake the Eris government."

Malkia scooped up the parchment she'd dropped, grasping Haltia's hand as they strolled back to the ship. "I had no idea it was that awful," Malkia replied, exhaling sharply. "When I remember my childhood, I recall how often you fought with Father, but it always appeared as if you started them on purpose. I was angry at you for battling him every chance you had."

Haltia kicked a small stone in their path and they watched as it collided with a distant tree, ricocheting off the bark and rolling to the side. "I hated him. I remained with him to protect Selen," Haltia stated, freezing in place to turn and face Malkia. "And you. He kept his distance from you, because I agreed to be his, and only his. I broke off my affair with Asha and focused on you and Palma, allowing him the freedom to deceive our entire group of friends and family." They began walking again, the large ship finally in view. "His dominion over the Artemisians and Elvens is because of my choice to ignore his plans and pretend he was working with our people to stop the wars in the heavens."

"You knew about his deceit?" Malkia asked, her breath coming in short.

"I suspected," Haltia replied, climbing up the ramp of their ship. "I was never privy to anything he did outside our influences on Eris. However, I spied on his correspondence and discovered he was creating a relationship with the Artemisians, while informing the rest of us that we were going to war with their civilization." Malkia and Haltia watched the ramp close and felt the pressure from the rise of the

171

ship, as they both took a seat near the exit.

"What about the Elvens?" Malkia questioned, turning to face Haltia, after her restraints were secured. "Who are they?"

Haltia sighed, wiping her face with both hands to clear away the remnants of her tears. "They are a devilish group of people, who reside on Thalia with the fallen angels and the pixies."

A laugh escaped Malkia's lips and she quickly placed her hand over her mouth, choking back any more surprise. "Fallen angels? What?"

"There is so much that you don't know," Haltia responded. "And for that, I'm at fault. I was determined to protect you from your father, and in the process I kept you from the knowledge of our star system. In time, I hope to teach you everything you were unable to learn on Esaki."

"Me too," Malkia said, leaning back on her chair.

The large ship quickly returned to Ustarum's land and Malkia and her group hustled towards his cottage. Damon insisted on carrying the container of moss and stayed close to Malkia, despite his resentment towards her. As they approached, Alyssa and Skye exited the home, racing to meet them.

"Were you able to retrieve the moss?" Alyssa asked, her eyes passing over each one in the group.

Damon handed her the container and a grin spread across her face when she glanced inside. "Fantastic. We'll just need to add this to our elixir and then we will be ready." She skimmed over the group. "Everyone wait by Tantiana and Ustarum and I will bring out everything that we require for the incantation."

The group followed Alyssa, stopping when they reached Tantiana.

Damon eyed Malkia, walking up next to her and gripping her arm, tugging at her to follow, as he edged away from the rest of their team. Halting just inside a group of trees, he turned to face her, the lines around his eyes etched with agony.

"Your disappearance was a dagger to my heart," he confessed, closing his eyes for a moment and breathing in deeply. "I understand that your heart was ripped out when your father kidnapped your daughter, but it was not my doing and I've grown weary of being treated like a punching bag for your anguish." He rubbed both his hands across his face, frustration crinkling the edges of his eyes. "I don't know if I will ever be able to forgive your misdeeds, but—" He paused, tilting his head to the sky, attempting to hide the single tears that kept escaping from his eyelids. "Damn it, Malkia, I love you." His eyes met hers. "I want to fix this. I want you and me to do this right."

Exhaling with relief, she stepped towards him, wrapping her arms around his bulky torso. Her sudden touch caused him to tense, but then he folded into her, curling his arms around her shoulders and squeezing her tightly. "I love you, Damon and I'm sorry," she whispered, craning her neck back to view his face.

Groaning, he picked her up and kissed her soft on the lips, reminding her of the first time he devoured her mouth. Swimming in his embrace, her fingers curled into his back muscles, sinking farther into his body and begging for more. One of his hands knotted in her hair, while the other one ran down her back, followed by a wave of shivers racing over her body, yearning for a chance to be alone again.

Coming up for air, she closed her eyes and licked her lips, a smile playing with the corners of her lips. Opening her eyes, she took in his gorgeous dark eyes and his chiseled face, drinking in his entire body as he grinned down at her.

"See what you've been missing out on?" He chuckled, winking at her.

Sighing happily, she jabbed him in the side with her finger. "I've missed you. From day one, I've missed you."

"You'd better have." He laughed, as she took another jab at him, missing as he sidestepped her. "If you need to wrestle, bring it on."

She pounced at him, hauling him to the ground, where both of them landed on their sides. He gripped her around the waist, dragging her around him and then back down to the dirt, as he pinned her beneath his weight. A wicked grin crossed her face as she wrapped her legs around his waist, skillfully throwing him to the side. Springing up from the ground, she twisted around, her eyes narrowing when she saw he had disappeared.

Her laugh echoed through the trees, just as she felt his arms wrap around her from behind. She leaned forward, grabbing both of his wrists and threw him over her shoulders, watching as he landed on both feet on the other side.

"You're making this too easy," he teased, growling in an attempt to rile her into being feistier.

"Alright, buster. You asked for it." She hurtled towards him, using her weight to knock him to the ground. She bounded on top of him, her hands pressing down his shoulders.

A slow and sexy grin spread across his face and his body relaxed as he reached up and drew her down, sealing his lips to hers. "This is exactly where I wanted to be," he breathed in her ear.

"Are we interrupting?" Skye asked, coughing softly behind Malkia.

Rising up from the ground, Malkia gripped Damon's hands and helped him up. Turning to face her friend, they both laughed when they saw half of their group staring back at them.

"Sorry," Malkia said, shooting Damon a sideways look. "We missed each other."

Ustarum stomped through the group, his eyes darting from face to face. "Let's do this. The elixir is ready."

Malkia and the rest of the group hurried after Ustarum, gathering together in front of Tantiana. Holding each other's hands, Malkia and Mataya began chanting the healing incantation, as Ustarum and Alyssa used a large syringe, pricking the dragon in the exposed flesh under her front legs. Pushing the elixir slowly through the tube, Malkia closed her eyes, feeling the powers of Eris rising through their bodies and entering Tantiana's body through the hand Malkia pressed against the dragon's neck.

The rest of the group lined up after Mataya, gripping each other's hands and chanting along with the sister's. The power surging into Tantiana's body was exhilarating, its strength creating a whirlwind around their group, making it difficult to hear each other.

Several moments passed, before the wind died down and the power began to dissipate. Malkia opened her eyes and glanced over at Tantiana. The dragon's eyes remained closed and she sighed heavily, sagging against the massive body in defeat.

Looking up at the group, her lips set in a thin line and her forehead crinkled in frustration. "Now what?" she asked, peering at Ustarum.

"Now we wait," he replied.

THIRTEEN

I Love You More

Malkia refused to leave Tantiana. All the excitement and happiness from her reunion with Damon vanished as she stroked her dragon's ear, occasionally scratching her favorite spot behind her ear. Her family and friends had either returned to the ship or had joined Ustarum inside his cottage for food and drinks.

After dinner was finished, Damon convinced Asha and Alyssa to assist him in loading the white dragon into their vessel. Malkia watched, as his body floated across the vegetation with the use of magic, and moved out of her view.

Remembering Adelina, Malkia hoped she had remained in the same place and that all three dragons were still safe and alive. Having all those dragons on board might be hazardous, but she'd made a promise and she wasn't about to break it.

Tantiana's breath came in short and Malkia jumped from the transformation, pivoting to view what was occurring. The dragon's eyes twitched and her head jerked backwards, as her exposed wing fluttered.

Stepping forward and touching her nose, Malkia sent her healing light into the dragon's body. "Wake up, Tantiana. We are waiting for you."

Tantiana's eyes twitched again, opening halfway and regarding Malkia. *What happened?*

Malkia sighed a big breath of relief, hugging Tantiana's neck. "You had me terrified," she said out loud to the dragon. "You were poisoned by a warlock's dart, but we discovered it soon enough to halt its destruction on your body." She stepped back, allowing Tantiana the space to rise.

I don't remember. Tantiana's thoughts shook with sadness as she rose on her legs, stretching her wings out and twisting her neck to relieve the ache.

Koleton and Skye exited the cottage, smiling wide when they saw Tantiana was awake. Mataya followed soon after, skipping over to the small group and nuzzling up to Tantiana. The dragon was beaming from the attention, but Malkia was now focused on who did this to her.

Ustarum must have been snooping in her thoughts again, because moments later he sauntered up, his brows furrowed and his lips pursed. Glancing at Malkia, he ran his hand over the end of his beard and stepped towards her. "After speaking with your mother, I'm beginning to believe this wasn't the work of a warlock, but of an Elven."

Rubbing her forehead, Malkia shot a look over at Tantiana and the small group. "I'm struggling to understand. Before today, I'd never heard of Elvens or Fallen Angels. What do I need to know about them?"

"Elvens are spry creatures, who appear nearly human, except they are slightly taller, with pointed ears and ashen skin." He edged in closer to Malkia, his voice sinking to a whisper. "Their magic is far more advanced then what most humans are used to, but they cannot outmatch a warlock." He paused, gripping Malkia's arm. "Or you. What they have on their side is experience, the ability to be light on their feet, and knowledge of most magical spells and powers. One of them is dangerous, but an entire civilization is deadly. If they've partnered with your father, he will be residing on Thalia under their care, and you'll have to move heaven and Theia to retrieve your daughter."

Malkia was holding her breath and it came out in a whoosh, her brows furrowing as her hands balled into fists. "Why would they work with my Father?"

"If he has promised them safe passage to meet our Creators, then he holds their loyalty in the palm of his hands," Ustarum spoke urgently, his eyes flashing around their surroundings. "If the Elvens are planning an attack, you can be sure most of us will perish, especially if it means they will be able to leave our star system for good. They've been methodically outlining a way to the blue planet for centuries and if your father has divulged any secrets to a clear pathway, they'll be delighted to oblige his demands."

Malkia growled under her breath. "I have to stop at the four moons between here and Thalia, before I can justify going there." She sighed, kicking the dirt with her toes. "What am I to do?"

"Go to Artemis first," Ustarum said, nodding his head in agreement. "And yes, you will need to stop at Enyo, Thallassa and Esaki before Thalia. Those four moons have the other pieces to your map, but you must ensure they don't fall into the wrong hands. So please conceal them before you move onto Thalia."

"Ustarum?" Malkia grasped his forearm, as he turned to leave.

"What is it?" He asked, peering back at her.

Malkia leaned in, her voice barely a whisper. "Can this map really lead us to the blue planet, without the assistance of the Aletheian's?"

Ustarum's jaw clenched and his body tensed, as he nodded. "I believe so. It was foretold that if the maps were united with one another, it would lead you not only to the blue planet, but would steer you in the direction to discover the whereabouts of the next star system to which our Creators traveled."

"I don't like this," Malkia grumbled, glancing over at Tantiana and her friends. "This entire situation, along with the origins of the map and everyone involved with retrieving it, doesn't sit right with me."

"Is isn't right," Ustarum hissed. "You have to stop him. His whereabouts are almost certain to be on Thalia, along with your daughter. Finish what you started and then destroy your father and the Elvens." He twisted away from her, rushing off before she could mutter another word.

Malkia plodded back to her friends and family, finally seeing Damon, Asha and Alyssa returning from the ship. Her eyes scanned the trees and hills, petrified of what or who might be stalking them and wishing she possessed the ability to sense when others were near.

"Now that Tantiana has been saved, it's time to depart," Malkia announced, strolling up to the group. "Damon has loaded the snow dragon and we need to make one stop before leaving for Artemis."

"What stop do we need to make?" Damon asked as he sauntered up towards them.

"There's another dragon and her hatchlings, residing in the forest, who were taken from Hemera by the Artemisians. I promised I would return and take them with us when we departed Eris." She could see everyone's eyes widening and Justin exhaled in a huff, before stomping away from the group. "We have the room. Why is this a problem?"

Damon gripped her shoulder, towering over her and peering around at the group. "It isn't a problem." He pointed to the sky. "The enemy is out there. We are all ready to finish this battle and it doesn't help to fight amongst ourselves. Malkia has owned her mistakes, now let's save these dragons and begin our journey."

Skye sighed, a tired smile settling across her lips and Koleton nodded, his usual cheerful face lined with a frown. The front door to the cottage creaked, as Haltia stepped outside of the cottage, hustling toward the group.

"It's time to leave," she said, glancing at everyone's serious expressions. "Whatever is the problem, we can work it out after we depart."

Ustarum opened the door, watching Malkia. She waved at him, unsure of how to bid him farewell. *You're my greatest accomplishment.* His voice entered into her mind. A sad smile bloomed on her face. *You're ready to face your Father. Remember all that I have taught you and you won't fail. Use the darkness, when it resides under your control, instead of the other way around.* He paused and closed his eyes. *You're stronger than you realize. Don't allow anyone to take your power and prevent you from fulfilling your mission. Protect your children, as they will be the key for our future. Good-bye, Malkia.* He opened his eyes, giving her one last pointed look before vanishing into thin air.

Good-bye, my dear friend, Malkia thought. She turned away, grasping onto Damon's hand and following along with the group.

They settled the ship into the clearing where Malkia had met Adelina a few weeks before. Stepping down the plank, Malkia shaded her eyes from the setting suns, gaining her bearings.

Adelina's silhouette could be seen in the forest and Malkia could feel her unease. Racing through the tall grass and into the coolness of the trees, she came face to face with the exquisite dragon.

You've been gone long, Adelina thought, curling around a thick tree and glancing back at Malkia. *Didn't think you'd return.*

My mission required more time than I anticipated, but I'm here now. We need to leave. Malkia eased forward, resting her hand against the bark of the tree and leaning against it, as she caught her breath. *There are two more dragons on my ship, but once we make a few stops, I will ensure your safe return to Hemera.*

Do these dragons pose any threats to my hatchlings? Adelina asked, her neck stretching to view the massive vessel.

Malkia shook her head, taking in a deep breath as she pushed away from the tree. *One dragon has been placed under a sleeping spell, as he was intent on taking me captive for the Artemisians. However, the other one is my best friend and was one of the first dragons I've ever encountered.*

Why was a dragon working for those barbarians? Adelina's eyes narrowed, her tail lashing in agitation.

He was taken from Hemera, just like you. However, he was convinced that his freedom came with my captivity. He wasn't giving up and I don't blame him. Malkia shivered, thinking of the battle at Ustarum's home. *I want to return him to his home, just like you.*

Adelina's head bobbed up and down. *I will retrieve my young ones and we will prepare for our journey.*

There is plenty of room, Malkia replied. *Just gather what you need and let's depart. We have a long way to go, before we'll have the chance to take you to Hemera.*

Adelina shot off into the forest, without another thought on the matter, a trail of broken branches strewn over her path. Malkia watched as she disappeared, leaving her to wait and wonder. Moments later, two smaller figures flew overhead, followed by Adelina, landing in the clearing near the vessel. Malkia raced to meet them, inhaling sharply when she approached them.

Follow me. She knew having three full-grown dragons on board was going to be a challenge, let alone two younger and more rambunctious hatchlings. It was only a matter of time before this voyage became a disaster.

Closing the dock door, after the dragons had entered, Malkia led them through the larger section of the ship and the only portion where the massive creatures could reside. Tantiana greeted her with a sideways glance and Malkia could see the snow dragon, enclosed in his cage. The young dragons were full of energy and Adelina wrapped her wing around them, dragging them close to her body and calming their anxiety.

Malkia pressed the button to speak with Damon, letting him know they were cleared to take off. She settled into a nearby chair, strapping herself in and waiting as the vessel shifted, shooting high into the sky and pressing Malkia into her seat, before gravity's pull dispersed and left Eris gliding away from them.

"Malkia," Damon's voice rang out over the intercom. "We are approaching Artemis. Will you please meet me on the bridge?"

Rubbing the sleep from her eyes, Malkia glanced around the large room, rising from the cot she had brought in to be near the dragons. Tantiana shifted from her position, twisting her head to look at Malkia and winking at her, before settling her head back down.

The walk to the main control room was a lengthy one and Malkia's tired body moved slowly through the corridors, sagging against the far wall of the elevator as the doors closed. Closing her eyes, she did her best to ignore her enclosure in the small space, with no escape until the doors opened.

Feeling the motion of the elevator come to a halt, her eyes flashed open just when the doors slid to the side. Rushing out of the tomb, she strolled towards the control room, dreading the view she would soon not be able to avoid.

Artemis was in the distance, a dark layer of smoke covering nearly every inch of it. Malkia cringed, clenching her fists as she edged up to Damon, standing to his side. "This is far more difficult then I imagined." She breathed in deep, her eyes wide from the sight in front of her.

"Why are we here?" Damon asked, twisting to look at her, his arms folded across his chest.

Malkia closed her eyes, her heart skipping a beat, before she opened them again and faced Damon. "Mataya claims I can fix my mistake. I don't know what that means, but I have to trust her, especially if it means I can heal Artemis."

Damon nodded, just as Mataya glided into the room, a smile rising on her lips and a peaceful expression spreading across her face. Malkia glanced over at her, relaxing when she saw her sister's happy expression and wondering how she missed this side of her. Mataya grasped ahold of her hand and kissed it.

"There's a ship approaching," Damon's voice rang out around them, bringing them out of their peaceful state.

Malkia and Mataya stepped forward, staring at the massive ship easing towards them. Glancing behind her, Malkia could see the dread crossing Damon's face, as his brows furrowed and eyes widened, while he shook his head.

"The shields are stable, but I don't think we could take on a ship of that stature. It will obliterate us." He ran his hands through his hair, then pushed an alarm button, signaling for the rest of their group to join them.

A chime rang and Malkia jumped, her hair settling around her shoulders as she twisted to find the reason for the extra buzz. A light flashed on one of the control panels and she stepped up to it, seeing the words "INCOMING CALL" just below the flashing light. Pressing down on the button, a loud voice greeted her.

"Who is the captain of your ship and what is the reason for your close vicinity to Artemis?" Malkia recognized the voice immediately and breathed a sigh of relief, before picking up the receiver.

"Is that you Apollo?" she asked, her eyes flashing over to Damon.

Silence filled the air for a brief moment, before the voice responded. "Malkia?"

Malkia laughed, a weight lifting from her shoulders. "Yes, Apollo, this is Malkia."

Another pause filled the room and she fiddled with her pendant, staring down at the floor. "Apollo, are you there?"

"Yes, Malkia." He cleared his throat. "You shouldn't have come here. My people are still seeking your life."

She swallowed hard, as she lifted her chin and peered around the room at the growing number of people. Her eyes settled on Haltia, who shot her a soft smile. "Apollo, I have to heal your moon. It isn't much, but it's something."

"How will you manage to heal my moon?" he asked.

Mataya curled her hand over Malkia's shoulder, nodding with a half-smile. Malkia pressed the button again, her hands shaking with uncertainty. "I don't exactly know the *how*, Apollo. However, I'm being told I have the capability." She paused, her eyes closing again. "Do you trust me, Apollo?"

"Yes, I trust you, Malkia. That isn't the issue. I have thousands of comrades who would be delighted to know you are sitting in the insignificant ship, just within their reach. They would eat you for dinner." He sighed, hesitating for a moment. "Luck was on our side, as it was my turn to monitor this area and most everyone else is asleep or tending to other duties. We will need to form a plan now, before the masses wake."

Malkia nodded, rubbing her hands along the sides of her trousers. "I need to make it to the surface of Artemis. How do I make that possible?"

"Do you have a smaller ship?" Apollo replied.

Damon shook his head, as Malkia looked over at him. "No, we don't." There was a brief moment of silence and Malkia could hear her heart pulsing in her ears.

"I will have to retrieve you," Apollo finally responded. "But first, you'll need to move your ship away from our monitors. There's a large asteroid, not far from us. It's superior to your ship and will keep it hidden until we return."

"When will you pick me up?" Malkia asked, ignoring the dread crossing Damon and Haltia's faces.

"My replacement will be here within the hour. Once he arrives, I'll make an excuse to leave," he replied, his voice barely a whisper. "Be ready. We won't have long, once we arrive to the surface."

"We'll be waiting," Malkia stated, setting the receiver down and looking up at all her friends and family. "It's the only way." Her eyes darted from one face to the next. "Mataya may accompany me, but the rest of you will need to stay behind."

Damon growled under his breath and turned away from her. The rest of the group nodded, as Asha spoke up. "Malkia, we all know you are capable of healing Artemis and I'll support you in this journey. It isn't easy to have you run off again, but this time we appreciate you doing it in a more respectable manner." She stepped up to Malkia, placing her hand under Malkia's chin. "I love you."

"Thank you, Asha." She gazed into the warlock's eyes. "You've been a constant support through this entire journey."

Haltia wrapped her arms around Malkia's waist. "We all support you, but it doesn't take away our fear. We wanted to be with you while you were on Artemis, but if that's not possible, we'll wait until you both return."

"Thank you," Malkia said, squeezing her mother's hand and glancing over at Alyssa who gave her a reassuring smile. "Thank you, everyone. Knowing I can trust all of you, makes this battle far less painful. I will do what I can to heal Artemis, find the pyramids and retrieve the next section of this map. Then we can move on to Enyo." She peered over at Asha. "I don't want to return there." She paused, a breath catching in her throat. "But for the sake of Esta and all the lives who've been taken or shattered because of my father, I'll do it."

Malkia could feel the shift of the ship, as Damon turned back towards the asteroid Apollo had spoken about. She watched the gigantic rock approaching and was relieved to see it could easily hide their ship. Damon was able to settle down into a crevice, giving them some time to relax while she was away.

After he finished securing the vessel, he stepped away from the controls and grasped onto Malkia's hands. "Will you please come speak with me in private?" he asked.

Easing away from the group around her, she followed Damon out of the control room and into a private conference room down the hallway. Nestling down into a chair, Malkia placed her hands on the armrests, watching as he shifted another chair to be close to her. As he sank down onto the cushion, he leaned forward and gripped her hands.

"Remember the first time we met?" he asked, his eyes searching her face.

Malkia nodded. "Yes. I was in your tent on Esaki. Why do you ask?"

"That seems like a lifetime ago for me," he mused, his thumbs rubbing over her hands. "I was an angry, intolerable man, but you saw something in me no one else had the ability to perceive. I believe I can understand the same in you." He paused, hanging his head and sighing. Looking back up, he continued, "When I first laid eyes on you, you were actually unconscious on a table in my camp. My heart skipped a beat from your beauty, but there was something familiar about you and it terrified me that you could pull at my heartstrings, even before we had a chance to speak. When we met in my tent later, I wanted to hold you and protect you, but I had to interrogate you instead and that broke my heart."

"Why are you telling me this?" Malkia asked, the line between her eyes deepening as she chewed on her bottom lip.

"We met before, when we were children. Do you remember that?" he asked, ignoring her question.

Malkia exhaled loudly, as her thoughts returned to that moment. "Yes, I do. You were at my house on Eris."

Damon nodded, a wary smile surfacing on his lips. "Yes, that fateful morning. My parents were a wreck and I was frightened before you entered the room." He smiled wide. "When you came around the corner, your hair in disarray and your eyes wide with curiosity, my fears ceased to exist. You're my calm. Even back then, you were what kept me grounded. When we met again, back on Esaki, I felt the same way and I cannot understand it. But I do know you're the reason I've become the man I am today."

"Don't give me that credit." Malkia half-smiled, winking as she continued, "Although, I have to admit, anyone who meets me is a better person afterwards." She laughed, her eyes crinkling slightly, enjoying the humor of the moment.

Damon's smile spread across his face, chuckling softly. "Yes, they are better for knowing you." Squeezing her hands, he pulled himself closer. "In all seriousness, I wanted you to know the effect you have on me. I wanted you to be aware of our connection and that my love for you runs deeper than any river or ocean on any of Theia's moons. When you channeled me earlier, I already knew it was going to occur. My dreams and visions are becoming more accurate and concise and I believe our connection is only increasing the strength of this ability."

Malkia leaned forward, pressing her lips against his, feeling the warmth and softness of his mouth. His tongue attacked her mouth, pleading for more as he drew her onto his lap. The kiss became frantic and she melted into his embrace, allowing him to pick her up and lay her on the table.

Their union was thrilling and Malkia moaned with delight. His energy coursed through her veins and they became one. A moment of ecstasy left them catching their breath as he settled down next to her on the table, a smile spreading across his face.

"I love you, Malkia," he whispered, breathless with relief.

"I love you, Damon," she replied, finally whispering the words she had held back for so long.

He glanced over at her, propping himself on his elbow and kissed her cheek and then her nose. "I love you more."

FOURTEEN

Artemis

Afterward, Damon had walked Malkia to her room, where she quickly showered and dressed for Apollo's arrival. She stared at her reflection in the mirror, as her nimble fingers plaited her long hair into a braid. The scars on her neck and running down her back, glistened in the mirror and reminded Malkia how much had changed since that day, nine years before.

Her hands shook slightly as a knock on her door startled her back to reality. She wrapped a hairband around the edges of her hair and straightened her shirt before walking to the door. Opening it, she gazed up at Apollo and Damon who stood on the other side of the threshold.

Malkia smiled, throwing her arms around the Apollo's large neck and body. "It's so good to see you again."

"Likewise," Apollo murmured, inhaling her scent, before she pulled away.

Damon's eyes narrowed, noticing the affection Apollo had for her. She grasped Damon's arm and looked over at Apollo. "Let's go meet the rest of my group and then we can depart."

Leading the way and dragging a seething Damon behind her,

Malkia relocated quickly to the control room where most of the group was already gathered. Mataya bounced up from her chair with a grin, prancing over to them and introducing herself to Apollo.

"You are Malkia's sister?" Apollo asked with a soft smile, attempting to hide his amusement at Mataya's fiery and energetic aura.

"Yes, I am," Mataya replied, her feet shifting underneath her as if she was dancing to her own music. "I'm looking forward to witnessing both of your healing abilities down on Artemis."

Apollo shot a quizzical glance at Malkia, who shrugged her shoulders, not understanding Mataya's meaning, but also knowing better than to question her newfound powers. "It's a pleasure to finally make your acquaintance." He nodded, grinning back at Mataya. "Your beauty is a gift that dives far beneath the surface."

Mataya's smile grew, her teeth catching a gleam of reflected light and her eyes beaming with joy. "Thank you, Apollo." She twisted towards Malkia. "We should leave now. We don't have much time."

Malkia nodded, following Apollo and Damon as they led the women to Apollo's ship. Once they had boarded, Damon kissed Malkia one more time before taking his leave of them. She watched as he left the vessel and closed the hatch door. Sinking into a chair near Apollo and Mataya, she strapped herself in and gripped the arms of the chair, anxious to begin this next step.

It didn't take them long to land on Artemis. The entire area was covered in blackened ash and a thick cloud of yellowed smoke. Apollo handed her an air mask, which at first she declined, but remembering the last time she had left a ship without a mask, she graciously accepted. Tugging the mask over her face, she stepped out of the vessel and down the stairs to the charred vegetation under her feet.

"Is there any place on Artemis that was untouched by the inferno?" Malkia asked, turning to face Apollo.

"Yes," he answered and Malkia breathed a sigh of relief. "The three pyramids that reside just past these hills, were unscathed by the fire."

"That's it?" Malkia questioned, her brows furrowing and the lines around her face creasing into a frown as she turned to face the blackened hills.

"That's all I've seen," he replied. "However, the good news is that nearly three hundred of my people were able to escape to the pyramids, before the blaze ran through their villages."

Malkia inhaled, her head nodding slightly. "That's better, but I wish I had the power to turn back time." Stepping farther into the murky smoke, Malkia noticed a few trees hadn't been completely obliterated by the fire and stood against the gray and yellow background like a beacon of hope.

Mataya's hand curled lightly around Malkia's forearm. "It's time you reach into the soil of Artemis and channel your healing powers." With her free hand, she grasped Apollo's wrist. "You will require the assistance of an Artemisian Demi-God." Mataya towed a confused Apollo towards Malkia. "Now, show the rest of our civilizations what you two are capable of creating."

"What do you mean *Demi-God*?" Apollo questioned, digging his heels into the ground, his eyes slanted and his jaw clenched, while glancing between Mataya and Malkia.

"You aren't like most Artemisians, are you?" Mataya asked, her perpetual smile showing through the mask.

Apollo stood silent, his entire face softening, as he relaxed. "No, I'm not."

"You and Malkia aren't much different from one another. The difference is, you were created directly from one of your Creators, while she was infused with magic and powers only our Gods would combine together." Mataya gave Apollo's arm a squeeze. "Malkia is the Chosen Heir of the human race, but you are the Demi-God of the Artemisians. Together, you will heal Artemis."

"How do you know this?" Malkia asked, her eyes wide with surprise.

"I don't know. I just do," Mataya responded, regarding Malkia as she she bounced on her toes. "When my powers began appearing, this deep awareness surfaced in my mind. At first, it was overwhelming, but as I've had time to piece together the puzzle, it has become exhilarating. You two are capable of healing an entire moon together, and possibly halting the conflict between the Artemisians and Humans, once and for all."

Malkia glanced over at Apollo and then back at Mataya. "Does this knowledge tell you how we are to do this?"

Mataya shook her head, chuckling softly. "Not really. If I had all the answers, then how would any of us learn and grow. You two are on your own. I divulged all the information I possess on this matter. It's now up to you two to discover the *how*."

Groaning, Malkia scanned the black smoke hovering just above the surface, but growing in density at the higher levels. She closed her eyes and fell to her knees on the charred ground, the burnt vegetation crunching under her weight. Reaching down with her hands, she dug her fingers into the ash dust, finally reaching the dirt underneath and connecting with the moon. She breathed in deeply inhaling the essence of the life beneath her.

Moments later, she sensed someone kneel in front of her and when he placed his hands on top of hers, she knew it was Apollo. Within seconds her connection with the moon and Apollo burst from her body and she felt the energy pulsating around her, creating a strong wind that caressed across her body, tugging at her hair and whipping it around her face.

She began chanting the words that Ustarum had taught her to control wind, while adding her own ending. "Mother of all strength, thrust forward and create a raging gust of wind, discarding the poison in the air and cleansing the soil and all that is living. Mother of all strength, thrust forward and create a raging gust of wind, discarding the poison in the air and cleansing the soil and all that is living."

Apollo could be heard through the wind, chanting an entirely different spell, but with it Malkia discerned a presence protecting them from the bellow of the whirlwind around them. "Artemis, goddess of all nature and wildlife, protect us while we cleanse thy wounds." He paused for a few seconds, before repeating his incantation.

The magic ebbed and flowed around them. Malkia sensed the pulsation of the energy and their combined powers cleaning the air and allowing the suns rays to warm the soil of Artemis. Opening her eyes, she tilted her face to the heavens, seeing blue skies once again, with the smoke disappearing to the north. Apollo was watching her as she glanced back down, a smile rising on his lips.

"Look at the trees!" he exclaimed, rising from his knees and drawing her up beside him.

Malkia's eyes flashed around at the vegetation and noticed that the colors of the trees, brush and flowers were returning. Mataya gripped her hand, jumping up and down as she beheld the view. *"You did it,"* she cried happily. "You both did it, and the vision was absolutely splendid."

The trio stood in silence, tugging their masks off their faces and breathing in the newly fresh air. Their eyes danced in amazement, watching as the winds rid the air of the smoke and the charred ground was overrun with a racing flood of color, spreading to the far off mountains. The plants sprouted from the ground, followed by blossoms bursting from their leaves, allowing the vibrant hues to dance with the wind. The trees spread out their branches, growing at a speed Malkia had never known possible.

"We did it," she whispered, a lone tear escaping and running over her cheek. "Artemis is healed." She glanced up at Apollo, squeezing his massive hand. "You and I did this."

He nodded, tears glistening in his eyes, as he stared out into the horizon and watched the magical episode unfold. "That was by far, the most exhilarating event I've ever experienced." He glimpsed down at Malkia. "Let's do it again."

Mataya giggled and Malkia laughed out loud, their joy echoing through the crisp air around them. "Let's go see those pyramids," Mataya requested, towing Malkia with her. "Your healing is not over, so yes you will have the chance to do it again."

"What do you mean, it's not over?" Malkia asked, freezing in place.

Mataya stared back at the two of them, a half-smile still on her face. "You have to spread the healing. We will need to move to the other side and do it again and keep doing it until the whole moon appears the way it does here."

"I see," Malkia replied, trotting after Mataya, with Apollo in tow. "I didn't realize it wouldn't spread on its own."

"It makes sense that it will require us to nudge it along," Apollo said, sprinting past Malkia with his long legs.

Malkia levitated, flying past the other two and winking at them. It wasn't long before they reached the top of the hill and peered down at the pyramids below. The structures were aligned just like the ones on Eris and Enyo, with a Guarding Statue not far off down the valley.

"Wait, why doesn't Enyo have a Guarding Statue?" Malkia asked, her eyes scanning the horizon.

"It did," Apollo breathed, his chest heaving in and out as he caught his breath. "It was destroyed by the Elvens years ago, before you were even born."

"Why?" Malkia twisted to look up at Apollo, shielding her eyes from suns.

"The Elvens are a force to be reckoned with. If they believe there's any threat presented that will make its way to Thalia, they'll attack before anyone has a chance. The Guarding Statue on Enyo became a cause for concern, when my people were told it was filled with the one spell that would annihilate the Elvens." Apollo shook his head, his eyes slanting and his jaw jutting out. "Word travels fast, even between moons. Only a few days after the revelation of this information to the Artemisians, the Elvens arrived in their high tech vessels and obliterated the statue. Just like they did back on Eris to the two pyramids and Duncan's village."

"You know it was the Elvens?" Malkia asked, clinching her teeth together.

"Yes. You asked me to find out, but I already suspected it was they, especially after you described the appearance of their vessels." Apollo began walking down a path towards the base of the hill, motioning for the women to follow him. "I did my investigation and sure enough, news had traveled through the star system about the pyramids of Eris. They claimed that inside the smaller two pyramids was the known whereabouts for all the Elvens' long kept spells and secrets and the village protecting the pyramids had already discovered these secrets." He paused, glancing back at Malkia. "I can only think of one person who would benefit from spreading that rumor."

"Me, too," Malkia mumbled, skipping over a large rock in the pathway. "Do you know where the map resides in these structures?"

Apollo shook his head, laughing at the notion. "Maybe I am a Demi-God like Mataya claims, but I have never been privy to the information of what lies inside the pyramids and statue. They've been a mystery to our people for ages, and we were forbidden to venture near them, told it was only to keep us safe from the hazards inside."

They traveled quickly down the hill, easing their way up to the first pyramid. Malkia had one mission and that was to find the map. After hours of searching for a way in, she sagged against the base of the large structure, wiping her brow with her forearm and shielding her eyes from the glare of the suns. Glancing around the area, she felt a bit hopeless, knowing there was so much farther to go before she would be able to free her daughter from her Father's grip.

"Any luck?" Mataya asked, skipping up to Malkia's side and scooping up the water container sitting on the ground.

"Does it look like I've found an opening?" Malkia asked, eyeing her sister with irritation, as she gulped down a large amount of water.

Mataya grinned, wiping the drops of fluid from her lips and chin with the back of her hand. "Don't be sassy with me, dear sister. We just haven't discovered the correct spell. We'll figure it out."

Malkia groaned, weary of Mataya's positive attitude and exhausted from the heat of the suns. "Maybe we should have allowed the smoke to linger just until the suns set," she grumbled, stomping towards the Guarding Statue, needing a change of scenery.

Mataya sprinted up next to her, giving her a sideways smile. "Cheer up, Malkia. Look how far we've ventured. You've already begun the healing of Artemis, and we're well on our way to acquiring the entire map that will lead us to our Creators. How marvelous is that?"

Peering over at her sister, Malkia's brows furrowed, thinking of the senseless map they were piecing together. "Why do we need to know where our Creators have gone?" Malkia exclaimed, halting in her steps and turning to face Mataya.

Mataya took a step back, her smile melting from her face as she stared at Malkia's frustrated expression. "I'm sorry, Malkia. I wasn't meaning to upset you. I was only doing my best to keep you cheerful, while we conducted our search." Mataya stepped forward again, grasping Malkia's forearm. "Let's take a break."

Malkia nodded, realizing she hadn't eaten since before they left the larger ship. She was famished and ready to rip apart anyone who crossed her unseen boundary. Letting Mataya drag her towards a large tree, she sank to the ground, resting her head on her pack and closing her eyes.

"I need to eat," she said, peeking under her eyelashes at Mataya. "Apollo has the food. Could you track him down and bring him and the food over here?"

Smiling wide, once again, Mataya nodded and skipped away as Malkia allowed her eyes to close, drifting quickly into the dark abyss of sleep.

"Malkia?"

She knew that voice, but couldn't quite pinpoint who it was. Malkia sat up straight, glancing around the darkened area, surprised to see how late it was. The fog had rolled in and the ground was wet from what appeared like a recent rain.

"What happened?" Malkia asked to the empty air around her, searching for the voice she had heard moments before.

A figure stood within the shadows of the Guarding Statue. Malkia rose, brushing off her clothes and keeping an eye on the mysterious person. Stepping closer to the statue, the figure shifted away from the statue, allowing Theia's light to illuminate his face.

"Jacob?" Malkia asked, rushing forward, smacking into an invisible force blocking her way. Rubbing her nose and face, she squinted as she scrutinized Jacob. "What's happening? Where did you come from?"

"Listen to me, Malkia." Jacob slid up to the edge of the force field, placing his hand up against it and staring at her. "You need to finish your mission before the suns set on the pyramids. The next section of the map is in the smallest pyramid. Retrieve what you can and finish healing the moon. You won't have much time once you wake and it's imperative that you have returned to your ship before the suns have set."

Malkia shook her head, the line between her eyes deepening in frustration. "Why? What will happen?"

"They're coming for you." Jacob glanced over his shoulder. "Find me on Thalia and I'll make sure you have an army to defeat your father. Now go." His body quivered and then vanished altogether, leaving Malkia staring at the spot he had once stood.

"*Malkia*," Mataya's voice could be heard all around her. "Malkia, wake up. I found Apollo and he's bringing the food."

Malkia closed her eyes, shaken by what Jacob had just said and wanting to return to her sister. As she opened her eyes, Mataya's face drifted into view and she smiled up at her. "I know where the map is hidden."

FIFTEEN

Returning to Enyo

After they retrieved the map, the trio raced back to their ship, realizing over half of their day was over. Apollo steered the vessel into the air, flying it over the mountains, searching for the black smoke. After some time, Malkia detected a dark shadow off in the western horizon and pointed at it for Apollo and Mataya to see.

"I think this is where the healing ended," Malkia said, noticing the vegetation below them turning into the ash covered, blackened landscape they had left earlier in the morning.

Settling onto the ground, the three of them pulled on their masks again and descended the stairs, into the gray smoke and charred terrain. Malkia found a clear spot and sank to the ground, sliding her hands through the ash and connecting with the soil below. She closed her eyes, just when Apollo joined her, his hands resting over the top of hers and together they began chanting their incantations.

The wind didn't abandon them. Within moments it was whirling past them, gripping onto Malkia's hair once again and dancing around her union with Apollo. The minutes ticked past, before the wind died down and Malkia sensed the growth of new vegetation around her. Opening her eyes, exhaustion swept across her face and a tired smile rose on her lips, seeing that the smoke had long dissipated and the trees and flowers were blossoming around them. It was magical, but the drain on her body was overwhelming.

They didn't wait long, returning to their ship at a sprint and following the wind and flourishing of the colors, knowing it would lead them to their next area. The moon was rapidly healing itself, having absorbed Apollo's and Malkia's powers, using it to redevelop her own land.

Before long, the trio finished and frantically ascended towards the stars, fearing for their friend's safety as Malkia recounted the warning Jacob had given her. When they reached their large vessel, Apollo flew the small ship into a bunker and switched it off.

"Won't you need to return to your people?" Malkia asked, her confusion spreading across her face, wringing her hands together, anxious to speak with her own group.

Apollo rose from his chair and shook his head. "I'll send them a message, informing them of what you did to Artemis and who's really behind the battles we have been fighting for years." He stepped towards the hatch, opening it with one hand and signaling for the women to exit first. "My place is with you, until your daughter is rescued and your father has been dealt with."

Malkia squeezed his forearm as she passed him and stepped down the stairs. The door to the docks opened and Skye rushed through, throwing herself into Malkia's arms. "Please, stop leaving me behind," she cried, her curly, black hair bouncing into Malkia's face and tickling her nose.

Brushing the hair aside, Malkia circled her arms around Skye's body and held her close. "I wish you had been there," she whispered in her friend's ear. "Watching the moon heal, was the most invigorating experience in my entire life."

Skye stepped back, a sad smile tugging on the edges of her lips as she curled her hands around Malkia's arms. "Let's finish this and go home."

Malkia's head bobbed up and down, as she wrapped her arm around Skye's shoulders and grasped onto Mataya's hand. Apollo led the way, with the three women gabbing and laughing behind him, as they rushed up to the control room.

Apollo explained their circumstances to Damon. Without a word, he and Koleton prepped for departure, as the rest of the group took their seats.

"You really saw Jacob?" Skye asked, her inky irises dancing with happiness, hoping their friend had really survived.

Malkia smiled, her hands clutching onto the arms of the chair, watching Damon slide the ship from their safe crevice and back out into the open space. "I didn't physically see him, but I believe he was sending me a message. I can only hope it was from him and not another ploy of my father's." Malkia's eyes fell to her lap as she inhaled a deep breath, before looking back at her friend. "He says they can help us, but we have to make it to Thalia first."

Skye nodded, her attention turning to Koleton as he gave her hand a squeeze. "Are you ready to return to Enyo?" he asked Malkia, running his hand down his beard.

"No," she replied, glancing over at Damon, his eyes glued onto her face. "The Artemisians that occupied Enyo were vicious creatures."

She peeked at Apollo, who was listening intently to her words. "But I've come to realize that not everything I witnessed was true. After my run in with the creature on Enyo, not to mention seeing all the human slaves, I was convinced they were all deplorable and disgusting barbarians." She paused, her voice catching in her throat, still remembering human eyes on the Artemisians she had destroyed. "The ones on Enyo deserved their deaths, but the innocent creatures on Artemis were unknowingly trapped by this war and became the target only because it would end their hold on my father."

Skye squeezed Malkia's hand, her eyes glossy with tears. "Is this map important enough to return?"

Malkia froze for a moment, her eyes glazing from the thought of passing by Enyo, but then nodded her head in reply. "Even if that map wasn't needed, my fear of those memories has to be faced eventually." Her eyes focused on Koleton, a tear sliding down her cheek. "But, to answer your question, I'm not ready to return to Enyo. Errandor was just as determined to see Artemis destroyed as my father and when I see him again, my conscience won't rest until I know the truth. I'll have to ask and I'm petrified to hear his answer."

Koleton pursed his lips, his head slowly nodding. "That's understandable." He leaned over Skye and grasped Malkia's wrist. "This time you have all of us and we're all going to face what is down on that moon. You saved those people from the dominion of ruthless creatures and, when it comes to their lives that is all that matters." A smile crept across his face. "Plus, I'll be there to dazzle everyone with my sparkling personality. There will only be drinking and laughing in my presence."

The group burst out with laughter and Malkia grinned, first at Koleton and then over at Skye. Her best friend winked at her, before elbowing Koleton back into his seat. Leaning in for the kill, he nuzzled Skye's neck making her howl from the tickle of his beard.

"Knock it off!" Skye cried, shoving him away from her, only to be tugged back towards him and smothered with kisses.

The laughter filled the room and Malkia's eyes scanned the group she now considered her family. She paused when she reached Mataya, receiving a soft smile, before she leaned back and whispered to Justin. Damon was at the controls, but his eyes kept wandering back to Malkia and she wanted nothing more than be in his arms.

As if he read her mind, he rose from his chair and signaled for Koleton to take control. Motioning for her to follow him, he stepped towards the door, with her right behind him. The dimly lit corridor was empty as Damon led Malkia to the elevator and up to her quarters.

"We have some time to spare before we reach Enyo." Damon opened her door and held it for her to enter.

She passed over the threshold and settled into her oversized cushioned chair at the far end of the room, exhausted from her time on Artemis, but thrilled they were finally making some progress. "What do you have in mind to pass the time?" she asked, leaning back and dragging her legs up onto the chair with her.

"I just want us to talk," he said, easing down onto her bed and undoing his boots. "It's been a long day for you and I would like to be able to take care of you."

She grinned, her eyes shutting. "I'm starving," she commented, her eyes still closed. "Could you bring me some food?"

"Absolutely," he replied, the bed creaking as he stood. "I'll return soon."

A blanket was tucked in around her and she smiled in return, her eyes remaining closed. The lights turned off and she faintly heard the door click shut, as her mind wandered off into the darkness.

"Malkia." She heard her name being called by Damon, but the exhaustion was overwhelming her body. "I have food. You should eat before you sleep."

Reluctantly she opened one eye, squinting at the dim light from the lamp in the corner. The scent of fresh bread filled her nostrils, willing her other eye to open. Damon had set a tray of food on the small table next to her chair and was settling back down on her bed.

"You really should eat," he suggested, yawning wide and stretching his arms over his head.

He didn't have to mention it again, as she reached over and gripped the tray, drawing it towards her and diving into the array of delicacies. The meat was warm and delicious, its tender juiciness making it difficult to chew at a regular pace. She wanted to shove more into her mouth, but with Damon watching, she resisted. A smile crept across her face, realizing she must appear like a famished beast, ripping into her prey.

Looking up from her tray of food, a laugh escaped her lips. Damon rested with his arm wrapped around her pillow, snoring softly as he slept. Eating what was left of her meal and drinking down a glass full of water, she washed her hands, tugged off her pants, turned down the lights and crawled into the bed next to Damon. Curling her arm around his chest, she was out within seconds.

Enyo loomed just ahead and Malkia stood stiff as a board, remembering the last time she witnessed this view. Her heart rose into her throat and she wanted nothing more than to fly away and never return. This place was the reason for her nightmares.

Sinking into a nearby seat, she tuned out the chatter of her family around her. Her thoughts went to the dragons, and she was grateful no disaster had occurred over the past couple of days. Watching their descent, she needed a distraction. But the dragons appeared to be sleeping, as she couldn't reach either of them with her thoughts. Giving up on having Tantiana talk her through this, she closed her eyes and leaned back against her chair, waiting for the vessel to land.

Errandor and Tarance stood in the landing docks, smiles spreading across their face when they caught view of Malkia. She didn't hold the same sentiment, but forced a smile in return, grasping tightly onto Damon's hand. "I hate this." Her eyes caught his and he nodded in acknowledgment.

"You can do this," he replied, squeezing her hand and kissing the top of her head.

Stepping towards the people thronging the end of the gangway, Malkia could see the two men were still surrounded by an array of their admirers. Finally reaching them, Errandor grasped her wrist, his feeble fingers shaking as he kissed her hand. She glanced over at Tarance, who smiled widely and nodded in gratitude.

"We believed we would never behold you again," Errandor observed, his eyes meeting Malkia's. "Why have you returned?"

Malkia placed her hand on Errandor's shoulder, as they meandered towards the bay doors. "I've been to Eris and have met with the warlock, Ustarum."

Errandor froze, his wide eyes flashing to hers. "What did you learn from him?"

Malkia eased the men back into a walk, squeezing Damon's hand once again. "He has shown me how to master my abilities and use what I've been gifted with to heal our star system. In doing so, he has let me in on the secret of our Creators and has instructed me to search the Enyoan pyramids for clues to our existence." The little white lie would have to do, as Malkia would never trust this man with the whereabouts to the blue planet.

"Does he believe our pyramids possess this clue?" Tarance asked, his hand grasping onto the back of Errandors arm.

"He believes it is possible and that I'm the only one with the powers to discover it," Malkia replied, glancing over her shoulder at her family and the crowd accompanying them. "I'll require full access to all the pyramids, along with room and board for all my friends and family until we are ready to depart."

"We would like to know the clue, if you discover it." Errandor stopped again, his hand gripping Malkia's forearm with the strength of a wolf-man. "I'm not a fool, Malkia. If Ustarum has sent you on this quest, he has a motive and a plan already in place for when you retrieve this clue. I want in or you will be banished from this moon."

Malkia sighed, stepping away from Errandor. "This is your moon and you have every right to know what we find, but I will travel on to the next moon before I make any more agreements with you." Her eyes darted from Tarance's to Errandor's and then over to Asha's. The warlock's eyes crinkled with a soft smile, giving her a slight nod of approval. Looking back to the two men, she continued, "I'm the only one with the knowledge and power to find this clue and as the Chosen Heir, I'm insisting that it be done my way."

"You're the Chosen Heir?" Errandor questioned, his brows furrowing.

"Yes, I am." Malkia tilted her head to the side, as she pursed her lips. "That surprises you. Why?"

"It—" Errandor began, but paused when Tarance tightened his hold on his partner's arm. Errandor shot an icy glance at Tarance, before staring back at Malkia, his eyes cold with malice. "You have your clearance to the pyramids, along with one of our empty homes for your family and friends. I'll instruct one of my assistants to see you to your new home and give you the keys to the pyramids as well." Without another word, he pivoted on his heel and, with Tarance in tow, stomped off down the opposite corridor.

Errandor's assistant was a tall, lanky man with snow white hair, and eyes swimming with a pale rose color, who called himself Ti. He led them back to their ship and asked them to follow his small vessel to their dwelling. After landing, Ti led them to a large cottage, with enough rooms for everyone to have their own space.

"These are the keys to enter the pyramids," Ti announced, holding out his hand.

The keys were each shaped differently, crafted from bone. Malkia gripped all three, running her fingers over the grooves before looking up at Ti. "Thank you for your hospitality. Once we discover what we have come for, we will depart immediately. Please let Errandor know we won't be any trouble."

Ti nodded, giving Malkia a half-bow before taking his leave. Watching his thin form retreat, Malkia wondered how many other people appeared as he did. His eyes appeared to be filled with a mist, which swam through his irises. It was unsettling and he was nothing like anyone she had met before.

Shaking her head, she returned to the ship. Tantiana, Adelina and the hatchlings needed to spread their wings. *You're all free to wander around the forest, but be careful to not be seen and keep close to our cottage. We are already on thin ice here and if Errandor knew I brought dragons on his moon, he would banish me for good.*

The older dragons nodded, stepping out of the ship, followed by the two hatchlings. Before Adelina could stop them, the two young ones bounded into the air and shot straight up into the air. Their mother was inches behind them, but Malkia could already tell this was going to be a battle.

Tantiana and she exchanged a pointed look, both sighing in frustration. *I'll assist Adelina and keep those two under close watch*, Tantiana thought.

Malkia forced a half-smile as Tantiana shot into the air, following the three other dragons. Watching for a moment, she saw Tantiana wrestling with one of the hatchlings and bringing him back to their small area. Shaking her head, she traipsed towards the cottage, ready to go to the pyramids and retrieve the next section of the map, so she could depart from this moon, once and for all.

Opening the door to the cottage, she found her family seated around the large front room speaking to one another. A hush rippled through the group when she entered, everyone's eyes turning towards her.

"Can we go to the pyramids?" Damon asked, leaning forward in his chair.

Malkia nodded, opening up her hand for everyone to see. "These are the keys. I would love for my time on Enyo to be brief, so the sooner we can finish this, the better it will be for all of us."

Mataya rose from her chair, gripping Justin's hand and pulling him up next to her. "The cottage is drafty and wet." She pointed at the water dripping in the far corner, from a recent rainfall. "Your friend doesn't want us to remain on Enyo any longer then we want to be here. If we can leave first thing in the morning that would be the best scenario."

Alyssa stepped forward, next to Mataya. "Before we separate, I need you all to know my discoveries." She intertwined her fingers, her eyes bouncing around the room, never fully making eye contact with anyone. "Part of the reason I became a deimos was to uncover the ties your father had on each of the moons. Ginny was his main contact, but Errandor was always loyal to your father. He's not blameless in the Artemisian war, although he was definitely kept in the dark about most plans." She glanced over at Haltia and Asha, calming her eye shift as she took in a deep breathe. "I believed your mother was just as much a part of the plot to blame the Artemisians for all the erroneous deeds of this star system and I warned Asha to keep her distance. I was wrong." Looking back at Malkia, she rubbed her thumbs together, fidgeting from one foot to another. "Errandor was instructed to bring you in and find a way to gain your loyalty. Dario and Kelsey went to Esaki under the direction of Errandor, not Emelia or Ginny."

Malkia's eyes widened. "What about the Enyoans?" She asked, gritting her teeth.

"Errandor doesn't care about his people. You've witnessed that firsthand." Alyssa's eyes fell to the ground, her fingers squeezing one another. "Emelia and Ginny were hungry for leadership and created a plan to eliminate Errandor, but it backfired on them and only eliminated his physical abilities, placing him in a state of pure mental awareness. Your father orchestrated the entire scenario, once he discovered your memories had returned. Dario and your father had the entire Enyo experience laid out for you, before you even set foot on this moon."

"What?" Malkia's cheeks flush hot and her hands began to shake, as her pulse quickened. "Everything? Even when the Artemisian nearly ripped me to shreds?"

"No." Alyssa shook her head rapidly, her eyes darting around the room at all the surprised expressions. "That is the only time they had no control over your movements. The amnesia only benefited Dario. He had intended on showing you the enslavement of his people and using your kind heart to convince you to annihilate the Artemisians, but that foolish barbarian did the job for him."

"Ginny made it sound like it was she and my father planning the entire experience," Malkia said, taking in a deep breath to cool her frustration and anger.

Alyssa choked back a laugh, her hands covering her mouth. "Sorry, it's not funny, just ironic." Clearing her throat, she continued, "Dario is a ruthless tyrant. He had no love for his mother or his mamu. The only love that man has ever possessed is for power, and he knew his ticket to amass the kind of power he was searching for was to do exactly what Thane asked of him."

Malkia bit her lip, battling the urge to recoil as she walked back to the door. "Let's go," she commanded, shooting a glance over her shoulder at the group. "I'm tired of the stories and the revelation of everyone who has deceived me. I was foolish, but now I'm learning my lesson." She yanked the door open and passed over the threshold without another word.

SIXTEEN

The Three Pyramids

The inside of the first pyramid was freezing, sending a shudder over Malkia as she nudged the cobwebs to the side, entering into the first chamber. Using her light from her hand to view the room, she noticed the same small statues from the Guarding Statue on Eris.

"I didn't see these statues on Artemis," she noted, turning to face Apollo. "But they were in the statue on Eris. Do you know what they symbolize?"

Apollo shook his head, his eyes scanning over the room and the statues. "They're quite peculiar," he said, sinking to his knees and running his fingers over one of the little people. "I've never come across anything of this nature in all my travels."

"Their faces seem peaceful, but their eyes appear to follow us around and that is why they disturb me." Malkia shone her light on one of the statues, its eyes lighting up, seeming to stare back at her. Its arms were folded across its chest, with one finger poking out and a crooked smile etched into its face, while standing on his tiptoes. "Every single one is posed differently, each with their own unique expression."

Flashing her light to another statue near Apollo, he leaned down to gain a closer view. "This one is winking," he said, glancing back at her.

Its one foot was crossed over its other knee and it was positioned in a near seated stance, while his hands were placed in front of its chest, all eight fingers spread out. "Eight fingers," Malkia mused out loud, wondering what it meant. She shined her light on the one next to it. This personage had one hand reaching for the sky, with two fingers being held up, while its other hand was placed behind its back. The face was staring at the floor, with its eyes closed and feet turned towards one another and toes touching. "Do you think the number of fingers they are holding up means something?" Malkia glanced over at Apollo who had stepped to the other side of the room, ready to move on to the next chamber.

He pivoted back, examining the statues again. "Maybe," he murmured, stooping over to view the closest statue. "This one has four fingers raised up, two on each hand."

"There have to be nearly three dozen, if not more, statues," Malkia replied, shining her light around the room. "Would you mind writing down the number of fingers and I'll continue the search for the map?"

Apollo nodded, drawing out a piece of parchment from his pack. "I'll come find you once I'm finished."

Malkia turned away, stepping to the end of the room and through the next doorway. Damon, Skye and Koleton had gone on to the middle pyramid, while Justin, Bella and Alyssa had entered the last pyramid. The rest of the group had remained at the cottage, preparing food for when the search came to a halt for the day.

The following chamber was warmer than the last and filled with rising columns, stretching up to the high ceiling. Malkia flashed her light around and noticed couches and tables placed purposefully around the room, indicating to her this had to be a common place for Errandor to visit. The chamber was clean and free of cobwebs, which seemed strange, considering the massive amount of cobwebs that lined the entrance.

Shaking her head in confusion, she swept through the room, finding another doorway at the other side. Gingerly, she stepped through, seeing only a wall on the other side, forcing her to turn down a corridor that led her straight to a long, dark downward spiral of stairs.

Shining her light down the middle, the stairs seemed to wind as far as the eye could see. She glanced back the way she'd come, hoping to see Apollo joining her, but found only darkness. Shifting her weight, she shone her light around the entire area, inspecting the ceiling and walls.

Groaning with frustration at the lack of symbols or maps, she stepped down the stairs, taking her time as the floor slowly moved above her. The darkness was everywhere, and the narrow stairs became suffocating, as she descended farther into the abyss. Her light was her only beacon and she cursed herself for not waiting for Apollo.

Glancing back up, she could no longer view the top of the stairs and surveying downwards, there didn't seem to be an end to the circle of steps. "What was I thinking?" she scolded herself out loud, continuing her descent while mentally kicking herself for not turning back.

Many moments later, the stairs came to an end and a large metal door stood in her path. Shining her light around the edges, she searched for a handle, concentrating on her breathing to keep her anxiety at bay. The handle was nowhere to be found and Malkia grumbled, as she let her light slide across the cramped quarters at the base of the stairs.

After examining every inch, she twisted back to face the door, unable to find a way into the next room, except through it. Unable to view what was on the other side, she didn't want to risk walking through and running into unknown danger or another one of her father's traps.

Instead she closed her eyes, concentrating on her light and allowing it to flow from her body, slowly wrapping it around the bulk of the door. Under her breath, she mumbled the incantation that had found the door at the Guarding Statue on Eris. The glow from the door permeated her eyelids and after invoking the spell, her eyes snapped open to see her light illuminating the handle.

Holding tightly onto the spell, she stepped forward and grasped the handle, pushing it forward and turning it to the left. She heard a faint click and the door gave way with a groan. Stale, dry air swept into her nostrils, pushing a gasp from her lungs. Coughing into her shirt, she eased the door open, shining her light around the entire room.

Edging gingerly into the room, her eyes grew wide and her hands shook as she was bombarded by the profusion of etchings. Without thinking about where she was stepping, her feet moved forward and into thin air. Her arms flailed out wildly, a scream burst from her lips and echoed against the stone wall, as she plummeted down the blackened chasm. Halting her descent with her levitation, her heart drummed against her ribs, making it difficult to catch a full breath. Reigniting her light, her hands shook as she flashed it downward to see what she almost plunged into.

Inhaling several rapid breaths, her light scanning the sharpened spikes at the bottom of the pit. Small insects scurried along the floor and the cobwebs stretched across the spears, making Malkia's stomach churn as her hands slid over her mouth. Fearing she would lose whatever food she might have inside her stomach, she shut her eyes and floated back up, settling on her feet just inside the doorway.

A hand curled over her shoulder, gripping her tight and she nearly hopped back into the pit as her heart jumped into her throat. Glancing over her shoulder, her breath came out with a whoosh, seeing Apollo with wide eyes standing behind her.

"You scared me!" She hissed at him, shaking off his hand, his long fingers sliding down her arm.

He shook his head, his eyes narrowing at her harsh tone. "You weren't at the door when I arrived and then you rose out of nowhere. I'm fairly sure you frightened me, first."

Malkia couldn't help but laugh, nodding her head and closing her eyes for a moment. "I nearly impaled myself on a dozen sharpened spikes at the bottom of this pit." She pointed into the chamber, her eyes focusing on Apollo. "This place is giving me the creeps and it doesn't help to have you sneak up on me with your lighter-than-a-rodent's scurry." She threw him a wide grin, winking at him, before turning again to face the eerie room.

"What does this chamber contain?" Apollo asked, stepping next to her and examining the deadly pit in front of them.

"There are writings all over the walls and ceiling, but my examination of the room was interrupted when I slipped into the pit," Malkia muttered, levitating and floating over the quarry to the other side of the room.

Touching the wall, she ran her hands down the first etching, noticing the many symbols of tall beings pointing to the skies, along with the small statues with the fingers and bizarre stances. The light from Apollo's lantern bounced around the room and Malkia could see hundreds of various etchings and writings.

She glanced over at Apollo, who had followed the wall to the right and was examining the writings in his path. "It will take us days, if not weeks to gather all this information. Do you think it's important for our mission?"

"We won't know how important it is until we go over all of it," he replied, his back remaining towards her.

She shook her head, pursing her lips in thought. Her eyes flashed around the room, using her light to see every inch of the walls and ceiling. "There isn't a map in here and I don't see any more doorways. I would like to return up the stairs and search for any other paths through the pyramid."

"I'll remain here and attempt to understand what the writers were attempting to communicate," Apollo stated, running his hands along the wall.

Standing on the far end of the room, Malkia squinted one more time at the ceiling and in the corner of her eye she noticed a glimmer. Her eyes flashed over to the side, trying to catch whatever had been there. Tucking her hair behind her ears, she bit her bottom lip as she studied the ceiling.

"Wait," she called out to Apollo, not exactly sure what she was looking at. He turned to face her and then followed her eyes to the ceiling.

"What is it?" he asked, tilting his head to try to see her view better.

She shook her head, her forehead furrowing. "I don't know, but I see something. Will you set your lantern by the stairs and close the door?"

He stepped lightly back along the wall and over the threshold of the door, setting the lantern down next to the stairs. Easing back into the chamber, he slid the door nearly shut, halting when the ceiling lit up.

Malkia gasped. "It's the map!" she exclaimed, flying up towards the ceiling. Touching the lights, she glanced down to see the silhouette of Apollo watching her. "We found it."

"How do we copy that onto the parchment?" Apollo asked.

"There are tiny holes in the ceiling. I'm not sure where the light is coming from, but there has to be a way to copy the holes." Malkia scanned the ceiling, realizing how large this map was. "It will take days to copy all the holes. There has to be a better and easier way."

"Let's return to the cottage and find out what everyone else has discovered. Maybe someone in the group will have an idea." Apollo turned towards the door, not waiting for an answer.

Malkia settled back on the same side of the pit as Apollo, following him out of the chamber. She left the door ajar and began the long trek back up the stairs, with Apollo following right behind her.

As they passed through the first chamber, Malkia checked for another pathway and was disappointed that there was nothing to be seen. Knowing how massive the structure was, she realized there had to be another entrance somewhere that Errandor was not disclosing or there had to be a hidden doorway. Considering the amount of cobwebs, she believed Errandor was determined to keep his entrance a secret.

The light from the suns was dimming as they emerged from the pyramid. Malkia still had to shield her eyes from the brightness, but she inhaled the clean, crisp air and was glad they had left that sepulcher for the day.

It didn't take them long to return to the cottage. Everyone, except Damon's group had made their way back and were helping Mataya and Asha prepare dinner.

"What did you discover in your pyramid?" Malkia asked Bella, sinking into the cushioned chair in the corner of the living area.

"Nothing too appealing," Bella confessed, leaning against her own chair. "The rooms were filled with old books and chairs. We found a few rooms with beds and a large chamber that appeared to be used as a kitchen. We finally realized that pyramid had probably been cleaned out years ago and was used as a shelter of some sort. Alyssa said it was the one where she and Asha hid with Errandor and Tarance, before they found you."

"Yes, that's right," Malkia replied, stifling a yawn. "I'm surprised the pyramid Apollo and I searched was not more like yours. It contained the same statues that I told you about back on Eris, along with a hidden chamber a few stories below the main floor. There was a pit, filled with sharpened spikes and cobwebs and insects running throughout the entire room." She leaned her head against the back cushion and closed her eyes. "But we found the map on the ceiling, so at least the search is over."

"*That's great,*" Bella's excited voice echoed in Malkia's ears. "Did you make a copy onto the parchment?"

Malkia shook her head, her eyes remaining closed. "It was made out of tiny holes in the ceiling, illuminated by some hidden source. We need to find a way to copy the map, without doing it one hole at a time."

"We'll come up with something," Bella reassured her. "Take a nap. I'll wake you when our meal is complete."

I just need to rest my—" her voice slurred just slightly and it made her jump. Her eyes flashed open and noticed Bella had already left the room. Closing her eyes again, the darkness enveloped her within seconds.

Supper was a party for the group. Damon and those who had accompanied him arrived shortly before it was finished and had woken Malkia when they entered the cottage. Their experience in the third pyramid had been exhilarating, and they were bustling with excitement as they spoke of their findings.

"We didn't find the map, but the vegetation that was growing in this pyramid had the most exotic and stunning colors I've ever encountered," Skye exclaimed, recounting their experience to the group. Koleton grinned as he shoved more food into his mouth, nodding in agreement. "It was everywhere. It must be where the Enyoans were keeping food in case they had to hide in the pyramids for a long period of time. I don't know how they accomplished the growth, but the entire pyramid had a feeling of enchantment."

"It wouldn't surprise me if they used the Thalians black magic that ensured their safety from the Artemisians and their deimoses," Malkia remarked, glancing over at Asha. "If it had a strong sensation of magic, it's a possibility they were involved."

Damon nodded, his brows furrowing. "It seemed to be filled with a hefty pulse of energy. My abilities have only heightened since Eris, and when magic is near, it throbs through my body—almost as if it is feeding an energy inside me."

"Really?" Asha and Alyssa both exclaimed at the same time.

Damon gave them a pointed look, folding his arms over his chest. "Yes," he affirmed, slowly. "Apparently, I have sparked your interest. Why is that?"

Asha and Alyssa glanced at one another and then over at Bella, who leaned forward in her chair, placing her elbows on the table. "It could mean many things," Asha replied, furrowing her brows in thought. "When creating the abilities in the Eris children, we used a small amount of magic from the Thalians—the Elvens. Malkia was able to absorb the magic when placed in the midst of it, and it would be interesting to know if you could do the same."

Instinctively, Malkia placed her hand over her stomach, realizing the powerhouse she and Damon had created together. "Ustarum must be right," she muttered under her breath.

Everyone's eyes swept over to Malkia, watching her hand rub her stomach, while she was in deep thought. Finally noticing the stares, she snapped her hand away and sat up straight.

"Would the Thalian's magic impact Damon the same way as myself?" she asked, attempting to steer the subject away from what she had been caught doing.

Asha's eyes narrowed, staring intently at Malkia, and traveling down at her stomach. Her eyes grew wide for a moment, as they traveled back up to Malkia's face. "It could," Asha replied. "The only way to know is to go back to the pyramid and experiment."

The group continued speaking, but Asha's eyes didn't stray from Malkia. Chewing on her lip, Malkia stared down at her hands, afraid she would reveal her secret to her friends and family before she finished her mission. Knowing they would insist on her staying out of the fight, she had to keep her pregnancy to herself.

Asha wasn't giving up easily and Malkia sensed her eyes on her for the majority of the meal. Excusing herself early, Malkia rushed out to find Tantiana and Adelina. The dragons had nestled into a nearby cave and were enjoying some much-needed rest after flying around the area, when Malkia called for Tantiana.

Tantiana? Malkia thought, once they were away from Adelina.

What is it? Tantiana replied, diving down into some trees and landing by a waterfall, where there was no one else around.

I'm with child, Malkia thought, raking her hands through her hair, before sliding off the back of Tantiana. *I don't believe the baby is in any danger, but if my family discovered this piece of information, they would insist I halt my mission.*

Your secret is safe with me, Tantiana winked at Malkia. *Dragons are involved in battle while carrying their children and we don't have the luxury of stopping whenever we desire. You're far better at protecting yourself and your child, than any other person in this star system.*

Agreed, Malkia thought, sitting on a nearby rock and pulling her legs up to her chest. *This war needs to end and we are closing in on the final battle. I just need a little more time before I reveal my circumstance.*

Tantiana nodded as she leaned her head down into the pool of the waterfall and sloughed gallons of water. After quenching her thirst, she nestled her head down next to Malkia, allowing her mistress to scratch her ears, while encumbered with her own thoughts.

Do you think I'm making another mistake? Malkia asked. *I've kept a great deal from Damon and he deserves to know he is about to become a father. Should I at least disclose this secret to him?*

Tantiana stirred slightly, her eyes glancing sideways at Malkia. *Maybe. He would want you to sit out from the fight the most, but he also knows you don't take orders from him.*

Malkia nodded and closed her eyes, leaning up against Tantiana's body for support. *I'm exhausted lately. This little fetus is taking nearly every ounce of my energy. I fear the group is going to discover my circumstances and be furious with me for not being upfront with them.*

How much longer do you think you can keep your secret, without causing an issue with the group? Tantiana asked, twisting her neck so Malkia would scratch in a different spot.

I don't know. Malkia sighed. *I would like to at least arrive on Esaki. Once we finish up here, Thallassa will be our next stop and that moon seems to be a quiet one. We should be in and out, before anyone notices we have landed.*

Tantiana closed her eyes. *Then you have your answer.*

Malkia's head bobbed up and down slightly, watching the water pour endlessly down the cliff side. The jagged rocks jutted from the cliffs, allowing the water to cascade over their edges and tumble down into the pool at the bottom. The sound was soothing to Malkia and she felt better about waiting a little bit longer before sharing her news.

SEVENTEEN

The Elven's Ancient Secrets

The pyramid was warm but humid, like a rainforest. Malkia wiped the beads of sweat from her forehead with the back of arm and tucked her moistened hair behind her ears. Surveying the large chamber, she paused in place, admiring the striking colors of the vegetation. A number of lanterns had been placed around the room, enabling them to view it in its entirety. It was breathtaking.

The fruits and vegetables were spread across the area, along with vibrant flowers and leaves, making Malkia feel as if she was in an enchanted forest of some sort. Skye hadn't been exaggerating on the robust amount of magic permeating around the room.

A hand curled around Malkia's waist and she smiled up at Damon. He seemed to realize something had changed about her, as both of his hands settled around her midriff and caressed her abdomen.

It's not possible he can know I'm with child. Malkia thought, glancing sidelong at his face. *Or has he had one of his visions?*

A smile surfaced on his lips, giving her the sense he knew, but it could just be the energy in the room. It was exhilarating. An invisible current within her kindled a deep longing for his touch. She reached up and touched his face. "What if we were alone right now?" she whispered.

He glanced down at her, his muscles tightening around her. "The things I would do to you—" His voice trailed off as a grin spread across his face, making his eyes sparkle. "We would create our own magic."

"It's nearly overwhelming." Malkia sighed in longing. "I can see why you three were on cloud nine back at the cottage. This place is filled with happiness."

"You're my happiness," he breathed, drawing her even closer to his body and kissing her neck. "We should kick everyone else out of this pyramid."

Malkia laughed, her eyes darting around the room at their friends. "You don't think they'll suspect our intentions?"

"I don't care what they think." He nibbled on her ear, as he swept her hair away from her neck.

"We could sneak back here tonight, after everyone else has gone to bed," she suggested, leaning against him, as her body yearned for him to be closer.

"You don't have to ask twice," he murmured in her ear, ignoring the growing stares from the rest of the group.

"Do you two need some alone time?" Koleton jested from across the room.

"Yes," Damon replied. "Great idea. You can all leave now."

Skye laughed out loud, covering her mouth as she ducked behind Koleton. Mataya and Justin were grinning, while Haltia rolled her eyes. The group didn't budge from what they were each examining, intent on annoying Damon.

"I wasn't joking." Damon growled in Malkia's ear.

She turned around and wrapped her arms around his neck, pressing up against his body. "They don't care, but I do." She pressed her lips against his. "We'll have our alone time. Don't you worry."

Asha slid up next to the two of them, shaking her head in disapproval. "Later, you two. Malkia, I think it would be best if you left the pyramid while we tested the Thalian magic on Damon. I think your presence will cause the experiment to be inaccurate."

Malkia withdrew her arms from Damon's neck, stepping back from him, her body still hot from the energy between them. Giving his arm a squeeze, she walked past him, smacking his backside before she left the room and throwing a smile over her shoulder at him.

Leaving the pyramid, she walked past the middle one, examining the distant building Errandor had constructed while she was away. It towered above the main city, just like his last building had, announcing his dictatorship to everyone passing by. She had wanted to trust the man, but seeing his lack of attention towards Haltia and his obvious disdain for her, caused her to wonder if he was in contact with her father. It wouldn't surprise her in the slightest.

She wandered back to the cottage and began searching the rooms for any sign of intrusion by Errandor and his guards. Believing he had to be monitoring them, only pushed her to find out what he was hiding. Before long, she discovered a device inside one of the walls in the kitchen area. She shook the small, motorized contraption, seeing what appeared to be an eye in the middle, zoom in and out. Tossing it on the ground, she crushed it beneath her heel until it shattered.

Sprinting out of the cottage, she raced back to the pyramid, hoping they had completed the experiment. She wanted to leave in the morning. Errandor wasn't going to control her movements any longer.

Skye and Koleton were sauntering out of the pyramid, with their arms around one another and speaking in a low tone, when Malkia came racing up to them. "How did it go?" she asked, looking over their shoulders.

"He was able to absorb the black magic, but Asha swept it away from him, before it consumed his body. He doesn't have any of it left in him, but he's definitely capable of doing what you can do." Koleton had been guarded, ever since he realized Malkia had a newfound darkness. He kept his distance and encouraged Skye to do the same.

"I've controlled the black magic," Malkia snapped, noticing the way Koleton protected Skye from her. "Ustarum taught me how to keep it at bay and only use it when I control its direction."

Koleton nodded and Skye shrugged her shoulders, as they walked around her and headed back to the cottage.

"You should know," Malkia shouted after them. "We're being watched by Errandor. I discovered a device in the kitchen area, which means there may be more elsewhere in the cottage." The couple turned back to face her, their brows furrowed. "Be careful what you say inside our temporary home."

She pivoted on her heel and rushed into the pyramid to find Damon. Running down the corridor and into the first room, she saw Haltia and Asha on the far end, speaking with Damon. Mataya, Justin, Bella and Alyssa were picking a basket of fruits and vegetables to take back to the cottage and Apollo was examining some of the inscriptions on the walls.

"What have you found in this pyramid?" Malkia asked Apollo,

watching Damon from the corner of her eyes.

"It's not much different than the one we explored earlier today." Apollo advised, running his hands over the etchings. "From the pictures, it appears the small humanoids that we keep running into have something to do with your Creators, and the number of their fingers does appear to be significant. The taller beings are continuously pointing to the stars, while the statues are either giving coordinates or information that will lead to the Creators' whereabouts." He glanced over at Malkia, his lips slightly pursed. "I haven't deciphered most of it yet, but I believe those statues are a key to finding your blue planet, as well."

Malkia nodded slowly, searching the wall Apollo had been examining. "I want to leave here tomorrow. I found a mechanical device in the wall of the kitchen area in the cottage, and I'm fairly certain Errandor is watching everything we do." She turned to look over at Mataya and her Esaki mother. "I would love to gather as much information as we can and depart first thing tomorrow. Would you return to the pyramid we searched earlier?"

"Yes, I will," Apollo replied. "We need to find a way to retrieve that map."

"I'll remain here and see if I can find anything that will assist us," she said, stepping towards Damon. "I'll have Asha and Haltia accompany you and see who wants to stay here. The sooner we leave, the better it will be for us. My father has been known to persuade stronger men then Errandor."

Apollo exhaled loudly and Malkia's eyes flashed over to him. "I wish we had the armies of the Artemisians to assist us," he stated, running his hand over his chin. "If they only believed your father's role in the destruction of Artemis, maybe they would turn their vengeance on him, instead of continuing their search for you."

"We can't worry about that at this time." Malkia gathered up her hair and twisted into a high bun on top of her head. "Let's collect the information from the pyramids and depart from this treacherous moon."

Apollo left without another word, and Malkia strolled up to Damon. "Koleton filled me in on the details of Damon's experiment. Now that we know his ability to absorb dark magic, can we proceed with assembling the information we have discovered and leave this forsaken moon as soon as possible?"

"What's wrong?" Haltia asked, curling her hand around Malkia's elbow.

"Errandor is keeping tabs on us," Malkia disclosed, grasping her mother's hand. "I found what appeared to be a spying device of some sort, inside one of the walls in the cottage. I wouldn't put it past him to bug our entire home, along with the pyramids as well. Could you two join Apollo in the first pyramid and collect everything you can find?"

"Absolutely," Haltia agreed, kissing Malkia on the cheek. Gripping Malkia's chin, she forced her daughter to look at her. "I love you, Malkia. I'll do whatever it takes to right my wrongs and bring Esta back to your arms. Please know I'm always on your side."

"Thank you, Mom." Malkia leaned in and gave her mother a hug.

Asha and Haltia left, leaving Justin, Mataya, Alyssa and Bella. Malkia could feel Damon's eyes on her as she approached the group and asked them to search the middle pyramid again, gathering up anything of value and copying any crucial information onto the parchments. The four of them departed from the pyramid, leaving Damon and Malkia alone at last.

She bounded into his arms, kissing him hard on the lips. The energy from the magic created a whirlwind within her body and she wanted nothing more than to touch the man she loved. He clutched onto her hips, tugging her into his body and wrapping his arms around her waist. Their tongues explored each other's mouths, slowly venturing to their neck and ears.

"I need you," Malkia moaned in his ear, her fingers caressing his back and arms.

"You don't have to ask twice." He picked her up, laying her on a bed of leaves, kissing her neck and face.

The energy pulsated ferociously around the room as their bodies became one. She rolled him on his back and straddled his body, grinning down at him as she felt waves of euphoria slide over her entire body, erupting like a volcano in the final moments. She moaned with delight, closing her eyes and allowing the powers of the dark magic to enrobe them in a state of ecstasy as she slid to the side and nestled into his warm body.

Staring up at the dark ceiling, she laughed out loud, seeing sparks fly through the air. "Did you see that?" she asked, watching the lightening sparks travel down the walls and converge together into the corner at the far end of the room.

"Yes, I did," he whispered, perching himself up on his elbows. "What's it doing over there?"

Malkia rose from the ground, tugging on her long pants and sliding her arms back into her shirt. "It looks like a passageway," she said, stepping towards it. Halting in her tracks, she waited for Damon to dress himself and pull on his boots.

He grasped her hand and led the way. Approaching the passageway, Malkia could feel the euphoria from the black magic once again. "We created this!" she exclaimed, bouncing slightly on the balls of her feet. "Our union produced enough of the magic to show us the way into this pathway." She pulled Damon close, her lips meeting his once more. She was hungry for more and could see he was as well. "I don't believe what Asha proclaims. Ustarum taught me how to control the darkness. It serves its purpose and once you learn how to use it to increase the light, together you and I will become far more powerful than my father."

Damon's hunger raced across his face and he pushed Malkia up against the wall, kissing her chest and neck. Pressing up against her, she sighed from his physical ache to take her again. She turned around, allowing him to disrobe her once more. As they both allowed the black magic to permeate them, the energy around them thickened and they both moaned as the pleasure raced through their bodies.

Exhausted from another climax, Damon leaned against Malkia, breathing rapidly. "This is the most exhilarating moment I've ever experienced." He kissed her on the back of the neck, heaving away from her, so she could turn around. Leaning over, she yanked her pants back up, grinning from ear to ear. "I love you, Malkia," he affirmed, kissing her again once they were dressed.

She beamed over at him as he gripped her hand, leading her into the passageway that was lit from their united energies. "Let's find out what

Errandor has been hiding from the rest of the star system." He squeezed her hand.

The corridor narrowed, leading down a long stairway. Malkia and Damon stepped lightly down the stairs, not feeling the least bit afraid of what they were going to find. The thrill was becoming more intoxicating as they sank farther below the main level. Eventually, they reached the bottom of the stairs, only to face another long corridor. However, there were dozens of doors along the way and as they entered the first one, Malkia realized this was Errandor's hiding spot for his people.

Beds lined the walls and had been cleaned recently. The room lacked the cobwebs and dust that the first pyramid had contained. Each room either had beds and closets filled with clothing and blankets or they were filled with books, food storage and games. Errandor had ensured they would be able to live in the pyramids in comfort.

After searching each room, they approached another set of stairs, leading upwards. They were more cautious as they climbed the stairs, worried they might run into one of Errandor's people, considering the obvious secrecy surrounding this area of the pyramids.

Once they arrived at the top, Malkia could tell they were in the middle pyramid. Voices could be heard through the stone walls and Malkia recognized Mataya's laugh. The room they were in was filled with plants, but not as luxurious as the ones in the third pyramid. There were cushioned couches running along the walls and lamps around them. At first glance it appeared to be a reading room, but Malkia noticed some of the couches had been shifted across the floor, peaking her curiousity.

"Why do you think they moved all those couches in that specific place?" Malkia asked Damon, pointing at the black scuff marks on the flooring, and then the place where the couches were set.

"Good question." He strolled over to the seating. Grabbing the end of one couch, he yanked it away from the area, setting it down in the middle of the room.

Malkia gripped another couch and did the same thing. A few minutes later, all the couches were removed and they stared at a trap door in the floor. "What is Errandor trying to keep from me?" she asked out loud, stepping towards the door.

Damon grasped onto her arm and held her back. "It could be a trap. Let me go first."

Malkia shook her head. "I can use my protective light." As she said it, her light came sliding out of her body, wrapping tightly around her. She grinned at Damon, before moving towards the door.

Clutching the handle, she yanked it up, a scent of musty air filling the space around them. Peering into the dark abyss, she spotted a set of stairs leading downward, once again. Gliding down the first few steps, she filled the darkness with her light and noticed Damon preparing to follow her.

At the bottom of the stairs, there was another long corridor that stretched on farther then her light would shine. This one was bare, with no doors leading to separate rooms. Following the path down the corridor they were silent. Her heart pounded in her chest and her eyes darted around, anxious for what they were about to find.

Another set of stairs met them at the other end and it led them up into a large chamber. The walls were filled with the same glow as the room Malkia discovered in the first pyramid and she realized that was exactly where they were. Shining her light around the room, she was shocked to see the boxes and crates that filled the room. This is where Errandor had hidden all his secrets.

Damon's eyes widened at the sight. He picked up a scroll from a pile and unrolled it on top of a crate. Malkia shone her light on the markings and noticed it was written in a different language, but recognized that most of the words were similar to what she had used in spells with Ustarum.

Grabbing another scroll, Malkia unfurled it and read the words on the top.

ELVENS UNITE

Underneath the title was a proclamation to the Elvens to rid Theia's Moons of the filth they called humans. It went on to declare war on all warlocks and witches, along with any human with special abilities. Malkia read on in her head, her brows furrowing with anger and disgust.

"They were going to annihilate the human race," Malkia growled, her eyes meeting Damon's. "We were always the target."

"How old do you believe these scrolls to be?" he asked, picking up another one and unrolling it.

"Hundreds of year's old, maybe." Malkia pursed her lips, reading the rest of the scroll. "It appears Elvens used to inhabit most of the moons."

"There must have been a war, many years ago. Us against them." Damon began to read the scroll in his hands. "*Human's superiority has evolved and they are intent on having equal rights to the Elven society.*

It is declared today that Humans are now the enemy of all Elvens."
Damon shook his head and looked at Malkia. "Humans only wanted to be equal to the Elvens. They didn't want us to be above them in any way, so they began a war." He paused, shaking his head, pulling another scroll from the pile and unrolling that one as well. After a minute of reading, he looked at Malkia again. "Humans won the war and banished all Elvens to Thalia. Enyo was their home, first. Eris was the Humans' home. Esaki was filled with dragons, pegasi and primitive humans. We took Enyo away from them."

Malkia sighed, sagging against the crates behind her. "Why did it have to come to that? What is the deal with all the separation and segregation between species?"

"I don't know," Damon grumbled. He continued to read, shaking his head as he finished. "There must be thousands of scrolls here. This is all part of our history and Errandor knew about it."

"I told you we can't trust him." Malkia wiped wisps of her hair out of her face, sauntering away from Damon to examine other areas of the room. Picking up another scroll, she gasped when she saw an outline of Theia, with all her moons. Grabbing another scroll in that pile, she grinned when she saw the moon Artemis, with a map to the pyramids and the significance of what was in those structures. "Damon, we need to take all of these with us. Come see."

He sprinted up to her, grasping the scroll. "Errandor already knew about the importance of the pyramids. What a low life snake."

Malkia nodded, picking up another scroll and unrolling it. It was the moon, Hemera, with a map to the three pyramids and Guarding Statue. She smiled, glancing around the room. "Out of everything we've discovered, these are the most valuable. Do you think we could take it all with us?"

"It would take days to gather it all up and sort it on the ship." Damon ran his hand over his chin, looking up at the ceiling. "If we are going to pack it up, we need to start now. However, I don't think we should take all this information with us to Thalia."

"No, that would be foolish," Malkia agreed, nibbling on her bottom lip. "We could hide it on Esaki."

"Where?" Damon asked, crossing his arms over his chest.

"I don't know yet, but we'll come up with something. For now, we need to pack it up and leave this place. It's only a matter of time before Errandor realizes we've discovered his secrets." She picked up an armful of the scrolls in the pile of maps and strolled over to a doorway at the far end of the room. "I'm taking these first." She pushed on the door and it slid open a few centimeters. Putting all her weight against the door, she pushed harder, only managing to move it another inch. "Will you help me with this door?" she asked Damon, throwing a glance over her shoulder at him.

He stepped around her and pushed on the door with one arm. Malkia grumbled when it swung open the rest of the way, revealing the first room she and Apollo had discovered, filled with the small statues.

Haltia, Asha and Apollo stood in the room, their mouths agape. "Where did you two come from?" Haltia asked, leaning to the side to see behind them, into the hidden room.

"We have discovered a mountain of information," Malkia said, strolling into the room. "We need to take it all with us. We'll bring the ship as close as we can. Then, using our combined powers of levitation,

I believe we can remove all of it before morning. Will you please pack as much as you can into the crates and boxes while Damon retrieves the ship?" Without another word she skipped out of the pyramid and raced for the ship, with Damon hot on her heels.

EIGHTEEN
Voyage to Thallassa

"Have you read these scrolls?" Haltia exclaimed when Malkia returned to the hidden chamber. "They're extraordinary!"

Malkia rushed over to her mom and yanked the scroll from her hand, irritated by the lack of work they had accomplished. "I asked to have these packed. We're on a tight schedule." She glanced around the room at the rest of the group, before meeting her mom's hurt eyes. "I'm sorry. I know they're wonderful, but we need to pack them onto the ship and leave. Errandor hid these for a reason."

"I see," Haltia murmured, stepping away from Malkia.

Mataya, Justin, Alyssa and Bella had arrived before Malkia and Damon had returned and were packing some of the crates near the entrance. After Malkia had snapped at Haltia, her mother began packing, avoiding Malkia's eyes and only speaking quietly to Asha.

It took them the rest of the night to sort through the scrolls and begin carrying them to the ship. Malkia set up a system, using her light and Asha's, Alyssa's, and Bella's levitation ability, where they placed the crates into the light, and it slid through a tunnel and into the ship. Koleton and Skye were on the other end to place the crates in the storage area.

By the time the first sun began to rise, they had nearly emptied the room. Apollo strode up to Malkia, gripping one of the scrolls in his massive hand. "We no longer need to find a way to copy down the map in the room below." He unrolled the scroll and turned it for Malkia to see.

Gasping, she gripped the scroll and ran one of her hands down the map. "They already copied it for us," she exclaimed, smiling up at Apollo. "How did you find this?"

"I ignored your request to not look at the scrolls," he scolded, his lips setting in a straight line. "You were awfully demanding of everyone around here, and although I understand why you insisted we move quickly, it was done in a disrespectful way. Next time you want something done, remember we are your friends, not your slaves." Without another word he turned on his heel and strolled back out of the pyramid and towards the ship.

Malkia stood watching him leave, her hands firmly on the scroll he had given her. Her eyes fell to her feet, as she realized her rude behavior and regretted her sudden outburst. "Where was my head?" she asked herself, looking up to make sure no one else had heard her.

Shaking her head, she rolled the scroll back up and walked to the back of the room to check all corners for anything they might have missed. Once she had examined the entire room, she followed the last of the crates outside and into the ship. Tantiana and Adelina, along with the hatchlings had all boarded and the group was arranging the crates so they could be examined, once they were on their way to Thalassa.

"Did someone grab all our items from the cottage?" Malkia asked, setting her jacket on one of the crates.

"I did," Skye answered, wiping her brow with the back of her arm. "If Errandor didn't know we were leaving before, he does now."

"I need to inform them of our departure, just in case." Malkia turned, saying it over her shoulder as she left the room. Walking down the plank of the ship, she could see the second sun had risen completely.

The suns' light beamed over the three pyramids and Malkia stood for a moment and admired the structures, realizing for the first time how truly ancient they were. Everything she had been searching for, had been hidden away on Enyo and now she would finally be able to find out what her Creators had left behind.

"This view never grows tiresome," a voice said behind Malkia.

Jumping in surprise, she whipped around to face Tarance and a few of his assistants. "You frightened me, Tarance."

"I apologize for sneaking up on you," the older gentleman replied, shuffling towards her and curling his hand around her forearm. "Can we speak in privacy for a moment?"

"Yes, of course." She glanced quickly at the three others they were leaving behind.

Tarance led the way to the other end of the first pyramid, stopping at a stone bench where he sank in exhaustion. "My energy dwindles quickly these days." He patted the seat next to him and Malkia settled down, turning slightly to see his face. "I'm here to say farewell, Malkia, but before I do that I would like to account for my side of the story."

Malkia nodded. "I'm listening." She brought her inside knee up on the bench, twisting more towards Tarance.

"Errandor has a good heart, but he is driven by a desire for human supremacy," Tarance disclosed, his eyes squinting against the light from the rising suns. "He feared that the secrets of the Elvens would be discovered and the news of their dominion over Enyo would be revealed. The Elvens have insisted on their possession of this moon for centuries, knowing the Humans drove them from their home during the ancient wars." He licked his lips, as he wrung his hands together, clearly overcome with emotion. "Errandor does *not* support your father. I want you to be clear on that." His eyes met Malkia's, as he paused in his story.

"Thank you for letting me know," Malkia responded, a wary smile surfacing on her lips.

"What you've discovered in the hidden room of this pyramid was always meant to remain hidden." His lips set in a straight line as he glanced over at the massive structure. "I understand your need for answers, but if the Elvens ever discover that their spells and history have been on Enyo all along, they'll extinguish us."

"I'm taking their secrets away from Enyo. You'll no longer be a target for the Elvens," she whispered.

"I want to believe you," Tarance quavered, scratching his cheek. "Once Errandor realizes you have emptied that room, he will declare you and your friend's enemies to the Enyoans. You will no longer be welcomed on this moon. He's terrified of the Elvens and considers them far more dangerous than the Artemisians."

"Then why did he run to the Elvens for their dark magic, to protect himself from the Artemisians?" Malkia asked, her brows furrowing in confusion.

Tarance sat up straight, clearing his throat, his eyes darting around the trees and vegetation. "He didn't receive the dark magic from the Elvens. The Fallen Angels stole the magic from the Elvens and brought it to him."

"Are the Fallen Angels at war with the Elvens?" Malkia asked, a sense of terror washing over her. She glanced behind her, realizing Tarance could be delaying her for a reason.

"In a way, they are." He placed a trembling hand on her knee, giving her a pointed stare. "Read through those scrolls. Absorb the information and then hide all of it away from Errandor, your father, and the Elvens." His hushed tone became more urgent with each word. "I love Errandor, and I don't want him to perish from his need of power. Please leave now and don't return until the war is over."

"What does Errandor want?" Malkia asked, leaning towards the older man.

"He wants to know how the Creators live forever," Tarance whispered, his eyes flashing around again. "He doesn't want to die and he believes if he can steal all the ancient knowledge of the Elvens and Humans, he will discover our Creators' whereabouts, joining them in their salvation."

"He's foolish." Malkia ran her hands through her hair, dread rising in her throat. "I cannot fight everyone. You must keep him here, while I finish this with my father and the Elvens."

"I'll do my best." Tarance nodded, trembling as he rose from his seat. "Now leave. You won't have much time before he checks the videos of your discovery." He grasped her arm, squeezing it one last time before he scurried back to his people.

Malkia sprinted back to the ship, closing the hatch and pressing the call button to the control room. "Damon, we need to leave now. Is everyone prepared for takeoff?"

"What happened out there?" Damon's voice was hushed over the speaker.

"I'll tell you once we're away from this place. I'm coming up there. Please prepare the rest of the group." She turned away from the speaker and raced for the door, tugging it open and running to the elevator. Moments later she was sprinting into the control room.

"Are we ready?" she asked, her eyes darting around the room.

"Yes," Koleton replied and Damon nodded.

Malkia sank into her seat and yanked the security restraints around her shoulders and hips, snapping in the locks. Gripping the arms of the chair, she watched as the ground gave way and they floated above the pyramids. Moving up and away from the city, Damon steered them through the clouds, turning on the thrusters once they were far enough away. The atmosphere dissipated into the background and the stars welcomed them back to space.

"What did Tarance have to say?" Damon asked, turning to face Malkia.

Malkia closed her eyes for a moment, propping her seat up straight and then opening her eyes to speak with him. "He told me that Errandor is not working with my father or the Elvens, but that he would consider us an enemy to the Enyoans once he discovered what we've stolen from him. He believes we would work with the Elvens to take back Enyo for their own."

"Will he chase us down?" Koleton asked, unstrapping his restraints and leaning forward in his chair.

"Tarance says he will contain Errandor for as long as he can, but I doubt that will be for long. We must take what we can from the scrolls and then hide them somewhere safe." Malkia exhaled loudly, her heart pounding in her chest. "I have made enemies from one moon to the next, and I apologize for that. If I had known the conflict between the humans, Elvens, and Artemisians, I would have stayed as far away from it as possible."

Haltia cleared her throat, shaking her head as her eyes met Malkia's. "You didn't have a choice in this war, and my desire to keep you safe from your Father has created the problem we face today. I should have rescued you years ago and brought you up to speed with our issues, before it became what it is."

Malkia stared at her mother, unsure of how to respond. If she had known her role and had been more prepared for what was to come, she might have made better choices. "What's done is done," she finally responded, looking around at the group. "We only have now, so let's make the most of it and learn as much as we can about the history of the Elvens and Human war."

In silent agreement, each member of the group nodded, before leaving the control room, either separating for personal reasons or following Malkia to the storage area. Damon and Justin remained on the bridge to steer them on to Thallassa. Just over a day journey and they would have another moon to explore.

Following Mataya and Bella down the hallway and into the storage area, she switched on the overhead light and shifted into the farthest area where they had left enough room to stack the crates after they had been searched. Picking up the first scroll, Malkia unrolled it and spread it out on the table, beginning the long search through the mass of information.

"These spells are ancient." Asha sighed, wiping away the dust from one of the scrolls and unrolling in front of Malkia. "I know a small amount of them, but the dozens we've rummaged through are mostly unknown to me or anyone I have associated with over my lifetime." She ran her fingers underneath the words on the scroll, uttering them under her breath as she went. "Chelia, chelia, dastar mes unta les kortum." She paused, her eyes narrowing. Breathing in sharply, her eyes flashed up to meet Malkia's. "It means, "Water, water, destroy all in your path"."

"Why is that important?" Malkia asked, her brows furrowing, as she pressed her back into the wall behind her.

"We're on our way to Thallassa," Asha replied, shaking her head and pointing back at the words on the scroll. "In all my life, I've never come across any incantation that would make water destroy everything that's in its path. I've heard of rain being turned to acid and I've also personally used rain to intensify a seer's sight, but I've never come across a way to lift water up from the soil and use it for destruction."

Malkia shrugged her shoulders, her eyes scanning over the words on the scroll. "It doesn't seem odd to me. After everything I've learned over these past few months, the idea that water could be used against me or anyone for that matter, doesn't surprise me in the least." She pointed at the next section on the scroll. "What does this mean?"

"Cast aside the trees and shrubs, ripping only the souls inside human flesh from their filthy shells." Asha's eyes closed, the palms of her hands covering her face. "This is ugly." She glanced up at Malkia, her eyes red from the dust. "There are several other incantations that speak of the deaths of humans. Although most of the spells are useful, there are many that should be destroyed. No Elven should ever know of their existence."

Malkia pursed her lips, surveying the piles of scrolls still to be read. "Let's begin a pile that will need to be burned."

Asha nodded, rising from her perch on the floor and holding out her hand to assist Malkia off the floor. "I need a break. I'll take the few scrolls that should be destroyed over to the entrance and mark a bin for destruction." Asha's tired eyes ran over Malkia's face, pausing for a moment at the left side of her forehead. Licking her finger, she reached up and wiped at the spot. "You're a mess." A tired smile rose on her lips. "Why don't you return to your quarters and take a break as well?"

"There's so much to learn," Malkia murmured, twisting to stare at the mess in the room. "Thallassa could possess its own mysteries and problems. If I rest now, I might not discover the most important information."

Haltia strolled over to the, curling her hand over Asha's shoulder. "Are you ready to eat and sleep?" she asked Asha. Her eyes wandered to Malkia, a deadpan expression on her face.

"Yes, I am," Asha responded, wrapping her arm around Haltia's waist. "I'm attempting to talk your daughter into taking a break as well."

"Malkia does what she wants," Haltia scoffed, a hint of frustration in her voice.

Malkia bowed her head, her exhaustion seeping deep into her bones, as her hand rested on her pendant. "Mom, I need you," she whispered. "I'm sorry I've been so selfish lately, and I promise to work on being a better person to all of you." Her eyes rose to meet Haltia's. "There's so much I don't know, and a great deal of information I learned from Ustarum and Duncan that I would like to discuss with you. When we have some free time, I would love to spend it with you."

"I would like that," Haltia replied, reaching out and squeezing Malkia's hand. "We can work this out, but for now I would like to fill my belly and then close my eyes for a spell."

"Of course. You two go ahead and take care of your needs. I'm going to finish rummaging through this bin and will follow shortly." Malkia smiled, as the two women turned, leaving her to finish her work.

Unrolling the next scroll, Malkia grinned seeing the moons of Theia illustrated on this parchment, outlining their names below each one. Hemera was the farthest away, nearly on the other side of Theia, while the six others were clustered closer together. This map gave her a clearer idea of each ones position relative to the others. Rolling it back up, she set it to the side, where several other scrolls lay. These, including the scroll that mapped out all the pyramids on each moon, she would take with her when she retired to her room.

Apollo appeared in the doorway, ducking to enter into the room. Smiling widely, he sauntered over to her, refreshed from his own extended nap. "Have you left this room since I departed hours ago?"

he asked, his eyes narrowing.

Malkia shook her head. "I'm leaving soon. How was the food?"

"Not exactly my choice in delicacies, but the bread was soft and warm, which helped with the overabundance of meat," he replied, his eyes scanning over the room. "Only Mataya and Justin have remained with you. Where has the rest of the group escaped to?"

"Most are sleeping or eating." Malkia tugged at the next scroll, unrolling it as she glanced over at her sister. "Mataya and Justin have been working non-stop and will require a break soon. Damon and Koleton returned to the main cabin to go over issues with the ship, and Skye left with Alyssa and Bella not too long ago."

"I'm here to assist. Just point me to where you want me to begin and I'll do the best I can," Apollo replied, his long talon-like fingers tapping on the top of a stack of scrolls.

"Asha marked a bin at the entrance for anything that we would want to destroy. If it contains any kind of incantations that were created to annihilate humans, or anyone for that matter, they need to be burned." Malkia indicated the bin, stifling a yawn with her other hand. "I've made a pile right here that I will take back to my room, but any kind of map, pyramid information or anything that mentions the Creators, I would like to go over extensively, so you're welcome to toss those in the bin behind me. Any spells that sound useful, go ahead and organize another bin for those and the warlocks can rummage through them when they all return."

Mataya and Justin meandered through the maze of scrolls, arriving just as Malkia finished speaking. "We're going on a search for food and a bed," Mataya spoke, her eyes bloodshot and drooping from exhaustion. "How much longer do you think you'll remain down here?"

"I'm leaving," she replied, another yawn overtaking her face. "I'll accompany you both up to the main deck, if you would be so kind to help me take this pile of scrolls to my room."

"We can do that," Justin muttered, reaching down and scooping up half the scrolls in his arms.

Mataya and Malkia gathered up what remained and said their good-byes to Apollo, before departing from the room. The trek back up to Malkia's room took nearly ten minutes, and as they stood in the elevator, Malkia sagged against the wall, her eyes closing and nearly dropped her scrolls on the ground.

Jumping ever so slightly, Malkia awkwardly laughed, tightening her hold on the scrolls and winking at her sister and Justin. "Just keeping us all on our toes."

Their tired laughs filled the small space, just as the doors slid open and allowed them to hurry to the end of the corridor, dumping all the scrolls on Malkia's cushioned sofa.

"I'm going to take a shower, before I eat," Malkia announced, shooing the two out of her room.

"Are you sure?" Mataya asked. "You could eat quickly, take a hot shower and then pass out on your bed."

"I'll be there shortly." She smiled, breathing in deeply, her hand resting on the wall next to her. "Make a plate for me."

Justin tugged Mataya along, giving Malkia the opportunity to wave and shut her door. The water from the shower head cascaded over her body and Malkia stood frozen beneath the stream, enjoying the soothing sensation of the warmth enveloping her body. Moments later, she finished scrubbing the dirt and grim from her hair and body and climbed out of the shower, wrapping a cloth around herself.

Opening the door from the shower room, into her quarters, she grinned wide, seeing a large plate full of food placed on her table with Damon settled onto the chair eating. "This is a pleasant surprise."

Damon shot her a closed mouthed smile, chewing on his food. He rose from his chair, pulling out the other chair and waving for her to sit. Within a few seconds she was digging into her own food and shoving it into her mouth, savoring each bite, as if it was her last.

"We will arrive on Thallassa in about seven hours. I thought I should eat and take a quick nap, before we are in close proximity." Damon paused, taking a quick sip of his juice. "Koleton has control of the ship for the next few hours, and then we will swap."

"Is that wise?" Malkia joked, winking at Damon.

He chuckled, shaking his head. "We could wake to drinks and dancing on the bridge or possibly mermaids swimming down the corridors. You never know with that man, but at least it will be interesting."

"It would be amusing to witness your expression if any of that occurred." Malkia laughed, sighing happily. "I'm just thankful I'm allowed a few hours of alone time with the most handsome fellow in this part of the universe." She ran her toes down his calf, nibbling on her bottom lip.

"Thank the Creators," he shouted before leaning over and kissing her on the forehead. "Finish your meal and come crawl into bed with me." He rose from his seat, tugging his boots off and setting them near the door.

Malkia closed her eyes, enjoying the taste of the food and thinking of the moment she would finally rest her eyes on Esta again. "So close," she whispered to herself. Her eyes opened, as she stabbed her next bite with her fork.

Finishing her food, she returned to the shower room, combing through her hair and hanging up her shower cloth. Naked and exhausted, she sank onto her bed, smiling to herself to see Damon already asleep.

Damon jerked awake, forcing Malkia to spiral out of her dreams. Perching up on her elbows, she looked over at Damon who was now sitting on the edge of the bed. "What's wrong?" she asked, touching his back with her fingertips.

He breathed in sharply, twisting to look at her. "I had another vision." Shaking his head, he rose from the bed, rubbing his hands over his face. "I don't think Thallassa will be a pleasant visit."

Malkia scooted over to the edge of the bed. "What do you mean?"

"We will be attacked before we have the chance to find the pyramids," he divulged, yanking on his pants and then his boots. "The merpeople don't want anything to do with our conflict with the Elvens or your father. This is what they'll tell you, and then we'll be forced to depart from their moon."

"Is there a way to avoid this outcome?" she asked, slipping her legs into some trousers.

"I don't know how it works," Damon replied, smoothing his shirt over his chest and abdomen. "I was able to plan for the moment you channeled me back on Eris, which prepared me and shifted the ending that I envisioned." He paused, giving Malkia a sideways glance. "I guess I never told you about that one."

Malkia laced up her boots, looking up at Damon, her brows furrowing. "You can fill me in later. For now, let's go see Koleton and run through the details of your vision." She swept her hair up on top of her head, twisting it into a messy bun and tucking the wisps behind her ears.

The two of them scooped up their weapons, wrapping the sheath belt around their waists and leaving the room in silence. Within a few minutes, they entered the bridge to see a half-asleep Koleton, sagging against the side of his chair.

Koleton opened one eye and stared at the two of them as he swung his chair around to face them. "You're late. Thanks for returning like you promised. I'm going to go find a place to nap." He rose from his chair, stumbling slightly as his legs grazed the corner.

"I overslept," Damon grumbled, moving towards the controls. "And I had one of my visions, which is what woke me."

Koleton paused in mid-stride, turning to look at Damon and Malkia. "And?" he asked, his eyes widening despite the crimson rivers spreading through them.

"The Thallassians won't be happy with our arrival," Malkia replied, watching Damon speed up the ship. "Why are you increasing our speed?"

"The merman we speak with—" he said, pausing and shaking his head, as he closed his eyes. "I'm forgetting the details, but I believe if we arrive earlier, the merpeople we would have encountered won't be present, and their influence on the other inhabitants will be non-existent." His eyes flashed open, returning his attention to the screens in front of him.

"How long until we arrive?" Koleton asked.

"Two hours," Damon murmured, rubbing his hands together and then glancing over at Koleton. "Why are you still here? It's now or never for some shut eye."

Koleton grumbled under his breath, turning on his heel and stomping from the room. Watching the door shut, Malkia sighed and walked towards Damon, running her fingers down his back when she reached him.

"Do you really believe arriving earlier will do the trick?" she asked, scratching in between his shoulder blades.

Damon rubbed his eyes, turning to face her. "No, I'm not sure this will work. However, the merpeople are the issue, not the Whalians."

Malkia threw her hands up in the air. "Who are the Whalians?"

"They are another ocean species who have the ability to walk on land for short periods of time," Damon said, his brows furrowing. "They reside on Esaki as well. Have you never heard of them?"

"Do they speak an intelligent language?" Malkia asked, a hint of sarcasm surfacing in her tone.

"Yes, they do." He shook his head and sank into the nearest chair. "Unlike the MerPeople, Whalians reside on several of the moons, but the most prevalent of their civilizations call Thallasa their home. The

Whalians are far larger than the MerPeople and they possess two separate fins, similar to legs and feet."

"And there are creatures like this on Esaki?" Malkia pursed her lips, tilting her head in retrospect. "Why have I never heard of them?"

"Why were you never told about anything, aside from the bare minimum?" Damon asked, giving her a pointed stare as he leaned forward in his chair. "Your Esaki parents weren't forthcoming about much."

Malkia nodded, her eyes slanting with irritation. "Tell me more about these different species."

"The merpeople like to keep to themselves. That's why any stories about them are always shaded with uncertainty. It doesn't surprise me that they want to stay out of battles with the Elvens, but I didn't expect a conflict with them." Damon rubbed his hands over the top of his legs, staring blankly out of the window. "From what I've heard, they're a community built around peace and structure. This is why the Whalians remain on that moon. They both desire a place of serenity."

"How do you know so much?" Malkia questioned.

Damon's eyes focused back on Malkia. "Unlike you, my Esaki parent's didn't keep my true identity a secret. I grew up knowing the stories of Esaki and all the moons around it." He breathed in deep, exhaling loudly. "I knew about the conflict, along with all the different species and civilizations that surround Theia. If there's one thing I'm grateful for, it's parents who didn't care to listen to Thane."

"What about your birth parents?" Malkia realized she had never asked Damon about his family on Eris.

He sank back into his chair, his eyes rolling to the ceiling. "My father was murdered by the Artemisians, shortly after we were placed on Esaki. My mother—" He paused, his eyes closing. "She had the spell tightened on me, because she never wanted to see me again and that is why I didn't return to Eris when they brought all the gifted children home. Her heartbreak from the loss of my father made her believe I was the reason for the conflict and therefore my father's death was my fault."

Malkia gasped unsteadily, staring at the man she loved in a new light. "I had no idea." Her head fell into her hands. "I'm so sorry, Damon. What a cruel position to place a child in."

"I didn't know she felt that way until I was older," he replied, his voice soft and quiet. "I blame your father and desire justice to be brought upon him, just as much as you do. Everything he has done has shifted my life to what it is now. I lost my children because of him."

A sharp breath escaped Malkia's lips as her eyes met his. "Damon—" she began, her voice shaking.

His eyes focused on her. "What is it?" he asked, twisting his chair enough to face her directly.

"There is something we need to talk—" she said, pausing when the doors to the bridge slid open and Mataya walked in with Justin in tow.

"Did you have a vision?" Mataya asked Damon, her eyes dancing between him and Malkia.

Damon sat up straight in his chair. "How did you know?"

"I had a horrid dream," Mataya whispered. "And I think it has to do with Thallassa and your vision."

NINETEEN

Elven's Curse

"What do you mean?" Malkia asked, rising from her chair, beads of perspiration forming on her forehead.

Mataya glanced over at Malkia, her eyes devoid of hysteria. "Koleton warned you of Damon's darkness, correct?"

Malkia's eyes darted over to catch Damon rising from his chair, the creases around his eyes deepening, as his expression hardened. "Yes," she spoke hesitantly. "But he has it under control, and besides, we all possess our own shadows in the abyss of our souls."

"I'm not accusing him of anything," Mataya explained, stepping towards Malkia, her eyes focusing on Damon. "You had a vision of the merpeople on Thallassa, right?"

"Yes, I did." He curled his arm around Malkia's shoulders.

"Do you remember what occurs after the merpeople demand our departure?" Mataya asked, a wary smile surfacing on her lips.

Damon choked out an unexpected laugh, covering his mouth with his fist, his eyes widening. "They don't demand our departure. Their weapons fire upon us without warning, and Koleton is struck and killed."

"You didn't tell me that!" Malkia exclaimed, twisting around to view Damon.

He glanced down at her, his brows furrowed and his muscles in his jaw twitching. "I was avoiding that outcome." A growl rose in his throat, as he focused back on Mataya. "This intrusion was unnecessary. My vision ended at the point Koleton was executed and I'm ensuring we don't encounter the merpeople."

"You will fail," Mataya whispered, her eyes straying over to the space outside the window. "And you'll succumb to the darkness, long enough to wreak havoc on the innocent. I highly encourage that we avoid Thallassa for now and return to Esaki."

Malkia's breath came in short, as her eyes darted between Damon and Mataya. "How do you know this, Mataya?"

"I have the sight, Malkia." Mataya's eyes met her sister's. "Just like Damon, I'm able to see what is to come. However, I'm also able to view all outcomes. This event will be a disaster, no matter which path we choose."

"There has to be a way around it." Malkia shook her head, sagging against the wall behind her. "Your visions are not meant to steer us away from our path, but to show you a better way. We need the information on Thallassa, in order to gain the upper hand with my father." Her hands pressed against the wall, looking up through her eyelashes at the trio in the room. "We will find a way to land on Thallassa."

Mataya's smile slipped from her face, as her face reddened. "Malkia!" she exclaimed. "Why are you being thoughtless?"

"We have this under control, Mataya." Malkia gave her sister a frosty glance. "Let's at least take a look at the moon and make a decision once we have scouted out the terrain and oceans. That's all I'm asking."

Mataya began to reply, but her mouth snapped shut, before she turned on her heel and glided effortlessly from the room trailing Justin in her wake. Sighing heavily, Malkia rubbed her eyes with the palms of her hands and stood up straight. Moving over to a nearby chair, she sank into it, scowling at the empty air in front of her.

"Tell me about your vision that you just had, along with the one you had on Eris." Her head tilted backwards, resting against the chair and her eyes looked heavenwards, waiting for Damon's reply.

"It's not a mystery to solve," Damon muttered, the sadness in his tone filling the space around them. "If my calculations are correct, we will avoid the entire episode between the merpeople and ourselves, shifting the outcome significantly."

"If—" Malkia said, pausing as she sat up to stare at him. "*If* your calculations are correct." She shook her head, pinning him with her eyes. "We cannot live by *ifs*. Tell me about your visions." She noticed his continued hesitancy and her eyes narrowed in return. "Please."

Damon shuddered, a line etching deep between his eyes, as he leaned back in his chair and crossed his ankles over one another. "We land on Thallassa and immediately encounter three of their species. The first will be the Whalians, who welcome us to their home and invite us to dine with them in one of their land establishments. However, before we have the chance to speak to them, the Merpeople arrive with another group known as the Jarians." He scratched his nose and then his chin, before focusing back on Malkia. "Neither of these species, desired our intrusion on their moon and the Jarians insisted we depart. Without

260

warning, the Merpeople attack with a weapon that fires from their wrists and strikes Koleton, killing him instantly." His jaw clenched, a haunted look spreading across his eyes.

"And that's all you witnessed in your vision?" Malkia asked, leaning forward in her chair.

A flush crept up his neck, settling over his face. "Yes, I woke the moment I viewed Koleton's dead eyes." His face quivered slightly, as he cast his gaze to the floor.

"Now tell me about the vision on Eris?" Malkia licked her lips and raised her brow.

Damon's eyes rolled upwards and he sniffed in reply, staring at the ceiling. "I knew you would channel me that day. I had a vision that morning, while I was awake, and I almost believed it was an actual event, until it ended and I was still sitting in the same place." His eyes strayed around the room, finally focusing on Malkia's face. "I was furious, and desired to take out all my frustrations and anger the moment you contacted me. However, as the day wore on, and I yearned to be reunited with you, I realized I had a choice. I could scream at you, as I had in my vision and say all the hurtful and awful words that were bouncing around in my head or I could take a breath and calm the storm within." He sat forward in his chair, sighing in between tight lips. "The shift in my thoughts changed me and enabled my anger to dissipate, although slowly, after we spoke."

Malkia rose from her chair and walked over to Damon, sinking down into his lap and curling her body and legs up against him. Kissing his neck, she ran her fingertips through the tips of his hair, as he wrapped his arms around her.

"I don't know why Mataya is concerned with your reaction on Thallassa, but I want you to know, I believe in you," Malkia whispered in his ear. "You and I are a powerhouse together and despite the worry spilling out from this group, we're the future. With our leadership, I believe we can build a better one for all the moons of Theia." She paused, as he tugged her closer to him. Her eyes shifted upwards, casting him a veiled glance. "However, we have to disclose the details of your vision to the group, especially to Koleton. This is his life at stake and he deserves the chance to decide whether we speak to these people or not."

Damon pursed his lips and nodded. "I know. Once he returns, we will speak. I promise to not make any moves without the entire group knowing the consequences." He smiled down at Malkia and kissed her on the forehead. "Thank you for loving all of me."

"You're welcome," Malkia replied, snuggling into his chest, enjoying the sound of his heart beating so close to her.

"It's a stunning view from up here," Haltia breathed, her face glowing from the sight.

Thallassa hung in space. The glistening of its periwinkle oceans was breathtaking, and Malkia stood next to her mother, remembering the last time she had landed on this beautiful moon. It seemed like ages ago, lying paralyzed inside Dario's vessel, agonizing over Misty's dire circumstances and having no idea where they were headed.

Now, she had returned, and knowing their chances were slim in having a peaceful meeting with Thallassa's inhabitants, created a heavy burden on everyone's shoulders. Malkia glanced over at Koleton, who stood near Skye and Damon, speaking in a hushed tone. Tears shone in Skye's eyes and her brows were knitted in sheer terror of what might occur on Thallassa.

"Koleton," Malkia called out, turning to face the trio. "If anything, you can remain on the ship. We need to have a few personnel on the vessel, while we are away."

Skye's eyes lit up, as her eyes flashed between Malkia and Koleton. "Yes. I'll stay here with you." She gripped his arm, her eyes pleading for him to listen.

"In these past few months, have you ever known me to back away from a conflict?" Koleton asked, his hand hovering near Skye's neck, while he twisted her hair in his fingers.

Skye shook her head, nibbling on her bottom lip. She stole a glance at Malkia, as a tear escaped and tumbled down her cheek. "I'm frightened, Koleton. I just found you and now you'll risk your life, just for some information that may prove unnecessary."

Koleton grasped Skye's chin, turning her eyes towards him. "It's bigger than all of us and you know that. What we accomplish on Thallassa could shift our advantage with Thane and Dario. We have to take that chance."

Her lower lip quivered, as she looked away from the group. Skye nodded in defeat, stepping away from Koleton and Damon and sinking into a chair away from everyone else. Malkia patted Koleton's arm as she passed him, her eyes focused on her friend.

Kneeling down in front of Skye, she clasped her hands and kissed them. "You and I have been through so much lately. I haven't been the friend that you need and I apologize for that."

Tears streamed from Skye's eyes and she choked back a sob as she stared down at Malkia. "Why are we doing this, Malkia?"

"Eventually, we will place all our lives in danger." Sorrow tore at Malkia's guts, as she realized there was no escape from their awful future. "You don't have to do this with us. I know you're here because of our friendship and your love for Koleton. However, you're not required to participate. You never were. But I have to halt the brutality and dominion of my Father and I don't have any choice, except to continue on this path and follow the instructions of Ustarum."

"Why?" Skye asked, her voice barely a whisper.

"He's seen things and knows how imperative it is to keep Thane from venturing away from this star system." Her forehead creased, as she fought back a fury deep inside her. "Plus, my dear friend, I won't stop until I've retrieved my daughter."

Skye's eyes dropped to her hands and her bottom lip quivered. "I'm sorry, Malkia. I haven't forgotten what he has stolen from you, but my fear of losing the one man who has brightened my entire life, grips ferociously at my heart and soul." Her eyes met Malkia's, sorrow etched deep within her inky irises. "I love him with all my heart."

"He's a brilliant man who adores you," Malkia replied, her eyes twinkling as she smiled at her friend. "He saved me back on Esaki and he's remained a loyal friend since that moment. It would bring me so much joy to see you two safe and sound, living a serene and calm life." Malkia squeezed Skye's hands tightly. "But first, we can't quit our mission. It's imperative that we make peace with the Thallassians and gather all the information we can on the Elvens and our Creators history. I have put on hold the retrieval of my daughter, in order to finish the necessary steps before we encounter our enemies. We're all making sacrifices, and it's crucial we remain united and supportive of one another."

Skye nodded, her eyes closing to fight away the tears in her eyes. "I understand." She shook Malkia's hands away. "I just need a few moments to myself." Opening her eyes, she gave Malkia a pointed stare. "I'll be fine, but I need some time alone."

Rising from her perch, Malkia pursed her lips, a weight settling over her heart. She turned away from Skye and walked slowly towards Damon, who was busy on the controls, guiding them towards Thallassa. Pausing next to Koleton, she touched his forearm and glanced up at his chiseled, redbearded face. "She needs to be reassured, even if you just remind her that you love her."

He nodded slightly, twisting his head to view Skye. "She's the best thing that has ever happened to me." He looked down at Malkia. "I'm not dying today, so don't you dare go into battle without me." He winked, before turning and sauntering confidently towards Skye.

Smiling to herself, Malkia continued towards Damon, just as Mataya and Justin walked into the room. Inhaling deeply, she halted in her tracks and turned to face her sister.

Mataya walked up to Malkia, leaving Justin to tend to other matters. "I apologize for my frustrations earlier," Mataya said, leaning against the table between them. "I understand it doesn't help our present situation and I'm aware I could be incorrect on what I perceived in my vision."

"Let's just finish what we started, so we can return to Esaki in the next few days." A cautious smile rose on Malkia's face, her pulse racing in her ears, anxious to see her home again.

Mataya remained aloof, but she stayed on the bridge, sitting in a chair next to Justin and Alyssa. Strapping herself in as well, Malkia watched their descent towards the beautiful oceanic moon, feeling awe blossom within as they broke through into the atmosphere and beheld the serenity of the water below them.

Flying over the waves towards a small landmass, Damon eased the vessel into a clearing and settled smoothly upon the soil. Unstrapping herself, Malkia joined the rest of the group, leaving Haltia and Bella to tend to the ship while they searched the area.

The air was cool and crisp, and breathing it in was refreshing to Malkia's lungs and brain. Glancing around at the terrain, she noticed a squat structure next to some tall trees, with moss threading from their branches. It wasn't too far from their ship. Waving at the rest of the group, she began the trek towards it, her hands firmly grasping the ends of her daggers.

As they neared the structure, a large figure emerged from a doorway. At first it appeared as an animal on all four legs, but it rose from the ground, standing tall above them. Breathing deeply, Malkia cautiously continued towards the creature, noticing that its long nose and large eyes covered most of its face. She held back a smile, seeing its body was nearly naked, revealing dark gray skin, with patches of hair spread over it and webbed feet and hands.

Malkia halted a few feet in front of the creature, tilting her head up to look at its face. "Do you speak our language?" she asked, unsure of how to begin this conversation.

Tilting its head as well, a smile spread across its face. "We aren't a primitive civilization, as much as your people believe that we are." It paused, staring over at their vessel. "What are your intentions with our moon?" Its eyes focused back on Malkia.

"We are in search for your pyramids, as they possess a piece to our puzzle to defeat the Elvens. They have began a war with us," Malkia replied, shading her eyes for a better view of the creature.

It nodded, stepping to the side and waving for them to enter the structure. "It appears we have been expecting you." His mouth set in a straight line, turning his eyes towards the ocean. "You won't have much time before others arrive."

Skye stepped forward, linking her arm with Malkia's. "Let's hurry."

Malkia nodded, and together they moved towards the structure, stepping through the doorway and into the muggy entrance, which immediately sloped downwards into a large room filled with several other creatures. The rest of the group followed behind them, with the first creature falling back onto all fours and squirming through the entrance.

Koleton grinned down at the creatures and Malkia followed his gaze, seeing the vast differences in humans versus Whalians. Their skins were a variety of bright colors, with smiles that spread easily across their faces. The group eased down the slope, stopping at the bottom, where they were greeted by a female Whalian.

"Is one of you named Malkia?" she asked, her periwinkle eyes twinkling with delight.

Malkia stepped forward, nodding. "I'm she." A warmth filling her chest as the air around her pulsated with joy.

The female Whalian grinned, revealing sharpened teeth, similar to the wolfmen back on Esaki. Malkia's heart skipped a beat, afraid that this might be a trap, but the Whalian reached down and patted Malkia's shoulder.

"My name is Sarela, and we've been awaiting your arrival." She pointed at the other creatures in the room. "We were contacted a few days ago by a man calling himself Dario and he spoke of a woman Malkia who was his leader's daughter. He asked for us to execute you, if you landed on our moon."

Malkia took a few steps back, encircling the group with her light and snatching her daggers from their sheath. "We will be leaving."

The Whalians only smiled, and Sarela stooped down to their eye level. "We won't be killing anyone today." Her eyes danced with amusement, as she licked her lips and winked at them. "We are a peaceful community and Dario's demand to kill anyone was comical, to say the least." She paused, rising back onto her back feet. "Although, the other people of our moon don't agree with our stance. It is a good thing you happened upon us first."

"Will you please take us to the pyramids?" Koleton asked, stepping forward next to Malkia and Skye.

"Yes, we will. Are you able to swim?" Sarela stared around at the group.

"I can swim," Malkia answered. "And we don't all need to accompany you. Some of our group should remain here."

Sarela nodded. "Whoever will be swimming, must wear a breathing device." She waved at her people. "We have enough for ten of you, but if some will remain here, then we will have plenty to go around. Please decide who will go and who will stay."

Malkia turned to face the group. "Apollo, I need you to remain here and watch over our ship. Who else will stay with Apollo?"

Alyssa stepped forward, her amber skin glistening with the moisture from the humidity. "I'll remain with Apollo." Her eyes flashed between Malkia and Sarela, fear crossing her face. "Malkia, don't trust anyone and watch over Mataya." Alyssa spoke softly into her ear.

"I will," Malkia whispered in return, her mouth twitching and her eyes narrowing at the thought of what they were about to do.

Ignoring the nagging sensation rising in her belly, she turned to face the Whalians. She was handed a small device and instructed to place the two tips in her nostrils and the larger one in her mouth. Following the group of Whalians, towards another slope that led to an underwater passage, she glanced back at her Esaki mother and Apollo, seeing the trepidation in their eyes and knowing that the risk she was taking could be the end of all their lives.

A sick feeling was worming its way up her throat and she placed the breathing device in her mouth to halt its ascent, as she waded into the pool of water, diving in to follow the whalians. Her eyes adjusted to water and she looked around to see Damon and Skye swimming next to her one side and Koleton, Asha, Mataya and Justin on the other. Sarela was just ahead and Malkia followed her through the pillars holding up their structure and out into the open sea.

The ocean life was full of peculiar creatures, and Malkia paused several times to admire the vibrant colors surrounding her. It was a watery dream land and her eyes darted around as she gathered a fist full of sand in her hand, letting it float away, clouding up the water around her. She grinned at the beauty around her and turned to catch up with the rest of the group, noticing that only one whalian had remained with her.

Moments later they emerged from the ocean onto a sandy beach, with the Guarding Statue greeting them at the edge of the water. It was different, like all the others, appearing as half merpeople and half whalian. As they stepped from the water and walked around the statue, Malkia noticed the backside continued on, turning into the tail of a snake.

"This island is secluded from any other land mass," Sarela said, stepping on all fours next to Malkia. "It possesses the three pyramids and our Protector Statue, along with a few streams and vegetation. Other than that, it falls into the ocean on all sides and never is disturbed by any of our storms."

Malkia tilted her head, remembering how the Enyo's pyramids had been untouched by the fires she had set to the land. "They can be destroyed, but it seems it is a difficult task. I have personally witnessed the protection of these structures, and it seems there must be some kind of sorcery keeping them out of harm's way, for the most part."

"No one has ever entered these pyramids," Sarela replied, nodding in agreement as her front feet rose from the ground. "I'm not sure what you will discover, if anything, but we are all aware if you're against this Dario person and his Elven leaders, then we are willing to assist you on this path."

The group moved into the trees, stepping towards one of the

pyramids that nestled against the one side of the ocean. Malkia touched it with her fingertips, a sense of dread once again rising from her stomach. Glancing around, her eyes stared out into the ocean, just as a snake like figure slid out of her view.

"I don't think we're alone," she shouted, her eyes flashing around the ocean, beach and trees.

"What did you see?" One of the other whalians asked, his eyes shining yellow like the suns.

"It had a snake like body and slithered through the ocean and off behind those trees," Malkia replied, pointing over to the ocean and trees where she had seen the figure.

"It's the jarians." Sarela's massive hand rested on Malkia's shoulder. "You must hurry. If they've arrived, the merpeople aren't far behind."

Malkia glanced at the pyramids, anxious to find what treasures they held, but knowing it was too late and not worth any of their lives. "We have to return. It's too late."

"Don't you know how to open the pyramids?" Sarela asked, her eyes narrowing.

Stepping away from the whalian, Malkia looked at her. "No, I don't. Every pyramid is different and the magic surrounding these could take days to break. I was hoping for a better outcome, but what's inside is not worth any of our lives." A sense of terror washed over her face, seeing more of the snake figures emerging from the water. "Let's go, now."

She took hold of Mataya and Skye's arms, dragging them behind her as she sprinted towards the Guarding Statue and the ocean on the other side. A flash of light struck a tree in front of her and she tugged both women in front of her, enclosing them all in her light. As they neared the ocean, they placed their breathing devices back in their mouths, diving into the ocean as soon as they could. Malkia glanced back to see the rest of the group hot on their tails and the whalians right behind them.

Swimming as fast as they could, one of the Whalians pulled ahead, guiding them over the ocean terrain and leading them back to their structure. Just as Malkia emerged from the water, she saw a slim figure swim past Damon and grasp Justin with its teeth.

Yanking the breathing device from her mouth, Malkia screamed, before diving back into the water and striking the snake figure with her light. Another jarian gripped Justin's leg with its teeth, dragging him away from the group and off into the depths of the ocean. Malkia fumbled with her breathing device, shoving it back into her mouth and then surrounded herself with her light, using it to push her after the snakes and Justin.

Moments later, she ran into Justin's lifeless body floating in the darkness of the water. She surrounded him with her light, healing him with her hands as she searched above her for any help from the whalians. Instead she was greeted with the faces of the merpeople and jarians, their teeth shining against her light, angry sneers contorting their faces.

Swimming up and away from them, she finally saw the light from the suns penetrating through the water, lighting her way to the surface. Reaching the top, she kept her light around both of them and floated out of the water. Breathing a sigh of relief, she wrapped her arms tightly around the muscular man and flew towards the Whalian structure and her ship.

Just as she was nearing the landmass, there was a tug on her light and it flickered slightly. Glancing around at the ocean, she noticed a mermaid peeking out from the water, her eyes bright like fire. Seconds later her light vanished and, forgetting she could fly without it, she lost her grip on Justin as they both tumbled towards the water.

Grasping Justin beneath the arms, Malkia steadied them both and flew back up into the air, missing the water and the teeth of the jarians by inches. Landing on the other side of the whalian structure, Malkia laid Justin down on the soil and kneeled at his side, her hands firm against his chest. She allowed her light to flow from her hands and into his body, seeing deep gashes covering his legs and torso.

She heard the footsteps and voices of her group and to help her concentrate she closed her eyes and envisioned the healing of Justin's body. Placing one hand over her heart and the other over Justin's heart, she invited the spirits of Theia to heal his wounds and ward off any evil residing in his body. "Oh Spirit of Theia, please send your mending light into this body, healing all that is injured from the inside out," she whispered, relaxing her body to enable to entry of the spirits. "Oh Spirit of Theia, please send your mending light into this body, healing all that is injured from the inside out."

Over and over, she mumbled these words, feeling the light twist into Justin and failing to completely heal him. Malkia opened her eyes and glanced down at his legs, seeing that his wounds had been repaired. However, his breath was shallow and she sensed that his life hung in a delicate balance

"What's wrong with him?" Malkia asked, staring up at Sarela. "Why is his body not fully healing?"

Sarela shook her head, falling down on all fours and sniffing around Justin's body. "It might be you, not him," she replied, her eyes boring into Malkia. "Did you encounter any of the merpeople out in the ocean?"

"Yes, I did. They surrounded Justin and me, down in the darkness of the water, and then another one seemed to attack my light when we were flying back to shore." Malkia rubbed her hands on her thighs, her voice shaking, as an intense fear twisted inside her gut. "My light disappeared and I nearly lost Justin. The mermaid had an evil in her eyes I've never encountered before." She stared back at Sarela, her eyes widening. "Who was she?"

"That was their version of a sorcerer, except the darkness she has inside her was a gift from the Elvens." Sarela backed away from Malkia, a sadness rising in her eyes. "She was taken away at a young age and kept prisoner in a glass cage, with tubes snaking from her body. For an entire year, she was locked away in her mind, forced to read the minds of others and reveal their secrets to the Elvens."

"Misty," Malkia whispered, a haunted expression spreading across her face as the color in her cheeks drained to a ghost white. She rose from her perch, turning to face her friends. "Apollo and Koleton, return Justin to the ship and have Bella, Asha, and Alyssa heal him with their magic." Returning her attention to Sarela, she strode towards her, an ache rising in her chest. "What happens to the mind reading children who are entrapped in these prisons? Do they all become like this mermaid?"

"Possibly." Sarela tilted her head, a deep line etching between her wide eyes. "Why do you ask?"

"Dario kidnapped a child named Misty to use in their wars against the Artemisians. She wasn't imprisoned for more than a few weeks, but I know her experience changed her." Tears gathered in her eyes and Malkia brushed them away, terror gripping her heart. "How do I prevent her from falling into the same darkness?"

"I don't think you can," Sarela muttered, her expression sobering. "This child will most likely succumb to the same fate, no matter what you do to prevent it. The Elven magic is inescapable, as far as I know, and if Dario used this on your friend, he knew there was no coming back from it."

Malkia's heart shattered, thinking of Misty and Rory as despair overcame her mind. "I don't know how to find her," she cried, allowing the tears to finally tumble down her cheeks. "She's just a child." Malkia covered her mouth, screaming as loud as she could. "I will destroy Dario for this." She bit her lip, forcing the sobs back down her throat.

Sarela squatted down on her knees, placing her massive webbed hands on Malkia's shoulders, twisting her to look at her. "You're not in charge of curing everyone's ills. Please remember this piece of advice, as it will save your heart in the future. The only person's path that you must be aware of, is your own. Do not allow the agony and sorrow of others to force your path. This will only create a hate in your soul, enabling that Thalian darkness inside of you to surface with a vengeance."

Guilt flooded over Malkia, as she stared into the depths of Sarela's periwinkle irises. "How did you know?"

"We are an intelligent species." A grin spread across Sarela's face. "From the moment I met you, I knew you had taken on the darkness." Sarela leaned in closer to Malkia, her eyes twinkling once again. "But you are the Chosen Heir and have the power to control the murkiness swirling deep within you." She winked, rising back off the ground. "Good luck, my new friend, and may Theia's light shine favorably upon you."

TWENTY
Damon's Darkness

Malkia stepped heavily onto the platform, trudging into the vessel and towards the bridge. Checking on the dragons, she noticed Tantiana lying with her back to the door and realized she hadn't spoken to her dragon in days.

I'm sorry, Tantiana, she thought, gliding into the room. *I've been consumed by my problems and forgot to check on your well-being.*

Tantiana turned to face Malkia, her eyes narrowed. *I should've been out there with you. Why did you leave me in here?*

We had too many worries already. I didn't want anything to happen to you. Malkia replied, chewing on her bottom lip and knowing she didn't have the right to choose Tantiana's battles.

Exactly. Tantiana huffed in her mind, responding to Malkia's thoughts that weren't intended for her. *I could've helped today and possibly prevented the outcome. There was no reason to swim to those pyramids, when I could have flown you all there.*

You're right. Malkia sank to the floor, the weight of the moons falling on her shoulders, as her soul crumbled inside her. *I was wrong to keep you from this expedition. The mistakes I continue to make are only hurting this group, not uniting it.*

I forgive you, but I don't want to talk any more, Tantiana replied. *Please leave me for now.*

Malkia's eyes flashed to her dragon, who had turned away from her. A sob rose in her throat, as she drew herself to her feet and walked towards the door. Tugging it open, she moved into the corridor, nearly colliding with Koleton.

"Damon has left the ship," he grumbled, pushing past Malkia. "He said something about destroying the creatures who attacked Justin and then barged off."

"Why didn't you stop him when he said those things?" Malkia asked, racing behind him, as they made their way back off the ship.

"I wasn't there and all the magical queens on this vessel were working on healing Justin." Koleton's expression hardened, and his eyes narrowed. "And why am I in charge of your partner? He's an adult and should have the capability to control his anger."

"Like you're doing that so well," Malkia muttered, nearly running into him when he froze in place.

"Are you serious, Malkia?" His face flushed crimson, turning to face her. "How dare you ridicule me, after everything I've given up to protect you and this group? Both you and Damon are acting like spoiled children and I'm tired of cleaning up your messes." He threw his daggers to ground and stomped back into the ship. "You're on your own."

Malkia's jaw clenched, watching his receding back. Bending over, she scooped up his daggers, sticking them in her boots and turning back towards the whalian structure, trudging regretfully to find Damon. Pausing in the tall weeds, she focused on channeling him, only to receive darkness and a heavy wall.

Groaning loudly, she continued walking towards the ocean, finally bouncing into the air for a better view. Scanning the area, she noticed a cluster of merpeople and maybe jarians out into the open sea, but had no idea how Damon could venture that far out. She searched around again, finally spotting him standing on the other side of the whalian structure, just inside the shadows of the trees.

Flying over the building, she could see the jarians were swimming towards him as well, followed by a few hundred merpeople. "Good thing Koleton remained on the ship," Malkia said to herself.

Moments later she settled down onto the beach, her eyes focusing on Damon and noticing for the first time his clenched fists and closed eyes. He was mumbling under his breath and red lightening was sparking across his skin. Malkia raced to his side, grasping his arm.

Pain shot numbly through her body, shaking her limbs and paralyzing her. Quieting her quivering body, she noticed Damon opening his eyes. A haze settled across them, as if he was no longer inside the shell. He shook her hands free of his arm and she collapsed into a pile as he walked towards the ocean to greet the Thallassian army.

"Damon. Stop." Malkia managed to squeak out, her voice shaking and stammering over both words.

He glanced back at her and what she saw filled her with horror. His eyes glistened yellow, while the color in his face had drained completely, leaving him pale as a ghost. Tears swam in her eyes, struggling to regain control of her body, restrained as if by a thousand hands.

He's using his mind to manipulate mine. The thought bounced through her head, echoing against her ears, as her stomach lurched in response. *How did he break through my barrier?*

Focusing on the wall, like Ustarum had taught her, her head ached and her temples throbbed. She was failing to find her barrier and the weakness was spreading throughout her body. Sagging back onto the sand, she pressed against Damon's magic, intent on breaking his hold on her, but only hearing the crash of the waves striking the rocky shore.

The touch of someone's hand brought her back to the surface of her mind and she snapped her eyes open to see Sarela curling her hands around her wrists. Dragging her back into the thick of the trees, Malkia began to feel the pressure on her chest decrease. Sitting up against a tree, she caught her breath, staring through the vegetation at Damon's legs.

"He's lost his mind." Malkia's eyes met Sarela's, sweeping her hair out of her way. "I knew his powers were increasing in strength, but I truly believed he had them under control. This is all my fault."

"Did you not listen to my advice earlier?" Sarela asked, her large lips setting in a firm line.

Malkia nodded, hiding her face in her hands. "I did," she mumbled. Breathing in deeply a few times, she looked up again, rising from the ground and walking past Sarela. "I have to stop his attack."

Sarela grasped her shoulder, her brows drawing together. "How can I assist?"

"If I fail, find a way to bring me out of his spell again," Malkia requested, patting Sarela's hand and then continuing towards Damon.

The jarians had surrounded Damon, but were frozen in place, as he waited for the merpeople to arrive. His hands remained balled into fists, but now his face was tilted towards the sky and a red light was ebbing and flowing from his body. Malkia gulped, swallowing the terror rising in her throat, as she rose from the ground and glided towards the man she adored with all her heart.

As she advanced on his position, the pressure on her chest returned, making her gasp for air and halt her progress. Inhaling, she closed her eyes and created the barrier between herself and Damon, holding it strong against his powers. When she opened her eyes, Damon was a few feet away, his yellow eyes boring holes into her soul.

Malkia's heart jumped into her throat, seeing the hatred boiling from his eyes and had to remind herself that the darkness had a hold of his powers, along with his soul.

"Damon, fight the darkness, please!" she begged, raising her hands ever so slightly, pointing her palms towards him. "We are stronger together, remember? Don't allow the evil creatures of this moon control the outcome of your life."

Recognition flashed across his eyes. But as quickly as it was there, it disappeared again, followed by a pain traveling from the back of her neck and spreading throughout her head. "Please, Damon!" she screamed. "Please don't try to push past my barrier."

The agony continued to swell, throbbing against her temples and pulsating behind her eyes. He turned to face the merpeople, who had finally arrived, paralyzing them in place, just as he had done with the jarians.

"Why are you doing this?" Malkia cried, pushing against his powers, her eyes squeezing shut. "Do you even remember why you want to destroy all these creatures?"

Damon paused, turning back around to face Malkia. His energy had been holding him above the water and as he blinked a few times, he began to sink into the water. Looking down below him, the yellow swirled back into his irises and he rose above the creatures once again, forgetting Malkia's presence.

"I'm carrying your child!" Malkia shouted, tears welling up in her eyes. "Stop this madness and return to the ship with me. Please." She wiped away the tears that had begun rolling down her face, the heat of her fear rising in her chest and spreading like fire to her face.

His face relaxed and he fell towards the water, just as Malkia swept over to him and wrapped her arms around his waist, carrying him away from the vile creatures he was about to terminate. She glanced back at the trees and nodded at Sarela, before landing in front of the ship and helping Damon up the ramp, closing it behind her.

She set Damon on a nearby chair, running her hands through her hair, and walking in circles, trying to calm her nerves. Glancing over at him, she was grateful to see his sparkling and mysterious, fog gray eyes staring back at her, despite the confusion spreading across his face.

Perching on her knees in front of him, she curled her hands around his arms. "We need to leave Thallassa. Are you able to make it to our room?"

He nodded, a sloppy smile rising on his lips. "I feel as if we just drank a barrel of liquor. Why can't I remember all the fun we had?"

"You will, after you rest," Malkia replied, tugging him off the chair and pulling his arm over her shoulders. "Let's go big guy."

"I was out of line," Malkia said, staring up at Koleton, who was leaning against the wall behind him, a look of disdain covering his face. "I have no excuse for the way I treated you and I apologize for messing up, once again." She fidgeted with the ends of his daggers, holding them out for him to take.

He grasped their handles and shoved them into their sheaths, snapping down the clasp. "This entire mission has been one shit storm after another," Koleton grumbled, avoiding her gaze. "I'm cranky and tired and I would love to have more than one hour of sleep sometime in the near future. However, your fearless lover has gone and poofed himself into a stupor—" His hands flailed around his body, demonstrating Damon's careless actions. "So now I—" He paused, pursing his lips and flaring his nostrils. "Little old me, has to be in charge once again."

Malkia touched him lightly on the forearm. "Go to bed, Koleton."

He glowered down at her. "I can't, Madam Queen. Someone has to fly us off this forsaken moon." Raising one of his brows, his arms waved over to the controls of the ship.

Malkia couldn't help but grin, his drunken hand movements reminding her of Damon's current state. "We will manage." She nodded at Skye and Asha, who were waiting a few feet away to help him to bed. "This Madam Queen will find a way to take us away from this awful place."

Skye wrapped her arm around Koleton's waist, pulling him away from the wall, and Asha placed his other arm around her shoulders, balancing him against her body. "Don't crash the ship," Koleton slurred, the side of his face leaning against the top of Skye's head.

Watching them leave, Malkia turned to face the controls and smiled at Apollo, who was already switching everything on to begin their takeoff. "He's an entertaining man," Apollo said, throwing Malkia a sideways glance.

"He definitely knows how to make an exit." Malkia joined Apollo at the controls, watching him maneuver the foreign buttons and touch screens. "How long until we can leave?"

"Just a few minutes," Apollo replied. "Enough time for them to put Koleton in his bed. We will be out of the Thallassian atmosphere soon."

Malkia stepped back to her chair, sinking gratefully on to its cushioned seat. Pulling the restraints around her body, she allowed her mind to wander for the first time in days. *I'm so close. A stop to Esaki and then I will finally be able to go find my daughter.*

Moments later, she watched the oceans disappear from her view and the beauty of space greet her once again. Apollo set the autopilot for Esaki, sitting in the chair next to her and turning to face her. "We haven't had much time to speak," he said, twisting one of his copper bracelets on his wrist. "Do you remember all that Ustarum taught you?"

She nodded, straightening up in her chair and undoing the restraints. "I have my moments, unfortunately in mid-action, where I forget his teachings. But for the most part I have become stronger and better at controlling all my gifts." She paused, running her hands through her hair, combing the knots from it. "Seeing Damon struggle to fight the darkness, terrifies me. Ustarum claimed that we have the ability to control the dark magic within us, so I believed Damon wouldn't have any issues, either." She hung her head, shame washing over her as she gripped the arms of her chair. "We should've been more careful on Enyo."

"Are you taking responsibility for a grown man's choices?" Apollo asked, cocking his head to the side. "Are you really that selfish?"

Malkia's eyes rolled upwards, staring at her friend through her eyelashes. "Maybe I am," she muttered. "I've led us down this path, all to save my daughter and execute the man who created me. Maybe I am selfish." She rose from her chair, toying with a lock of her hair. "I need to return to the storage area and finish rummaging through those scrolls." She changed the subject, brushing her hands together while avoiding Apollo's eyes. "Did you happen to find anything of value down there?"

"Yes. I placed them in a bin, near your position when I saw you down there last." He turned to check on the ship, the lines around his eyes deepening in frustration. "I shouldn't have called you selfish," he called out. "Your need to absorb everyone else's problems and choices, is agonizing to witness. I hope, for all our sakes, in the future you'll allow each of us to take accountability for our own mistakes."

A weary smile surfaced on her lips as she turned to leave, remembering Sarela's advice, and knowing they were both speaking the truth. Exhausted from the day's events and knowing by the time she organized herself in the storage room, she would only want to crawl into bed, she headed for her room. Crawling into bed next to Damon, she squirmed into his arms, wrapping herself up in his warmth.

TWENTY-ONE
Losing Her Again

"Are you messing with me?" Koleton choked through his tears, laughing at the faces around him. "I called you Madam Queen?"

"Do you seriously not remember the events on the bridge?" Malkia asked, her eyes dancing with amusement, as she reached for her drink in front of her.

Koleton shook his head. "After I left you outside the ship, I waited on the bridge for you two to return. There was a point, somewhere during that time, where my life became a fuzzy memory." He pointed at Skye, who was sitting next to him. "I do remember my sweet lady coming to visit me and lecturing me on going to bed." He looked over at Skye, winking and squeezing her leg enough to make her burst out with laughter.

"Stop it, Koleton." Skye grinned, pushing his hand away. "It's a good thing you enjoy my lectures or we would be sitting at the bottom of the ocean, cursing you for your impaired driving."

"Oh, really?" Koleton asked, turning to face Skye and grabbing her around the waist, tickling her sides with the tips of his fingers. "Are you sure you want to stick with that story?"

Skye screamed with laughter, making everyone else at the table smile and laugh as well. Malkia stole a glance towards the door, hoping Damon would join them soon. He hadn't wanted to speak when they woke, leaving as quickly as he could to relieve Apollo from the bridge.

"When will we arrive to Esaki?" Haltia's voice interrupted Malkia's thoughts.

Malkia focused back on the group, smiling over at her mother. "I believe we will arrive within a few hours." She sighed, leaning back in her chair. "I cannot wait to see Parowan and all our old friends." She glanced around the room, noticing Mataya had remained aloof throughout the conversation. "Are you excited to return, Mataya?"

Her sister's eyes turned to face her, shooting her an icy glare. "Have any of you asked about Justin since we returned to the ship? Do any of you care about him?"

"Of course we do," Alyssa replied, curling her hand over Mataya's. "What's wrong? Justin is completely healed. Why are you so upset?"

"Because—" She paused, pushing away from the table and rising from her chair. "If my sister had just listened to me in the first place, we wouldn't have needed to heal Justin at all." She turned on her heel, stomping from the room.

Silence spread across the room and Malkia sighed as she heaved herself off her chair. "She's right. I have my own sins to amend." She shot a sad smile around to the group and left without another word, following her sister down the corridor. "Mataya wait," she called out.

Mataya turned to face Malkia, her eyes narrowed to crinkled slits and a scowl rose in her expression. "You should've listened to me. I know you view me as the naïve younger sister, who's frightened to leave the town she grew up in. But I'm no longer that person and I would appreciate it if everyone would stop treating me that way. Especially you." She gestured with her thumb, pointing towards her room at the end of the hall. "I'm going to check on my man and see if he's ready to have his breakfast. If you're done speaking with me, I'll take my leave."

Malkia nodded, watching as her sister stomped away from her. Exhaling in a huff, she licked her lips and turned towards the bridge, anxious to have a conversation with Damon.

Moments later the door to the bridge slid open and Malkia stepped over the threshold, seeing Damon standing against the window, staring mindlessly out into space. Malkia tiptoed towards him, not wanting to disturb his thoughts, but not wanting to leave either. She watched him in silence, wondering if he remembered what she had said back on Thallassa.

"Are you going to say anything?" Damon asked, after a few minutes, twisting slightly so he could see her.

"Are we close to Esaki?" Malkia asked, smiling at him and hoping he knew she didn't want any conflict with him.

He turned to face her, his expression hardening. "That's it? You have nothing else to say to me?"

Her smile melted from her face, and she tasted the bitterness in her mouth, as her anxious heart fluttered. "I'm not here to argue," she said, rising from her chair and regretting her decision to come see him. "Please just spit out what you want to hear from me."

He tapped his fingers against the wall, his eyes boring into her and his mouth setting into a straight line. "I had absolutely no control on Thallassa. You told me I would have the ability to keep the darkness under my thumb. Why did it explode from me like a volcano, spewing a blackness from my soul and strangling anything good from my heart?"

"I don't know," Malkia croaked, a wave of nausea rushing through her body. "I was told the dark magic could be contained and controlled. I never imagined you would have the difficulty that I witnessed yesterday."

He stormed towards her, grasping her by the wrists and yanking her towards him. "You never imagined I would have the difficulty you witnessed?" he screamed at her, fury pouring from his eyes. "I was a prisoner behind the walls of that darkness, unable to control my own body or actions. You have no idea what difficult position you've placed me in." He twisted away from her, storming from the room, leaving her to chew on his pain and agony.

Standing still, Malkia allowed the quiet to seep into her bones and numb her throbbing mind. She closed her eyes, wishing for time to wind back to the moment she heard Damon was approaching her Esaki town. "Oh, how I would do things differently," she whispered out loud, a tear tumbling down to her chin.

Wiping the fluid from her face, she opened her eyes to face the space outside the ship. It was calm out in the blackness, and Theia's light shone brightly against it, reassuring her heart. Sinking to the floor in front of the window, she stared across the vast darkness, yearning for an opportunity to end the conflict right away. She leaned her forehead against the glass, allowing her tears to fall without restraint, as the sobs rose continuously one after another, rocking her body with their force.

As her sobs receded and she began wiping her nose and face, a motion outside the ship caught her eye. She sat up straight and searched the space around them, searching for whatever had moved, a dread rising in her chest. Scooting away from the window, she pressed the call button, her eyes never straying from the darkness.

"I need someone on the bridge, immediately," she announced into the speaker, squinting her eyes as they darted around space. "And how do I ensure our shields are secure?"

Moments later she heard thundering footsteps racing down the corridor, followed by both doors opening. Koleton, Skye, Haltia and Mataya came running in, all focusing on Malkia.

"What did you see?" Koleton asked, sprinting to the control area.

"I don't know," she replied, following him to watch what he did. "Show me where the shields security is on the panel."

Koleton pointed to a large screen, where there were rows of green lights stacked on each other. "This shows our shields are strong and holding. If any of the bars turn yellow, that indicates a weakness, but if they start turning red that means the shields are failing." He pointed to the screen next to it. "This will show where the shields are struggling, if there are any issues. Right now, we are safe, but if we took on too much fire power, we could become vulnerable, slowly or quickly, depending on the strength of the weapons." He stood up straight and turned towards her, his fists squeezing together. "Now, what did you see?"

"It could be nothing," Malkia said, walking towards the window. "I was watching the darkness, when I noticed movement in that direction." She pointed towards the left and slightly down. "I've been searching to find the disturbance, but I haven't caught the movement since that moment. It could be an asteroid for all I know, but I wanted to know what needed to be done, in case it was a threat."

Skye scowled at Malkia, as Koleton curled his arms around her shoulders and led her away and out of the room. Mataya stood in quiet retrospect, eyeing Malkia with icy contempt, before turning on her heel and leaving the room as well.

"They all hate me," Malkia mumbled, looking at her mother. "I've done nothing, but anger the people closest to me and I'm struggling to fix what I've broken." She pressed her hands to her cheeks, controlling her unwanted tears. "Damon despises me for allowing him to absorb the dark magic and seeing what it can turn him into, I don't blame him." Sinking into the nearest chair, she pulled her knees into her body, hiding her face against them. "And the rest of the group has various reasons to be disgusted with me. Why can I not please anyone in this group?" she muttered, behind her barrier.

Malkia heard her mother exhale and moments later her soft hand touched her forearm. "Let's talk in private for a moment. This is our chance, before chaos controls our world once again," Haltia spoke, running her hands through Malkia's long hair.

Easing her knees away from her, she tilted her head to see her mother, her body feeling leaden with grief. "It seems there is so much to say to one another, but where do we begin?" she asked, tucking her hair behind her ears.

"Let's start with your sister, Mataya." Haltia replied, gracefully sinking in the chair next to Malkia. "You two are close, am I correct?"

"Yes," Malkia affirmed, sitting up straight in her seat and gripping the arms of the chair.

"Do you give her the credit she desires or do you see her as someone you are required to protect and in some sense, mother?" Haltia raised an eyebrow, a cautious smile surfacing on her lips.

Malkia eyes wandered heavenward, thinking of her sister and how much she had matured. "When I saw her magical abilities, I felt inferior to her," she confessed, her heart thumping in her chest as she chewed on her bottom lip. "It's not that I want to mother her, although I do desire her safety, but I possess an insecurity of being small compared to my younger sister."

Haltia's smile spread across her face. "You're not small, Malkia. It's actually refreshing to know you're still human." Haltia held up her hand when Malkia started to object. "Hold on and allow me to explain." She paused, the lines around her eyes deepening, as she smiled again.

Malkia nodded and leaned back against her chair, waiting for her mother to continue.

"After years of being able to channel you while you slept, my heart shattered when your father discovered my treachery and barred my ability to see you without his knowing." Tears festered in Haltia's eyes and for the first time Malkia recognized the woman who had raised her to the age of five. "I adore you with all my soul, my dear child and I believed if I kept you on Esaki, your father would focus on other matters and leave you at peace. However, his revenge ran deep and his desire to control you never faltered. In fact, over the years, it only grew in strength, controlling his life and guiding his every move."

Groaning, Malkia leaned forward in her chair, grasping onto her hair and screaming at the floor. Rocking, as the tears once again tumbled from her eyes, she stared up at her mother. "I don't want to hear of my father's hatred for me, any longer!" she cried, her throat thickening with sobs. "Please, stop." She sat back in her chair, her vision blurred from the tears, as despair ripped through her soul. "I can't, mother. I understand his loathing towards me, but I don't want to hear of it ever again, as it creates an agony deep inside me that I cannot control. I want nothing more than to forget my own father's hatred of me, so please stop reminding me."

"I had no idea it pained you this deeply," Haltia whispered, rising from her chair and embracing Malkia. "We are experiencing a great disconnect within our group." She pulled Malkia's chin up, wiping the tears from her face. "I can see that now. I wanted you to know my story and I was mistaken that you had no feelings for your father. I was incorrect and I apologize." She kissed Malkia's forehead. "Let's start over."

Malkia watched as her mother returned to her seat, taking in some deep breaths, and gaining control of her emotions. The embarrassment of the situation coiled around her. "I'm sorry for my outburst," she mumbled, hiding her face behind her hands. "Thank you for not judging me harshly."

"I love you, Malkia," Haltia replied. "Do you want to know about your biological grandparents and the mysterious blue planet?"

"Yes!" Malkia exclaimed, her eyes opening wide, as she wiped the remnants of the tears from her face. "This is what I want to talk about. Where do we really come from?"

"What do you know already?" Haltia asked, crossing her leg over her knee.

Malkia's breath came in short, as a smile rose across her face. "I've been to the blue planet," she whispered, her green eyes twinkling as she recalled the memory.

"How?" Haltia asked, her eyes widening and her brows furrowing.

"The Angels took me there to speak and show me my true heritage," Malkia replied, her hopes rekindled. "I saw your mother and father."

Haltia's head snapped back as she shook it in denial. "That's not possible. My mother was executed, along with my biological father."

"That's what your father wanted you to believe, but they discovered the way to the blue planet and have been living there in safety ever since." Malkia tilted her head with an afterthought. "At least that is how I perceived it."

Haltia closed her eyes, relaxing the muscles in her face, before opening her eyes again and focusing on Malkia. "I thought my mother was dead. This news is not what I expected to find out, and as much as I desire to see her again, we need to focus on what we definitely know." She leaned forward in her chair, her elbow resting on her knee, as she placed her chin in her hand. "The blue planet exists, as you've been shown, and your father has been instructed to discover its whereabouts and a route to it. The Elvens are bound and determined to find the Creators of humans and annihilate them all."

"This entire conflict is grotesque and petty," Malkia said, her annoyance flaring. "The Elvens have used a human to search for the Creators of the Humans, in order to eliminate the humans. All the while, they have created more wars and division between families and species than ever before known in ours or their history." She scooted off her chair, rising and strolling back to the window. "I've grown weary of this disgusting behavior."

"Let me reassure you, this will not end until someone forces its ending." Haltia joined Malkia at the window. "I've seen what your father is capable of creating and he doesn't struggle to enlist followers and warriors for his cause. His entire agenda is to discard our star system of all creatures that aren't human and he'll use everyone, including his own flesh and blood, to ensure its success.

Malkia shot her mother a sideways glance, her lips setting in a tight line, and releasing a loud sigh of frustration.

Think about it for a moment." Haltia's hand curled over Malkia's shoulder. "He convinced the Artemisians of a conflict that never existed, then used his own daughter's life to force a battle between humans and Artemisians. Furthermore, he worked with the Enyoans to destroy the Artemis moon, using that same daughter by enlisting our own people to manipulate your path." She paused, her forehead creasing and her grip on Malkia's shoulder tightening. "All the while, he's been forging alliances with the pixies and Elvens, pretending to assist them in their mission to annihilate the humans. Do you see what he has created in our lives?"

Malkia turned to face her mother, shaking her head, as she finally was able to put the pieces of the puzzle together. "He's a master manipulator." Her eyes widened as her breath caught in her throat. "Damon is just like him."

Haltia nodded, her eyes casting down to the ground. "Your father would destroy everyone if you and Damon created a child with one another. He knows how powerful that child would be and if he knew you two had joined together, he would move heaven and Theia to possess any child you two had together."

Malkia covered her mouth, swallowing the terror that was rising in her chest. "He knows of Damon's abilities?"

"Of course, he does," Haltia responded, threading her hand through Malkia's hair. "He was the one who manipulated me into believing we had no other choice but to infuse the children with these various powers, in order to protect them from the Artemisians. Damon, you, Rory, Palma and any children you created, were all part of his plan."

Malkia's expression hardened and for the first time since her true reason for existing had been revealed, she knew there was no turning back and despite all the hurt and broken feelings among her friends, they had to forge on. Even if it meant they would all perish.

"You said earlier, you wondered if I was human any longer," Malkia spoke, her eyes searching her mother's face. "Why?"

"Dark magic can change a person, especially a woman. You spoke of your friend, Misty, and the awful circumstance she was placed in." Haltia shivered, her eyes closing for a moment. "Chances are, she won't be able to resist her journey down into the darkness. It will consume her entire soul."

"I can't change what has been done." Malkia stepped back, walking towards the doors. "I need to speak with—."

A red light began flashing throughout the room, as the sound of an alarm ripped through the air, making Malkia jump and cover her ears. Her light naturally flowed outside of her, protecting herself from the sound, just as a flash of light ripped a hole through the window, tearing a startled Haltia out into the quiet of space.

"No!" Malkia screamed, sprinting towards the window.

An emergency wall shot up from the floor, halting Malkia's rescue, and securing what little air was left in the room. She closed her eyes, tightening her light around her body and stepped through the wall and into the silence on the other side. Glancing around, she searched for her mother, but only saw another vessel firing its weapons towards her ship. She moved in between the ship and the blast and felt the impact judder through her body as the electricity snapped and fizzled around her, nearly snuffing out her light entirely.

What happened to the security of the shields? She thought, reaching out to Tantiana and channeling Mataya.

Her sister's image appeared in front of her, where she was racing in midstride towards the bridge. "Our shields, Mataya. Someone has to repair our shields. I'll take care of the filth who has attacked us."

She dropped the channel, without hearing Mataya's response, flying towards the ship and recognizing the Elven warrior vessel. "Are you following us?" she asked out loud, allowing her light to burst from her hands, aiming at the heart of the smaller ship.

It crumbled from the strike, floating away from her, as the Elven's bodies froze instantly after they were exposed to the merciless vacuum of space. Malkia's eyes darted around, searching for her mother and finding her far off in the distance, an icy sculpture against the light of Theia. Racing towards her, she pulled her mother into her light, shivering from the chill.

Moments later she stepped back into the ship, laying her nearly defrosted mother on the ground in front of her. Placing her hand over Haltia's chest, she pled with her mother to regain consciousness, muttering her healing incantation under her breath. Several hands settled around her and she looked up to see a terrified Asha and wide-eyed Bella using their magic to help heal her mother.

It seemed like an eternity as the scene before her tumbled forward in slow motion, closing and opening her eyes to check on her mother and weeping after she finished each incantation. Haltia's body remained cold, and Asha leaned forward sobbing over her partner's body, while Malkia kneeled next to her, gripping her mother's icy hand, her body trembling with grief.

Kissing Haltia's hand, her mouth warming the areas of the skin and she continued to will her mother to wake. "Please!" Malkia cried, tilting her head to the heavens, sobs rising one after another. "I just got you back in my life. Please don't leave!"

An arm circled around Malkia's body, hauling her off the floor and away from her mother's lifeless body. "No!" she screamed, her arms reaching out for Haltia. "Take me back!"

Damon held on tight, holding Malkia against his chest and allowing her to weep in his arms. She clung to him, biting down hard on her lip, tearing through the tender flesh and mixing blood with her own tears. The despair swirled through her heart, and she swallowed hard to halt its consumption of her mind.

Her eyes wandered over to her mother and she hiccoughed at the sight of her blue lips and frozen face. Squeezing her eyes shut, she attempted to drown out the sight, but failed miserably.

"How did this happen?" she cried out, opening her eyes and focusing on the startled faces of her friends and family. "Why was that Elven vessel able to blast a hole right through our ship?" Her eyes landed on Koleton, who was avoiding her gaze. "How Koleton? You told me we were secure." She wiped her nose with the back of her arm, pushing away from Damon and rising to her feet. "There was absolutely no warning." She pointed around at Skye and Mataya. "You all ignored my caution that something was out in space, allowing your emotions to cloud your judgment and now my mother is dead, because of your failure."

Pivoting on her heel, she sprinted from the room, racing down the corridor and back to her quarters. Inside her room, she locked the door, barring everyone from entering and crawled under the covers, wrapping her arms around the pillow.

The tears stung her face, as the fire raged inside her. She breathed deep, but was unable to quiet the inferno, finally allowing it to surround her heart and soothe her into a vision of revenge she would eventually rain down on her father.

TWENTY-TWO
Life Ceremonies

The descent into Esaki's atmosphere had lost its excitement. Malkia watched, her expression hardened and her lips set into a firm line, ignoring the quiet chatter around her. Seeing the ruins of Domesca rise up in the horizon, her heart ached, but she chose to keep her pain buried. No one would be able to penetrate the wall she was building around herself.

Landing in a clearing just outside the crumbled walls of the fortress, Malkia unstrapped her restraints and rose from her chair, feeling the eyes of the group watching her as she left the room. Rushing down the corridor and into the elevator, she sighed when the doors shut and sagged against the wall behind her.

She opened the bay door to the dragons' quarters, allowing the four conscious ones to race out and fly into the sky, delighted to finally be able to spread their wings. Glancing over at the snow dragon, she watched as his chest rose and sank with each breath, and wondered if he would ever accept her friendship.

Footsteps in the corridor turned her attention to the door, as Apollo appeared, his hands clasped behind his back. "I believe I would not be welcomed here on Esaki. Maybe I should remain with the ship."

Malkia strolled over to her friend, lightly touching his forearm with her fingers. "No. You're one of us now and my people should be familiarized with your face." She threw a look back at the snow dragon. "Will you ask Asha or Alyssa to end the sleep spell encircling this beast? Set him free into the sky, after you've made it clear to him that he can remain here on Esaki or join our fight and give up his need to complete his mission."

"I would be happy to assist with this task," Apollo replied, giving her a sideways glance. "I'm sorry for your loss, my dear friend."

Malkia nodded, her jaw clenching. "I'll meet all of you outside the ship." She patted his arm, before leaving the room and walking off the ship.

Tilting her head towards the suns, she closed her eyes and spread her arms out, as she sank to her knees. Bringing her hands down to the ground, she pressed them deep within the soil. "Thank you, Theia. I'm finally home," she whispered, opening her eyes and surveying the area.

A number of figures stood on the stones next to the walls of Domesca. Malkia rose from the ground, brushing the dirt from her hands and stepping towards the group.

"Malkia has returned," a man shouted over his shoulder.

She smiled, recognizing the deep voice of Cormac. Moments later, dozens of people rounded the corner, walking towards her, just as Parowan came tearing around them, galloping full speed in her direction. Malkia's hands swept over her mouth, hiding the smile that was rising on her face.

Parowan halted in front of Malkia, tilting her head down and nuzzling her face against her mistress's cheek. Malkia sighed, wrapping her arms around the pegasus's neck. "I missed you, too," she whispered in Parowan's ear. "I'm sorry my return took so long." She closed her eyes and laid her head against the pegasus, breathing in the familiar scent of her exquisite beast.

"Our people were slaughtered in your absence," a voice intruded upon her thoughts, the words plunging into space between the speaker and herself, like stones into water.

Malkia stood up straight and squared her shoulders, glancing around at the old familiar faces of her town's people, along with the residents of Domesca. Recognizing the voice, her eyes rested on Dominique. Being a head taller than most others, he was easy to spot.

"My dear friend." Malkia stepped towards him, her lips setting in a straight line. "I was informed of the executions, and have been on a journey to end the wars in the heavens, but we still have so much more to accomplish." Reaching Dominique, she embraced him tightly. "My sorrow for the bloodshed here on Esaki runs deep within my soul and I won't rest until those responsible are halted in their conquest." She leaned back, staring into his forest green eyes. "I'm here to celebrate the lives who were spared and mourn the ones we have lost, amongst many other things. Let's go welcome the rest of my group."

They turned to face the ship, leading the people towards it. "Malkia, we've had one attack after another, ending just about a week ago," Dominque disclosed, holding out his arm for her to take. "The lives that have been lost are too many to count and there are several more bodies who wait for their ascent to our Gods. Our next death ritual begins at the setting of the second sun. We would be honored if you spoke some words of encouragement to the people of Esaki."

She patted his arm, smiling up at him. "Of course, I will." Licking her lips, she relished in the memories of the moon she grew up on, knowing their rituals and beliefs were completely far-fetched and unrealistic. Keeping it to herself would be difficult, but at this point, necessary.

Stepping towards the ship, Malkia noticed the rest of her group was converging just inside. As they approached, Koleton shifted out into the sun, grinning widely and waving at all his old friends. "I returned! Let the celebrations begin," he crowed, pumping one fist in the air and wrapping the other one around Skye's waist.

The crowd laughed, but halted as Apollo moved up next to Koleton and Skye, his eyes squinting at the townspeople and falling on Malkia. Without warning, a stone was hurled at Apollo, striking him in on the chest, followed by a number of objects thrown his way. He stepped back in the shadows, Koleton's face draining of all color as his arms flailed around widely.

"Stop!" Cormac bellowed over the crowd, as he sprinted up the plank of the ship. "We aren't barbarians, and if our friends brought this creature to our moon, they have a good reason for doing so." He held his arms up, his focus resting on Malkia. "Let them explain."

Malkia eased up the plank a few steps and twisted to face the group. Waving at Apollo, she waited until he stood next to her before clearing her throat and shielding her eyes from the suns. "I think we all know humans aren't similar to one another. Am I correct?"

The group was silent for a moment, but stirred when Dominique nodded in reply. The rest of the crowd followed suit, with a handful shouting in agreement.

"Alright, since we are aware of human difference from one another, I would like to point out the mere fact that the Artemisians also possess this trait." She turned and faced Apollo, reaching up and touching his cheek. "This fellow saved my life and has proven to me that not all of his kind are the evil, cruel savages we've come to know." She grinned up at Apollo and winked at him, before pulling her hand down and looking back at the group. "He's my friend and comrade. I understand your reasons to not trust him, however if it weren't for him, all of us—" She paused, jabbing her thumb back towards the rest of the group. "Would've perished a long time ago. Give him a chance. Please."

The townspeople nodded, talking excitedly amongst themselves, with Parowan stomping her hooves on the ground before running around in circles. Malkia knew she could smell the dragons and was probably anxious to know if Tantiana was being held in the ship. Smiling at her people, she raised her hands in the air to gain their attention once more.

"One more issue at hand," Malkia said, lowering her hands and sweeping her hair behind her shoulders. "We have returned with Tantiana, but have picked up four other dragons as well." A hush fell over the crowd, as they all glanced behind Malkia.

"How did you possibly—" Cormac began, his brows furrowing in confusion.

A burst of laughter escaped Malkia's lips, even surprising herself as she reached over and slid her hand on Damon's bicep, looking up at him with sparkling eyes. "This ship is massive, but not that large." She focused back on the town's people. "Two of the dragons are hatchlings, along with their mother. The last dragon has been subdued and will be trained by Apollo and Koleton, once they release him in the drylands just north of here."

"I'm famished," Koleton hollered above the crowds whispers. He threw Malkia a sideways grin, his hand gripping Skye's as they stepped off the plank and into the crowd. "What does an old man have to do, to get fed around here?"

The crowd burst out laughing, and Malkia welcomed the interruption as the dragons were forgotten and Apollo was accepted into the midst of group. They moved towards the broken fortress, steering off to the left and around the corner, where Malkia could see a small grouping of huts and tents set up just inside the trees of the forest.

Malkia stopped in her tracks and waited for Alyssa and Asha to catch up to her. "When will you release the spell on the snow dragon?"

"We wanted to settle in first," Alyssa replied, kissing Malkia's forehead. "I know you're grieving and I don't want to hurry you through it, but I do want to remind you that your mother needs you to finish this." She glanced over at Asha and back to Malkia, taking her hands in her own. "We all know the risks. Haltia knew them better than anyone, here. Her past contains stories that would rip your heart apart and now she's at peace with Selen and her mother."

Malkia's eyes shot up to meet Alyssa's, but fell again when she decided to wait on divulging the information about her grandmother. "I want to know these stories." She paused, pursing her lips, fighting a sob rising in her throat. "I want to know my mother, and I would like to perform her life celebration here on Esaki."

"That's a great idea," Asha replied, curling her arm around Malkia's shoulders. "She would love to be connected with this exquisite moon."

The trio walked behind the rest of the group, catching up after a few minutes. Malkia joined Damon at a table filled with the familiar dishes of Esaki, and she inhaled the delicious aromas saturating the air around them.

"After everything we have been through—" She paused, her eyes trailing over the crowd until she met Mataya's gaze. "It feels surreal to be home again." She lifted her cup of juice, wiping away a tear sliding down her cheek. "Thank you to my team, my friends and family, for standing by my side and fighting a war to keep our people safe. Without you, I would have lost my mind, if not my life."

The group around her lifted their glasses, saluting her toast and ceremoniously sipping their drink before returning to their socializing. Cormac approached her, sinking into a chair next to her and twisting to look at her.

"What's happening up in the stars?" he asked, his lines around his eyes deepening and his brows furrowing.

Malkia sighed, leaning back in her chair. "Before I answer that question, what do you know about the other moons around Theia?"

"Just the stories that have been told throughout my childhood," he replied, his elbows resting on the table. "Why do you ask?"

"The people of Esaki seem to only be a nuisance in the war out there." Malkia swept her hand across the sky, numbness infusing her body. "I think back to my childhood and all the information I was given about the inhabitants of other moons and it seems this place is different from the others." She wrapped her finger around a lock of hair, tilting her head to stare at the sky.

Cormac nodded, pursing his lips in thought. After a moment he focused back on Malkia's gaze. "I don't know much about the other moons, and I have to admit my lack of knowledge is embarrassing." He gripped her wrist. "Tell me more."

"The Enyoans were enslaved for years by the Artemisians. But the Artemisians were also seeking revenge—all the while being manipulated by my father. The Erisians were gaining power over the other moons, by way of my father, while the Elvens were working with him to create complete chaos and disconnect. And we were just here." Closing her eyes, she inhaled a long breath, forcing the air through her lungs as her mind turned to her deceased mother. "I don't understand why our moon was kept in the dark. We were civilized people, not to mention intelligent and strong. Why is this place different?"

"It does seem odd." Cormac rubbed his hands together, his eyes darting around at the others. "I want to join your fight." He exhaled loudly, his eyes resting on hers.

"We could use you," Malkia replied, nodding. "Let's talk more after the life ceremony tonight. I have my own mother to give back to soil. I would like to finish eating and return to the ship to prepare her body."

"I'm sorry for your loss," Cormac said, rising from his chair. "There is so much of that going around this place—" He paused, his eyes wandering to the rubble of Domesca. "Who knew this would be our fate, back when we first met? At that time, I believed the darkest force we had to battle was a disillusioned man and an army of savages." He patted Malkia's shoulder, giving her lopsided smile. "Who knew?" he asked again of no one in particular, his gaze turning inward

Cormac walked away, leaving her to chew on her own thoughts. "Can we talk in private?" Mataya's voice returned her mind back to the present.

Tilting her head up, Malkia stared into Mataya's bright, hazel eyes. "Of course. Lead the way." She rose from her chair and smiled over at Damon, before following Mataya back to the broken homes of Domesca.

Mataya was once again light on her feet, skipping her way to the debris. Halting near one of the homes, she turned to face Malkia. "Remember how you and Apollo healed Artemis?"

Malkia nodded, placing her hands on her hips and surveying the charred landscape of Esaki. "Do you believe we can do the same to Esaki?"

"Not you and Apollo," Mataya replied, placing her hands on her hips and twisting around. "But you and I could heal our moon. Our connection to its soil and our combined powers could be exactly what this moon needs to recover."

"Let's do it." Malkia grinned, her eyes dancing with light again.

Mataya touched Malkia's arm. "I'm sorry for the way I acted on the vessel. Fear has a funny way of gripping a person's heart and causing unnecessary worry to surface." She paused, searching Malkia's face. "Your mother was a wonderful woman and my heart breaks knowing you won't have the time that you deserve with her."

Closing her eyes, Malkia held back the tears and swallowed the ache that was rising in her throat. "Thank you." She opened her eyes and stepped away from Mataya. "For now, I need to focus on other things. Where do you think we should begin?"

"Right here," Mataya replied, sinking to her knees in the spot that she stood.

Malkia shifted in front of her sister and knelt on the ground facing her. Together they dug their fingers into the soil and closed their eyes.

Changing her words slightly, to fit the needs of her moon, Malkia began chanting, followed by Mataya. "Mother of Esaki, rise up and wash your light upon this land, cleansing the soil and all that is living. Mother of Esaki, rise up and wash your light upon this land, cleansing the soil and all that is living." They both paused, feeling a warm sensation slither across their bodies. Taking in a deep breath, Malkia kept her eyes closed and repeated it one more time.

After the third repetition, Malkia heard the gasps of several people and opened her eyes to see the residents of Domesca clustering closely about them, her own people peppered among the crowd. She rose from the ground and offered her hand to help Mataya up. Glancing around, a smile spread across her face as she watched the charred areas begin to blossom once again—flowers uncurling and opening bright faces to the light of the suns, new leaves, golden and wrinkled, stretching forth from the magical profusion of buds.

"What did you do?" Alyssa asked, touching Malkia's forearm.

Turning to face her Esaki mother, happiness sparkled inside her for the first time since her mother's death. "We healed the vegetation. Mataya is truly remarkable."

"Yes, she is," Alyssa replied, grinning over at her younger daughter. "You are both my angels."

"I was beginning to wonder when you two would stop dilly-dawdling and actually put your powers to some good use," Koleton boasted, sauntering towards them, a wicked grin plastered across his face. "We didn't have the opportunity to see Artemis's transformation.

This is really a treat." His eyes danced around the trees, twinkling from the ever-expanding colors and crisp, clean smell of rejuvenated foliage.

Malkia's eyes scanned over the faces of all her friends and family and she drew in a long breath, relishing the sweet scent of the newly budded vegetation. "If only we could create this feeling across all the moons," she whispered to her Esaki mother.

"We will do our best," Alyssa replied, squeezing Malkia's shoulders.

The life ceremony ended with a flame touched to each corpse. Within seconds, the searing heat and light claimed the tightly wrapped bodies and Malkia stepped away from the inferno, watching with a heavy heart.

Everyone who had survived the attacks had converged together in their makeshift homes, just beyond the broken ones of Domesca. Cormac had told Malkia that only one hundred and eleven people were alive in this area and, because of their small numbers, they had been able to hide away in the lower caves of the mountains during the last battle. The witches had helped by casting invisibility spells over as many people as they could.

"The Artemisians sought to destroy the city and homes, but when those peculiar, pointy-eared humans arrived, they were out to annihilate every living person and creature." His voice had shaken from the memory and he had left abruptly, leaving Malkia to fume over the heartache on her own.

Now she surveyed the small group of people and the burning fire in the center, consuming the dozens of bodies, while her mind returned to her daughter and the stars above. She yearned to remain on Esaki and fix the damage that the Artemisians and Elvens had inflicted upon it, but her heart was with Esta.

Damon curled his arm around her waist and drew her close. She had been distant from him since her mother's death and now her desire for his nearness had intensified. She looked up at his scruffy face and rose up on her tiptoes to kiss his cheek.

"I love you, Damon," she whispered into his ear. "How would you feel about having a baby with me?"

He glanced down at her, a lopsided smile rushing across his face. "Are you suggesting we go make one?"

A quiet laugh escaped her lips and she covered her mouth to suppress the sound, looking around to see if anyone had heard. "We can do that too, but no that isn't what I'm implying."

His smile faded and he touched her stomach with the palm of his hand. "Are you saying—" His words caught in his throat, as he glanced down at her stomach and back at her face. "Are you?" The color in his face had drained and his jaw clenched, waiting for her response.

"I wanted to make sure it was true, before I broke the news to you," she said, only partially telling the truth. "I suspected a couple of weeks ago, but now I can sense the tiny energy within me. It's like nothing I've felt before." Her hand trailed to the one he had on her stomach, and she placed it over his, pressing firmly.

Sliding his hand away from hers, he grasped her around the waist,

311

picking her up and swinging her around. "There's no one else I'd rather have a child with," he exclaimed, kissing her on the forehead. "This is the best news!" He set her back on the ground, squeezing her tightly and planting another kiss on the top of her head.

"Now to end this war of my father's, so our child can grow up in a safe environment." Malkia sank into Damon's embrace, turning to face the fires and surveying the sullen people in the group. "The carnage and death toll has risen to a point where we have no choice but to end the Elven's domain, along with my father's. They came here to hurt me and possibly to force my hand, but either way, it has to be done."

Damon's chest rose and he held his breath for a moment, before exhaling loudly. "I know," he breathed, squeezing her once again.

After the townspeople left for their homes, Malkia waited for Damon and Koleton to bring her mother's body over to a secluded funeral pyre that they had made just for her. She had asked that her mother be left free of any bindings, so she had the option to fly if she desired. They laid her body down and Apollo helped Malkia arrange her arms folded across her chest, placing small stones over her eyes.

Asha stepped up and grasped Malkia's hand, while Mataya wrapped her arms around her shoulders. Malkia nodded at Damon, who lit the torch and handed it to Asha.

"Be at peace," Malkia gulped, her vision blurring as the tears swam in her eyes. "You were a warrior in this life and an example to us all. Thank you for your protection, patience, and undying loyalty and love. Until we meet again."

"Until we meet again," Asha declared, stepping forward and lighting the branches underneath Haltia's body.

Within seconds the flames grew and spread, engulfing her body and the wooden planks. Asha sank against Malkia, her own body trembling with the sobs rising in her chest as they watched Haltia's corpse turn crimson. Mataya muttered under her breath and waved her hand in front of the flames, invoking a spell to speed up Haltia's ascension. Moments later, small pieces of her body flaked away and slowly floated away into the twilight. They stood in silence for several hours, staying frozen in their spots until the last of Haltia's body had either united with the soil or risen to the heavens.

Mataya gave Malkia one last squeeze, before leaving with Justin. Asha had sunk to the ground, sitting with her eyes closed and her palms to the heavens. Most of the group departed with Mataya, leaving the two of them to say their good-byes. Breathing in deeply, Malkia tilted her head the sky and stared at Theia and the stars around her.

Moments later, she felt a hand on her shoulder and turned to see Asha had risen from the ground. "I'm going to remain on the ship for the night," she whispered, her face covered with the remnants of her tears. "It was the last place that I held your mother and I need to end this ceremony with her smell."

Malkia nodded, a silent tear trailing down her cheek. "That's exactly where you should be. I love you, Asha."

"I love you, too." Asha turned away, leaving Malkia alone with the dying embers of the wood and her own thoughts.

She stood quietly, allowing her mind to empty all dark thoughts and the light to fill her body, remembering all that her mother sacrificed to keep her safe from her father. "Thank you, mom," she whispered to the heavens. "You're my shining star, my protector, and my guarding angel. May peace be with you, on the other side." She paused, grief shattering her heart and her body shaking with the thought of not seeing her mother's face again. "I love you."

TWENTY-THREE

Esaki's Secrets

Damon's eyes scanned the terrain, his lips setting in a straight line. "I don't see them," he said, glancing over at Malkia and Mataya.

"There's only one pyramid," Malkia replied, pointing off to the left. "It was on the edge of the ocean, one side partly within the waves. You'll need to move along the shore."

He nodded, steering the vessel over to the one side. The surf from the ocean was intoxicating to Malkia, and reminded her of the two different oceans the Aletheian's had taken her to, intensifying her desire to be near the water.

Damon had been distracted since they had woken in the early morning and wouldn't make eye contact with Malkia. Glancing over at him, she noticed his clenched jaw and the rigid lines of his posture, as if he were holding the burden of their collective fate on his shoulders.

"There it is," he muttered, wiping the beads of sweat from his forehead with the back of his arm. "I'll circle around and land the ship in the closest clearing I can find."

"What's bothering you?" she whispered, curling her hand around his forearm.

He quickly glanced up at her, before looking out the window again.

"I had another vision last night." He gritted his teeth, a flush creeping up towards his face.

"Tell me about it," she coaxed, sinking into the chair next to his and twisting to focus on him.

"Dario was in it." His eyes fell to his hands and he expelled his breath in a whoosh, before turning and grabbing her hands. "We were fighting on top of a roof. I've never felt so much anger in my entire life, and it had something to do with protecting you and our unborn child." He glanced over at Mataya, who had her eyes closed in a chair at the other end of the room. "The worst part is when I stole a glance over at you and I saw you kneeling in front of a young girl with dark hair. I'm not positive it was Esta, but who else would it be? The last thing I saw before I woke, was you embracing her, followed with her pulling your daggers from their sheaths." He hung his head, a line etching between his eyes.

Malkia sighed, thinking of what it meant and who the child might actually be. "We have to remember that if I do perish in this battle and our child's life is extinguished, it is still better than allowing this tyranny to continue." She squeezed his hands when he arched his eyebrow up at her. "This isn't easy for any of us, but we have to stay the course."

He shook his head, turning his focus back upon the ship and navigating a clean landing into a clearing not far from the pyramid. "You know I don't like this and if I had my way, you would remain on Esaki."

Not wanting to start an argument, Malkia ignored the last statement, turning to face forward, waiting for Damon to finish landing the ship.

It wasn't long until the three of them stood outside the stones of the pyramid, peering up to the top.

"Once we find the map, we can return to Domesca and plan out our departure for Thalia," Malkia said, turning to look at Damon and Mataya. "With Sirath on our side, we'll have five dragons to accompany us to war."

"Apollo was able to coax the snow dragon into giving up his need to capture you?" Mataya asked, her eyes dancing with mischief.

"They've taken a great liking to one another," Malkia replied, smiling over at sister. "Let's begin our incantation and see if we can break into this pyramid."

Mataya nodded, shifting around and grasping onto Malkia's forearms, before closing her eyes. Malkia did the same and within seconds she felt the rush of Esaki's energy run through her body, connecting Mataya and herself. The light bounded from their bodies and they stood in silence, waiting for Damon to give them the all clear.

Moments later, Malkia felt a hand on her back and opened her eyes to see Damon standing next to her, staring over at the pyramid. "The door's open," he told her, shifting his eyes to look at her and Mataya. "It's on that side over there." He pointed to the left, and then clasped his hands behind his back. "Lead the way."

Malkia followed Mataya around the corner, seeing the doorway opened wide and leading into a dark tunnel. Flashing her light within, she noticed two winged human statues standing a few feet in, facing one another. Their hands were folded in prayer, held before their lips and closed eyes as if to forestall speech.

"I haven't seen those before," Malkia said, stepping towards the entrance and glancing up at the tall statues as they walked by. She shone her light down the corridor and noticed it branched out into two rooms. "Should we split up?" she asked, turning to look at the other two.

"No," Damon replied, his eyes narrowing and his expression hardening. "We will stay together for this." He stomped past her, and she cringed back, knowing his temper was flaring because of his vision.

The two women followed after Damon, who veered off to the left side of the pyramid. It opened into a massive room, with a spiral staircase in the middle that led upwards to other floors. The walls were lined with the little statues, similar to those the other pyramids contained, and Malkia smiled with recognition. She knelt in front of the first one she came to, seeing his eyes closed and his hands held together in a fist in front of his chest, with one finger sticking out.

"We need to document the number of fingers on each of these statues," she requested, looking over at Mataya. "Could you write them down, starting with the first one when we enter? I really believe they are a code of some kind."

"Of course I will," Mataya answered, tugging out a piece of parchment from her pack. "What will you do?"

"Continue to explore and hopefully find that map, so we can leave," Malkia replied, touching Damon's arm.

"Why don't I begin on the other end with the statues," Damon suggested, grasping his own parchment and sauntering towards the last statue. "Just wait until we have the numbers and then we can continue on together."

Malkia sighed, but settled back, examining the rest of the room with the light from her hand. The staircase had several etchings on the base and she scanned upwards, squinting to see what was up above, but only seeing murky air through the aperture in the ceiling. Her fingers traced along some of the etchings in the stone staircase, seeing a pattern as they spiraled upwards. Recognizing some of the symbols, she pulled out her own parchment and began to copy them in their patterns. Just as she was finishing, Mataya touched the small of her back, making her jump.

"Are you finished?" she asked, holding the parchment over her heart and taking a deep breath to calm her hurried pulse.

"Didn't you hear me?" Mataya questioned, her brows furrowing.

She forced a smile, glancing around to find Damon. "I guess I was in my own world." Worry snaked through her chest, realizing while she copied the symbols, any outside noise had dissipated completely.

She stuffed the parchment in her pack, sighing with relief when Damon walked towards them, his own parchment in his hands. "Are you two ready to make our way up?" he asked, grabbing hold of the stone railing.

Malkia looked down at him from the fourth stair and then glanced upwards, peering into the dark hole above. "Here goes nothing," she whispered, flashing her light inside and stepping up.

As she grew closer to the aperture, the air dropped in temperature and she wrapped her arms around herself, sending out her light around her in order to illuminate the room. She peeked over the ledge and saw an empty room that seemed to stretch in every direction. Stepping up to the top, she cast her light around, waiting for Damon's torch to help.

It smelled fresh and damp, the petrichor that follows a long rainfall.

Malkia felt as if they had stepped into another dimension as her eyes scanned the blank walls. Damon and Mataya shifted away from her, using their own lights to see more of the room. As Damon moved to the other side of the pyramid, Malkia gasped at what she saw.

Near the middle of the room was a massive sphere suspended above the ground. Gingerly, she stepped towards it, noticing that it was sculpted with topography like a planet or moon. It slowly rotated on its own and she peered around and under it to see if it was being held up by any rope or object but couldn't find anything.

"Damon?" she called out, not seeing him any longer.

"I'm on the other side," he said, bringing his light down so she could see it under the object. "Are you checking this out? It's absolutely extraordinary."

Mataya touched Malkia's shoulder, her eyes wandering over the round object. "What is it?"

"A sculpture of a moon, maybe." Malkia stepped away, her head tilted up. "Possibly Theia or another planet." Out of the corner of her eye she noticed another object above her. She shone her light up and saw that it was a smaller, round object orbiting the larger one. Her eyes widened and her jaw dropped. "I think this might be the blue planet that the Aletheian's took me to," she whispered, her breath catching in her throat. "You're right, Damon, this is extraordinary."

"Why is this blue planet so significant to us and our moons?" Mataya asked, licking her lips and she stared at the smaller moon.

"Our Creators have something to do with all of it, but the blue planet connects us to them, I believe. It's a stopping point or a clue in their whereabouts," Malkia replied, her fingers running over her lips, as a sense of elation suffused her being. "My grandparents reside there. Everything we have uncovered has something to do with this planet. From what I know, it is far larger than Theia and supports billions of people and creatures. Our connection is becoming increasingly important and I'm beginning to think if the Elvens ever invade that planet, it will begin a revolution that will terminate more than we could ever imagine."

"Shouldn't we destroy any route or information we have on this planet," Mataya asked, pressing her lips together.

"Probably," Malkia answered, walking around to meet Damon. "We need to keep this place a secret. There is a reason the Elvens and my father don't know what is in here, and we need to keep it that way." Her eyes scanned around, finally seeing Damon a few yards away. "Do you see any map over there?" she asked him.

"No, but I'm thinking this pyramid doesn't contain a map of the stars." He pointed to the side of him. "Come see this machine."

Malkia and Mataya sprinted over to Damon, halting in their tracks in front of a bizarre looking table, filled with scribbles and buttons. Malkia reached forward and pressed the closest one. The words lit up, but nothing else happened.

"What do those words mean?" Malkia asked, running her fingers over the strange letters.

"It says, *Teotihuacan*," Mataya replied, turning back to see the planet behind them.

"How do you know?" Damon asked, his brows furrowing, as he examined the other words. "These symbols are like nothing I've seen before."

"I don't know why I know," Mataya said, pointing her finger at the sculpted planet. "But those buttons show us points on this planet."

Malkia and Damon both whipped around, and Malkia gasped at the light shining at a point just below the middle of the planet. Reaching over she pressed another button. Another point lit up, not too far from the first one.

"We have to keep this a secret from everyone. The points on this planet have some kind of meaning." Malkia turned and faced Mataya and Damon. "Those small statues below us, have to hold the key to the star map we have been piecing together. It's all connected to our Creators, and the Elvens will do anything to have this information." Her hands wrung together, sweat trickling down her spine, despite the coolness of the air. "This right here would be detrimental to our mission. We have to agree to never breathe a word of it to anyone. We can tell the others about the statues and whatever else we discover, but this—" She swung her arm out towards the planet. "This has to remain our secret, until we know what we are dealing with."

"Agreed," Damon and Mataya said in unison.

"Let's find out what the other side of the lower floor holds and then return to our group." Malkia swept past them, searching for another staircase and finally seeing it near the end of pyramid.

She rushed over to it, seeing that it was a straight stairway. Stepping down the first few steps, she turned to see Mataya not far behind her and Damon still looking at the planet. A moment later, he pressed the buttons again, turning the lights off on the planet and moved around the machine, following the two women.

At the bottom of the stairs, Malkia turned to the right and entered a tight corridor, running alongside the staircase. She tiptoed down the hallway and could see a slight purple glow at the opening. Peeking around the end of the corridor, she breathed in the soft scent of the purple algae. The same vegetation had been growing in the Eris Guarding Statue.

"This is the healing herb that is needed to ward off the Elvens poison. I wonder if we brought it with and created a protection elixir, if it would keep us safe during out battle with them." Malkia stepped towards it, followed by Damon and Mataya.

"It wouldn't hurt to bring some," Damon replied. "I'll gather a bundle and meet you two outside."

"We can help," Mataya said, a wary smile surfacing on her lips. "Plus, you're the one who insisted we not separate." She winked at Damon, as she moved around him and quickly grasped onto a handful of the algae before it could shrink away.

"Good call," Damon muttered, gathering some of the algae as well.

Malkia examined the room, letting her light shine into the darker corners and making sure they didn't miss anything of importance. Reaching the doorway to the opening corridor, she looked back to see Mataya and Damon had filled their packs with the algae and were already following her out.

Before long, they were back in the ship. They had closed the doors to the pyramid and replaced the magical incantation that hid them from everyday travelers. Their secret was safely tucked away.

The rest of the group had returned to Domesca as well and Apollo had been successful in teaching Sirath their plans to overthrow her father and the Elvens, while they had been gone to the pyramid. They stood around a large table near the townspeople homes, sharing findings and ideas for the battle ahead.

"Malkia, I know I offered to accompany you to Thalia, but these people need leadership here on Esaki," Cormac said, folding his arms across his chest. "With so many of our people deceased, it would be reckless to leave now. Dominique is the only other one who has stepped up to lead and with both of us, it has been a chore. I shouldn't abandon him."

"I understand," Malkia replied, pursing her lips and glancing around at the group. "We have the dragons, and Jacob is waiting for us on Thalia." She extended a hand and grasped his wrist, as he gripped hers. "I only hope we will see each other again and that when we do, our moons will be a safe and serene place to live, once again."

"Thank you, Malkia." His eyes fell for a moment, before focusing back on her. "You're a brave warrior, and I'm honored to have known you."

"Until we meet again." She shot him a wide smile, before releasing his wrist and turning to face her group.

"Are we ready?" she called out, her eyes scanning over her friends and family.

"Let's get this show on the road," Koleton shouted over the group, his smile wide and his eyes dancing with hope. "No time for good-byes. We will see you heathens on the other side of victory." He winked at the townspeople, gripped Skye's hand and kissed it tenderly. "Let's go, lady love."

Skye grinned up at her bearded man and turned away from the people with him in tow. The rest of the group followed after, with

Malkia and Damon taking up the rear.

After closing the loading dock of the ship and checking on the dragons, Malkia settled into the seat next to Damon on the bridge, watching Esaki disappear beneath them and welcoming the stars again.

She leaned over and kissed Damon on the cheek. "Good luck, handsome man."

TWENTY-FOUR
The Fallen Angel's City

"We have to find a safe spot to land our ship," Damon said, throwing a pointed look at Malkia. "Did Jacob say where he would find us?"

"No, he didn't," Malkia replied, raking her hands through her hair, as she glanced over at Mataya. "What do you think we should do?"

Mataya smiled, rising from her seat and stepping towards the window. "I think we are overthinking this whole scenario. We have to begin somewhere. Pick a spot and let's see what is waiting for us and if we can reach Jacob that way."

Malkia nodded, turning to face Damon. "She's right. It just has to happen. We have no idea what we will find, and it's best to just dive in and see what is out there."

Damon's jaw clenched, obviously not keen on their plan, but he steered the vessel towards an immense mountain range, easing into a crevice on the side of a cliff. After they disembarked, Malkia stood on the edge of the cliff and stared down at the valley. She was overwhelmed by how similar Thalia looked to Eris.

Tantiana's warm breath swept across Malkia's neck as she nuzzled up close to her mistress, grateful to be free of the close quarters. Skye stepped up next to Malkia, curling her arm around her shoulders. "Are you ready to face him?" she asked, picking at the lint on the front of her shirt.

"Which him?" Malkia sighed, tilting her head to stare at the gray sky.

"Your father," Skye replied, her obsidian eyes watching Malkia.

She faced Skye, her eyes bloodshot from the past few days traveling. "I'm ready for this to be over, so yes, I *need* to face him, more than ever now."

Asha and Bella slipped around Tantiana and joined the two women. "We need to find a way to contact Jacob," Asha said, her hand resting on Malkia's shoulder.

"What do you have in mind?" Malkia asked, sinking down onto a large rock, crossing her arms over her chest and peering at the three women surrounding her.

Asha glanced over at Bella. "We could use one of the Elven's communication spells," Bella whispered, her eyes flashing around the rocky terrain. "I've never performed such an intense incantation before, but if we succeed, Jacob will be able to tell us his exact whereabouts."

Pursing her lips and leaning back on her hands, Malkia's eyes met Tantiana's who seemed to be anxious to fly. "Let's do it," she replied. "Where are the other dragons?"

Tantiana rose from her perch, her head swinging around to view the rest of the group. *They're stretching their legs and wings over by the waterfall, on the other side of this crevice.*

Nodding, Malkia rose from the rock and grasped Skye's hand. "Tantiana will join the other dragons and keep them away while we work on finding Jacob. Is there anything in particular that you require for this spell?" she asked, her eyes falling on Bella.

Bella licked her lips and glanced over at Asha. "I don't think so. It only requires ten drops of blood from the witch performing the spell, mixed with the dew drops of the Thalia moon. Give me a few minutes and I'll have what we need."

Sprinting away without another word, Bella left the three women and disappeared behind the vessel and into the trees. Malkia nodded at Tantiana, before the dragon twisted away from them and followed Bella. Squeezing Skye's hand, Malkia tugged her along, with Asha tagging along behind them.

Gathering around a small fire that Damon had started, Malkia stretched her hands towards the flames, warming her chilled fingers, and smiled to herself. *Esta is close. I can feel her presence,* she thought, losing focus as she gazed into the heart of the fire.

Out of the corner of her eye, she noticed Bella's return and watched as Asha met her over by the rocky wall. Closing her eyes, she focused on her daughter, hoping she would be able to communicate with her. Blackness encircled her and a dark tremor of dread knotted in the pit of her stomach, before spreading numbly throughout her body. Breathing in sharply, her eyes flashed open, twisting frantically to view her unknowing friends.

"I don't think we have time!" she cried out to Bella and Asha, her voice rising an octave as the panic rose in her throat. "The Elvens know we're here."

As one, the group turned their eyes to Malkia, then focusing quickly over to the cliff side opening to their hideout. "How much time do we have?" Damon asked, racing towards the ship.

"Minutes, if that," Malkia breathed, her light bounding from her body and spreading over the ship and all her family and friends. "My father is with them. Damon take the vessel, and I'll ride Tantiana. The rest of you either go with Damon, find a dragon to ride or find shelter."

Malkia whistled and Tantiana flew next to her, slowing down just enough for Malkia to hurdle onto her back. As they dove over the cliff and Damon eased the ship into the air, the Elven vessels appeared on the horizon. Asha, Alyssa, Mataya and Bella remained just inside the woods with the young dragons. Skye mounted Adelina and followed closely behind Malkia, while Apollo raced off on Sirath, directing the dragon towards Damon.

Shooting down along the closest river, Tantiana glided just above the water's troubled surface, as Malkia searched the area for any hidden foes. Moments later, one of the Elven vessels settled in behind the dragon, their shots careening across her light, creating sparks of silver around the duo.

"Where are you Jacob?" Malkia whispered, her eyes darting over the mountainsides and examining the wooded areas.

The Elven ship slowed down and Malkia twisted her head to guage their trajectory. Suddenly, another, larger ship appeared above her, its base doors opening and a light encircling both dragon and rider.

"Can you escape their light?" Malkia cried out to Tantiana, gripping the scales in front of her.

Tantiana pressed against the light, just as it began to rise towards the ship. Breathing deeply, Malkia closed her eyes, pushing her palms out to the sides and focusing her light into her arms. *When my powers*

329

obliterate their hold on us, turn to the left and fly into the trees. Malkia commanded her dragon.

The light burst from Malkia's palms, making contact with the Elvens tractor beam. The backlash embraced them in a maelstrom of flame, sparks careening against her protective barrier. For a split second, the beam faltered, and Tantiana slipped free before the energy stabilized itself once more. The dragon raced over the treetops, deftly angling below their cover and concealing them amongst the branches and rocky spurs that broke the planet's surface.

Flying off of Tantiana, Malkia settled onto the soil, her eyes frantically combing the patches of sky visible through the greenery. *Settle in, Tantiana and wait until I require your assistance.*

Tantiana stepped quietly back into the darkness, folding within herself and turning her face out to watch her mistress. Giving her dragon one last look, Malkia stepped through the trees and down towards the river, hoping to keep the Elvens away from Tantiana.

As she prepared to move into the open, a flash of movement caught her eye. Carefully concealing herself behind the trunk of a large tree, she combed the forest for signs of who or what had followed her.

"Malkia, you can reveal yourself." She heard Jacob call from a few yards away.

Breathing a sigh of relief, Malkia eased away from the safety of the tree and encircled herself with her light. Arrayed before her in the dappled shade was a motley band. Jacob stood at the periphery, sunlight pouring down over his head and shoulders

"Jacob," she breathed, her eyes darting around at the strangers. "How did you find me?"

"It's a long story," he replied, hurrying towards her. "We need to move from this area and plot out a more effective counterstrike against the Elvens." He grasped her elbow and smiled down at her. "It's so great to see you again, Malkia."

"What happened to you?" she asked, her hand gripping the top of her dagger, her eyes never leaving the strange figures arrayed silently behind Jacob.

Jacob glanced over his shoulder and then back at Malkia. "These are my people," he told her, touching her chin and bringing her eyes to focus on him. "They won't hurt you or anyone with you. In fact, they desire the end of the Elvens and your father's dominion over Thalia." He paused, shooing his friends away with a snap of his wrist. "Take a breath and look at me. They're on your side and have been waiting for this moment for many years. Let's proceed to my village and I'll fill you in on the details."

Malkia relaxed slightly, her thoughts returning to the rest of her group and Tantiana. *Do you want to stay here, until I'm positive Jacob's people are safe?* She asked Tantiana.

We are stronger together. Stop protecting me, Malkia. I want to be with you. Tantiana thoughts sounded frustrated for the first time since Malkia had met her.

"Tantiana will be joining us," Malkia said, stepping back from Jacob and surveying the area. "Will that be a problem?"

"Of course not," he replied. "We're in this together, Malkia. Our main goal here has been to gather intelligence, which I'll pass on to you once we've reached the safety of the village. Your father's history is tangled with the Elvens and Artemisians, touching every part of

Theia's star system." A smile had crept up on his face as he spoke, and Malkia couldn't help but be intrigued.

"What about the rest of our people? Damon, my sister and the rest of the group are scattered over miles, searching for you." Her eyes returned to the sky, as she chewed on her bottom lip.

"We'll find them. Our numbers are small, but we possess powers that no warlock, Elven or Demi-God, retains," Jacob replied. "Call your dragon and follow us through the trees. We have a hidden passage that leads to our village."

Tantiana appeared suddenly from the dense screen of foliage, nuzzling her face against Malkia's back. Startled, Malkia laughed uncomfortably when she turned to find Tantiana staring innocently back at her.

I love you, Tantiana, but please make more noise when there's no danger, Malkia thought, a smile tugging at the corners of her lips.

The duo trailed after Jacob and his people, swerving around the rocks and vegetation that ended abruptly in the steep escarpment of a rockface.

"Why have we gone this route?" Malkia asked, taking a step back, and grasping her daggers. Instinctively she enrobed both her and Tantiana within her light.

Jacob glanced back at Malkia and smirked. "Relax. You'll find out soon enough why this way is safest."

A few of Jacob's friends held their palms against the rock, closing their eyes and chanting in a language unfamiliar to Malkia. She listened to their words, hoping to recognize some of them.

Jacob curled his hand over her shoulder, staring down at her. "You have no idea how important you are, do you?"

She released the breath in her lungs with a loud sigh, her eyes falling to the ground. "This talk needs to end. My importance is insignificant and I'm tired of hearing what everyone thinks I should be doing. I'm about to battle my father and hopefully save my daughter from his grasp. The last thing I care about is who everyone else believes I am."

"Just wait," he said, his eyes straying over his people.

Malkia's eyes grew wide as the rocks and soil began to disappear and a door appeared. "I should've known," she whispered, biting her bottom lip as she sucked in the warm air. "Who are you?"

A half-smile rose on Jacob's face, as he stared at the magic swirling around the mountain. "I'm a descendant of the Fallen Angels and I was brought back to Thalia by my father." He turned to face Malkia, his eyes dancing with amusement. "If I'd known what powers I possessed, I would have never been that terrified boy back on Esaki."

Malkia nodded and smiled, her hand lightly touching the side of Tantiana's face. "I know the feeling. Why did your father keep you away for so long?"

"Just like you, I was left on Esaki, for my protection," Jacob replied, as he stood up straight to follow his people into the cave. He grasped Malkia's hand and tugged her along. "The Fallen Angels are a dying race. Keeping me away from the Elven conflict allowed me and others like me to grow up and join the fight at an age when we were capable of protecting ourselves."

Malkia's feet stilled and she stood just inside the massive doorway. "I've been researching the history of Thalia and the other moons of Theia and there is absolutely no mention of the Fallen Angels. Why is that?"

"I'm not sure," he answered, his eyes darting back behind them. "I do know that my people have kept themselves hidden for thousands of years. But, shortly after my birth, their existence was revealed and it created a rift between the Elvens and Pixies."

Tantiana nudged Malkia forward, and once the dragon had entered the passage, the wall behind them closed in as if the aperture had never existed. Following Jacob's people through the dirt-and-rock-filled cave, Malkia was reminded of the Artemisian's bunker back on Eris, although this one was far larger and could easily accommodate Tantiana.

The path was lighted by hundreds of electric lanterns. Jacob's people remained quiet, and Malkia examined them as they hurried through the passageway. All five women wore their hair long and braided, while their clothes fit tight as a glove, allowing them to move with ease. Most of their skin was as dark as the bark of the trees, save one woman whose skin and hair were the pure white of bleached bone, a carnelian mouth blossoming against her pale skin. They captivated Malkia, with their stone-faced expressions and smooth faces, and she wondered what kind of people they really were.

"What happened to you?" Malkia asked, shooting Jacob a sideways glance as she wiped away the quickly-forming beads of sweat from her brow.

Jacob stepped lightly around a curve in the path and Malkia noticed how different he appeared, with his nearly white hair and bright blue eyes. His skin remained dark, like the four ladies in the group, which only heightened his angelic features.

"The Artemisians attacked Domesca after Dario took you away from Esaki. I was with Damon and Cormac, when a bright yellow light surrounded me, swirling like a whirlwind and blocking me from seeing anyone. Moments later, it dwindled, revealing one of Thalia's wooded forests. My people were clustered nearby, waiting for me." He shot her a sideways look, a weary smile turning up the corners of his mouth. "I was told that my father was a Fallen Angel, who had loved a human woman, and in turn created me. At first, they believed I would never show the signs of the Angels, but when they were told of my ability to speak to Pixies without restraint, they brought me here for testing. Just in time too."

"Do you know what happened on Esaki after you left?" Malkia asked.

He nodded, pursing his lips and pointing forward. "We are almost to the half way point." Looking over at Malkia, she noticed the tears glistening in his eyes. "The pixies from Esaki have returned here, as well, and have described the destruction and death toll. The thought of what those monsters did eats at my heart every single day."

"Me, too," Malkia whispered, holding out her hand and squeezing his when he grasped it. "It's been a long road, and I'm sure you've had your own battles to fight. When I first began this journey to Thalia, it seemed like this day would never arrive, but here we are. I'm anxious to end my father's dominion and be reunited with my daughter."

Jacob nodded, his eyes remaining sad, as he threw her a crooked smile. "Let's finish this."

It took some time weaving through the large tunnel, but the group trudged along with Tantiana in tow. The group of Angels remained a few yards ahead of Jacob and Malkia, and she noticed a slight disdain in their attitude towards her if she attempted a conversation with them. After the last time she was rejected, she glanced over at Jacob, raising her eyebrows and sticking out her tongue at the group ahead. He shook his head and covered his mouth with his hand, trying to hide his smile.

Finally, a light beamed through an exit up ahead, and Malkia sighed with relief when she noticed it. "Thank Theia, we are finally done with this cryptic cavern," she whispered loud enough for only Jacob to hear.

The group of Angels stepped out into the light first and moved out of the way for Malkia and Tantiana to follow. The dragon cautiously poked her head out and squinted at the suns. From this vantage, a massive city could be seen cupped by the valley, with buildings similar to Errandor's and homes strewn on the outer edges and into the trees. The pathway to the city had a canopy of tree branches, with vibrant flowers filling in the gaps, all the way down to the entrance.

Malkia heard scurrying and the chirps of animals and birds, and allowed herself to drink in the peace that surrounded their hidden town. She pondered how the settlement remained hidden from the rapacious Elvens. Her brows furrowed. Stepping away from the side of the mountain and glancing up to the top, she mused, "Once again, why did we use this route?" She could have flown Tantiana over the mountain.

The pale female Angel tilted her head towards Malkia, raising an eyebrow and pursing her lips. "Your dragon is easily detected by the Elvens. She shouldn't be in the sky, until we are prepared for this battle." Her voice was quiet, but the strength of her rebuke forced Malkia to take a step back. "As well, our town is protected by dark, concentrated powers. The same that you have coursing through your body. It's unbreakable by the Elvens." A smile that didn't touch her fathomless eyes stretched her lips for a moment, gone almost before Malkia could note it.

Jacob leaned in close to Malkia. "There is a reason the full-blooded Fallen Angels don't speak often around humans." He muttered. "Although your jests are comical, these beings give you the cold shoulder so they don't overwhelm you. Especially in a closed space like the caves."

Malkia's eyes widened and she nodded her head, surveying the mysterious but wondrous group around her. "Now I understand." She glared at Jacob, punching him in the arm. "You could have warned me."

"What fun would that be?" He chuckled, gripping his arm where she struck him. "Good grief, lady. You have some power behind that fist."

She winked at him, as they linked arms. "You haven't seen nothing, yet." Pointing toward the city, a wide smile rose on her face. "Now where does a girl find food on this moon?"

"Follow us." A dark-eyed man spoke near the front of the group, stepping forward on the path.

Malkia admired his well-built and chiseled body, with skin the color of chocolate and hair as white as snow. It was cut short, but just like Jacob, the contrast between his skin and hair was fascinating.

One by one, the Angels followed this chocolate god and Malkia realized he was probably the highest ranked among them. "Where do you fall in line with your people?" she asked, twisting to view Jacob.

He laughed, patting her hand, as they followed his people. "I'm a nobody to them. A servant in some ways, but useful because of my relationship with you and the pixies." He lowered his voice, although Malkia had a feeling the Angels could hear every word. "They need you, because of your connection with the Aletheian's and they know the only way to end the Elven's dominion over the moons is to ally themselves with you."

"I see," Malkia replied, narrowing her eyes. "What about the pixies? You said they returned to Thalia. What's their role in this war?"

"Their loyalties are divided between the Elvens and the Fallen Angels." Jacob exhaled with a huff, a frown covering his face after the breath was expelled. "It hasn't been easy, speaking with both sides and hearing their reasons for choosing their paths. The pixies who reside with Elvens, believe that the discovery of the Creators whereabouts will bring the peace we desire here on Thalia, while the Angels know the Creators will only bring more destruction and chaos into our star system." He paused, shaking his head and tilting his face to the sky, for a moment. Coming to an abrupt halt, he turned to look at Malkia. "The Creators are not gods, although many species of this star system believe they are. There are few of us left who know the truth. The Creators are travelers of our skies, savages who bring torment to the heavens. We don't ever want them to return again."

Malkia's mouth gaped as she struggled to find a response, and finally snapped her jaw shut. Ever-deepening furrows of consternation between her brows echoed the implacable line of her mouth. Taking in a few deep breaths, she turned and began walking again. "How do you know this is accurate information?"

Rushing to catch up to her, Jacob wiped the beads of sweat from his chin, giving her a sideways look. "These people are the Fallen Angels. Do you have any idea what that means?"

Malkia shook her head, watching a small creature race across the path in front of her. Knowing Tantiana would want to catch it, she turned and stopped her dragon with a frosty stare. "You have some kind of Angel mojo coursing through your body. That would be my guess," she replied, her mood plummeting and a weight settling on her shoulders.

"Yes, but that's not all." Jacob stopped again, grasping Malkia's shoulders and twisting her to face him. Tantiana, still focused on the animal, nearly ran into them and danced off the path to avoid the collision. Jacob's eyes never left Malkia's face, and when she focused back on him, he continued, "Fallen Angels are Aletheian's who have chosen to give up their celestial status and become mortal beings."

The lines on her forehead deepened significantly as she stepped back and shook her head.

Jacob stepped after her and placed his finger up to her lips, stopping her from speaking. "Listen. When a Light Being chooses to discard their outer light, they're forced to live as any mortal being and therefore we can perish, just as all life will. If we live well, we have the capability to survive in the mortal state for centuries, but just as a sword can make you bleed, it can do the same to us. We are choosing to end the battle before it becomes unstoppable." He gripped her hand, tugging her down the path to catch up with the group, who were waiting for them. "If our Creators return and realize all the species they created, they might choose to destroy us. The reason we know this information, is because the Fallen Angels who were once Aletheian's never lost their memories from before their fall."

Malkia yanked her hand away from Jacob, slowing to a walk, just as she noticed the shadow of a large bird fly overhead. "I agree. I don't want to bring the Creators barreling back to our homes and disrupt our lives any more than they already have been. That being said, I need answers." She glanced up to find the bird, but not seeing it through the vegetation she stared down in the city that was now so close. "The blue planet. How did my biological grandfather fly to our star system and how did he and my grandmother return?"

"Your grandparents reside on the blue planet?" Jacob asked, his eyes darting over to the group of Angels who had began to walk again.

She nodded, her pulse racing as anxiety swirled inside her. "Does anyone in your city know—" She stopped talking, her arms flying out to guard Jacob, as what she had thought was a bird descended into the city. An Elven ship fired its weapons onto the innocents below them.

The leader of the Fallen Angels pointed to each member of his team and they shot off in different directions, as if knowing instinctively what he wanted. His eyes fell on Malkia's alarmed face. "Can you halt their invasion?"

"How did they find your city?" Malkia shouted, fear clawing through her chest.

"We don't know," he blurted, closing the gap between them. "Are you able to protect my people or not."

She nodded, leaping into the air and landing on Tantiana's back. Her dragon raced through the enclosure of trees, bounding into the air when she reached the light of the sun and flying towards their city. Closing her eyes, Malkia's light flowed from her body, strengthening as she increased its size. *Tantiana, take me to the center of the city.*

The dragon tilted to the right and moments later landed in an open courtyard, close to the center. Malkia's light was already folding over most of the buildings and homes. The Elven vessel had escaped into the sky and Malkia breathed a sigh of relief when she knew her light had encompassed the entire city.

Now what? Tantiana asked, snorting and stomping her foot.

Malkia patted her beast's side, twisting to view the buildings around her. *I don't know. I thought this place was protected. How did they find us?*

As she jumped off Tantiana's back and landed on the ground, she noticed four figures sprinting towards her. *Someone's coming.*

As they neared, Malkia recognized Mataya, Asha, her Esaki mother and Bella and raced towards them, embracing her sister and kissing her forehead. "When did you four arrive?"

Asha gripped the tender flesh of Malkia's forearm, making her look over at her. "I believe I possess one of those devices Dario placed in your back on Enyo," she whispered, her eyes flashing around the area.

"How do you know?" Malkia asked, her eyes widening, running her hands over her face and running them through her hair.

"There was a small bump on my lower back at your father's fortress. It wasn't excruciating, so I assumed it was caused by something the Artemisians did to me." Asha turned and lifted her shirt up, showing Malkia an area on the small of her back that had webs of crimson flowing all over it. "However, just after the Elvens' ships showed up earlier, a dull ache began to pulsate from that area and it has only grown worse since. Now that they just attacked a hidden city, I'm positive they have me bugged."

Malkia groaned, turning to face Bella and Mataya. "You two have to expel the device from her. If this contraption is the same Dario forced into me, he'll have the power to find and hurt her whenever he pleases." She bit her bottom lip, looking over at Asha. "This must be how they discovered the whereabouts of the Fallen Angels' city. I hope Damon and the rest of our group finds us before they execute us all."

"You'll hold them off," Jacob said, strolling up beside her.

Mataya's eyes widened, screaming and throwing her arms around his neck. "Where have you been?" she asked, pulling back, her eyes narrowing as she met his.

"Here," he said, smiling and kissing Mataya on her cheek. "It's great to see you again, Mataya."

"You look fantastic," Mataya replied, grinning from ear to ear, as she unwrapped her arms from his neck. "Something has changed about you."

"Everything has changed." He folded his arms across his chest, turning to face Asha. "What has enabled the Elvens to break through our spells?"

"It's a long story," Malkia replied, pulling him away from the four women and throwing them a sharp look, before focusing on Jacob. "Let them halt the problem at hand, while you and I find someone to distract the Elvens and my father."

Just as she mentioned her father, five Elven vessels appeared in the sky, hovering just above her light. Malkia shaded her eyes from the suns with her hand and tilted her head to see the ships. A door to the larger vessel opened and a figure glided out, staring down at Malkia with eyes bright like the flames of a fire.

"Who is that?" Malkia voice shook, the color draining from her face.

"I can't tell," Jacob replied, as the courtyard filled with other Angels, who were examining the sky as well.

The figure eased downward, growing closer to Malkia's light, and was revealed as a figure of a young girl. Malkia squinted, eyeing the vessels and the girl hovering below them. She clutched her chest, fighting the panic knotting inside her.

Her light quivered and she gasped as her eyes darted around at the crowd, realizing what was about to happen. Terror gripped her throat, making it difficult to catch her breath. "Run," she cried, stuttering when her breath caught in her throat. "*Jacob, run.*" Her scream echoed through the crowd and seeing the hot flush run over her face, they turned without another word and sprinted away from the area.

Closing her eyes, she focused on her light, blotting out the screams of terror surrounding her and the sharp breath of Tantiana stirring next to her. Whoever was up there, she had been snatched up by the darkness and Malkia cried out desperately in her mind, hoping it was not the one child she had prayed would never return to this war.

Silence filled her head and she screamed up at the sky, petrified to look at the child again, but instead forced her eyes open and stared up at her friend. Misty was merely a vessel for the Elvens and her father's cause. Her twisted face and crimson eyes shook Malkia to the core, and she fought desperately against the power that was extinguishing her light.

Angry tears flooded her eyes and as they tumbled from her lids, she felt a snap in her mind and watched in horror as her light fizzled, weakening rapidly around the city. Misty descended, followed by the five vessels, landing in the courtyard, in front of Malkia and Tantiana.

That's the child who cried in my mind back on Eris. Malkia shivered, her gut wrenching with the realization. *Misty never stood a chance.*

One of the vessel doors opened and three figures descended the plank. Malkia's heart dropped into her stomach when she saw Dario, followed by Palma and her father. The pain gripped her chest and she took a few steps back, terrified by what they planned next, as she reached with her mind to speak with her blood sister.

It's over Malkia. We've won. She heard Palma in her mind, seeing a smile creep across her face.

What have you won? Malkia's eyes narrowed, pressing her lips together as she drew out her daggers.

Her father strolled past them, placing his hand on Misty's shoulder as he paused right behind her. "Malkia, this was never supposed to be a war between us. You were always going to be our final weapon. Since you turned on me, I had to improvise." He patted Misty's shoulder, his expression remaining stone-faced.

"*You're a disgusting bastard,*" Malkia shrieked, focusing on her light and the mind barricades Ustarum had taught her. *Shield of protection, safe within my space.* The spell rumbled through her mind, as she squared her shoulders, glaring at her father. "I'll never understand your reasoning for this entire battle." Her tone quieted, as sparks crackled around her. "I only wanted what was mine, but you insisted on dragging us all into a war that we didn't start, and have destroyed one life after another, just so you can have power over all these moons."

She cringed, as a soft smile surfaced on his lips, showing a gleam of devilry in his eyes. "Having power over all these moons is just the beginning," he disclosed, leaning down and whispering in Misty's ear.

He stepped a few feet back from the young girl and Malkia skipped farther away, bumping into Jacob and the leader of the Fallen Angels from their earlier hike through the mountain. "You shouldn't be here," she mumbled, her eyes darting between them and Misty.

A flaming red light tore past Malkia, striking Jacob in the chest, throwing him dozens of feet backwards, where he skidded to a halt on a pebbled pathway. Screaming, Malkia raced after him, just as Damon's ship appeared above them, shooting at her father and Misty, forcing them to dash back to the safety of their ship. Tantiana released her fire, consuming one of the Elven ships in her inferno. The other three vessels shot off into the sky, chasing after Damon, with the one carrying her father following shortly after.

TWENTY-FIVE

Divided We Fall

Malkia sprinted to Jacob's side, dropping down next to him and holding her hands over his chest. Gagging from the blood rising in his mouth, he gripped her wrist, pulling her towards him.

"I'm sorry, Malkia," he gasped, a trail of blood dripping from the corner of his mouth. "If Chantum surv-v-vived, find him and make him fight alongside y-y-you. If you d-do it together—" He choked, coughing up more blood as he turned away from Malkia.

She watched in agony as his eyes rolled backwards, exposing the white of death, just as his body violently convulsed. Her hand trembled as it covered her mouth, feeling like a knife had ripped open her heart. It was only seconds later when his body quivered one last time before it relaxed, his last breath expelling from his lungs.

Sitting back on her heels, Malkia rocked back and forth, weeping and allowing the tears to fall without restraint. Jacob's dead eyes stared back at her as she chewed on her nails, unable to tear her eyes away from his.

A figure moved in her peripheral vision, spiraling her back to reality and she leapt to her feet. Looking around she saw thousands of Fallen Angels walking down the roads toward the center of the city. Malkia raced over to Tantiana, jumping onto her back and turning to face the Angels.

The leader, she had encountered earlier, wove through the crowd, his eyes pinned on her. "Malkia, my name is Chantum and Jacob was my brother and friend." His resonant voice bit into her heart and she had to use her inner block to tone down his effect on her body. "With this attack today and the death of one of our people, we insist upon a collaboration against the Elvens and your father." He halted a few yards in front of Tantiana, his palms coming together in front of his face. "I beg of you to assist us. The Aletheian's have known of your birth for centuries. Knowing that you will bring peace to our moons once again only deepens our desire to fight by your side."

"They will return soon," Malkia replied, pointing to the skies. "That child has extinguished my ability to shield your city for the time being, so I suggest you prepare yourselves for a battle to the death." She glanced around at the throng of Angels surrounding her and noticed Bella, Mataya, Allysa and Asha's faces in the crowd. The burning Elven vessel caught her eye, and she realized their technology surpassed the Angels powers, despite what they believed. "Ready your people now, so when they return, we may possess the upper hand." She focused back on Chantum, panic squeezing her chest while a knot tightened in her stomach.

"We are ready," Chantum said, pivoting to face his people. "Angels of Thalia," he shouted over the crowd, forcing Malkia to shield her ears with her hands. "We have known this day would arrive, and this is a battle we have prepared to fight for many centuries. Prepare your powers within you, along with your outward weapons. When the

Elvens return, they won't hesitate to slaughter any of you, so do *not* second guess your chances to strike."

"Vetestium." The crowd roared as one, pumping both their fists in the air. "Vetestium, vetestium."

The group thinned, as each of the warriors sprinted out of the courtyard and off to their appointed stations. Chantum shielded his eyes from the suns as he looked up at Malkia. "It means victory," he told her, pointing his thumbs over his shoulders at the receding Angels. "We have waited for this moment for many years and welcome the victory we will have in our near future."

Malkia nodded, watching as he strode away, his boots silent on the pebbled ground. He stopped next to Jacob's body, leaning over him and whispering something undiscernible as he used his finger to outline a symbol of some sort over his body. After he finished, Jacob's body quivered and faded completely, leaving Malkia's gaping in surprise.

Twisting ever so slightly, Malkia noticed a sly smile rising on Chantum's lips, but as quickly as it was there, it was gone. He closed his eyes, raising his face to the sky and stood in silence for several minutes, before opening his eyes and sprinting into the shadows of the buildings.

Shaking her head, Malkia slid off Tantiana's back and walked over to the four women. "Have any of you seen Apollo and Skye?"

They all shook their heads and searched the skies. "Skye left on Adelina, right after you, but she steered off in a different direction. And Apollo rode on Sirath, following Damon's ship," Asha replied, rubbing her temples and closing her eyes. "The Elvens will return soon. What would you like us to do?"

"Fight," Malkia replied without hesitation, fear hitting her like ice water. "This is it, ladies. Just like Chantum told his warriors, we cannot hesitate in this battle. We thought the Artemisians were wicked, but it was an illusion to distract us from the real threat. Misty was never going to be free from the damage Dario inflicted upon her. From the moment they discovered her abilities, my father knew she would be used for this exact purpose." She sighed, rubbing her tense shoulder with her hand. "I will do my best to shield us, once my light is at full capacity again, but be prepared to protect yourselves."

"There are four of us," Mataya spoke up, moving to the center of the group. "I propose we each take a corner of the city, stay hidden and connect our incantations to protect Malkia and the Angels while they attack. We can do this."

Asha shook her head, surveying the city. "How will we connect over such a large area?"

"Like this." Mataya's eyes shut, bringing her palms together, connecting them with her lips. "Between we four, create an armor, protecting all who dwell inside." A light shone between her hands, spreading through her fingers and beaming out around her.

Asha, Alyssa, and Bella all closed their eyes, bringing their palms together and connecting them with their lips. "Between we four, create an armor, protecting all who dwell inside."

Light burst from their hands, twisting around their bodies and encompassing the five of them inside the light. Malkia's lips quivered with delight as a smile spread across her face, watching the beauty of the four women around her.

"This is astonishing!" Malkia exclaimed, turning around in circles and watching the light ebb and flow around her.

A flash across one of the suns, caught Malkia's attention and her head snapped up to look at the sky. Over a dozen ships were approaching and Damon was nowhere to be seen. "Go!" she shouted, pulling the four witches from their reverie. "They've arrived."

The light from their bodies disappeared, as they turned to see what Malkia was pointing towards. Mataya embraced her sister. "Remember what Ustarum taught you," she whispered in her ear, her fingers digging fervently into the muscles of Malkia's back. "Keep the darkness hidden and use your amulet to guide and strengthen you. And don't forget to protect your mind. You know he will attack there first." Mataya stepped back, kissing Malkia's cheek and turned to face the other women.

"Let's do this, ladies!" She cheered, holding her hand out in the middle of them. Malkia, Alyssa, Bella and Asha all placed their hands on top of Mataya's and shouted, "Vetestium, Vetestium, Vetestium." They pumped their hands up and down each time they yelled the word, thrusting them in the air, after the third.

Malkia watched as the four women dashed off towards the corners of the city, then eyed the ships that approached, breathing steadily to calm her nerves. Feeling a presence behind her, she turned to see Chantum and a handful of his warriors watching the vessels as well.

"They are coming in slowly," Malkia said, walking over to them. "Why do you think that is?"

"They must be bringing in foot soldiers, as well." Chantum's smooth features remained calm, but his eyes danced with terror. "Be prepared for their weapons and sorcery." He pinned her down with his eyes. "To counteract their sleep agents is nearly impossible, so it would do you well to protect yourself at every angle."

"Are your warriors in place?" she asked, searching for more than the few that were there.

His lips trembled with a hidden smile as he focused on her. "Don't worry about my warriors. They are well prepared."

Malkia rolled her eyes as he turned his attention to his people. It was then she saw Misty, standing behind the Angels, just inside the shadows of one of the buildings. Her carnelian eyes focused on her. *You left me.* Malkia heard Misty's voice in her head. *You're the reason I'm stuck in this hell.*

An arrow whizzed through the air, striking one of Chantum's female warriors, slicing clean through her body. Shock spread across the woman's face before she slumped over, her face colliding with the soil. Jumping to attention, the rest of his group spread out around the area, just as hundreds of Elvens exposed themselves in the light of the suns.

A red light flashed from Misty, spiraling toward Malkia. Holding out her hand, her own light burst out from her palm colliding with Misty's light and exploding in multiple directions, causing Elvens and Angels to duck away. Malkia's powers rose inside her, as she allowed her amulet to strengthen her light. Levitating away from the chaos and back onto Tantiana's back, she watched as Misty followed, throwing another flash of red in her direction. She drew up her light, surrounding the dragon and herself as the crimson light crackled around them, threatening to extinguish it once again.

From the corner of her eye, Malkia noticed Apollo and Sirath dive from the clouds, his bow and arrow drawn out to attack. As he neared them, he aimed his first arrow at a dark-haired Elven who was racing towards the group of Angels, striking him in the back. He hollered obscenities at the Elvens as he soared over their heads, allowing Sirath the chance to cover them in his flames.

Tantiana jumped into action, turning her long neck to face Misty and released her fire towards their old friend. With a flick of her hand, Misty redirected the flames towards a building filled with Angels, setting the entire structure on fire.

Their screams of agony rocked through the murky air and Malkia leapt from Tantiana's back, searching for a way in to the building to save the Angels. A wicked smile rose on Misty's face and twirled in her crimson eyes as she raised her hands, causing the flames to spread and build in strength. She was using Malkia's own powers against her.

A deep growl rose in Malkia's throat as she focused on blocking Misty from her mind and twisting just enough to catch Dario slipping out of the shadows, with Palma tailing right behind him. Their bows were held firmly in their hands, their eyes boring into Malkia. She encircled herself with her light again, sending Tantiana to help the Angels around the city.

The light from Mataya and the rest of the witches had enrobed the city within it, but not before thousands of Elvens had intruded on its boundaries. Malkia knew it would be only a matter of time before the rest were able to penetrate it.

Her eyes flashed between Dario, Palma, and Misty, watching as the fire leapt from the first building it was consuming, to a neighboring structure. The smoke was invading their air and Misty was grinning as one of her hands pointed towards Malkia. She balled it up into a fist, freeing her red light from her body and ramming it against Malkia's light, instantly extinguishing it. The force of the blow tossed Malkia across the courtyard like a doll, where she jolted into stillness just above the pathway.

She glanced over at Dario and Palma, recoiling as she saw them both release arrows trained on her position. She jumped into the air, the edge of Palma's arrow grazing her right calf. Gasping from the pain, she swerved away from their position and noticed they were completely surrounded by the Elvens inside the city, as well as the ones barricaded outside the light.

Apollo and Sirath were attacking from the air, striking the Elvens with fire and arrows, but there were too many of them and the Angels were already drawing away, searching for shelter. Frantically searching for Damon and Skye, she noticed another dragon shooting through the clouds, with two adolescents on her tail. They soared towards the city and Malkia caught sight of Skye, screaming at the top of her lungs and thrusting her hands in the air.

She drew her arrows and aimed one after another at the Elvens outside the light, striking them in their surprise and turning their attention towards her. The three dragons released their fire breath, creating another inferno outside the city.

Focusing back on Misty, Malkia could see her eyes narrowing as she watched the scene that was beyond her reach, scanning the light that was blocking the other Elvens from entering. Malkia's body shook, feeling Misty's rage speak inside her mind, begging for Malkia to join her in the fight. Without a word, Misty's red light burst from her body, just as Malkia's did when shielding others, but instead it shot through everyone in its path, pulling their souls from their bodies and pushing against the light of the witches.

Malkia's amulet warmed against her chest and she looked down to see it swirling with a dark and bloody hue. Eyeing Misty, she knew what she had to do as her powers grew deep inside her, finally releasing her purple light from her hands and enclosing the young girl within. Gulping in anticipation, she focused on the witches' light and felt her heart drop into her stomach when it shattered into pieces, crumbling into the air and blowing away with the wind.

Too late, she heard Misty laugh in her mind.

Taking in a deep breath, Malkia twisted to see Misty's laugh turn into a scream, tugging at her own hair and throwing daggers of light in Malkia's direction. As each of them bounced off her prison walls, she screamed louder. *Why are you imprisoning me again, Malkia? Wasn't the first time horrific enough? Why are you doing this to me again?*

Malkia's breath caught in her throat and she paused in the midst of the fight. *I've never imprisoned you. Why would you think such a thing?*

Liar! My glass prison that you forced me in, so you could strengthen your powers. You have destroyed my entire life. Misty screamed in her mind.

Malkia's light around Misty shuddered and Dario raced towards Malkia, his sword drawn and a sly smile surfacing on his lips. Her eyes darted between the two, all the while wondering where Palma had gone.

Terror washed over her, seeing hoards of Elvens racing through the buildings towards them. She jumped into the air, searching for Apollo and Sirath, just before Dario swung his sword at the empty air she had left.

Chantum stood in the center of the courtyard, his shoulders slumped in defeat as he surveyed the slaughtered Angels around him. Swooping down towards him, Malkia curled her hands under his armpits and tugged him off the ground and into the air.

"Leave me!" he shouted, squirming to look at her.

"No. Your people need you. I don't know what has happened, but we are losing, and unless we find all the survivors soon, we will all perish in this battle." Malkia's words were met with silence as she flew away from the mayhem. She caught a glimpse of Apollo and Sirath on the outskirts of the city, fighting the Elvens there, alongside the four other dragons and Skye.

Landing near the spot where Mataya was hidden, Malkia whistled, patting Chantum's chest and searching the area for any enemies. Mataya appeared from a building, followed by a large number of Angels, some of them children. Asha, Alyssa and Bella sprinted up to them, halting next to Malkia.

"Where can they hide?" Malkia asked, turning to face Chantum.

"Inside the tunnels of the mountain. My people can take them there safely." He signaled for his people to move onto the tunnels, fear racing across his face. "Now what? We have failed. How will we ever win this battle?"

"Find protection for your elderly and children, then gather your warriors inside the forest over there." She pointed to the right of the mountainside. "My friends will hide us there until we have a better plan. This time there is no division between your people and mine. We do this together. A unified plan."

Chantum nodded, as his people raced up the path to their tunnels, with the four witches shielding the entire path from the view of the Elvens and her father. "I should have listened to Jacob," he muttered, soft lines creasing around his eyes for the first time. "By choosing mortality, our powers have decreased, but my ego convinced me that you were unnecessary in this fight."

"If you didn't think I was necessary, why all the psycho-babble about knowing of my coming and needing my assistance?" She quivered with indignation, her eyes flashing around at the chaos, feeling her gut wrench from the realization that this outcome could've been prevented.

"It's all true," Chantum whispered, his eyes examining the inferno that was his city. "But Jacob was only a half-angel, and his insistence on your help, fueled my desire to exclude you from our fight. He may have been my brother, but he wouldn't exist if my father hadn't strayed from my mother's arms." He jammed his hands into the pockets of his black trousers, heat staining his cheeks. "Jealousy even intrudes the minds of Angels."

Malkia's mouth set in a hard line; her eyes pinned on the hundreds of Angels rushing for the mountain. "Now you know. Let's do what Jacob wanted and work together to execute my father and all his Elven followers."

Chantum nodded, turning to face his people, just as the last of them fled beneath the canopy. "I will meet you in the forest." He bowed his head and raced off after his people.

Twisting to face the four witches, she scanned over Asha's body. "Did you remove the device?"

"There was no bug inside me," Asha responded, her fingers trailing to her back. "With the pain and vibrant red lines, I was positive that was why the Elvens discovered our whereabouts, but it wasn't there."

Malkia turned in a circle, chewing incessantly on her bottom lip while scanning the sky, searching for any sign of Damon. The ships of the Elvens had landed on the other side of the Angels' city and had overtaken the area, waiting for the Angels to return. *Tantiana, round up the others and meet me near the tunnels we were brought through.* She reached out to her dragon, her eyes still examining the sky.

"Let's go see to those Angels. Everyone but Damon, Koleton and Justin will meet us there." Malkia stepped onto the path, followed by the other four women.

TWENTY-SIX

Better Plan

The crowd in the trees had dwindled since the last time the Angels had converged around Malkia. She waited until all five dragons had descended into the safety of their defensive bubble, before having the witches completely enclose them.

Apollo and Skye jumped off their dragons' backs and joined Malkia in the middle of the group. "We are outnumbered," she shouted over the silence of the group. "When I arrived, I was told you were prepared for this battle, but what I witnessed out there was complete and utter chaos. There was no structure and, with the Elven's technology, along with their fighting skills, we never stood a chance with that attack." She paused, twisting around to see the many faces.

A number of groans filled the air and Malkia held up her hand to stop them.

"However, I don't think all is lost. We need to think smarter and move faster. The dragons give us an advantage and, once our ship returns, we will have that assistance as well. For now, we need to devise a strategy that involves every single person and dragon here." Her eyes fell on Chantum. "You have the ability to lead well, but your organization skills are lacking. Appoint someone who has that skill set, along with a number of others and make a plan that will force those heathens out of your city."

Chantum gave her a firm nod, his eyes straying to gaze at the many faces and finally falling on a petite woman. Her eyes shone like Theia during the setting suns, piercing everyone at whom she looked. A grin gathered on her amber cheeks as she noticed Chantum's gaze.

"I choose Thora." His eyes shone with admiration, and he bowed to her after saying her name. Rising back up, his gaze settled back on Malkia. "She has a brilliant mind, and has kept us together throughout these years since our existence was discovered by the Elvens."

"Great," Malkia said, stepping through the crowd and stopping in front of Thora. "Keep him in line." She winked at her as heat rose on Thora's cheeks.

"I will, Malkia." Thora's resonant voice shook Malkia, but this time she held it together as the female Angel stood straight and looked around at the group. "You heard the woman. Let's fall into our teams and spend ten minutes outlining our next moves."

As the Angels organized, Malkia stopped Thora from leaving. "What about the pixies? Jacob mentioned that the ones who resided on Esaki had returned here. Are they going to assist?"

"They already are helping," Thora affirmed, clasping her hands together. "If they need to speak with one of us, we will be summoned away, but the pixies always assist from the shadows."

Malkia nodded, searching the trees and vegetation around them. "Are they here now?"

"A few, but you won't see them unless they want to be seen." Thora rubbed her hands together, her gaze darting around at the others. "Now if you'll excuse me, I have a job to do."

Thora skipped away and Malkia turned to find her friends. Her small family stood near the dragons, waiting for her return. Weaving through the crowd, she expelled a deep breath when she reached them.

"I'm worried about the three men," she said, focusing back on the sky. "And how did the Elvens find the city? It makes absolutely no sense." Her brows furrowed, while her heart drummed in her ears.

Apollo curled his hand over Malkia's shoulder, his long, talon-like fingers rubbing against her shoulder blade. "If I may say, Damon and the other two men are capable of defending themselves, and I do believe if the ship is still functional, they will arrive in no time at all."

"It doesn't help, Apollo, but thanks for trying," Malkia replied, her eyes slightly rolling at the gesture. "Until I see their faces and know they are alive and well, I'll continue to worry about them."

"Humans and their emotions." Apollo grunted, throwing his arms in the air.

"You realize the Elvens are only preparing themselves for the next attack. We shouldn't wait any longer." Skye stepped toward Malkia, her arms folded over her chest. "I vote we swoop in right now."

Malkia shook her head. "You're right about preparing for us, but I think we can be sly with this next attack. The first sun is about to set and the decrease in light could be an advantage." She leaned in, Skye shifting closer to hear. "I have some ideas, one including me going in first, but I want to hear what the Elven's have decided."

"What about Misty?" Skye asked, as a brief flash of rage swam through her eyes.

Malkia inhaled slowly. "Leave her for me. I'll dismantle her powers, if I find a way to do so." Her throat clenched with grief. "I want to save her, but if I fail, I'll end her life myself."

"What if they have a trap set for us?" Alyssa said, interrupting the conversation and curling her arm around Malkia's waist.

"You'll know if there's a trap, once I arrive. I'll let Tantiana know to stay away and she will relay my message." Malkia lifted her head, looking at her odd pieced family and smiled at the thought, before focusing back on the issue at hand. "We have to be the ones who implement a sneak attack. My father believes we aren't prepared, and because of that we need to use our enormous loss today to our advantage."

"Agreed," Alyssa replied, gripping Asha's hand in her own. "We both know Thane well, and after witnessing the damage the Elvens inflicted upon this city, he will believe he is already victorious." Her eyes strayed back to Malkia. "The only problem will be his desire to end your life."

Malkia's heart felt the now-familiar ice pick stab through it when her Esaki mother mentioned her father's need for revenge. No matter how much she detested the man, he held a piece of her heart in his clutches. As much as she wished for his death, she felt it would only broaden the darkness within, instead of dissipating it.

"Then, I will give him that chance and we will find out who is the actual victor," Malkia muttered, twisting away from her group and looking over at the Angels. "We need to move quickly," she shouted.

Thora bounced up from the ground, her eyes twinkling with delight as she approached Malkia. "We have an idea, but it will require your dragons' assistance. Could one of them enter the city first, lighting up the center area with its fire?"

"That could be arranged." Malkia pursed her lips.

"After the city is on fire, we will wait, allowing the fire to spread. After it has grown, we will send in a small group of our finest and fastest warriors, allowing them to sneak up and extinguish as many Elvens as they can." Thora waved her hand at the group of Angels she had just left.

Six females and five males stepped towards them. Each of them wore a stony expression, as they each examined the group around Malkia. Seven of these warriors possessed hair as dark as an obsidian rock, while the other four wore fire red locks that traveled down to the base of their backs. Malkia's gaze wandered around the large group of Angels and realized these were the only ones who did not have the white hair like the others.

"Why this group?" Malkia's curiosity spoke before her logic could stop her.

Thora grinned and her eyebrows waggled with delight. "These are the newest group of Fallen Angels. They abandoned their exalted positions at the time we discovered you had been taken away to Enyo and their powers are by far the strongest among our numbers."

Malkia's eyes flickered with surprise and she took a step back to gain a better view of the group. "Have I spoken to any of you before?"

A female Angel, with eyes the color of blue sapphires and hair as black as night, stepped through the group. "I accompanied the Aletheian's when you first met us on Esaki, but I never spoke to you." Her voice chilled Malkia to the bones, forcing her to encircle her and her friends in her light. "When you traveled to us for the first time, we knew you were the child from Eris who the pixies had visited on several occasions."

Malkia took another step back, her eyes narrowing. "The Aletheian's seem to be all-knowing." She pursed her lips and glanced around at the group. "If you all were once these omniscient beings, why did you not foresee this entire outcome?"

"We aren't Gods," Chantum replied, swerving through the crowd and standing next to Thora. "We catch glimpses of paths that could be taken and we are warned of the troubles stirring in our areas. We have seen the end result, if the Elvens and your father succeed at traveling to the blue planet. It will be the end to that world as they know it, not to mention massive destruction will rain down upon the moons of Theia."

"What you're telling me is that you know we could lose, but you've also seen the path of our success, right?" Malkia asked, the lines in her face deepening as she wrung her hands together.

Chantum glanced over at Thora, exchanging with her a guarded look. "We've seen thousands of different outcomes, but the one where the Elvens succeed is by the far the most devastating to everyone."

"I'm ready to end this," Malkia croaked, her jaw clenching. "Your intro plan sounds excellent. After these warriors begin their intrusion, when do the rest of us attack?"

"They will signal us with a flash of bright white light, letting us know they have completed their assignment." Thora said, smiling again and pointing at the eleven Angels. "At that point, I would like you to use your own light and distract the Elvens, while half of our group descends on the city, slaughtering any Elven in their path. We will give them enough time to advance toward the center before the remainder of our warriors wipe out whoever remains."

"Do you believe this strategy will succeed?" Apollo asked, his arm grazing Malkia as he stepped forward.

Thora's eyes narrowed and her expression melted into a frown. "Do you have a better proposal?"

"No, but I'm curious to why you would send the entirety of your most valiant warriors first," Apollo replied, his long fingers resting on the end of his dagger. "What if they are ambushed and slaughtered before the battle even begins?"

"They can't slaughter us." A male warrior spoke up from the group. His violet eyes sparkled against her light and his obsidian hair glittered from the second sun's fading rays. "In the first year of falling from the status of an Angel, we are indestructible. This is why we are the only ones who should venture into that city and clear the path for the remainder of our warriors."

Apollo nodded tightly and Malkia lifted an eyebrow at this revelation. "Do the Elvens know of this?" she asked, her eyes falling on Chantum.

"We don't believe they do, but anything is possible," Chantum replied, tilting his head to the side. "We are wasting too much time with all this talk. I realize you have many questions and, after we have won this battle, I promise to sit down with you and give you what you need."

Malkia nodded. "Thora, give the command."

Thora bowed toward the eleven Angel warriors and they immediately raced from the group's veiled spot, using the edge of the mountain to keep themselves concealed. All lights were extinguished, as they waited for the mighty eleven to reach the city. After they believed enough time had passed, half of the group crept through the trees, spreading around the city in an attempt to attack from all angles.

This was the dragons' signal. Malkia closed her eyes, focusing on Sirath and Tantiana. *Light up the entire center of their city and then return to Mataya's concealment.*

Both dragons leapt into the air, as Malkia followed Chantum into the trees with the first group. Moments later, the sky lit up with the fire of the dragons and Malkia heard the whistle of hundreds of arrows flying through air. She breathed a sigh of relief, when both dragons communicated they had safely returned.

The sounds of arrows whizzing in the air, continued to fill the silence of the forest and Chantum signaled that the first eleven had began their attack. Apollo and Skye had returned to the backs of their dragons and were waiting on the second group to fight. Malkia had brought Asha and Alyssa with her, leaving Bella and Mataya to keep the groups safe until they all made their advancement.

Just as they reached the homes on the periphery of the settlement, a bright light shone out from the city, illuminating the wisps of clouds in the darkening sky. Chantum nodded at Malkia and she looked over at the sisters, breathing deeply one last time before jumping into the air and flying over the structures of the city. Encircling herself within her light, she tightened the barricade within her mind.

Her light pulsated around her and the silver streaks flashed brightly against the shadowed buildings. The fire was raging in the center of the city and Malkia could see the Elvens retreating from the area. Her eyes flashed around, searching for Misty and her father, but she only saw the flames consuming one structure after another.

As she settled on top of a building, away from the fire, an arrow whizzed by her light, followed by dozens more. She glanced toward the direction they had come, and her eyes narrowed, noticing a large group of Elvens being led by Palma.

Why do you want me dead? she asked her sister, allowing the barricade in her mind to waver.

You are the reason our parent's struggled. Palma shouted in her head. *And I detested the way our mother showered you with affection, but ignored me completely.*

Did you need both of our parent's full love and affection? Because our father has never loved me. Only you. The pain in Malkia's heart was growing and she felt the darkness unfolding within her, as she witnessed the hatred in her sister's eyes.

You should have never been created, Palma replied, her hand waving to the side of her.

Malkia's looked to the edge of the building and gulped when Misty and her father stepped onto the ledge, encircled with the young girl's crimson light. A pounding ache pressed against Malkia's skull, causing her to take a hurried step back, falling on her backside as she tripped over a raised area on the roof.

Grunting from the impact, she rubbed her temples and focused on her light and barricade, attempting to push Misty and Palma out of her head. "Why are you allowing him to control you?" she screamed at Palma, her face reddening while her fury trembled inside her.

Palma chuckled, but her eyes shot daggers of hate at her sister. "I'm the victor," she snapped, moving a few feet closer toward Malkia and drawing an arrow back, aiming directly at her sister's chest. "I begged you to return and join us, even though I despised you for the love our parents had for you. Instead you spit in my face with your self-righteous words." She twisted to look at Misty. "Extinguish her light, now."

"Misty, no!" Malkia cried, rising from her perch. The battle below them raged, with the clanging of metal colliding against each other and the arrows whistling on all sides, along with the roar of the flames, consuming everything and everyone in its path. "Is this what you want?" She gestured her hand toward the chaos. "If you want the secrets of the Aletheian's, why are you slaughtering their people?"

Adelina shot past the building and Skye dug her heels into the dragon's side with an arrow pointed at Palma. Before she released the arrow, the Elvens turned and struck Adelina multiple times with their deadly aim.

"Jump Skye!" Malkia screamed at her best friend, as a look of terror wash over her friend's face. Adelina plummeted to the ground, landing with a sickening jolt that shook the structure they were standing on.

Racing to the edge of the building, Malkia searched for Skye, but instead watched in horror as more Elvens bounded from their hideouts and struck Adelina with their swords. She attempted to jump down to save her but was pulled back and forced to turn and face her enemies.

Barely able to breathe, a pressure built in her chest and her heart drummed maddeningly in her ears, seeing that Misty was controlling her movements. She fell to the ground, with Palma only a few feet away, menacingly drawing a finger across her throat and laughing out loud from the gesture.

Misty and her father walked over to the group of Elvens and Palma.

Her father wore a lopsided grin, greeting Palma with a kiss to the forehead and pat on the shoulders.

"Malkia," he said, raising an eyebrow as he gave her the once-over. "You're the reason these Angels are perishing. If you hadn't sought refuge within their city, we never would have discovered their whereabouts. You've caused all this turmoil."

Malkia searched the skies, hoping the attack had gone as planned. "How is this my fault?" she asked, bitterness filling her mouth, as she struggled to inhale a full breath.

"Your connection with Misty was never broken." He winked at her, waving his arms around at the broken city. "We just had to encourage her desire to find you. As you can see, her memory of your barbaric imprisonment is all the coaxing she required." He hid a smile, as Misty glanced up at him.

"Take your filthy hands off of me." Skye's shouts filled the air from behind the group of Elvens.

Malkia watched, helpless to assist her friend as the crowd separated and a lanky Elven dragged Skye toward her father. Dropping her in front of Palma and Thane, Skye's eyes met Malkia's and she mouthed, I love you.

Thane wrapped his fingers in Skye's hair, yanking her up beside him and drawing his sword in front of her. Malkia trembled, reaching out to her friend as the tears flooded her eyes. "Please, no," she begged, her gaze flashing between her friend's terrified expression and her father's icy glare. "Please, take me instead."

"What's the fun in that?" Her father asked. He pursed his lips, his arm relaxing, allowing the sword to fall to his side as his eyes narrowed. "I'll capture each and every one of your friends, along with any allies and one by one I will slaughter them, just so I know you're suffering the deepest pain that a person could ever experience." He tightened his grip on Skye's hair, drawing a cry from her lips and tears from her eyes. With a flash of his hand, he brought the sword up to the tender flesh of her neck, slicing it deep and clean.

Blood poured from the wound and Malkia pushed against Misty's powers, trying to reach her friend. "No!" she cried, her hands reaching and pushing, as she watched the pain wash over Skye's inky irises, before rolling back into her head. Thane released his grip, allowing her to tumble forward and land face first in the gravel at their feet.

Out of the corner of Malkia's distorted vision, she noticed an Artemisian vessel descend from the sky above them, firing its laser weapon at the group around Thane. Misty deflected the blows, wrapping the three of them in her light and moving them away from the area, freeing Malkia from her grasp.

The Elvens scattered, shooting at the ship, as her shaking legs sank down to Skye's body and she turned her friend over, cradling her head in her lap. She shielded them both from the blasts around them, faintly aware of her body shuddering. A flood of tears wet her cheeks, and her sobs rose, one after another as she tugged her friend closer to her body, ignoring the sticky residue that was soaking her trousers and shirt.

"I'm so sorry." She wept into the dark curls of Skye's thick hair. "Thank you for always standing next to me and loving me." A sob caught in her throat and her vision blurred from the tears. "I love you, too." She kissed Skye's forehead, before rising and heaving her friend into her arms.

Ignoring the battle around her, she flew from the chaos and headed for the forest where Mataya and Bella were hidden. Landing in the safety of the trees, she found a spot near the mountain and settled Skye's body onto a bed of leaves and twigs. Mataya and Bella raced over to where she stood, gasping at the sight of Skye's lifeless body.

Mataya grasped Malkia's arm and back, sobbing as she sank to the ground next to her sister's legs. "Wh-why?" she screamed, crawling to Skye's side.

"I have to return," Malkia whispered, turning to Bella, whose own face was overrun with tears, her lips pressed together. "Please stay here with Skye." She rested her hand on Bella's shoulder.

Bella nodded, her eyes briefly meeting Malkia's, grief clouding her features. "We won't budge from this spot."

TWENTY-SEVEN

The Final Battle

Racing away from the women, Malkia leapt into the air, flying back to the charred remains of the city, praying to find Adelina and everyone she loved safe from her father's grasp. Landing on the same building, the flames had consumed everything up to that point and were dancing on the edges of the structure. Malkia searched for Adelina, but only noticed Sirath and Apollo off in the distance, with Tantiana and the two hatchlings close behind. She searched the ground below, but the smoke filled the air, making it impossible to see anything a few feet down.

Keeping her light wrapped around her body, she jumped off the edge of the building, gliding down to the terrain below. Her eyes focused through the murky air, catching a glimpse of Adelina's crimson and black scales. Settling next to her, she enclosed her half charred body within her light and touched her leg.

"Thank you, dear friend," Malkia spoke out loud, petting the deceased dragon. "Your sacrifice won't be forgotten."

A weight settled on her heart as she shot up into the air, searching for her father and Misty. The Artemisian ship had landed on another building and Malkia watched as three men raced down its plank, their boots clanging loudly against the metal. Damon's eyes met hers and she flew towards him, tossing herself into the safety of his arms. Hiding her face against his chest, the sobs rose without restraint, not knowing how she would ever halt her father's destruction.

Moments later, Damon pulled back, his hand touching her chin and turning her face towards him. "I'm here now. Is Skye alive?"

Her eyes fell, the sorrow shedding her insides, knowing Koleton was watching her. "She didn't survive," she whispered, a wave of nausea hitting her and dread snaking its way through her body. Her eyes rose, twisting to face her friend, and wanting nothing more than to ease the pain she witnessed rushing over his expression.

Koleton heaved slightly, his eyes narrowing to crinkled slits as he twisted away from her, a trail of bile streaming from his mouth. He leaned over the edge of the building, gagging and screaming, as he held the sides of his head. Feeling helpless to comfort him, Malkia sagged against Damon, watching the murky sky.

"Misty is approaching," she mumbled, sensing her near for the first time. "Someone should take the ship and use it to protect us."

Damon nodded at Justin, who raced back up the ship's plank and flew it into the air, just as an Elven ship approached from the opposite direction. The flames were dying out on this side of the city, casting dancing shadows across the darkness. The Elven vessel landed on the other side of the building's roof, catching Koleton's attention. He rose from his perch on the ledge and stood next to Damon and Malkia, anticipating the next attack.

Malkia surrounded the three of them with her light as the ship's door opened and out floated Misty, followed by Thane, Palma and a number of Elven warriors. They stood in formation around Thane and Palma, with Misty taking the lead.

Thane curled his hand over Misty's shoulder, preventing her from moving forward. "Malkia, I've come with a proposal," he shouted across the distance, blotting his forehead with a cloth.

"What would that be?" Malkia answered, gripping onto Koleton's forearm to hold him back from attacking.

A wide smile covered her father's face, the light of the flames glisten against his teeth. "If you come with me now, I'll discontinue our advancement on the Fallen Angels and your people. You'll give me the map to the blue planet and will instruct the Elvens on the knowledge you've acquired in your travels to all the pyramids of Theia."

Damon growled under his breath, his hand firm on his daggers, ready to strike at a moment's notice. "Don't listen to this savage," he muttered, pinning her father within his glare.

"It appears your current lover is envious of your former." Thane nodded and Malkia heard the whiz of the arrow, just as Misty reached into her mind and instantly extinguished her purple light.

Damon fell against her, groaning and grabbing his upper thigh, just as Dario came into view on the roof across from them. Eyeing him with icy contempt, Malkia built her inner light up and flung it at the brute. He grinned as he dodged it.

Koleton wielded his sword and dagger, bringing them around to protect Malkia, as she knelt to examine Damon's leg. A large gash was streaming blood, underneath the grip of his hand. Easing his hand away, she placed her own hands over the wound and infused her light into his body. Just as it began to heal, another arrow flew by her head, barely missing Koleton.

"Stop," Damon demanded, jumping up from the ground and pulling Malkia up next to him. "It's healed enough." He turned to face Dario, every muscle in his body tensing. "I'm going to kill him." He sprinted across the roof, dodging the arrows and laser shots and leapt the gap between the buildings, landing like a panther on the other side.

"Take the deal!" Thane bellowed over the commotion. "Take it, before anyone else is hurt."

Malkia twisted to see her father, squaring her shoulders and standing tall next to Koleton. "You just executed my dearest friend and her partner stands next to me, seething desperately for the revenge he deserves," she shouted, flames of fury shooting through her. "You're a coward. A man who will do anything to gain supremacy over others, include risking and sacrificing your own children." Her lips drew back into a snarl as her eyes darted between her father, Palma and Misty. "You've turned my sister against me, kidnapped my child and ripped this child's soul from her body. I will *never* assist you."

Her father's eyes narrowed and he took a step back, allowing the Elvens to shelter him from any danger. Palma moved forward, her bow raised and an arrow pointed at Malkia. Attempting to raise her light around her and Koleton, it sparked and fizzled, only allowing her to use it as a weapon.

Stepping out of the line of sight of her sister, Malkia tossed a look over her shoulder, seeing Damon and Dario attacking each other with their fists, nailing each other in the face and stomach. Her heart pounded in her ears, focusing back on Palma and Misty and allowing her light to target them both, as each of her hands shot off her powers towards them.

Once again, Misty deflected her light, but Palma was hit directly, rolling away from the Elvens and nearly tumbling off the edge of the building. Koleton swept his sword around, racing towards the Elvens who protected her father. Just as he reached them, Apollo and Sirath appeared near Palma and his first arrow sunk deep into her sister's torso, causing her to shudder while attempting to crawl away them.

Apollo sprang from Sirath's back, landing on his feet near Palma. Sprinting towards them, she felt Misty's eyes on her as she reached Apollo and grabbed his wrist, just before he swung his dagger to end Palma's life.

His serpent eyes widened and he took a step away from her. "Why did you stop me?"

"This is my sister," Malkia whispered, her knees buckling, as she sank to the gravel below. "Her death is necessary, but I'll be the one to finish her." Her shoulders sagged and expression sobered, drowning in the grief of her sister's betrayal.

Apollo nodded and patted Malkia's head, before pivoting and racing towards the battle Sirath and Koleton were fighting on their own. Malkia leaned over Palma, placing her hand on her sister's trembling body, seeing the blood ooze from the wound and the copper stench filling her nostrils.

"Why?" Malkia asked, gripping Palma's hand and searching her emerald eyes for answers.

All the color in Palma's face drained as blood trickled from the corners of her mouth, choking from the remnants of the fluid. "I just wanted—" She coughed, turning her face away from Malkia, wiping away the flood of tears falling down her cheeks. "I wanted his love."

She squeezed Malkia's hand, pulling her close. "I don't want to die."

Malkia bit hard on her bottom lip and released her sister's hand. She reached to her sides and tugged both of her daggers from their bindings, gripping them tightly in her hands. "Where's Esta?" She asked, pursing her lips together.

"The Elvens have her secured in one of their vessels, waiting for father's order to execute her in front of you." Palma's lower lip trembled and her body shuddered. "I'm sorry." Her eyes rolled into the back of her head and her back arched violently, her whole body trembling.

Malkia rose from the ground, watching as her sister's body relaxed and an emptiness filled her eyes. "Go in peace, sister," she whispered, her body feeling leaden.

Slowly turning away to face the other fight, she nearly toppled over Misty, her eyes crimson as the fire consuming the city. "You won't reach your daughter in time," Misty whispered, a muscle in her jaw twitched.

"Please come back to me, Misty," Malkia begged, sinking down to look the child in her eyes. "I've never hurt you. Please remember."

Misty's eyes lit up from Malkia's words and a tear slid from her eyelid. "Please free me from my prison, Malkia. I don't want to cause any more pain." Her hands trembled, grasping onto Malkia's wrist.

A sharp breath escaped Malkia's lips, as she reached up and swept a wisp of hair behind Misty's ear. Blood caked the edges of the child's ear and Malkia noticed it was slowly oozing from the inside. "What has he done to you?" she muttered, searching the child's red eyes.

"I can't fight it," Misty cried, covering her ears with her hands and slamming her eyes shut. "Stop the noise in my head, Malkia. Please. Make it go away."

"How do I stop it?" Malkia gripped the child's arms, pulling her hands away from her ears. "How do I save you?"

Misty tugged at her hair, wiping blood over her face and neck. "Kill me, please. It won't stop." She yanked her arms away from Malkia, clasping them back over her ears. "Please, stop it!"

Malkia's eyes fell on her father, who stood away from the battle, his stare trained on her and Misty, a sly smile surfacing on his lips. "We have to be able to halt his control on you, without ending your life," Malkia said, tugging the child into her chest and holding her tight. "There has to be another way."

Her father winked at her, just as she felt her daggers rise from their sheaths. "There isn't," Misty breathed. She pushed away from Malkia and sank both daggers into her own chest, slicing through the bone and cutting through her heart.

Malkia eyes widened in horror, as the child smiled and sank to the ground. "Damn it!" she screamed, rushing to grab Misty before her head hit the ground.

She cradled her head and ran her hands through Misty's dark hair, noticing the crimson light leaving her eyes and returning to their chrome color. Misty smiled up at Malkia. "Thank you," she croaked, closing her eyes, before slipping away completely.

A tear ran down Malkia's cheek. She leaned down and kissed Misty's forehead, running her thumb over the child's cheek. "I'm sorry I couldn't save you." She hiccoughed, sorrow shattering her heart. "I hope wherever you fly away to, it will bring you the joy and peace you deserve." She kissed her forehead again, resting her head on the ground.

Twisting to see her father, her body locked up with rage, eyeing him with freezing contempt. The darkness swirled within her heart and its powers surged inside her, strengthening her light and enrobing her within its protection. She rose from the ground, gliding toward her father, his eyes widening as he shrank back, skipping backwards towards his ship. The Elvens surrounding him shot their arrows and laser weapons, striking her light and failing to break through. Tossing the first few Elvens to the side with a sweep of her hand, brought her closer to her staggering father. His wild eyes looked back at her as he ducked into the vessel and slammed the door in the faces of the remaining Elvens.

Seconds later the ship flew off into the sky, leaving Malkia staring at its underbelly. She glanced over at Apollo and Koleton, who had just killed the last of the Elvens left on the roof. Koleton wiped his brow with the back of his arm and Apollo swept his daggers against the sides of his trousers, before settling them back in their scabbards.

Damon leapt across the gap at that moment, racing towards them, his eyes trained on Malkia, knowing his vision had just played out. What they thought it meant was far different from the reality. "A large group of Elvens came to Dario's aide, but he didn't escape without being injured," Damon said, leaning down and resting his hands on his knees, attempting to catch his breath.

"My father escaped as well," Malkia replied, wiping the blood and sweat from her face. "Misty and Palma have perished, but before my sister died, she told me that Esta is near, hidden away on one of the

Elven vessels."

Tilting his head to look at Malkia, Damon's chest heaved in and out and his forehead creased. "We need to end your father's life. Dario is of little concern, but Thane will continue this battle to your last breath."

She nodded, a weight settling over her heart. "The Elvens have retreated, the Angels' city is charred to a crisp, and I have lost more than I've gained in this war." She inhaled deeply, her stomach churning from the failure. "My daughter remains in the grips of my father and this time she will be all alone. I'm not sure how much further I can pursue this maddening quest."

Apollo's massive hand curled over Malkia's shoulder and she twisted up to look him in the face. "Your friends and family have sacrificed their lives for this cause. We will continue on, despite our weariness and we will find your father once again and end his life, along with his destructive quest." His brows furrowed and his breath caught in his throat. "If your child is alive, we will find her."

Standing off a few feet, Koleton raised his eyes to meet Malkia's, his face and beard covered in soot, blood, and tears. "Skye wouldn't want you to quit," he choked out, his shoulders sagging. "Please don't let her death be in vain."

Malkia stepped away from the other men and moved towards her friend. "For Skye, I will continue." She touched his face and then curled her arms around his large body, embracing him tightly. "For my mother, for Misty, for Adelina, for Jacob, and for all the Esakians and Angels who have been caught in the middle of a war they didn't start— I won't stop until all their lives have been avenged and we can live in peace, once again."

Koleton's body trembled under her embrace and he squeezed her tightly. "Thank you. I will fight until my very last breath," he muttered near her ear.

Justin had returned with the ship, and Apollo mounted Sirath again, as the rest of them followed the dragon to where Tantiana and the hatchlings were waiting with the victorious Angels. Settling onto the soil, Malkia's eyes wandered over the terrain, noticing the charred structures and the hundreds of bodies strewn in the streets. Tantiana nuzzled her face against Malkia and absentmindedly she stroked the dragon's ear, continuing to survey the destroyed city.

Chantum moved through the crowd, followed by Thora, Asha and Alyssa. "The Elvens have retreated and their numbers have dwindled significantly," he announced, pinning Malkia down with his intense eyes.

"All of our numbers have dwindled," Malkia replied, watching the Artemisian ship land. Justin, Mataya, Bella and Damon exited, followed by Koleton cradling Skye's body close to his. "We will need time to regroup." She turned back to face Chantum. "Although it will allow the Elvens and my father to regroup as well, I believe we all need the time to bury our dead and clean up the mess." Sadness crushed her heart as her thoughts returned to the loss of her daughter, along with Misty and Skye. "I need some time," she whispered, giving Koleton and Skye a sidelong glance.

"Of course," Chantum replied, snapping his fingers and waving at several of his soldiers. "We will establish a base and clean up a home for your people to reside in for the time being. Please do what is needed and we will reconvene soon."

Malkia nodded, shuffling her feet to turn and face her friends and family. Feeling a hand on her arm, she twisted to see Asha's purple eyes staring back at her, wearing the same grief that she was feeling.

"I would like to take care of Skye's life celebration," Malkia said, her lower lip quivering. "And we will need to retrieve Misty and Palma's bodies as well and give them a proper ceremony, as they were victims in this war as well."

The group nodded in quiet agreement, all bearing a heavy heart, as they turned away from the Angels. The air around them remained murky, even as the first sun's light dawned on the horizon.

There's movement in the shadows. Tantiana said. *Look toward the light.*

Malkia stopped walking, her arms shooting out to stop Asha and Mataya from continuing as well. Her eyes squinted, searching the misty air. A slight breeze swept through the crowd, twirling the remnants of the smoke away from them and she noticed a dainty shadow staggering in the distance.

Rushing through the small crowd, Malkia sprinted towards the figure, seeing her confused, inky irises staring back at her. "Mom," the child muttered, coughing and falling forward on her knees.

Scooping Esta up, Malkia cradled her daughter in her arms for the first time in nine years, joy dancing through her heart. The child relaxed in her embrace, curling into her body and closing her eyes, a sigh escaping her lips as she hid her face in her mother's chest.

Malkia kissed the top of her daughter's head, pivoting around to see her people staring back with wide eyes and gaping mouths. Alyssa and Mataya both rushed forward, curling their arms around Malkia and Esta and kissing the child as they squeezed her.

"He let her go," Alyssa whispered, her eyes focusing on Malkia. "Why do you think he allowed her to go free?"

"I don't know," Malkia muttered, feeling a sense of relief, mixed with a rush of dread as she tilted her head to the sky. "At this moment, I don't care." A sob rose in her throat and the tears flooded down her cheeks, creating rivers through the blood and soot covering her face. "My baby girl is here." Her voice was barely a whisper as she leaned over and kissed the child's head again. "I finally have her again."

"It's not over!" Koleton yelled, his deep voice startling Esta. "He's not letting her go as easily as you believe." He pointed towards the rising sun, all color draining from his face.

Malkia turned to see what he was pointing at and took a step back when she noticed the massive shadow moving through the misty air. Tantiana and Sirath eased forward, and Malkia encircled everyone with her light.

The shadow kept moving toward them, shifting into the clearer air and focusing on the two dragons holding flank in front of her group. Its eyes darted around, resting on Mataya and sinking to the ground, bowing toward her sister.

"I don't think this creature is here to hurt us," Alyssa said, stepping forward and placing her hand on Malkia's shoulder.

"He's here because we called for him," Mataya interjected, skipping toward the creature. "I know him. I sense his soul connecting with mine."

"Wait," Malkia shouted, tightening her grip on Esta, her blood running cold. "What do you mean, Mataya?"

"She means, this beast is here to assist us," Apollo replied, his fingers gliding over Esta's hair and his eyes dancing with joy. "He's an ancestor of the dragons, but smaller and more agile, like the deimos. They are ancient and wise and if they're here to assist us, we have gained a magnificent ally."

Mataya had reached the fiend and was stroking its nose, its wings twitching from the attention. "He speaks to me." A smile crept across her face. "Like you and the dragons." Her eyes fell on Malkia. "They're our friends and will support us in this war."

The cloudy air stirred around the creature, as dozens of other beasts came into sight, kneeling like the first one as they reached the group. Malkia breathed in deeply as the smoke twirled up into the sky, revealing hundreds more perched along the horizon.

Her eyes darted around her group, seeing the men's hands resting on their weapons, but frozen in place as they attempted to grasp what was before them. She pivoted on her heel, focusing on the hundreds of Angels standing a few yards back, smiles spreading across their faces. Her Esaki mother's hand curled around her waist.

"Just like the deimos, these nesoi creatures are not meant to be our enemies. Let's not allow your father to turn them against us, like he has done with so many others," Alyssa advised, her silver eyes glistening from the rising sun's rays. "We may have lost loved ones today, but our Goddess and God haven't left us to battle your father alone. Be of good cheer, my dear daughter. We will win this war, after all."

Malkia closed her eyes and thought of her mother, Skye, and Misty, before opening her eyes again, a fresh smile spreading across her face. With her Esaki mother by her side and Damon next to her, she stepped towards the nesoi beasts, her spirits soaring for the first time in weeks.

Epilogue

Ti cringed, standing in the shadows of the trees and listening to Thane and the Elven leader, Dasco.

"You failed," Dasco barked, his hand gripping his staff as he leaned forward in his chair. His eyes had narrowed, an icy look of contempt covering his ashen facial features. "You allowed the one last vantage of ours to escape, and now we have nothing to convince her to give up the information."

Thane didn't budge, but glowered over at the Elven. "I didn't fail, you imbecile. Your warriors are the failures." He paused, waiting for a rebuttal, but when he didn't receive a reaction, he continued, "My daughter is with child." He held his hand up, seeing the leader was now ready to interject. "And this child was the making of her and Damon. We will have our information, don't you worry." He chuckled to himself, rubbing his hands together. "And we will have the most powerful child on our side. He won't need any dark magic infused into him. He already possesses powers far beyond what you and I have ever seen."

A smile spread across Dasco's face as he sank back into his chair. "How do you know all of this?"

Rising from the stool, Thane's eyes danced with amusement.

"Misty sensed the child. She divulged the information to me and that was when I gave her permission to end her life." He laughed to himself, his eyes glazing over in thought. "That daughter of mine believes she saved the young girl, but she was always under my control to her very last breath."

Ti shrank back into the forest, afraid he would be detected if he eavesdropped much longer. His feet were light on the ground, which is why Tarance had sent him in the first place. Now to make it to Malkia before her father began the next attack.

Keep going! *Guardian* is available now!

If you enjoyed this story, please leave a review on Amazon!

The final adventure is available now!

Guardian

Acknowledgments

This story has been an exhilarating one to weave together. I've loved the journey, along with the growth in myself as I've refined my writing skills and storytelling. My family has been a steady and strong support. Thank you for loving me through the difficult moments and cheering me on when it would've been easier for me to give up. You have all been my supportive rocks and I love and appreciate each one of you. Steven, you are my constant, my love, and the best support system I have ever had. Thank you for all you do!

Once again, thank you to my editor, Erin Sandlin. She keeps me steady and grounded, urging me to excel in my craft of writing. Erin, you are a saint, and I know I can always count on your guidance to mold my stories into a masterpiece. I couldn't have created this story into what it is today without you. Thank you!

A BIG thank you to Niki Ellis Designs for creating an updated book cover for Malkia's story. Thank you for sticking with me and listening to my thoughts and ideas. You have been a joy to work with and I appreciate your insight and wisdom on all things design and beyond. It was a long journey, but we made it!

Brandon Burgon's book covers will always have a special place in my heart. Someday I hope to use them for special editions and will continue to use his brilliant talent to market this series. Thank you, Brandon! You have been a good friend. You can find more of his work at: www.burgonartworks.com

I want to give a gigantic shout-out to all my readers, friends, extended family, and all the other authors who have supported me through these past few years! Thank you! Without your support, I couldn't have continued on. The loving words, the kind messages, and the constant reminder of my book's worth, have helped keep the fire burning within, driving me to keep writing and pursuing my passion. Thank you! Thank you! Thank you! I have been overjoyed by your love and support!

More by the author

Theia's Moons Series

Eyes Wide Shut

Enyo's Warrior

Protectors of the Stars

Guardian

The Chaos Awakened Saga

Marked Chaos

Expanded Chaos

Transformed Chaos

Novels

Be My Leprechaun

Novellas

Wrong Side of the Mirror

Novelettes

A Web Through Time

Wicked Heart

Wicked Soul

Jolly Old Monster

Unable to Wake

About the Author

International Bestselling Author Niki Livingston writes tales of epic and dystopian fantasy worlds filled with magic, mysticism, and mystery.

When she's not busy writing enchanting stories of diverse women rising in their power and strength, she spends her time walking her rescue puppy, quieting her mind with meditation and yoga, diving into the newest books of Veronica Roth and Laurie Forest, and binge-watching The 100 and The Wheel of Time.

For all her latest releases and updates, subscribe to Niki Livingston's newsletter!

www.NikiLivingston.com